FEET OF CLAY

FEET
OF CLAY

✦

Roddy Wright

HarperCollins*Publishers*

HarperCollins*Publishers*
77–85 Fulham Palace Road, London W6 8JB

First published in Great Britain in 1999

1 3 5 7 9 10 8 6 4 2

The Scripture quotations contained herein are
from the New Revised Standard Version Bible,
copyright © 1989, by the Division of Christian
Education of the National Council of the Churches
of Christ in the U.S.A., and are used by permission.
All rights reserved.

The quotation from C.S. Lewis on pp. 262–3 is taken from *On Love*,
compiled by Lesley Walmsley, HarperCollins, 1998, pp. 46–7.

A catalogue record for this book
is available from the British Library

ISBN 000 274016 8

Printed and bound in Great Britain by
Creative Print and Design (Wales), Ebbw Vale

◆

CONTENTS

◆

INTRODUCTION

'BISHOP WRIGHT, IS IT TRUE you've sold out to the *News of the Screws*?' The drunken shout through the letterbox curdled my blood. I was sitting on the stairs of a dark hallway in a cold house in Kendal. On the landing above me was a journalist, notepad in hand, tape recorder running. Kathleen sat close by as we struggled to answer the prying questions of this stranger in our house. Outside we could hear the continuous noise of the media pack, raised voices, fists banging on the fragile door, and all the time the click and flash of cameras. We were both so tired. All we wanted was to be rid of this suffocating attention.

What were we doing here? Kathleen and I are private people, yet here we were answering searching and intrusive questions from someone we did not know. Throughout the previous week the attention of the nation's media had increasingly focused on us as we made headline news for newspapers, television and radio. We wanted none of this. We felt as if we were on the run, two fugitives without a hiding place.

The media attention was to become a painful and lasting reality in our lives. At the time, in 1996, I thought it might just last a few more days, until the story was no longer new. That attention has continued on a regular basis since then, however, and has been mostly unfriendly. The shouted question through the letterbox that

Saturday night in Kendal was intended to be offensive – but it was also full of bitterness and disappointment. We were not speaking to *his* newspaper. The truth was that we did not wish to speak to any newspaper. Neither of us has ever wished to live in the glare of such publicity. An ordinary man from an ordinary background who had lived, for the most part an ordinary life: that is how I saw myself. But recent events had altered that.

This is the account of an ordinary life – though a rich and rewarding one – and how it was changed by events. Faith and doubt, joy and sorrow, happiness and pain, trust and betrayal, all have a shaping influence on most lives. I am aware of them all in my own. I am also acutely aware of the pain I have caused my loved ones and my Church. That is now a part of my life too. Life does not stay still, however: we move on, changed by experience. This book describes the past, but the future is still waiting. It is my hope that, with God's help, that future will be a meaningful and positive one.

I

✦

GLASGOW AND ISLAND CHILDHOOD

TO MOST PEOPLE THE GLASGOW TENEMENTS looked grim and forbidding. Built to accommodate the rapid population growth resulting from the Industrial Revolution of the nineteenth century, for a
hundred years they were essential to the industries which were so
important to the city and the country. Engineering, steel-making,
shipbuilding and shipping had made the Clyde world-famous, and
they depended on the thousands of tenement dwellers who made
up the vast workforce. By the 1920s and '30s the sturdy sandstone
of the tenement buildings was blackened by years of soot, smog
and neglect. They were widely regarded as hopeless slums, but
within those darkened facades there was a real richness of life, with
all its beauty and culture, as well as real poverty, with all its hardship.

The tenements were home not only to Glaswegians, but also to
thousands of Gaelic-speaking Scots, mostly from the Western Isles,
and a large Irish contingent, mainly from counties Donegal and
Mayo. By the start of the Second World War the Gorbals was home
to many Irish families, just as Kinning Park, Govan and Partick had
become home for the Gaels, known as 'Glasgow Highlanders'. The
Potato Famine of 1846 and the following years had driven thousands of starving Irish families from their homes to seek life and
work, no matter how meagre, in Scotland. The same potato disease

had forced an already impoverished people from the Highlands and islands of Scotland to seek employment and food elsewhere. Added to this suffering was the great injustice of the infamous Highland clearances – but that is another story. When they settled in Glasgow the Gaels brought with them their language, their culture and their Christian faith of whatever denomination. The generations who followed them held firmly on to these links. As late as the 1950s Gaelic was a living language in those Clydeside areas where the Glasgow Highlanders lived.

Many of the islanders were seamen, earning their livelihood in the Merchant Navy. One of the first places to be visited by young islanders arriving in Glasgow was 'the Pool', by the docks in Carlton Place in the Gorbals, where all the hiring was done by the shipping companies. Here the new arrivals were introduced to the deep-sea life which took them far from their island homes and from Glasgow. The New Zealand Shipping Company, Donaldson's Shipping Line, P & O, The Blue Funnel Shipping Company, and others no longer in existence, all benefited from the ability of these men born so close to the sea. When they eventually married and settled, usually among their friends and relatives in Glasgow, many found local work with the Clyde Port Authority as ship's riggers, dockers, crewmen for the tug-boats on the river, or for the ferries on the Clyde and round the west coast of Scotland. Mementoes of their far-flung travels were often on display in their drab tenement homes – beautiful Japanese tea sets, intricately woven tablecloths from South America, and ornaments fashioned by the Aborigines in Australia or the Maoris in New Zealand.

The Irish, for the most part, worked in the construction industry – they were the navvies who were so important in the building of the hydro-electric plants, tunnels and other projects vital to Britain's post-war recovery. Like the seamen, they had to spend long periods away from home, leaving wives and mothers to live as best they could in the city. Life was hard, mutual support essential, and the first generation of both Gaels and Irish in Glasgow tended to stay close to their own. Their children grew up as Glaswegians yet were, somehow, different.

This is the world into which I was born on 28 June 1940. I was born in our house, a two-room and kitchen, two stairs up, at 218 Watt Street, Kingston, Glasgow C5. The district known as Kingston was really part of Kinning Park, but it has long since disappeared to make room for the Kingston Bridge and the M8 motorway. My parents were Andrew and Dolina Wright and I was their second child, my sister Chrissie having been born in November 1938.

My father had been brought up on the little island of Eriskay in the Outer Hebrides. He was known as a 'boarded-out child', having spent his infant years in the care of the Sisters of Charity in Edinburgh (it was a custom on some islands to board children out in this way, until they could return to the island and earn their keep). His real home was provided in Bun a Mhuillin, Eriskay, by Chirsty Campbell, who fostered him. Until his death he loved that island and its people. I think I must have met most of them in the first years of my life in the warm and welcoming kitchen of our Glasgow home. My mother was a daughter of Roderick and Effie MacInnes of South Boisdale in South Uist. This is a township on the southern end of South Uist and, on a clear day, one can see across to Barra Head, as fine a view as anywhere in the British Isles. My mother was one of a large family raised on a croft in the thatched cottage where she and most of her brothers and sisters were born. These islands and people would play a very important part in my own life – as much as Clydeside where I was born.

Is it really possible to remember events that happened when one was still an infant? To this day I have some 'images' which are quite clear in my mind, but are they genuine flashbacks retained by my memory? Are they formed by what I saw or by what I heard my parents discuss at a later date? I was born just as the bombing of Clydeside was beginning, which reached its crescendo in 1941 with the famous blitz of Clydebank. I have a very vivid flashback of being carried by a man in a helmet. I can feel the rough blanket in which I was wrapped rubbing against my face, the distinct smell of burning still in my nostrils, and the sound of crackling in my ears. Much later in life my mother told me how the air-raid warden had carried me to the safety of the shelter when a bomb had fallen on a factory at the back of our tenement in 1941. But I still do not know whether I remember it as it happened or whether the image is the result of my mother's story. Whatever the answer, it is my earliest memory of the tenement where I was born.

◆

Looking back on my life, I am painfully aware of the debt I owe my parents. Too often I feel that I failed to appreciate their love, and the efforts they made on their children's behalf.

My father had very little schooling after the age of 12. I know from him and from others of his generation that he became a part-time crewman on the *Saint Winifred* at that early age. She was a large fishing boat, under sail, working out of Eriskay. By the time he was 16 he had left the island and joined the Merchant Navy, sailing deep-sea immediately. I recall him telling me that in those days, about 1924, the ordinary seaman had to take his own blanket, tin mug, plate, knife, fork and spoon on whatever ship he joined. Where and when he sailed in the years before marrying my mother I cannot say in any detail, but I know he travelled to Australia and New Zealand, a country he loved, and that the harbour into Rio de Janeiro was, in his view, one of the most beautiful in the world. They were never long enough in port to see much more than the dockside, however.

In 1926, during the General Strike, he had to abandon the sea for a while because the docks were at a standstill. No work meant no money and therefore it was necessary to do what one could just to survive. He and three others heard there was work in Fort William where Balfour's were building a pier. Today it is known as the British Aluminium Pier. The four of them walked all the way from Glasgow in search of that work, sleeping rough in the fields and bothies. They were successful and earned £1 a week working all daylight hours. For that sum my father rowed a boat, towing timbers out in Loch Linnhe to where the construction was taking place. Telling me about this episode in his life, he described the lodgings he had shared with George Skilanders, also a boarded-out son of Eriskay. 'We had a great landlady who gave us a warm room, a good meal each day and enough change from our pound to buy a pint and a packet of cigarettes on a Saturday night,' he told me. This was indeed luxury.

Many years later, in 1976, I was the curate of St Mary's, Fort William, and my father was long dead. Every few weeks I brought Holy Communion to a young mother who was housebound, suffering from multiple sclerosis. After a few visits, her mother called me into the kitchen and asked if she could talk to me.

'Are you related to anyone called Andrew?' she asked.

'My father was called Andrew,' I replied, 'but he's been dead for 12 years.'

'It's just that you resemble him, but—' she shook her head. 'I don't suppose it's possible.'

Curiosity aroused, I pressed her on the matter, and she took a photograph from her bag and placed it face down on the table. On the back was written one word, 'Andrew'.

'That's my father's handwriting!' I exclaimed. Turning the photograph over, I saw my father, aged about 18, looking right back at me.

'Can I have this, please?' I asked.

'Oh, no!' she replied. 'I've kept it until now.'

I voiced the question which had formed in my mind as soon as she had produced the photograph: 'Did you have a crush on my father?' But she just smiled and would say nothing further. I worked out later that she would have been about 14 years old when my father was there. Her mother was the landlady of whom my father had spoken so highly.

Some days later, on my daily visit to the local school, two children ran up to me in the playground. Giggling, one of them said to me, 'My granny says she's got a picture of your father, but I don't believe her. He looks *much* younger than you!'

But I digress. After the Fort William episode, my father returned to sea and about 10 years later he met and married my mother.

She, like most of her generation, left school at an early age. Leaving school most often meant leaving home as well. Such was the poverty in South Uist in the early 1920s that leaving home in search of work was the norm. The girls would return if needed at home, or if they managed to find a husband with a croft! My mother's first leaving took her to the fishing ports around the east coast of Scotland. Girls from the islands made this journey every year during the herring season. Normally they would be chaperoned by an older woman, working together as a group alongside similar groups from Lewis, Harris and Barra. The work was hard – long hours from before dawn, in the winter months, gutting and cleaning the huge numbers of fish unloaded from the fleets of fishing boats. Cuts and abrasions, callouses and frostbite were the marks of their trade. They lived in a world still to discover moisturizing creams and gentle soaps. Many years later I marvelled at my mother's skill with a sharpened knife cleaning herring or mackerel. The pennies earned from such hard work were saved for the family at home. At the end of the season the girls returned to the islands, where they were needed to work on the family croft.

The following year my mother left again, this time to work in Glasgow. Two of her older sisters already had positions as domestic servants in the Helensburgh area. She began her work in the same way, entering a very real world of 'upstairs and downstairs'. She moved from the cramped life of a small thatched house on a croft to a large dwelling in a teeming city where, amongst the servants, there was a strict hierarchy of order, the youngest being given the most menial tasks. Such a change must have been very difficult because of the strangeness of both house and city, but it was simply accepted as being necessary. Those girls worked for a pittance – their keep was their wage. The little actual money they earned was saved and sent home where any such help was appreciated. My mother moved up the ladder a little to become the domestic servant for a business family whose large house was by the River Cart, which divides Paisley from Glasgow. Here she remained until she married my father. Her employers thought a great deal of her and when she left they asked her to find a replacement, preferably from Uist. She introduced them to her cousin, Bella MacInnes from Smerclate in Uist, and Bella stayed with the family until she retired, by which time she was companion rather than servant.

My parents were married in Glasgow, in the church of Our Lady and St Margaret, on 25 January 1938. The officiating priest was the Very Rev. Dr Leydon, and the witnesses were John Alex MacInnes from Eriskay and Morag MacInnes from South Uist. The reception was held in the Wheat Sheaf Restaurant, Paisley Road. The couple set up home at 218 Watt Street, where they were to live for the next 25 years.

◆

My brother, Donald John, was born in 1943 and as the war progressed we spent more time in the islands. It was safer than risking the bombs in Glasgow. Like many families at that time we were divided, my sister Chrissie living with the Campbell family (my father's foster family) on Eriskay while my brother and I were with our mother at my grandparents' home on Uist. My father was working on the Clyde or at sea. Like many seamen he continued to work aboard boats as his 'shore job'. The Clyde was frenetic with a variety of wartime shipping and dock work was an essential part of the war effort. Plantation Dock, Queen's Dock, Prince's Dock, Rothesay Dock and Kingston Dock were very busy, working round the clock. Where the Clyde opened to the Firth at Greenock – the 'Tail of the Bank', as it was known – ships would wait on anchor for their turn in one of the docks up-river. Today the docks are no longer in use and few, if any, merchant ships sail up the Clyde.

I spent the last year of the war in South Boisdale, and it was there that I began my schooling. Chrissie and I were sent to Ghearraidh na Monaidh School, where the headmaster was Iain MacKay and my teacher was Miss MacEachen. I have vivid memories of walking barefoot by way of my grandfather's croft to the school, which was built on the brow of a hill. Opposite was the lovely little church of Our Lady of Sorrows, known locally as Eaglais Ghearraidh na Monaidh. The school day was divided by the 'little break' and the 'big break'. During the 'little break' we played outside, come hail, rain or snow. The 'big break' was at lunchtime and each day Chrissie and I went to school prepared with a bottle of milk, a little tin of cocoa and a scone. These we brought to an old lady called Kate Iain Bharraich, who lived with her even older sister near the school. In the warmth of their little kitchen we had our hot cocoa and scones. After school each day we made our way back over the croft to the house that was for the present our home.

My memories of Uist in those childhood days are all happy. Some days, Chrissie and I would be kept at home by my mother to help on the croft. Grazing the few cows and heifers was very important, grass being sparse on such rocky ground. *Buachalachd* – watching the cattle – was a legitimate reason for not being at school and accepted by the headmaster. It was fine by us: Chrissie and I would play, keeping an eye on the few cows and moving them to other areas of grass when the need arose.

Sunday was always an important day. We would wear our best clothes and walk as a family to the little church by the school. The men always stood in groups outside, smoking pipes or cigarettes, chatting and sharing news and views. The women and children went straight in and took their places in the pews. I can still, in my mind, hear the 'pitter-patter' of bare-footed children making their way to the front where they had their places. (From Easter to October we never wore shoes to church, school, or anywhere. My mother and her generation never wore shoes as children. At least we were provided with some footwear during the winter months!) The lighting of the candles was the signal for the men to make their entrance and they usually squeezed into the very back pews. After Mass friends and relatives would often make arrangements to meet later in the day. Sunday night was a 'ceilidh night' and in those days, without television, such visits and entertainments were very important. One of our regular visitors was Ruaraidh MacPhee, a tailor, who shared stories with my grandfather, marvellous stories which have become folklore. Much later in my life, I was sitting at my desk on a Thursday evening, preparing material for the classes I taught in Lochaber High School on a Friday. I was listening to a Gaelic programme on Radio Highland, presenting some archive material on folklore to do with story-telling. A shiver ran down my spine as I suddenly realized I was listening to my grandfather and Ruaraidh MacPhee arguing over the validity of a story about which they very obviously differed. Sitting at my desk, I could clearly picture my grandfather taking the pipe from his mouth to empha-size a point, sitting on the bench (*an beingidh*) as was his wont. The shiver was one of pure nostalgia, as that recording took me back 40 years to those lovely nights by the fire in South Boisdale.

It was in those early days that my Uncle Angus taught me how to make a *sgoth seallaister* – a little toy boat made from wild iris leaves. The art was to make a boat with just two leaves – sail and longboat complete; the fun was sailing it in a stream or little loch.

Occasionally my mother would take us down to Orosay, a little peninsula stretching out into the Atlantic on the shoreline of our township. Taking a sack and some food for a picnic, we would spend hours paddling around the rocks, using a stone to prise limpets and winkles from their firm grip. With the sack well filled, we would return home where our catch would be cooked and the limpets served with a delicious white sauce. Another memorable dish was the crab food provided by my Uncle Angus and his partner Calum. Weather permitting, they sailed daily out to the west where they lifted their lobster pots. I can still picture their little craft with the brown sail, looking like a dot on the horizon, so far out to the west did they seem to sail. In reality they would only be about a mile offshore. They always brought crabs home, but the lobsters were the money earners and we seldom sampled their luxury.

Spring and summer were the busiest seasons on the croft, as on any farm. Shortly after Easter we would make our way to the *bogach* to cut the peats. The instrument used for this is known as a *cas-chrom*, a crooked spade wielded from the top of the ditch by the cutter. Below, ankle-deep in the water, his partner would catch the soaking sod as it was cut and lay it on the top on dry ground. It was back-breaking work and we children would not participate at this stage. However, some weeks later we would return to make lit-tle stacks of the drying peat so that the wind would hasten the process. After another few weeks the horse and cart would be brought along to begin the important work of bringing home the winter fuel. The better the summer the quicker the work was completed. It was hard work, with bothersome flies adding to the discomfort. But they were such happy days for us children – the freedom of the hill and the bogland, the excitement of lighting the peat fire and brewing the tea, the satisfying taste of scones newly baked on the *greideal* (griddle) at home and eaten with home-made butter and cheese. We also had something called *aran Innseannach* – Indian bread – made from an imported, dark-coloured flour, speckled with red from some kind of spice: perhaps an odd thing to find in a crofter's house in South Uist, but it was commonly available then.

In addition to the few cows, sheep were very valuable and were carefully tended from lambing until the sales in the autumn. All the local crofters could use the common land for grazing and that land included the hills. Here the sheep grazed freely, each marked in such a way as to be easily recognized by the owner. The crofters from the township would gather with dogs and helpers to round up all the sheep on the same day for dipping or shearing. Such a day began very early, with everyone heading for the hills to gather the sheep, and some would walk miles before all the animals were satisfactorily penned in the *fang*, as it was known. The bleating of sheep and lambs would ring in your head for days afterwards. Such working together was taken for granted then, unlike today. It was simply the natural way of life.

Spring also meant major washing days for my mother. Carrying a sack of peats down to the loch-side and building a large fire were the first tasks of the day. Then a large tub was filled with water from the loch and set to boil on the prepared fire. With the water ready and soap added, my mother began to wash all our blankets, boiling them individually in the tub, turning them with a large stick. When this was done she rinsed them in the loch and we helped her by stamping on them until the soap had been completely washed out. When that part of the exercise was over we stretched the blankets out on the ground, anchoring them with large stones. The drying was left to the sun and the breeze. On the hot fire my mother would boil eggs and make a large pot of tea, and we would enjoy our picnic by the loch. I could never forget such a vivid childhood memory.

◆

Sometime in 1945 we all returned to Glasgow, together as a family once again. I doubt if the contrast could have been more stark. The loch, the stream, the hill, the croft, the silver sands and the rolling waves of the Atlantic were overnight replaced by the street, the close, the 'stair-heid', the back court, the midden, the cellar and the 'dunny close'. Still central in life, however, were the church and the school. We settled in quite happily: it is remarkable how adaptable children can be.

My first visual memory of Glasgow, apart from the flashback of the 1941 bomb, is of a street gathering full of cheering people, a bonfire, and some kind of effigy being gleefully burnt. It was VE Day and the effigy was that of Adolf Hitler. The great family story of the day was of how I got lost in the crowd, to be found later wandering in some street nearby. I had been wearing a new pair of trousers which had somehow split at the crotch, and I returned wearing a skirt! It was back to old trousers for Roddy.

Chrissie and I had to start school again, going to Our Lady and St Margaret's Infant School on Admiral Screet, near the Paisley Road Toll. It was a long, L-shaped building edged all round by a verandah. The headmistress was Miss Gaffney and my teacher was Miss Hamilton, a stout, elderly lady with white hair and a red face. I remember her clearly and I know I liked her despite her use of the 'strap', as the tawse was known. Our first difficulty arose when she demanded that I catch up with the rest of the class in learning my catechism. This seemed unfair to me, since I already knew the first chapter off by heart. The problem for Miss Hamilton was that my answers were in Gaelic. She won the day and I learned that first part all over again in English.

Throughout my tender years my spoken language was, for the most part, Gaelic, whether I was in Uist or Glasgow. Now that I was in school, however, English – or, more accurately, Glaswegian – became increasingly my primary spoken language. We Glasgow Highlanders were truly bilingual. It was not a change that my mother relished. She herself, until the day she died, never lost her soft Highland accent.

A big feature of the tenements were the cellars – truly a world of difference compared to the abundant fresh air and light of the islands. These were, for the most part, disused wash-houses, many still having the old boilers intact. During the war years they had been used as air-raid shelters and brick walls, known as 'dykes', had been built in front of the doors to prevent blast damage. After the war they became play areas for children as well as, unfortunately, dumping areas for various forms of rubbish and convenient toilets for some people. There was always a smell of dampness mingled with other unpleasant odours in the cellars. The 'dunny close' was the last in the building at the corner and was so named because of the large dark cellar, or dungeon, at its base. It had a number of passages and one of these had a 'stank' − a grating opening on to the street above. These cellars were part of our playground, sometimes our gang hut, and sometimes a place to smoke that illicit cigarette. Indeed, amongst our street songs was a little one about a cigarette that was often the only one available because of wartime restrictions. The brand was called 'Pasha' and, to the best of my memory, the ditty went something like this:

> *Pasha, Pasha, Pasha,*
> *I don't want to smoke a Pasha*
> *I don't want to die on. (Repeat)*
> *Give me my Capstan, Woodbine, Gold Flake'll do,*
> *But, whatever you give me*
> *I won't smoke you.*

The cellars, although exciting places for us children, were really hygienic nightmares. We seemed oddly immune to their perils, although the results of poor hygiene, sewage, and the various effects of malnutrition were, at times, all too evident in tenement life. We were constantly reminded not to play in puddles − stagnant water lay all around the back courts, attractive to children at play, but also attractive to various forms of bacteria. 'Don't play there or you might catch scarlet fever!' was an admonition too often ignored. In the middens where household ashes and rubbish were binned, flies abounded. Perhaps it is remarkable that there was not a higher level of disease. Tuberculosis and other related diseases were facts of life, however, as were real poverty and bad living conditions. Thankfully, many parents were very good at managing with so little and we mostly lived healthily despite the difficulties. I may have made tenement life seem terribly grim, but that is not my intention at all. I don't think I ever saw it like that. Some of my happiest memories relate to my life there: Watt Street was a good place to live. There was a strong sense of community, and a readiness to help out those who were struggling.

We were parishioners of Our Lady and St Margaret's, Kinning

Park. In those days there were between 10 and 11 thousand Catholics in the parish and the large, beautiful Pugin church was packed on a Sunday, especially at the 10, 11 and 12 o'clock Masses. Five priests served the parish, living in the large house attached to the church on one side and the school on the other. Some of those priests are very much alive in my memory and had a very definite influence on my life.

After my First Holy Communion I became an altar boy. My mother had a surplice made to fit and she made sure it was starched white and ironed every Sunday. I loved serving Mass, even as early as 7 o'clock in the morning. During my first year I was always 'in the care' of an older boy, and I remember being allowed to move the Mass book, or Missal, from the Epistle side to the Gospel side of the altar. It was even better when I was allowed to ring the Sanctus bell or, more importantly, at the Consecration. I can still visualize myself reading that little book, stumbling over the Latin words that every altar server had to learn by heart.

By the time I made my First Holy Communion I had moved from the Infant School in Admiral Street to the 'big school', as it was known, St Margaret's in Stanley Street. It still stands, though derelict today, a large edifice which can be seen clearly from the M8 motorway. In those days it housed a Junior Secondary and Primary School. There were three playgrounds, one at ground level, one inside on the first floor of the three-floor building, and one on the roof. The one on the first floor was used by the boys and had bars on the windows! I cannot tell you how many pupils attended, but with such a large Catholic population, there was always a full school roll. Being an altar boy had its benefits during the week too, as our teacher, Miss Smith, would name some of us to serve Mass on the occasion of a funeral or wedding, usually at 10 o'clock. An hour away from class was always very welcome, and even more so was the gift, or 'tip', we received afterwards from relatives or the bridegroom. Invariably I brought my tip home to my mother, who would give me a little of it for my own use.

At about the age of nine I started as a paper boy, delivering the *Evening Citizen* to customers in the surrounding streets. My work consisted of folding the papers for sale in the shop and then taking those ordered to their addresses. The shop was owned by the MacPhee family, who came from Ballachulish in Argyll. They were well known in Gaelic circles and James and Hugh were important figures in the BBC Gaelic Department. I remember them with fondness, not only because they paid me 4/- a week but because of their kindness. The shop was beside the dunny close and on the other side was Mr Young's shop. He was the local cobbler and I can still smell the leather and polish. Very often he would stand at the door, in the leather apron he always seemed to wear, smoking a ciga-rette which he held with very black hands permanently stained with dye. He was important in our community as new shoes were a rather rare commodity for many families. Some children wore clogs while others seemed to wear wellingtons or sandshoes (sannies) almost the whole year round. On a few occasions I had to put cardboard inside my shoes to keep my feet temporarily dry until my parents could afford new shoes. Such little hardships did not really bother me too much: many of my friends had to put up with much more.

As I write I have before me a class photograph taken at about this time. They were all, in varying ways, important to me over the short number of years we were at school together and yet I cannot remember all their names. I see Malky and Francis Clark, James Adams, Matthew Grant, Angus MacDonald, Peter Mitchell, Robert Paterson, Brian Browne, Mary Doherty, Sylvia McLoughlin, the Keegan twins, and so many others whose faces I recall so well, but whose names have disappeared from my memory. I do remember very vividly, however, that we had some excellent fun together.

The winter of 1947 was one of the coldest this century. There were great snowfalls followed by a severe and long-lasting freeze. For us children, no matter the footwear or the weather, it was a time for fun. We went up to Pollokshields, to a field near the Pollok Estate where we went sledging. For the most part we used old tin trays or flat boards as our vehicles, hurtling down the 'Cunion' as it was known. Progress was halted by hitting the fence at the foot of the hill. It is extraordinary that none of us suffered more than cuts and bruises and we always arrived home in one piece. However, during that very severe winter, being at home was far from com-fortable for many families. To add to the cold there was a miners' strike and coal was precious. I remember my mother being worried because our bunker was empty and she was now having to use the coal stored in old tin baths under the recess bed in the kitchen. This was her reserve, stored away there during the summer months when coal was cheaper and no fire was needed. The man with the wee pony and cart who came around shouting 'Coal brickettes!' to advertise his products was never more popular. I think these were made of compressed coal dust; they were a poor substitute but they did give off some heat. Some of us children would go scavenging at the railway sidings in Shields Road where coal and coke which had spilled from the wagons could be found. Keeping an eye open for the Railway Police, my friend Sandy Kay and myself managed to fill an old pram on more than one occasion. Despite my mother's remonstrations I am sure she was glad of the little help. The coke, although giving off a good heat, also produced a rather unpleasant smell, but the smell was better than the cold!

The extreme cold also meant that the close and the cellar became our permanent playground that winter, no doubt to the despair of our parents, who were more aware of the health risks than we were, in our unthinking pursuit of fun and games. It was in the close that I learned to play 'keepie uppie' – bouncing a ball on to the wall with your head as many times as possible without stopping. Some of my friends were excellent at this, but I could only be described as mediocre. One person who did not appreciate this game was 'the lampie', the man who came round every evening as darkness fell to light the gas lamp in every close and on each landing. Too often we would strike the gas mantle with the ball, leaving the close or landing in darkness. In the cellars we played other games, and it was here that I experienced my first cigarette and my first kiss.

One other event during that cold winter remains clear in my mind. Six or seven riggers, including my father, were given the task of crewing a ship which was being towed to a breaker's yard in the south-west of England. On the day he was due home I was serving the 7 o'clock Mass and called into Cullen's dairy for rolls and milk on my way home. There Mr Cullen showed me a picture in the morning paper. It was of a group of sailors shipwrecked off the Isle of Man – the riggers who had left Glasgow's Plantation Dock some days earlier. Armed with the paper, I ran up the stairs and breathlessly banged on the door. My mother quickly opened the door.

'What on earth is wrong?' she demanded.

'Mammy, mammy, daddy's been shipwrecked! Honestly! Mr Cullen gave me the paper. Look, he's on the front page!'

My mother grabbed the paper from me and looked at the picture of seven bedraggled seamen, one of whom was my father. 'And he hasn't even shaved,' she said.

Apparently the tow had broken and they had drifted on to rocks, where they were rescued by the local lifeboat. My father returned the following day, not to a hero's welcome but to a wife and mother begging him not to go to sea again.

I have often thought how hard he must have worked as a Clyde rigger. Often his day would begin as early as 3.00 a.m. when he would walk to one of the docks to help move a cargo boat from one dock to another – work which could only be done at high tide, and the tide depends on the moon rather than the clock! When that work was done he would go to 'The Corner' on Plantation Dock to seek other work for the remainder of the day. The work was often very cold and wet and poorly paid, yet I can still see the disappointment on his face when he returned after a fruitless journey to 'The Corner'. There were many days when there was no work and only worry because no money was being earned. Whatever the earnings, the unopened paypacket was always handed to my mother so that she might manage the household budget. Considering our circumstances, my parents managed remarkably well on very little income.

Our parents tried so hard for us and took good care to instil strong values in us, even when we were very young. They were strict with us, especially when it came to honesty, and when I failed myself in this respect I always had the feeling I was failing them. It is a fact that guilt over wrongdoing in childhood can remain throughout one's life. I still feel ashamed of a few such episodes which are engraved deep in my memory.

Auntie Pene was a fascinating little lady. She was the oldest living member of the Campbell family who had fostered my father, so although she seemed like 'family' she was not a blood relative. In my memory she was always very old and rather strict. After her retirement she lived with us for long periods. The incident I remember happened when she was still working as a housekeeper to a family in Dennistoun. On her day off she would visit us and share a meal with us, nearly always bringing us cakes or sweets – she may have been strict, but she was always welcome! On one occasion she brought us balloons, enough for all the children living in our close. A balloon was at that time a very special gift. I was playing with mine on the stair-head when it hit the lighted gas mantle and, of course, it burst. Downstairs in the close-mouth, Margaret Webster, who lived on the ground floor, was playing with her own balloon. I managed to bully her into giving me her balloon. It was mine by right, I argued, since it was my aunt who gave it to her. And off I went to play with my new balloon. Meantime, Margaret ran upstairs to complain to my Auntie Pene about my behaviour. Immediately I was called home by my mother, made to hand over Margaret's balloon, and banned to the wee bedroom to await my father who was on his way home. Margaret got her balloon back and I got my due reward. I feel ashamed about this episode even now.

Another incident of rule flouting which still brings me twinges of guilt could have had rather more disastrous consequences. About 10 minutes' walk from our street there was a rubber dump in Shields Road. To us it was an attractive place to play, although (or because?) it was out of bounds to the public. The gates were always padlocked and the surrounding walls were made of corrugated iron. Inside beckoned a great mound of tyres, along with discarded war materials of various kinds – all of great interest to three little boys. One day Donald White, Sandy Kay and I went on a secret excursion. Sandy took up his position as lookout for the police while Donald and I scaled the wall. Inside we looked for some 'good' tyres to bring back with us for use in our back court. But Donald discovered something far more interesting – a large bundle that turned out to be a parachute. Excitedly, we clambered back to the wall, tripping and stumbling over the tyres as we hauled our heavy package. With much heaving and pushing, we managed to get it over the top of the wall and it landed with a thud beside a startled Sandy. I wonder what we looked like to the quizzical adults who watched our progress – three little boys struggling with a large canvas bundle down Shields Road, across Scotland Street and down to our own close in Watt Street? Donald issued instructions as we pulled it into the cellar, where we all collapsed panting on top of our prize. But, what to do with it? Donald went up to his grandfather's house and returned with some rope. He would show us how a parachute worked!

A perimeter wall ran along our back court. Originally it had been the outer wall of the factory bombed in the blitz of 1941 (the time of my earliest memory). To make this wall child-proof, pieces of glass had been cemented in along the top. This was completely ineffective and we used the wall for climbing and a game called 'dreeps', which entailed scaling a high wall or dyke and dropping, or 'dreepin'', to the ground. On this wall Donald said he would demonstrate how a parachute worked.

By this time we had been joined by others and, having tied the rope to the bundle, Donald began to pull it up the wall while we helped by pushing from below. Eventually he managed to balance it precariously on top and I ran to a nearby dyke, using it to help me climb on to the perimeter wall. However, Donald was impatient and began to pull the large canvas straps round his small shoulders without waiting for assistance. As I was slowly making my way along the wall to join him he was demonstrating to the open-mouthed children below how to pull the correct string so that the parachute would open and allow him to float down to the ground. Just before I reached him he gave a big heave, trying to pull the awkward bundle more securely on to his back. He stumbled, lost his balance and, arms flailing, jumped off the wall, the parachute falling with him. He certainly forgot to pull the string! His landing was sudden and heavy, and he writhed on the ground in obvious pain. By the time I got down by a safer route, adults had arrived in response to his shouts of agony. He was carried off on someone's shoulders to the doctor's surgery. I was taken upstairs by a very irate mother and punished for taking part in a dangerous theft. Donald recovered, but I never discovered what happened to that parachute.

◆

By this time I had a little sister, Effie, who was born in 1947. I remember coming home from school one day to be told by Auntie Pene that I had a little sister. It was a shock and complete surprise to me, and I was none too happy, probably because I would have to push a pram again. I had thought we were finished with that kind of nonsense. Donald John was a lively four-year-old by then. My first reaction to the news was to run off down the street to the river, where I took a comforting trip on the little ferry which sailed from Kingston to the Broomielaw.

Chrissie was at this time already an accomplished Highland dancer. By the age of nine she had won a clutch of awards at various competitions. Amongst the medals which adorned her braided tunic, however, there was one notable absence. My father never allowed her to wear the first medal she ever won, because it was a Masonic emblem which had originally hung from some worthy's watch chain!

Often in winter, on a Friday or Saturday night, we would go to a ceilidh in St Margaret's Hall, or Lorne Street, or the Kingston Halls, or Overnewton in Partick. The stars at these gatherings were mostly past winners of the gold medal at a National Mod (annual Highland Gaelic meeting). At that young age I was more aware of their names than I was of the stars of the Celtic or Rangers football teams. That changed before long! Chrissie was often asked to perform during these events and did herself proud. My mother thought I should learn to dance too, so I was sent to Chrissie's teacher, Miss Munro, for the necessary instruction. After two weeks the good lady sent a polite note to my mother explaining that I might be better suited trying something else, as her floorboards were suffering from my efforts. I was delighted to accept her verdict.

Our Gaelic culture was a very important part of our lives in those days. Our home entertainment was often provided by the Gaelic department of the BBC Scottish Home Service. Request programmes for families back home in the islands or separated from relatives on the mainland were most popular, as was any programme including piping or Scottish dance music provided by the likes of Jimmy Shand and Bobby MacLeod. The best entertainment, however, was provided by the friends who came to visit. These were nearly always islanders and while the men went for a dram to Scott's Bar or the Shandon, the women would enjoy tea and scones at home. Some were apparently good at 'reading' the tea leaves and my mother was always happy to have her fortune told. I could never tell if it was innocent fun or something more serious on the part of the participants.

It was not unusual for Donald John and myself to go to sleep in the recess in 'the big room', as we called the front room of our house, only to wake in the morning on a makeshift bed on the floor. In our place there would be someone from Eriskay or Uist, usually a seaman, who had arrived late at night off the London or Liverpool train. My parents always made them welcome and we were accustomed to having these friends live with us for short – and sometimes long – periods. Regular visitors were my mother's brothers, Donald and John, Norman and Duncan MacInnes from Eriskay, and various other relatives from Eriskay and Uist who had to attend the hospital in Glasgow.

My mother, and later my Uncle Donald, told me a story of something that happened during one of Donald's visits when I was very young. My mother left me one day in Donald's care while she went shopping. It was past 5 o'clock, the pubs were open and my mother had still not come home. Donald, in need of a pint, but stuck with me to look after, simply took me along. Children were not allowed inside the premises, of course, so he tied me to a lamp-post outside, intending to make just a very quick visit. Unfortunately my mother came up the street at just the wrong time. Seeing her lovely son tied to a lamp-post, she understood immediately what had happened. Quietly, she untied me and took me home. Donald came out after his quick pint to discover the disappearance of his charge. He later told me how he panicked and searched desperately around the vicinity. I think he feared for himself as much as for his darling nephew! Eventually, with dread, he climbed the stairs to our house – where my mother was waiting for him. Neither of them would tell me what was said on that occasion.

◆

Many years later, driving around the West Highlands and Argyll on church business, I was filled with nostalgia. I had come to know many of the places and names as a child, looking out of the train window on our way home to Uist. This was an event we looked forward to so eagerly each year. It was in a real sense a pilgrimage undertaken annually by many Glasgow Highlanders. As soon as the school term was finished early in the summer our preparations began for a return to our roots. The day of departure would find us up and ready at about 4.30 a.m., heading off to Queen Street Station for the 5.30 train. Cases packed and sandwiches made, we children would keep an excited lookout for the approach of the taxi, usually ordered the previous day from the Co-op undertakers – it was normally a Rolls-Royce, much to our wide-eyed glee. When it arrived we would stagger down the stairs, heavily laden and whispering lest we waken our neighbours. Comfortably seated in unaccustomed luxury, we would say goodbye to our sleeping street for a few months.

On one such morning as we waited for the taxi, I heard a knock on the door. Thinking it would be the driver, I excitedly ran to open the door and was shocked to be confronted by a large policeman, who stood there holding his helmet. In Gaelic he asked: '*Suil a leag thu leam seo a ghlanadh?*' (Can I clean this?) I was struck dumb and my mother, who had come to the door after me, nervously asked him what was wrong. He held out his helmet, which was covered with wet tea leaves. Earlier, my mother had swilled the teapot and thrown the contents out of the window, not thinking that anyone would be in the back court at that early hour of the morning. Unfortunately the policeman had been having a quiet smoke below as he took a break from pounding his beat. Blushing with embarrassment and confusion, my mother invited him in and cleaned his helmet herself while he had a cup of tea and a blether with my father. The policeman came from Skye, and happily chatted away in Gaelic, managing to calm my poor mother. As he left, the taxi arrived and we got on with the business of the day.

Our taxi took us to Queen Street Station where we joined the queue – there was *always* a queue – waiting to board the Mallaig train. Here we met many friends about to start their journey to Skye, South and North Uist, Harris and Lewis. The train would take us all to Mallaig, where we would join the various steamers taking us to our destinations. Once on the train we quickly passed through the tenements, factories and shipyards on the north-west of the city, alongside the Clyde, and then through Helensburgh, Garelochhead, Arrochar, Ardlui, Crianlarich, Tyndrum, Rannoch Moor, Tulloch, Roybridge, Spean Bridge, Fort William, Corpach, Kinlochshiel, Glenfinnan, Lochailort, Arisaig, Morar, and finally into Mallaig. All these places were to become much more significant later in my life. For now, I just stared happily out of the window. That journey took us through the finest scenery in mainland Scotland but I knew there was still better to come.

Mallaig pier was always incredibly busy, noisy with the bustle of boarding passengers and fishermen unloading their catches. Screaming seagulls were everywhere. MacBrayne's had their special ferry berths and we said goodbye to our friends from Lewis who made their way to the *Loch Seaforth* as we headed for the *Lochmor*, a sturdy but remarkably uncomfortable vessel. My poor mother seemed to feel seasick as soon as she saw the steamer's funnel, partly, I'm sure, from apprehension as she had experienced some terrible journeys on much earlier travels from her island home to the mainland. We always travelled in 'steerage' – a large saloon in the bowels of the *Lochmor*. MacBrayne's kept a definite distinction between their First and Second Class travellers. Most of us in steerage brought our own food, although we were allowed to eat in the First Class Dining Room with its beautiful oak panelling, silver cutlery and a white-jacketed steward in attendance. I don't ever recall eating there! The bar, on the other hand, was a busier place from the moment we sailed, growing noisier and smokier by the hour. The men tended to congregate there while the women would find a place in the saloon and, if possible, lie down. Cases and trunks were used as makeshift seats for the journey.

As for the children, we had a whole boat to discover and made the most of the opportunity to play with schoolfriends who were about to spend the summer in the same islands. The sail would last at least eight hours, often much longer, depending on weather and freight. MacBrayne's carried not only passengers but also the Royal Mail deliveries, cars and other cargo. A few cars would be winched aboard at Mallaig and the operation was carried out in reverse when the steamer arrived in Lochboisdale, Lochmaddy or Tarbert. Passengers always watched such manoeuvres with great interest.

Leaving Mallaig, the *Lochmor* headed first for Eigg, clearly visible with the prominent An Sgurr cliff on the port side as we left the harbour. Just behind were the beautiful mountains of Rhum. On the starboard side the jagged outline of the Cuillin mountains of Skye looked strangely close. Eigg had no pier and an open boat came out to ferry passengers and cargo ashore. In summer that little ferry would make two or three trips before the *Lochmor* could move on to Rhum, where the same procedure took place. Then we headed out into the Minch to Canna – a flat but very green island in comparison to Rhum. Canna boasted a pier and almost the whole population came down to meet the steamer. There is a lovely natural harbour there and in summer yachts would often be at anchor, perhaps sheltering from the strong south-westerlies, or just sampling the peace and beauty of the island. Leaving that harbour we could see, floating on the horizon, Barra and the Uists, growing ever larger and clearer as we steamed towards them. It was the first real glimpse of 'home', and Watt Street seemed suddenly far away.

To describe the journey and all its breathtaking beauty as if there were never any difficulties is only to give one side of the story. A large factor in the enjoyment of the journey was the weather. On a fine summer's day nothing could be better, and the trip was one of life's delights. But even at the height of summer the weather could be far from kind, with gales sometimes preventing sailings. Wind and rain, for which the Minch and Northern Atlantic are notorious, often meant little visibility and a continuous, rolling motion of the otherwise sturdy *Lochmor*. Seasickness, often violent, was a fact of life for many of the passengers. My poor mother suffered a great deal from this, although she had to make the journey so often in her life. My father, who had sailed all over the world, said that the motion of the *Lochmor* was strikingly different from anything he had experienced in the larger deep-sea vessels.

Entering the mouth of Lochboisdale on South Uist always brought about a spate of activity: the women tidying their hair and rounding up the children ready to go ashore; the men, some of them sheepish and unsteady, making their way back from the bar for the last time, organizing the luggage, and joining the queue already forming near the starboard side where we would disembark. As we looked out to the pier we would see a large group of people waiting to greet the passengers, amongst them our own relatives eagerly scanning the faces of those on board.

And then we were home to the sweet smell of burning peat, the warm welcome of our grandfather, and the exciting prospect of two months living in the beautiful surroundings we had come to love during our extended wartime stay. Glasgow was far away in every sense.

On our return to Watt Street at the end of every summer life continued as if we had never left. Our neighbours always seemed glad to see us back, especially those close to us who benefited from my mother's generosity as she gave them a feathered chicken, fresh eggs, or the delicious potatoes grown on the machair of Uist. They were less likely to enjoy the home-made butter and cheese which were always packed in the large box of stores which travelled back with us. They were too precious to share and besides, the salty butter and sour cheese were acquired tastes.

My mother's first concern was always to have us properly prepared for our return to school. The need to replace worn shoes or various garments, and the payment of bills became the priorities. The holiday was soon a distant memory. Often, because of his work, my father was unable to join us in Uist for the holiday, but on our return we would find a room decorated or woodwork freshly varnished. The peace and quiet while we were away must have been his only opportunity to see to such necessities.

◆

From this distance in time it is difficult to remember anything in detail of people's religious beliefs when I was a child. There were several churches in surrounding streets and most of them were Church of Scotland. Although they were generally large and beautiful buildings, they did not attract large crowds on the normal Sundays in the year, as our own church did. Many of my friends were in the Life Boys and the Boys' Brigade, however, which were almost exclusively for church members of the Protestant religion. I knew no Catholics who attended or wore the uniforms. We would greet our Protestant neighbours on the way to their church services as we made our way to or from Mass at St Margaret's on a Sunday morning.

Our own background was staunchly Catholic. The island of Eriskay at the time was 100 per cent Catholic and South Uist and Barra about 90 per cent. We had a picture of this in miniature outside St Margaret's in Glasgow after the 11 and 12 o'clock Masses on Sunday. Groups of men would gather in Stanley Street, usually in island groups – the *Barraich*, the *Uistaich* and the *Eirisgaich* – and no doubt sharing news of home. On the islands, however, there were no Catholic schools in the sense that they existed in Glasgow and in Uist everyone went to the same school. Here in Glasgow, we attended St Margaret's, which was a specifically Catholic school, while most of the others living in our street attended the Protestant Scotland Street school (designed by Charles Rennie Mackintosh, the famous architect, and still standing today as a museum of his work). The religious difference thus meant separation in some aspects of our lives, but it did not affect our relationships too much. We were always brought up to accept people as they were and give them respect.

In my case our Catholic faith was a central and important part of life. At home saying Grace before and after meals was the norm, as well as night prayers. No matter the weather we never missed Mass on Sunday except in the case of a bad illness such as chickenpox, measles or mumps. In addition, each Sunday evening we attended Rosary and Benediction, and on Tuesdays we attended Novena and Benediction. Throughout the months of May and October we attended Evening Devotions as often as possible, when the rosary was publicly recited in the church each evening except Saturday. In those days such evening services were well attended: regular church worship was a natural and expected part of life, following the pattern of the church year.

The parish priests became important figures to me. Five served the parish at any one time, and I particularly remember Canon McCarthy and Fathers Rawlings, Quinn, Carter, Kane and O'Hara. The parish was divided in such a way that each priest was responsible for the visitation of all families living in their allotted streets. We were accustomed to visits from our 'allocated' priest and he was always made most welcome by my parents. For the young people there were all the usual established organizations such as the Cubs, the Scouts, the Girl Guides and Brownies, and the Guilds for both boys and girls. I was a Cub and a member of the Boys' Guild (the chance to play Saturday afternoon football was too good to miss), and of course I was an altar boy from a young age. This meant that I was involved in parish youth activity on at least three evenings a week. The Church thus played an important part in my childhood, providing me not only with a pattern of worship and a foundation of belief which formed the bedrock of our family life, but also with much companionship and entertainment alongside my friends.

It is difficult to say when I first thought of becoming a priest. As a boy I wanted to be a seaman like my father, and I think that is what he expected. The majority of the men who came to our house were seamen and I loved listening to their tales of dramatic weather, crews they had known, and the far-off places they had visited. On our holidays I loved my time in Eriskay, being taken along on the Campbells' boat, the *St Clare*, for gentle fishing on a summer's day. I will always love the sea.

In my schooling I was just average at most subjects – keen to learn, but showing no special promise. I did love to read, however, and was a regular visitor to the local Kingston Library. It was here that I discovered Biggles and the Famous Five, and I have been an avid reader ever since.

There was something about the Church and church activities, though, which caught and held my imagination. Several factors probably sparked this off. The word 'catholic', of course, means universal and it was through the church that I learned about the wider world, beyond Glasgow and my beloved islands. I met the visiting missionary priests and listened, open mouthed, to their extraordinary sermons about life in the African bush. Like any small boy I was attracted by such an exciting and adventurous life. I remember asking my father if he had been to Africa and, when he replied in the affirmative, pestering him to tell me more about life there. Like most seamen, however, his experience was only of short stays in various ports along the west coast, and he could tell me very little. At school we were encouraged to bring our pennies each week to help the missions – our 'pennies for the Black Babies' as it was referred to then. Today, this small enterprise is known as 'Missio', and I am sure that our original, innocent terminology would no longer be allowed by the laws for race relations.

Perhaps some might think me too involved with things religious at such an early age, but many of my schoolmates were just the same. It was all really very natural and did not signify any particularly fervent commitment to Christianity on my part. We all accepted our church involvement without question as a normal part of a balanced life. I felt at home at the altar, at Mass or Benediction; I was aware of right and wrong – sin – at an early age; I was well versed in the details of the life of Jesus and the lives of some of the saints, and the first prayer I learned (in Gaelic) was the Hail Mary, '*Failte dhut a Mhoire ...*' From a very early age I was always comfortable with the faith of my family and with my Church.

Some special church events stand out in my memory as having a particular impact on me. I think it was about 1950 that a Religious Exhibition was held in the Kelvin Hall, which ran for two weeks. The altar boys or the whole school class was taken – I cannot remember which. It was a great outing for us and we came home brandishing literature from all kinds of sources. I can still see the little leaflets depicting the life and work of the Alexian Brothers, the Marist Brothers, Mill Hill Fathers, White Fathers, Columban Fathers, Maryknoll Missionaries, Redemptorists, Passionists, Jesuits, Dominicans and Franciscans. I picked them all up, and my head was full of images of tending the sick, teaching little Africans, working with Indians in the Andes, of men languishing in Chinese jails, martyrs for their faith. Whatever, each new image looked like an exciting life and I visualized myself in a white robe, a black soutane, or a brown cowled habit and bare feet. Our local priests, in comparison, seemed to live very dull lives. The exhibition had a tremendous effect on me at the time, although it would be hard to say how much, if any, influence it had on my later decision to become a priest.

One of the high points in our church life was the two-week Parish Mission which took place every five years. It was advertised for weeks beforehand and eagerly anticipated. A time of spiritual renewal for the whole parish, the Mission also offered a chance for those whose church attendance had lapsed to 'come back to the fold' without feeling too conspicuous. The priests tried to visit everyone (a tall order, given the size of the parish) and there were special events and services every day.

Being an altar server I would be present at a number of the Mission services. Each day began with Mass and a sermon at 7.00 a.m. and this was repeated at 8.00 and 10.00 a.m. The day ended with a long service which began at 7.00 p.m. I can still see the Mission Father, a Passionist, with a crucifix in his hand, preaching with that loud, booming voice of his. I was spellbound, listening to the teaching enriched by great stories. But he put the fear of God into us and I would run home at night convinced I was a great sinner. Looking back, I know his sermons were really intended for the adults, but I had ears and a very vivid imagination.

When the Mission was over there was a real sense of sadness among the parishioners as we came back down to earth. The priests must have felt it too – how could they be expected to continue with such intense preaching and prayer? Many older priests must remember those days with nostalgia, because very large churches like St Margaret's were invariably packed at the main Masses on a Sunday (60 per cent of the parish attended church then) and on an occasion such as a Parish Mission there was standing room only. In the smaller buildings of today, just a few short decades later, there are plenty of empty places.

The Boy Cubs, of which I was a member, was a parish organiza-tion and, with many of my classmates, I enjoyed our Friday night meetings, with the games and the tests for badges, the days away in the Scout Camp at Auchengillan, and the friendship. Once a year there was a National Pilgrimage to Carfin Grotto and the Scouts, Cubs, Guides and Brownies from all the Catholic parishes would attend, converging on the mining village by bus or train. The Grotto was the vision of the then parish prist, Monsignor Thomas Taylor, who had persuaded the miners to build a shrine in honour of our Blessed Lady, Mother of Christ, during the terrible days of unemployment in the 1930s. Today it is an important venue for many Scottish Catholics, used annually by different groups as a place of pilgrimage and prayer.

Although it was an exciting day out for us all, our visit to the Grotto was also a religious occasion and we prayed the rosary with the thousands of pilgrims who were there. We were led in prayer by the old Monsignor himself, his high-pitched voice reaching us through a microphone. I suppose it was the first 'sound system' I had ever seen or heard used. There were some funny moments when he would interrupt the Hail Mary or the Our Father with admonitions such as 'Keep off the grass!' or 'Keep moving!' But we prayed seriously and knew how to use our rosary beads. Today my rosary changes pockets as I change trousers, which is not the case with most young Catholics now. When I was a child, daily prayer and religious observance were a very natural part of life, and they remain so for me.

✦

The school I would attend on leaving St Margaret's Primary depended on how well I performed in the Qualifying Exam, the equivalent of the eleven-plus. An 'S' pass would mean my progress to the Senior Secondary school, which for us was St Gerard's in Govan. A poorer pass would mean going to the Junior Secondary, which was situated closer to home, in the same building as the Primary. I managed to gain an S2 pass, which was average, and so followed my sister Chrissie to St Gerard's. She had gained a very good S1 pass two years earlier. Over the years I have come across a number of people who did not seem to advance in life to the extent which had been indicated by their school results and early academic ability. Chrissie comes into that category, but perhaps it was not meant to be otherwise: she gave so much to life that did not depend on paper qualifications.

Attendance at St Gerard's meant travelling on the Underground – the subway as it is known in Glasgow – from Shields Road to Govan Cross. Wearing my new green blazer and carrying an empty school bag, I accompanied Chrissie rather apprehensively to my new school. She had her own friends, of course, and at that age did not want a little brother tagging along. So I was left at Govan Cross to see if I could meet up with any of my old classmates from St Margaret's. As I stood there, feeling lost, I was approached by two boys wearing the black blazers of Govan High School and without warning one of them punched me on the side of the head, calling me 'a Fenian bastard'. Shocked, I chased after them shouting wildly, 'No I'm not!' For my part I did not have a clue what a Fenian was, and in hindsight I am sure that my assailant was similarly ignorant. In the tribal atmosphere of Glasgow there is a long history of rivalry between the supporters of Celtic and Rangers football clubs. 'Fenian', from the Irish Republican term Sinn Feinn, is used in a derogatory way of those whose allegiance is to the green and white hoops of Celtic, with its Irish Catholic origins. That was my first experience of direct Protestant/Catholic bigotry in the context of Rangers and Celtic in Glasgow. Fortunately I met a friend from St Margaret's soon after that and made my way safely to St Gerard's.

'What's your name?' Mr O'Carroll was asking each new pupil in the First Year English class to introduce him- or herself to the rest of the class. Being last in the alphabetical order I was the final pupil to be asked to give my name.

'Are you a brother of Christina Wright?' Mr O'Carroll asked me.

'Yes, sir.'

'I won't like you, sonny!' he replied abruptly.

I was dumbfounded. What had I done? From that moment I think we never spoke to each other again. I was placed in another class with an excellent teacher called Mr Hill.

As soon as I met Chrissie on our way home I demanded to know what had caused him to say such a thing. 'Oh,' she said offhandedly, 'he doesn't like me because Bridie Coll and myself talk too much in his class.' It was certainly an odd welcome to my new school.

My first day at St Gerard's does not sound very happy, but I settled in well and loved the school. It was, in a sense, like moving from a village to a big city. Kinning Park was not such a small place, but we all knew each other and everyone in the school came from the same area. At St Gerard's, by contrast, I met children from Whiteinch and Partick, on the other side of the Clyde, and from Govan, Hillington, Cardonald and Pollok. These were places I barely knew, and some I had never visited. We tended to keep our friendships with those living in the same area as ourselves, but my horizons broadened nonetheless. The academic scope was greater, too. Here I was introduced to Latin and French, History and Geography, Maths, Science and Physical Education. Gaelic was not on the curriculum. It was a whole new world and I was excited by it all although it was tough going and some of my classmates were rough and strange. It was certainly far removed from my introduction to formal education in Ghearraidh na Monaidh School, South Uist, some seven years earlier.

As best I can remember I was not called 'Teuchter' until I went to St Gerard's. This was a term used unflatteringly to refer to Highlanders in the city. Personally, I resented the name – at the age of 11 I was intent on being like my pals and had pretty much lost my Highland accent. In the same way, however, some of the people in Uist called me a 'Keelie', a term used in other parts of Scotland for somebody from Glasgow. I suppose I was, in a real way, both Teuchter and Keelie.

One Sunday afternoon, returning from Maxwell Park where we often went for a walk at the weekend, I realized it was getting late because the No. 12 tram car passed, well lit. 'Maw, the cars are lit!' I exclaimed, in the kind of accent I heard every day at school.

'Don't speak like that!' replied my mother, cuffing me across the ear.

She was obviously disappointed to hear me speak with a Glasgow 'twang'. All of us are influenced by our environment, however, and it was natural that I should pick up a Glaswegian accent. It still clings to me and I am proud of it. My mother was rightly proud of her own island heritage and because I share it I am proud of that too. At the time, however, I just wanted to belong where I was.

✦

'What, Roddy? Och, don't be silly! I'm sure Father Rawlings asks that question of *every* altar boy.'

'But I didn't speak to him about it – it must have been John Armour, the head altar boy.'

My father and I were walking home from Sunday evening Benediction. Father Rawlings had spoken to me in the sacristy afterwards, asking if I had thought of becoming a priest. Actually I had been thinking quite a lot about it, since a classmate, Brian Browne, had recently gone to Blairs College, the National Seminary near Aberdeen. I was impressed by this and John Armour, whom I respected, was another positive influence, the examples of these two friends adding to the pull of what I had seen of the Church at work during the Parish Mission and the Religious Exhibition. Even then, although I could not explain it, I felt this was possibly the life for me.

My father rejected the idea out of hand at this stage, however, hoping that I might go to sea as he had done – although I am sure he wanted me to be on the bridge rather than on the deck. Studying for the priesthood was simply not something that ran in the family. I did not mention the subject again for some time, but it stayed in the back of my mind and I concentrated harder on my Latin studies at school, encouraged by the teacher, Mr MacDonald.

In fact, like most boys of my age, I was in trouble at school, perhaps too often. I had my fair share of 'scraps' and came home with a bloodied nose on more than one occasion. Thankfully, my mother did not fuss too much, unless I had dirtied my shirt or jersey. By the end of my first year, when I turned 12, I was well used to St Gerard's, had learned to stand up for myself, and had a wider range of friends than ever before. Already I was stretching in size and my poor mother was bemoaning the fact. Shoes and trousers were too small, too short, too soon!

Once more we made our longed-for summer pilgrimage to the islands. By this time, however, I was growing into adolescence and experiencing those difficult, changing moods: not so keen to do the simple tasks around the croft, wanting to do 'my own thing', preferring to speak English because I was lazy about using Gaelic, and generally not pleasing the adults. It was not the best of summers.

On my return to St Gerard's I found myself upgraded in some classes and downgraded in others. The group of us who had left St Margaret's together were scattered and new friends were made. I had spent what little time I had in Glasgow during the holidays with my friend Brian Browne and discovered a great deal more about his life at Blairs. Also, at this stage, I was teaching much younger boys how to serve Mass, showing them the various movements required around the altar in the celebration of the Tridentine Mass as it was then (i.e. the old Latin Mass which had remained unchanged for 400 years – the vernacular rite was not brought in until 1964/5). I also had to assist them in the pronunciation of the Latin responses. More than ever I was occupied around the church in Stanley Street. As the first term of my second year progressed I was writing on a regular basis to Brian in Blairs College, but little did I understand then what a major part this establishment would play in my life in the years to come.

Strangely, as I thought more and more of the priesthood, I was also becoming acutely aware of other changes in myself. Adolescence progressed as normal – the physical changes, the overnight awareness of girls, the disturbing thoughts kept in the closet ... Strange how those I had resolutely and happily avoided were now sought out – I was suddenly quite happy in the company of girls! On a winter's evening one girl and I found ourselves alone in the 'dunny close' during some back court game. She kissed and hugged me, and I responded. I went home overexcited and feeling very guilty. I had begun to have a real conscience about right and wrong by then, and I was particularly concerned about Mortal Sin which meant I could not go to Communion until I had been to Confession. I started to go to Confession every week and sometimes I had some dreadful wrongdoings to confess.

At school there was a group of very streetwise lads in my class and occasionally I joined them in their shady activities. On a Saturday morning close to Christmas in 1952 I met with them and we walked, via the Kingston Ferry, to the 'town', as the city centre was known. In Argyll Street we visited Lewis's store. This was, if not *the* largest, one of the largest shops in the city. We darted around from floor to floor, up escalators and down lifts – great fun and excitement! When eventually we emerged back into a crowded Argyll Street my friends showed each other what they had managed to gather – socks, pens, a pack of cards, penknives and, I remember clearly, one tennis ball.

'Teuchter, did you no get anything?' They looked at me expectantly.

In a strange way I felt ashamed. Was I so feeble? 'No, ah didn't know we were doin' that,' was my reply. Determined to put things right, I followed the others into another shop and was duly inaugurated into shoplifting. Very nervously I stood at the counter as the assistant approached.

'Yes?'

'Eh, see that clock?' I asked, pointing to an upper shelf behind her. 'How much is it?'

As she turned and stood on a stepladder to reach the clock, I hastily lifted a diary from the counter and stuffed it in my pocket. Perhaps I could give it to Chrissie for Christmas. When she turned round and told me the price of the clock, I stammered that it was too expensive and hurried out to the street where the others were now waiting. Proudly (peer pressure is a powerful force), I showed them my booty. But the diary turned out to be an autograph book – why would Chrissie want an autograph book for Christmas? It had all been rather stupid and pointless. This was my first and last act of such criminal behaviour, and I still feel guilty. Years later, when I worked in Secondary Schools, I became aware of just how powerful peer pressure can be – the influence, usually negative, that some pupils can exert on others. It is necessary to be a strong person to resist such pressure, and many youngsters are simply not so equipped.

◆

All my life I have enjoyed – yes, enjoyed – Lent. Setting oneself a task of any kind and completing it is always very satisfying, but when this is done in a spiritual manner it is even more fulfilling. All of us at home would try and 'keep Lent' in our own individual ways. In Lent 1953 I decided to do this by going to Mass every morning at 7.00 a.m. The other altar boys were probably delighted, as not too many of them wanted to start the day quite so early! I did not find it too difficult, as I still enjoyed serving Mass. ('Giving up sweets', the kind of thing many people did during Lent, was not a real penance for us as we were not tempted by such luxuries too often anyway.)

At some time during that Lent I spoke seriously with my mother for the first time about the possibility of going to Blairs College. She was not overkeen, pointed out the many difficulties, and suggested that I leave such a decision until I was much older. I was determined, however, and kept writing on a regular basis to Brian at Blairs.

A year passed, and eventually my parents, having obviously conferred, responded to my persistence and made an appointment to see the parish priest, Canon McCarthy. He spoke at length with them and later with me. It was agreed to put my name forward for consideration and arrangements were made for me to sit the entrance exam, go for interview and undergo the medical tests that were necessary. Throughout Lent that year, Blairs was foremost in my mind and I was inspired to work harder at school – albeit with limited success.

Holy week, especially the Triduum – Holy Thursday, Good Friday and Holy Saturday – was the climax of the Church's liturgical year, ending with the joyous celebration of Easter Sunday. On Holy Thursday we had a custom called 'the Seven Churches' in Glasgow. This day is the most solemn celebration of the Blessed Sacrament, the Eucharist, when we remember and re-enact the Last Supper. In those pre-Vatican II days there was a day-long adoration of the Blessed Sacrament in each parish church. Many Glaswegians, especially the children, who were always on holiday in Holy Week and Easter Week, made a pilgrimage on foot to visit seven of the main churches before returning to their own parish. With some friends I made the pilgrimage on at least three occasions. We took a different route each year. That year, for example, we walked to Govan, visiting St Saviour's in Merryland Street and St Anthony's at Govan Cross. Then, taking the Govan ferry to the other side of the river, we visited St Simon's in Partick and walked the length of Argyll Street as far as St Patrick's, Anderson, then on to St Andrew's Cathedral in Clyde Street. From here we crossed the suspension bridge over the Clyde into the Gorbals, where we called into St Luke's, Ballater Street and St John's in Portugal Street. Having completed our pilgrimage we made our way by West Street and Scotland Street back to our own church in Stanley Street. My memory is of a happy day and we had much fun on our journey, cheerfully comparing the adornment and decoration of each church's altar with our own in Kinning Park. Naturally, we always judged our own as the best!

Sometimes after Easter I received a letter informing me that I would sit the entrance exam for Blairs in St Aloysius College, Garnethill, on a Saturday morning in May. It was a very nervous Roddy who made his way to Cowcaddens on the subway and then walked, pencil in hand, to the college. I honestly cannot remember any details of the exam now, but I am sure I returned home with little confidence. About a week later, accompanied by my mother, I went to 19 Park Circus, the Archdiocesan Office. There I was to be interviewed by His Grace, Archbishop Donald Campbell. I was one of a group, each boy accompanied by parents or guardians. We sat tensely in a large waiting room from which we were individually summoned. It was all quite nerve-wracking, especially for my poor mother, and I think we were quite overawed. All I remember of the interview is that theArchbishop and my mother had a conversation about Uist and her family. He had been parish priest in Daliburgh for five years and knew them all well. It certainly helped my mother relax, but I am not so sure about me!

A short time later I received word to attend a medical examination. This was carried out by a Dr McGuire and he used a little hammer to see how quick my reflexes were. My leg did jump so I suppose everything was in order.

During all these procedures my parents told no one of my intentions and I was ordered to silence on the subject outside our home. They felt it was pointless to say anything until it was certain I was going – perhaps trying to shield me from any embarrassment if I failed. Certainly my father was not at all convinced at this stage that my application would be successful. I continued as normal, hoping but still uncertain that I would be accepted.

At the end of June 1954, just as we were preparing to set off to Uist for the summer, a letter arrived confirming my acceptance. With it was a long list of necessities: two suits, two shirts, two pairs of shoes, two pairs of pyjamas ... I did not even have one suit to my name, so my parents compromised by buying me a blazer and a new pair of trousers. Even that was quite a demand on my parents then, and this was only the beginning of their struggle to support me on the long road to the priesthood – just one of the reasons why I should be forever grateful to them.

We had to cut short our time in Uist so that my mother would have enough time to prepare me for my departure in August. I can still see her sewing little tags marked with the number 44 on to every single item of clothing, as directed in the letter from the college. Oh, and I got my first pair of football boots!

2

✦

SEMINARY LIFE:
BLAIRS AND CARDROSS

THE POST-REFORMATION HISTORY of the Catholic Church in Scotland owes a great deal to the seminaries. After Catholicism was outlawed in Scotland, the training of priests for the underground Church was heavily reliant on establishments abroad, especially in France, Spain and Rome. The priests returned to Scotland to work in strict and risky secrecy. Scotland was thus regarded as 'missionary' territory, but later managed to set up its own training establishments, of which Scalan, situated in the Braes of Glenlivet, was the foremost. Despite rough and threatening intervention by the forces of the Crown since the time of the Jacobite Rising of 1745, Scalan continued the work of producing 'the heather priests', as they were known, and these men were vital to the survival of the Catholic Church in Scotland.

By the end of the eighteenth century the college had moved to Aquhorties on the River Don, where it grew in strength until, in 1829, the year of Catholic Emancipation, it moved to Blairs. The generosity of the benefactor, John Menzies of Pitfodels, provided the house and estate of Blairs, on the south side of the River Dee about five miles outside Aberdeen, for the education of young Catholic men wishing to study for the priesthood. The old house still stands alongside the 'new' college building built in the 1890s. The magnificent church was built in 1903 and another wing was added to the college in the 1920s. Blairs closed its doors for the last time in the mid-1980s, and with it ended a remarkable era in the story of the Catholic Church in Scotland. I was privileged to have been a part of it.

✦

Buchanan Street Station was very busy that August day in 1954. A large group of boys in black blazers were gathered on the platform with their families, waiting to board their reserved coaches on the train to Aberdeen. Apprehensively, I joined them, recognizing some of those with whom I had shared the exam room and the Archbishop's waiting room. My father had said goodbye early that morning. Chrissie, Donald John and Effie had said their farewells at lunchtime before returning to school. Having spotted Brian Browne in the crowd, I boarded the train with him and found my seat. My mother stood alone in the crowd as the train slowly pulled out of the station. We waved to each other, although I found it difficult to see her through all the tears. I was 14, and this was much, much more than just a simple train journey.

The first sight of my new home transfixed me – the granite edifice, glimpsed through the trees, was large and very imposing. Chattering, excited and a little uncertain, we entered through the outer arch and arrived in the front hall, to be greeted by the Rector, Canon McGill, and other priests on the teaching staff. The priests took our names and told us our cubicle numbers – mine was in St John's dormitory. Then we were asked to hand over whatever money we had, the total being noted against our names. We were not allowed any pocket money.

Years later, when I was assistant to Father Roddy Macdonald in Dunoon, he told me a lovely story of his experience on entering the portals of Blairs for the first time. On the train journey he met up with Angus MacQueen from South Uist and, being from the same diocese, they struck up a friendship which has lasted to this day – they are now both over 70 years of age. Roddy's father was a train driver on the West Highland Line and poorly paid. Angus was a crofter's son, but had more money in his pocket because of the generosity of his neighbours and relations in Iochdar parish in Uist. Roddy spent most of the single shilling in his pocket on the train journey. He was in the queue immediately behind Angus as they entered the front hall of Blairs. Sitting at one table was Father Ewan

MacInnes, who was Master of Discipline in the college at the time and a native of South Uist. He asked Angus his name and then counted his money, both notes and coins. Next in line, Roddy gave his name and handed over his one remaining penny: 'Perhaps you could help me count this!'

◆

On reflection, it is surprising how easily I slipped into the rigid routine of the college. It was very different indeed from life at home. In most respects, our day was timetabled from rising to sleeping. The rules of the college were strict and demanded self-discipline, even at that early age. Yet most of us accepted all this in a positive way, with little or no difficulty.

On many occasions over the years I have been asked my opinion on the value of the Junior Seminary. Changing attitudes amongst the clergy, very different views on education and straightforward economics eventually led to the closure of Blairs. The question so often put to me was whether it was ever a correct way of preparing young boys to consider a life in the priesthood. I think the distin-guished history of the college – the educated men it produced over all the years of its existence, and the knowledgeable and committed laymen it helped form – is the only, and the best, answer. It is true that by the time I was there, in the mid-1950s, the majority of the students did not continue on to the Major Seminary. However, they did go on to become doctors, educationalists, lawyers, professionals of all kinds. This was of real value to the Church.

Was I, at the age of 14, too young to go to the Junior Seminary? It is the firm view of many that there should never have been such an establishment. Such decisions can only be taken at a much later stage in life, they say. But when I left St Gerard's to go to Blairs, my classmates were already making decisions about their future lives. By the age of 15 they were seeking apprenticeships in the shipyards and engineering works where they expected to spend the remainder of their working lives. Was it so different for me? The fact is that I did not make my decision about entering the priesthood for certain until I was 23 years of age, after a very thorough course of study and spiritual formation. By that time my old classmates from St Gerard's were long committed to a particular industry or area of expertise.

Throughout my time in the Junior and Major Seminaries, I never had any fears about pulling out and returning home if I should decide that the priesthood was not for me after all. Unlike some boys I knew, there was no pressure from my family to go through with it if I did not want to. Indeed, on several occasions my father asked me directly if I was still intent on becoming a priest. He reminded me that the door was always open if I wanted to turn round.

I honestly believe that the majority of us who went to Blairs were aware of the decisions we were making. Now we would be regarded as too young, but I do not remember ever feeling that I had committed myself to a course of action without understanding what I was doing. In the last 30 years, however, there have been dramatic and historic changes in attitudes to the Church and religion in general. Matters which were earlier accepted as quite natural – such as the Junior Seminary – are now viewed with scepticism and disapproval.

Today, I cannot visualize a young lad of that age accepting the regime that then existed. Perhaps it is all a question of comparisons. Home life at that time was not easy in the sense of comforts, possessions, entertainments. Our luxuries were an old wireless and a gramophone that had to be wound up before it played. I well remember Chrissie and I excitedly playing our first 78 record, the voice of Slim Whitman scratchily filling the room singing 'Rose Marie'. Today young people have televisions in their bedrooms, Sega and other computer games, personal stereos and much else. The comparison between home life now and the Blairs regime I knew would demand far greater sacrifice of any young boy today. What we did not have, we could not miss.

The normal weekly timetable in the college was as follows:

6.30 a.m.	Rise.
7.00 a.m.	Morning Prayer, Talk, Mass.
7.40 a.m.	Bedmaking and cubicle tidying.
8.00 a.m.	Breakfast. The Grand Silence ended with Grace at this meal.
9.00 a.m.	Classes.
1.00 p.m.	Lunch.
2.40 p.m.	Classes.
5.00 p.m.	Tea.
5.30 p.m.	Study.
7.30 p.m.	Talk, Rosary, Spiritual Reading.
8.00 p.m.	Supper, followed by recreation.

9.30 p.m.   Night Prayer. Start of Grand Silence.
10.00 p.m.   Lights out.

We were wakened by a loud bell every morning and greeted by the words *'Benedicamus Dominum'* shouted by the senior student in that dormitory. (There were four dormitories, named after the evangelists, housing over 200 students.) We gave a sleepy *'Deo Gratias'* in reply. Apart from this exchange, it was forbidden to speak from the time of Night Prayers until Grace was said before breakfast. This was regarded as a sacred time, the monastic 'Grand Silence', and it was a major breach of the rules to break that silence in any unnecessary way. Prayer and discipline were essential parts of the normal daily programme.

Every Tuesday and Thursday afternoons we played football, went for long walks along Deeside, or ran cross-country on the moors between Blairs and Stonehaven. In the summer term we had to play cricket instead of football, not the most popular of sports amongst the majority of the students. The game was deemed to be of value, however, so we played it! Also in the summer term we participated in all the normal athletic disciplines and until the closure of the college I held the record for putting the 10lb shot (perhaps it is significant that this weight was withdrawn from use two years after I had set that record).

On Saturdays we had a full morning of classes followed by a free afternoon. Sunday was special – we had a lie-in until 7.00 a.m. Best clothes were the order of the day and there was always a High Mass sung in plainchant, which we were all taught to read. Everyone had to use the *Liber Usualis* which contained all of the Church's sung liturgy in Latin plainchant. In the afternoon we had the opportunity to play football again, which I always enjoyed, or we could go for a walk. We were instructed always to walk in groups of at least three. This was to prevent the formation of cliques – two being friendly to the exclusion of others.

Discipline was strict and enforced by the presence of senior pupils who were called censors, similar to prefects in other schools. Every Friday evening they met with the Master of Discipline to give their report on the behaviour of the pupils and every Sunday night the whole student body gathered for the 'Report', which named students who had broken the rules regularly or were unfortunate enough to be caught. If a student accumulated more than a certain number of points for wrongdoings, he would spend

Tuesday afternoon in detention – in the study hall writing out some given work while the rest of the boys were out enjoying recreation. I remember once having to write out the Pythagorus theorem, with diagrams, 25 times. Sadly, I still failed to learn it properly – Mathematics was not my strongest subject. Sometimes detention was actually preferable to a game of football, or worse, a long walk, on a cold and windy winter afternoon. In certain circumstances a student who was unable to live with the disciplinary code would be given a 'domi' as we called it, and was asked to remain at home after the end of that term.

Every day the Spiritual Director would address the students. The fifth and sixth forms had their own oratory and were separate from the Junior House for all services and spiritual exercises, except on a Sunday when the whole House gathered in the main church. We had to read daily from a spiritual book for at least 15 minutes and most evenings we recited the rosary before supper. It was a foundation that has been of great benefit throughout my life. The daily involvement with prayer and the Sacraments was not, as some might think, too intense. It was natural and we grew to feel at home with that aspect of life. The example of the priests was also very important, some inevitably making a deeper impression on us than others. The man who struggled to instil in us a basic grasp of the Greek language was also the centre-half we all wanted on our side in a game of football and was the man with an obvious, simple and deep spirituality. I found him to be a level-headed individual full of common sense where others lacked that important quality.

When I was 16, like any other lad of that age I was aware of my sexuality and tended to daydream. My conscience weighed heavily on me. Put simply, in the language of those times, I was having 'bad thoughts'. Feeling guilty, I went to Confession early one morning, an opportunity offered to us each day before Mass. I told the priest that I had these thoughts.

'Do you have them often?' he asked.

'Eh, quite often.'

'As often as five times.'

'Oh, I have about 20 before breakfast!'

'Oh ... Oh, I don't think you should think of being a priest.'

I was really downhearted. This was clearly the end of my hopes. After breakfast I made my way to the 'prof's corridor', as it was called, which was out of bounds at that early time of day. I stood glumly outside the Rector's room waiting for him to come along from breakfast. It was my intention to inform him straight away of my need to go home and to make the necessary arrangements. As I stood there my Greek teacher, the centre-half, came along and, seeing me, asked why I was there so early. With an embarrassed shuffle of my feet I told him of the advice given me earlier by the other priest. He laughed.

'What? Don't think of leaving because of that! I'm afraid you'll have those thoughts until they screw the coffin lid down!' he said cheerfully.

After a few more words of sensible advice and encouragement I went back downstairs to prepare for class and another day in college – and to suffer, no doubt, a few more 'bad thoughts'. Despite them, and heartened by the realism of my Greek teacher, I still wanted to be a priest.

◆

Holidays came and went, and every summer I spent the usual weeks in Uist and Eriskay before returning to Blairs and an ever-diminishing number of fellow seminarians (at the end of every term some boys were asked not to come back, while others decided for themselves not to continue).

My holidays were always so refreshing – it was good just to be back in the warmth of our home in Watt Street, or relishing the freedom and fresh air of the islands.

It was always a pleasure to catch up with relatives in the islands, and interesting to see how my cousins' lives were changing as they grew up. They were fascinated by my life at Blairs, but none of them wanted to follow me there. One cousin, Angus, made a sudden decision about his future and left South Uist on the *Lochmor*, heading for the mainland without telling any of his family. A day later he arrived on our doorstep without warning. None of us had the luxury of the telephone in those days, and telegrams were only used in emergencies.

I had been at Blairs about a year by then, and was at home on holiday. I showed Angus round the city and, never having left South Uist before, he was enthralled. My father took him down to 'the Pool' and after a medical examination Angus signed on as an ordinary seaman on a ship leaving for Cadiz that very night. This was what he had left home to do. A day or so later, my mother received a worried telegram from South Uist: 'Angus has left home.

Have you seen him?' My mother calmly sent her reply: 'Angus in Cadiz. He is well. Letter following.' I would love to have seen the faces of Angus' family when that telegram arrived.

I was already losing touch with the boys and girls who had played such an important part in my childhood: their lives were now very different. Everyone had changed. Chrissie left school at 16 and trained as a Contometer Operator (a form of mechanized book-keeping), working for the Scottish Co-operative Society at their headquarters in Dalintober Street. That large and impressive building still stands and can be seen very clearly on the south side of the Kingston Bridge. Donald John was in the second or third year at St Gerard's, a lad with a touch of mischievousness and full of fun, but doing well in his schoolwork. Effie was by now in the Upper Primary at St Margaret's. My parents were happy to see us all grow and flourish. My friends now were mainly boys in the same year as myself and, at holiday time, we would meet, go to the cinema, and spend time in each other's homes. Brian Browne left Blairs when his family emigrated to America. I am sad that I lost contact with so many old friends with whom I had shared so much, but at the time it seemed inevitable.

◆

By the time I was 17 I was in the sixth form and studying assidu-ously for my Higher Grade exams. I was also *Decano* – the head stu-dent – which entailed being the go-between for staff and students, something that often felt like walking a tightrope. By this time there were only 11 of us remaining in the top year. When the sixth form played the fifth form in the annual football match all of us had to play, regardless of talent. I remember we managed to win that game – I hope fairly!

The Higher exams were in March, which left us free of serious classwork from Easter onwards. This time was used to prepare us for the Major Seminary with lessons in Italian and Spanish, offered on a voluntary basis. I had been told by the Archbishop that I would probably go to the Scots College in Rome, so I took some lessons in elementary Italian.

At the end of each year the sixth form traditionally presented a play and we were no different. The theatre was in the old chapel of the original John Menzies house which had become the college in 1829. It was really quite well equipped, with an excellent stage and props. Much of the summer term was spent there in rehearsals for our first performance at Pentecost. The audience was mainly the students and their relatives, who were invited to visit the college on this Feast day each year. We had to produce both male and female parts from our little group of 11 and I was given the role of a Highland policewoman named Sergeant Fire. The jacket of my uniform was borrowed from the local policeman. I cannot remember where my skirt came from, but I know it was too tight around the waist and the open zip was fortunately covered by the long jacket. Thick black stockings were borrowed from one of the nuns who looked after us all in the college – with string for garters the stockings stayed more or less as required throughout the performance. It was all great fun and the play was remarkably well received by our captive audience. My mother and Chrissie were there, on their only visit to the college in my years as a pupil. Afterwards, my mother's only comment was, 'You're the ugliest woman I've ever seen!'

When the Higher results came through I was satisfied. I was never a great student, but I had gained average passes, sufficient for University or Senior Seminary entrance. I had been told to expect to go to Rome, and was quite pleased with my fledgling Italian, but when the end of term arrived the Archbishop informed me that as he only had four students for the Archdiocese this year, all of us were being sent to the Diocesan Seminary in Cardross. I accepted his decision happily, but have often wondered how life would have turned out had I gone to Rome.

My years at Blairs were contented ones and I owe a great deal to the priests and the students with whom I shared so much, for the lasting friendships I made and the knowledge of the Faith I received. When I left for that final time I had no idea I would one day return in another capacity.

◆

During the summer of 1958 after leaving Blairs I spent some weeks of my holiday fishing herring on an Eriskay ring-netter. At that time there were four large boats fishing out of Eriskay, the *Virgin*, the *Santa Maria*, *Sancta Virgo* and *Our Lady of Fatima*, known for short as 'the *Fatima*'. They were all crewed and owned by Eriskay men and contributed to the economy of the island in a way that is difficult to measure. Their grandfathers and fathers had laid a foundation which enabled them to be one of the most successful fishing communities on the west coast of Scotland. Three of the boats were owned by the MacKinnon family and the other by the MacInnes brothers.

I was very kindly given a place aboard the *Virgin*, skippered by Calum MacKinnon. His brother Hector was skipper of the *Sancta Virgo*, and a cousin, Murdo, was in charge of the *Santa Maria*. On Monday afternoon they would sail from Acairseid on the east side of the island and head for the fishing grounds, ranging from Harris in the north to Barra Head in the south, and east to waters off Canna and Rhum. These men gave me a marvellous experience of life and work. I gained my sea legs with them and it is a love that has never diminished.

With herring plentiful in those days and market demand high, one of the MacKinnon boats would take the full catch to Mallaig for sale, while the other two would shelter in Canna, Lochboisdale or Castlebay, depending on where the final catch was made. By dusk, together again, we would set out in search of the shoals. Herring fishing in those days was done at night.

The darkness emphasized the blinking lights of the other boats around us on the same search as ourselves. On a clear night the stars appeared so plentiful and so bright that I felt I had never seen them properly before. We would regularly see shooting stars plunge, as it seemed, straight into the vast ocean. It was an experience of God and His creation that made a deep and lasting impression on my very soul.

As we approached known fishing grounds, two of us lay on the foredeck looking at the white-capped waters rushing past, searching beneath for signs of the herring. At the same time the skipper in the wheelhouse was keeping his eye on the echometer, which printed out the evidence of their presence. The sea would give off a phosphorescent glow created by the movement of hundreds of the silver-bellied creatures deep below the surface. It is an experience I yearn to relive again, but that is most unlikely: today there is a terrible dearth of the 'silver darlings' in our seas.

As soon as we knew there was a shoal the radio of the discovering boat would crackle into life.

'Hello, *Santa Maria*, hello *Sancta Virgo*, *tha sinn a cuir a lion*.' (Hello, *Santa Maria*, hello *Sancta Virgo*, our net is out.)

Arrangements were then made for one of the other two boats to come across and pick up the end of the *Virgin's* ring-net, identified by the attached light bobbing on the sea. A 'ring' was then formed and a sweep of the area undertaken. This completed, the other boat came alongside and, apart from the man at the wheel, the other crew (judging the roll of the boats) leapt aboard the *Virgin*. With the help of winches we physically brought our haul aboard. We were so accustomed to the movement of the boat that, no matter the swell, we took little notice as we brought the ring-net closer and closer. Meanwhile in our arc lights we could see gulls in large numbers filling their bellies, their necks swelling to a size I found astounding as they swallowed their thrashing victims whole. The water boiling white now with the trapped fish, the screeching gulls, diving and swooping and fighting, the shouted instructions to crewmen, all had my adrenalin flowing, filling me with a surging energy. When the catch was aboard, disentangled and emptied into the hold, the net was wound up and prepared at the stern for the next shoot. Leaping at the appropriate time, crewmen rejoined their own boat lying alongside in the rolling sea, while aboard the *Virgin* we set about the task of separating and boxing the still thrashing catch – herring, mackerel, ling, even sea trout and an occasional salmon, all caught in the one sweep. When this was done there might be a call to join one of the other boats to go through the same process again.

The night's work over, one (or two, on a good night) of the boats would set off for Mallaig, sometimes a six-hour sail away. The others would rest up in the nearest harbour, most often Canna or Lochboisdale. Aboard all the boats dinner would be greedily gulped down – freshly caught fish, potatoes and UHT milk. It was a way of life I loved.

◆

Sometime in August of that year I returned to Glasgow to prepare to go to the Seminary in Cardross, or to be more precise to the House of Philosophy in Darleith (the Seminary had two Houses, three miles apart, the House of Philosophy for students in the first two years, the House of Theology for the final four years). Once more my parents and I had to set about acquiring the items stipulated as necessary by the college authorities: black suit, black coat, black hat, biretta, surplice and collar, and a soutane. The textbooks for the various subjects of the two-year Philosophy course could be bought through the college book service or from students who had already finished that part of the course. Again these needs were an extra burden on my father's meagre wage.

The Scottish Education Department was very fair to 'Church students' as we were termed. We received the same bursary benefit as students of a similar age studying at the universities, and this also applied to those studying at seminaries in Rome or Valladolid in Spain. Because of my father's lowly wage I was to receive the full bursary available. His earnings averaged, I discovered in my application, approximately £8.00 per week. Even in 1958 this was a low wage, and I knew how hard he had to work to earn even that. When the bursary was paid I hoped that my parents would be given the full assistance stipulated by law for the expenses they incurred on my behalf. I am still resentful to this day that this was not the case: we did not receive a penny directly, the total grant being paid straight to the college for my board and tuition fees, including the amount set aside for clothes and books. This made life hard, and my family was not alone in this difficulty. Students complained about the arrangement to no avail, and it was some years after my ordination that this injustice was rectified. In my case I was greatly assisted by the generosity of relatives and friends, who were unfailingly kind and supportive. Anything I did receive I gave to my mother, knowing the difficulties she and my father faced almost daily.

◆

Even in its current state of dereliction, Blairs College has a majestic appearance, especially when seen from Deeside. Darleith House, once a manor house, then a convalescence home for service-men of the Second World War, and now housing students for the priesthood, was anything but majestic. It was a grey, squat building, with steadings some three minutes' walk away where the first-year Philosophy students were housed. Our rooms – really cubicles – held a bed, a tiny desk, bookcase and a simple chair which at night became a clothes horse. It was sparse, but I must say I was happy there. The daily timetable was based on the monastic life, beginning at 6.20 a.m. when we rose for Morning Prayer, meditation and Mass, and ending with Night Prayer at 10.00 p.m.

Philosophy was a new and difficult world for me and, I am sure, for many of my fellow students. From French, Maths and Latin we stepped into the heady world of Plato, Aristotle, Thomas Aquinas, Hume, Descartes, and so many others, studying Logic, Metaphysics, Cosmology, Epistomology, Physiology, Ethics (General and

Moral) and History of Philosophy. These were the subjects which taxed my mental ability for the first two years at Cardross, an ability which is best described as 'average' and left at that.

The spiritual life was very important in the Seminary and our day was structured around a programme of prayer and spiritual reading. Each year of study began with a three-day retreat, which was conducted in complete silence, and it ended with a similar exercise as some of the senior students prepared to be ordained to the diaconate or priesthood, or to receive what were known as minor orders.

Of all that happened in my first Senior Seminary year, the date 11 June 1959, the Feast of St Barnabas, stands out in my memory. We were completing our first year of Philosophy and struggling, like most students, with our exams. As a distraction from study I had enjoyed a very competitive game of football earlier in the day and in the evening I played a game of tennis. Afterwards, I sat on the front steps to have my last cigarette of the day and to watch the game being played by Father John Rae and another student on the court which was in front of the main building. The priest was a popular man, an excellent lecturer and an all-round sportsman. He had gained his 'Blue' in football and tennis while studying at Oxford University, something rather unusual for a lad from Lanarkshire. As I and one or two others watched, we saw Father Rae chase a ball and then fall as he tried to make a shot. He was dead. It was the first time in my life that I had witnessed a death. The suddenness of it left us all deeply shocked and the remaining part of the term, after his funeral, was rather sombre. Father Rae's death at the age of 38 from a brain haemorrhage was to be my first of many experiences of death's unexpectedness and seeming unfairness.

After that first year in Cardross I returned to Uist and Eriskay for the summer, where again I was happy to take part in a few weeks' herring fishing, this time aboard the *Santa Maria*. Indeed, I enjoyed the experience so much that I felt quite unsettled on my return to the seminary. For a number of weeks I seriously contemplated leaving and approached the Spiritual Director to discuss my concerns.

'What is it, Roddy?' he asked after a few minutes. 'Is it a girl? Have you fallen in love?'

'Actually, I have,' I replied. 'It's a boat. I've fallen for a boat and fishing.'

He began to laugh, but quickly became serious again when I explained how much I loved the life. It took a few visits and much discussion before I decided to continue with my studies. In reality, of course, I was dreaming. My experience of fishing was thanks to the kindness of the Eriskay fisherman and not because of any natural talents I possessed.

From then on I approached the priesthood with sureness and firm intent. The following summer I went with my sister to visit relatives in Donegal, where I had a wonderful holiday in another very beautiful part of the world. As a result, my time in the islands was curtailed and I did not return to fishing seriously again, limiting myself to less exhilarating fishing with mackerel gut two or three times a week.

◆

At the end of my Philosophy course in 1960 I transferred to the Theology House at Kilmahew. Here I shared a room with Eugene Connolly in the tower of the impressive building, a far cry from the cubicles at Darleith. We had a marvellous view of the 'Tail of the Bank', the opening of the Firth of Clyde, and could clearly see Gourock, Dunoon and the industrialized areas of Greenock and Port Glasgow.

At Kilmahew the subjects we were studying, in addition to the presence of deacons and those in minor orders, made us even more aware of the priesthood towards which we were working. Now we were getting close. I enjoyed the various subjects of the Theology course much more than Philosophy. Over a period of four years we studied a full course of Moral and Dogmatic Theology, Scripture, Canon Law, Liturgy, Church History and Spirituality. Most of these subjects demanded much concentrated work and the college timetable ensured that this was possible. Ample time was also set aside daily for the spiritual exercises which were now a vital part of life. In this aspect we were given a great example by Monsignor Traynor, the college Rector. He had been involved in the training of priests all his working life and was himself a theologian of note.

He could regularly be found in the college chapel, deep in silent prayer and meditation. His spiritual talks were very much appreciated and he managed to convey the most profound Dogmatic Theology by the use of very simple language. As in most things in life, the simple way is clearer and more certain.

My happiness in those years of study was proven by the speed with which time seemed to pass, each year bringing me nearer to the priesthood. There was also a cameraderie among the students which grew stronger by the year and lasted well beyond our time in the seminary. I have a photograph of a group of seven of us which was taken in June 1966. We were on a driving holiday on the continent and had hired a minibus for three weeks. We visited Belgium, Holland, Germany and Austria, stopping for a few days here and there as we travelled (the cost for the whole holiday was about £200 – how prices and times have changed!). The seven of us, pictured in a Munich beer hall, had been friends throughout our college days and stayed so long after we had left Kilmahew. Two of the group, Peter Gorman and Peter Marr, are now dead; may they rest in peace. Pat Joe Loughran and Eugene Connolly left the active ministry a few years later and married, while Sean Fitzgerald and Joe Cairns continue as active priests in the Archdiocese of Glasgow. If the cameraderie we enjoyed has failed since, then it has been in the main due to my own negligence and stupidity, but I still value the friendships, the closeness, the fun of those days.

◆

Rules, it is said, are made to be broken, and there were a few that rather constantly came into that category at Kilmahew. In those days most of us were already smokers by the time we were 18. Capstan and Senior Service were my regular brands. The college had strict rules which curtailed our use of tobacco to short periods after meals, and this only outside the building or in the recreation room at the front. It was strictly forbidden to smoke in one's room, but some of us were rather relaxed when it came to adhering to these rules. Eugene and I had a bin in our room which also did duty as an ashtray. We were also not allowed to have personal radios. There was a communal one available in the recreation room, and we all gathered round it when there was a major football match, especially involving Celtic or Scotland. However, many of us also had our own illegal little transistors hidden away in our rooms.

Those illicit radios came into their own a few years later in 1963, on the day President Kennedy was shot – as the first Catholic president of the United States, he was something of a hero to us. I was deep in study that November evening when Paddy Joe Loughran, a deacon in his final year, knocked on my door.

'President Kennedy has just been shot!'

'What? How do you know?'

He had heard it on the radio he kept hidden in his room. I switched on my own illegal radio, and others came into the room and for a while we just listened silently, smoking our illegal cigarettes and trying to follow all the conflicting news reports.

Later that evening, when the Spiritual Director announced Kennedy's death to us all, we had to pretend we knew nothing about it, and prayed solemnly for the repose of his soul. It is strange to look back today and think that we had access to a television only on very rare occasions then. The President's funeral was one of them, and it was only the second time in my life that I had ever watched the small screen.

◆

As I was approaching the time to receive minor orders in June 1962, my father was very badly injured at work and was hospitalized. We had no telephone at home, so communications were normally by letter and my mother wrote to tell me about the accident. My father's back and neck were badly damaged. He had already undergone surgery and was in the Southern General Hospital in Glasgow. I informed the Rector of what had happened and was given permission to travel to Glasgow to see him, provided I returned in time for evening rosary. By this time it was already two weeks after the accident.

When I saw my father I was shocked by the extent of his injuries. He was encased in some kind of straitjacket to restrict most movements, his large, hard-working hands lying apparently useless on the bedcover. Only then did I find out from my mother exactly what had happened. He was working aboard a ship in dry dock and was pulling a hawser up to where he was positioned on the superstructure. The hawser touched a live bare wire and had it not been for the rubber boots he was wearing, my father would have died there and then. As it was, he was thrown by the shock and fell a long distance down into the ship's hold, hitting a generator on the way. His back and neck were broken, but the surgeons managed to save his mobility, although it would always be severely restricted. His hands and one arm were still black, the result of internal bleeding and burns caused by the high voltage that had surged through him. Knowing how hard my father had worked all his life and painfully aware of the many sacrifices he had made, I was numbed by the thought that he would never be able to work again. Life can be so unfair.

On my return to college that evening I reported to the Master of Discipline on my father's grave condition and was told that I could visit him just once a fortnight. In those days ridiculous rulings of that kind were accepted as the norm. We were living an almost monastic existence in the Seminary and there was much emphasis on adherence to strict rules and undeviating obedience to authority. It was how things were, quite simply, and we very rarely questioned it, although I did just that when my father later died. How attitudes on all sides have changed! Shortly after the shock of my father's accident, I received word that my grandfather, Roderick MacInnes, had died in our old home in Uist. I loved him and knew I would miss him greatly. But the rules did not allow me to go and comfort my mother, who was in mourning, and I was certainly not permitted to travel to Uist with her for the funeral.

◆

In June 1962 I duly received minor orders and, being a cleric now, was forbidden by the Archbishop of Glasgow to do any kind of secular work for money. It was a ruling much resented by many of the students, as money was often scarce, but again, we accepted such an order as part of the 'package'. I was fortunate that I spent my summer in the islands where at least there was plenty to do at that time of year, taking home the peat and harvesting the hay. And I happily spent some days at sea, tugging on the line of mackerel gut and filling the odd box with a mixture of mackerel, ling and cod.

I made my way to Mass at 8 o'clock every morning, normally on foot. Monsignor Neil MacKellaig had been my parish priest in Uist for as long as I could remember and gave me great encouragement. In Eriskay at this time was Father Angus John MacQueen, who was always friendly, encouraging and helpful to me. He had a remarkable rapport with the parishioners, encouraging a community spirit amongst young and old alike.

Throughout that summer my parents were unable to travel to Uist because of my father's injuries. Although he was mobile, his movements were still very restricted and my mother was working as a domestic help for two different families, trying to earn enough to support them both. Now that my father could no longer work, he had no income at all. As ever I was the lucky one able to have a holiday, fit and rested on my return.

◆

I continued with my studies, now the proud possessor of a room all to myself. After my third-year theology exams were over, I entered into retreat to prepare for the next important step, entry to the sub-diaconate in June 1963. This was the time when I would make the solemn promise of obedience to my bishop and bind myself to a life of celibacy. The Code of Canon Law (Canon 1037) states that the candidate for the priesthood 'is not to be admitted to the order of diaconate unless he has, in the prescribed rite, publicly before God and the Church undertaken the obligation of celibacy'. This was when the real commitment began. It was what I had prayed about, thought about, discussed in depth with my Spiritual Director, and lived for up until this point. It was a big milestone, but I felt ready. I had no doubts.

The retreat helped us all to focus on the profound meaning of what was to happen, and provided a vital breathing space of peace and calm. Inevitably, the retreats also had their lighter moments, very often provided by the Retreat Master himself, the priest specially brought in to lead us through the programme. Most often, the Masters were excellent, providing us with material for serious thought and also lightening the occasion with wit and laughter. Silence was strictly kept throughout the three full days. My birthday, 28 June, normally fell on the last day of retreat because ordination day was on 29 June, the Feast of Sts Peter and Paul. Two years before, on my 21st birthday, the students had stood after supper and silently mouthed 'Happy Birthday' to me, while I, feeling very foolish, had silently mouthed back 'Thanks!'

After the retreat, and the solemn occasion of ordination day, I spent some time relaxing in Donegal, a place which I had grown to love.

It was only now at this late stage of my progress to the priesthood that my father really accepted that I would be ordained. Perhaps he never truly believed that I would successfully stay the course. Be that as it may, he never put me under any pressure to continue, and I was always assured that there would be no disappointment or shame if I wished to pull out. Some of those I knew at the Seminary had to endure this kind of parental pressure and it created great unhappiness in their lives. I was allowed to choose my course in life freely, and I know I benefited greatly from my parents' loving support. My father finally had to recognize that I was not going to follow him to sea after all, but perhaps my brother was about to offer some consolation: as I entered my final year of study,

Donald John was in his own final year at college, qualifying for a Radio Operator's ticket. It was his intention to join the Merchant Navy.

On my return to the Seminary after our summer break, I again entered into retreat to prepare for the diaconate. In July, Archbishop Donald Campbell of Glasgow had died very suddenly while on pilgrimage to Lourdes. His auxiliary, Bishop James Ward, ordained us deacons in Clerkhill Convent, Dumbarton, in August 1963. I was pleased and moved that my parents were both present for the occasion – my father wearing a neck truss of some kind and obviously very uncomfortable. After a cup of tea and a brief chat, which was all we could manage, they returned home and I went back to college.

✦

Sometime in September I had occasion to go to Glasgow and, my business done, I paid a short visit home to Watt Street. My mother was delighted at my unexpected visit and said she would waken my father, who was resting.

I asked after his health and she replied with a serious look, 'Oh, I'm worried about him.'

'What's wrong?' I asked in alarm.

'I think he's in love with someone else.'

'Och, Mammy, don't be daft. How can that be?'

'Well, he keeps asking to see Ena, whoever she might be!'

A twinkle appeared in her eye, and it was then I discovered that because my father was at home all day with nothing to do, she had rented a television set, our very first. My father's favourite programme was *Coronation Street*, which I had never heard of: it was not on our timetable. Ena Sharples was, of course, a principal character. I should have been warned; my mother's sense of humour was always present in any adversity.

About a month later my mother wrote to tell me that we were to move to a new house in the Corkerhill area of Pollok. The housing schemes were gradually drawing people away from the old and shabby tenements to houses built after the war. These had baths and hot and cold water, luxuries we had never experienced in Watt Street. Some of our neighbours had already moved and the close community into which I had been born was disintegrating. As I read the letter I knew I would never go home to Watt Street again.

I would miss it. An added sadness was that the move would mean leaving the parish of Our Lady and St Margaret's which had been such an influence on my life. All at once I was surrounded by change and it was disconcerting.

When I went home that Christmas it was to 32 Hardridge Road, Corkerhill. Despite his injuries my father had struggled on doggedly and had managed to paint and decorate the house. Having an extra bedroom made such a difference, as did the availability of hot water. My mother even had a washing machine which she had managed to purchase secondhand. There was no further need to go to the 'Steamie', although she kept her old washing board to hand, just in case. Despite the space and the smart newness of it all, however, we missed 218 Watt Street. The memory of our home there still fills me with nostalgia.

During this holiday I noticed that my father seemed to have aged a great deal and was suffering discomfort and pain. He had always been a fit man, having worked hard all his life. The sudden destruction of his normal active life and the continuous pain from his injuries were very hard to bear. We were all concerned by his deterioration, although we did not think to attribute it to anything except the accident of the previous year. The Transport Union was still fighting a claim for compensation on his behalf. Unfortunately the company, Simon and Lobnitz, had gone into liquidation which complicated matters. Aware that he could never work again, my father refused, on legal advice, a paltry sum offered by the liquidators. Culpability for the accident was wholly attributable to the firm's negligence, and he was advised to push for more. This ongoing worry was obviously taking its toll.

When I returned to the Seminary in January 1964 for the last months of preparation before ordination to the priesthood, I felt strangely homesick. I was worried about my father's health and felt guilty that I could do so little to help. It was hard to be so cut off.

A few weeks later I received a letter from my mother. My father was in hospital and had undergone a stomach operation. On the first free day I got permission to visit him and travelled to the Southern General Hospital once more. As I entered the ward I could see my mother sitting beside him, holding his hand. I was shocked by his appearance. My mother's eyes betrayed her distress and worry, although her welcoming smile tried to hide that truth. My father claimed to feel better.

As we left the hospital together, my mother broke the news to me that the surgeon had discovered inoperable cancer – it had spread from the stomach to the liver. Like any family in the same circumstances, we were devastated. My mother decided to hide the whole truth from my sister Effie, who was the youngest and still at school.

I returned to college that evening with a very heavy heart and determined to see my father as often as possible. It emerged that this would only be once a week: every Thursday I would be allowed to travel to Glasgow to see him. I accepted this ruling, although with some desperation, despite the fact that I was technically free on two other afternoons in the week.

As Easter approached, I could see clear and rapid deterioration on every visit, but I was still only allowed that one weekly journey. At my mother's suggestion my father was brought home so that she might care for him in comfortable surroundings for the remaining time.

◆

As deacons we were required by ordination, and also as excellent practice, to preach at Mass and the people of the surrounding parishes in Dumbartonshire had to suffer our efforts. When the others were out visiting these churches, one of us had to remain in the college to preach at the High Mass which was celebrated every Sunday, and this was the most nerve-wracking experience of them all. To be faced by some 30 biretta-clad heads bent over surpliced bodies, either willing one to finish or fall flat on one's face, was intimidating to say the least.

I still remember the embarrassment of hearing one deacon who began, as expected: 'In the Name of the Father and of the Son and of the Holy Spirit.' This was followed by a silence, most of us reacting with nervous coughs and shuffling of feet.

After what felt like eternity he spoke again: 'Aw, jings, I've forgotten what I was going to say!'

Despite the urge to give way to appalled laughter we kept our silence. Then all heads came up as the celebrant, Monsignor David MacRoberts, poker-faced as ever, intoned, *'Credo in Unum Deum'* and the poor deacon had to continue with his role in the celebration of the Mass.

In Holy Week all of the deacons participated in the ceremonies which were celebrated in St Andrew's Cathedral in Glasgow. We were all schooled in the various rites and most of us seemed to be better trained that the other participating clergy. Instead of going to St Andrew's Cathedral with the rest that Easter, however, Hugh McGinlay and I were sent to help with the Easter Vigil Ceremony in St Columba's Cathedral in Oban.

On the Saturday afternoon we travelled by bus to Oban and went to the Columba Hotel where a room had been reserved. It was my first experience of hotel life. In the evening, at about 9 o'clock, we made our way along the promenade to the Cathedral House and were invited into the sitting room where we sat nervously in the presence of Monsignor Ewan MacInnes, the Administrator. He immediately ordered us some tea, which we drank while he continued to smoke his pipe and watch television. After a short time Father Calum MacNeil, who was curate in Barra, came in to join us. He had been retained in Oban to assist the bishop as Master of Ceremonies.

We relaxed in his company as he spoke of college life and entertained us with some of his stories. At about 10 o'clock we realized that on the television was a slightly risqué French film with English subtitles. Monsignor MacInnes had studied in France and had no need for such aids. Soon afterwards the door opened and there was Bishop McGill, in most of his regalia, announcing that it was time to greet the Risen Lord. 'Yes, my lord,' replied the Monsignor. 'But, tell me, did they kiss in France like that in your day?' There was no reply from the bishop. We trooped silently into the cathedral sacristy and then, properly vested, into the candlelit darkness to begin the solemn celebration.

Hugh and I were well versed in the liturgy and the rites, but obviously Father Calum had never paid too much attention to detail. On a number of occasions the bishop intervened with a question – 'Shouldn't I be at the back of the church just now?' or, 'I think I should be wearing my mitre now.' Father Calum's response was the same each time. He put his hand into his soutane pocket, produced a little book, sought out the appropriate page and, looking up and nodding, answered, 'Yes, my lord.' We then proceeded until the next pause for question and answer.

Hugh and I had increasing difficulty keeping a straight face as the service went on. At the end, when we reached the safety of the sacristy, the bishop turned to us and said, 'That is how we do things here. It's called the Celtic Rite.' I think he was unamused.

◆

From Oban I returned to Glasgow and home for my last holiday before ordination in June. As I entered my father's bedroom I could not conceal my shock. It was obvious that he was close to death. Sitting by his bedside, I noticed that the mirror had been removed and later discovered that my mother had done this so that he might not see in his reflection the deterioration taking place in his body.

After a while he asked if I could help him to the toilet. I gave him my arm, but he looked at me with knowing eyes and said, 'You'll need to carry me.' I found myself lifting my father as if he were a child, his body so wasted, once-powerful arms and legs now skeleton-like. Giving him the privacy he deserved, I waited outside until he was ready to be lifted back, trying to hold back the rush of tears. I returned him gently to his bed and he looked directly at me as he lay back exhausted. That look told me everything. He knew that death was very near.

Not just for my own sake, but also to help my mother, sisters and brother, I spent a great deal of time with my father that holiday week. On the Friday he became so ill and distressed that the doctor arranged for him to be readmitted to hospital. When we arrived shortly afterwards, he whispered to me that he wanted to see the lawyer handling his compensation claim as soon as possible. Immediately I made my way by bus to the city centre where the lawyer, Mr McCann, had his office. I informed him of my father's condition and asked if he could visit him in hospital very soon.

On the Sunday I had to return to the Seminary to prepare for my final exams and ordination. My thoughts were constantly with my family, and the following Thursday I travelled back to Glasgow and the hospital to see my father. There was so little left of him that I wondered how he was still alive. He could barely talk but managed to whisper to me that he doubted if he would see my ordination. Again he mentioned the lawyer and said that he had not come.

Knowing that I might never see my father again, I phoned the college, explained the situation, and asked if I might stay at home for a few days. This permission was not granted and I returned that evening with a feeling of despair, having called once more on the lawyer, pleading with him to visit my father. In fact, the compensation issue was never resolved, and neither my father nor my mother after his death ever received a penny. I was late into college and was reprimanded by the Master of Discipline for my tardiness. Numbed, I did not know what to say.

That Saturday we had a two-hour lecture from Barnabas Ahearne, a noted American Scripture scholar and writer. My mind was elsewhere. The lecture over, we made our way to the refectory for tea before evening study. The head student approached me at table and told me that Father McKay was at the door wishing to speak to me.

'Your father is dead,' Father McKay told me briefly. 'Your brother will phone back later.' He had nothing else to say.

I then spoke to Tony Bancewicz, who was the driver of the college vehicle and in third-year theology, and asked him if he could drive me to the station. Then I knocked on the door of the staff refectory where they were entertaining Barnabas Ahearne. Father McKay opened the door. 'Yes, Mr Wright?'

'I'm going home and will be absent until after my father's funeral. Tony Bancewicz will take me to the station.'

I was shocked by the reply. 'Oh no, he's not,' said Father McKay flatly. 'There's no need for you to go home tonight. Your family will have enough to do and your presence isn't needed.'

'I'm going home now,' I stated firmly. Having already packed a bag, I made my way to the front door, where Tony was waiting with the Land-Rover.

Father McKay appeared and spoke to Tony: 'You don't have permission to take Mr Wright to the station.'

'Let's go,' I said to Tony, ignoring Father McKay. 'I'll answer for you and take the consequences.'

After the funeral I returned to college knowing I had only a week to do some serious study before the final exams. With my father so ill, I had found it almost impossible to concentrate. First of all I satisfied myself that Tony Bancewicz had not been disciplined for taking me to the station, then I reported my return to the Rector, who gave me support and encouragement. On leaving the Rector, I was met by Father McKay, who asked me to come to his room immediately. There he confronted me with a little transistor radio and an obviously used ashtray. In my absence he had inspected my room and found these illegal objects.

'You have been in flagrant breach of college rules,' he told me stiffly, 'and this must bring your ordination into question. And don't expect kid-glove treatment in your exams just because your father has died.'

I was at this time just two months from ordination, the culmination of many years' work and the realization of long-held hopes.

Father McKay's words had little effect except to make me angry, however. I refused to take them seriously: the Rector had not referred to any such problems when I had seen him earlier.

I did not complain then, and have no wish to do so now. The apparently harsh college rules which hemmed me in during the illness of my father would not be tolerated now, but we accepted them then, more or less, as part of life. Petty behaviour and rigid insistence on rules in inappropriate situations are always unacceptable, but such things are also to be expected as a part of life, even today. I had no regrets about defying the rules when my family needed me most, and the Rector, at least, understood and showed compassion. In the event, I surprised both myself and certain others by doing rather better than expected in my final exams.

3

✦

DRUMCHAPEL AND

BARLANARK

I WAS ORDAINED PRIEST ON 29 JUNE 1964, the day after my 24th
birthday. The ceremony was conducted by the Archbishop of Glasgow, James Donald Scanlan (the successor to Donald Campbell, he
had not long been appointed to the Metropolitan See of Glasgow,
having previously been Bishop of Motherwell), and was in Latin,
following the Tridentine Rite.

First came the 'laying on of hands', when the Archbishop and
other priests present placed their hands on the head of each ordi-
nand, praying that the Holy Spirit touch us with his gifts. This part
of the ceremony goes back to the very beginnings of Christianity:
'What they said pleased the whole community, and they chose
Stephen, a man full of faith and the Holy Spirit, together with
Philip, Prochorus, Nicanor, Timon, Parmenas, and Nicolaus ...
They had these men stand before the apostles, who prayed and laid
their hands on them' (Acts 6:5–6). Then we went through the ceremony of the 'anointing of hands', when each of the new priests had
their hands anointed by the Archbishop with oil of Chrism – sacred
oil. Our hands were anointed because we would be using them to
administer the Sacraments, especially in the celebration of the
Eucharist. After the anointing we each received from the Archbishop a chalice and paten (the cup and plate used for the bread
and wine), emphasizing our important role in the celebration of the

Eucharist on behalf of the faithful. It was a solemn and moving occasion.

After the ceremony the newly ordained priests had breakfast with the Archbishop and on my plate was a letter informing me that I had been appointed as assistant priest in St Laurence's, Drumchapel, and that I must be there on 28 July. All I knew about the parish was that it was situated in a large housing scheme on the north-west side of Glasgow.

A number of my relatives had travelled from the islands for the ceremony and I was delighted to have them there, although I was keenly aware of the gap in the family ranks left by the death of my father. After a low-key reception in a restaurant, we all went home to Hardridge Road. It was very crowded and some of us had to sleep on the floor that night, but nobody seemed to mind. It was just good to have the family together.

The following morning we returned to Kinning Park, to the familiar and much-loved church of Our Lady and St Margaret's. Here I celebrated my first Mass. It was, and still is in my mind, a beautiful and moving occasion. The Mass was still in the Tridentine Rite, and therefore in Latin (for the first year of my priesthood I said all my Masses in Latin, until the vernacular rite was introduced), and I was assisted by Father Fred Rawlings, who had been a curate in the parish since I was a year old. It was the last occasion on which I would have around me so many people who had influenced my life and encouraged and supported me on my progress to that day.

A few days later I accompanied my mother to Uist. For her the return home was very much tinged with sadness this time. Her sister, Mary Kate, had been widowed just 12 days before my mother and both families were still in deep mourning. After several days I took my mother over to Eriskay, but we did not stay long. My father had loved this island and my mother was keenly reminded of him in the people she met and the landmarks we saw. She was very emotional throughout our visit, and it was better not to linger.

✦

On 28 July I took a taxi from Hardridge Road to Drumchapel. It was my first visit to the area and I looked around with curiosity as we passed through Knightswood and into the housing scheme where I expected to spend the next period of my life. I was driven into the grounds of St Laurence's, a modern but simple church and house linked by a patio-style area. The door was opened by a tall, straight-backed priest who, cigarette dangling from his mouth, welcomed me with a broad smile and a warm handshake. That was my first impression of Father Charles Duffin, the parish priest under whose charge I would live for the next year and a half.

The following morning, after celebrating the early Mass at 8 o'clock, I asked him what I should do. Jimmy Reilly, the other assistant priest, was still on holiday and I expected to be busy with pastoral duties.

'Well, Roddy,' Charlie replied, 'the schools are still on holiday and everything is quiet. Are you able to use a paintbrush? I'm painting the hall these days.'

At the rear of the building was a wooden structure that had once served as the church until the present one was built. I would become well acquainted with that hall because it was the centre for many parish activities, especially for the young people. So here I began my active ministry, painting a hall. That work continued for almost two weeks, by which time the schools had reopened and my daily timetable was fairly full.

At that time Drumchapel was a vibrant and young community. For many in the new houses it was a luxury to have hot and cold water and a bathroom, having spent 'a previous life' in a tenement in Govan, Partick, or Maryhill. They had most likely begun life in a 'single end' – a very small flat with only the one room and a kitchen, often home to a family of six or eight. Now, by contrast, they had a mansion – two or three bedrooms, a living room, a bathroom, a large kitchen and, in many cases, a verandah. Yet they still referred to themselves as coming from Partick, or Govan, or Maryhill – another part of the world. But a new community was gradually being formed, especially when the young generation began to find their own identity in Drumchapel, through school and youth clubs.

The parish community was at this exciting stage of growth when I arrived and it was a positive place to be. For the adults there was also the added bonus of good work opportunities and unemployment was not a factor in the lives of many. The world-famous John Brown's Shipyard was nearby in Clydebank, as was Singer's, the great sewing machine company. Many of the men worked in these establishments and there were genuine opportunities for the young people in various apprenticeship schemes. Others continued to work in the engineering plants, factories and docks as they had always done. Also locally there was a large biscuit factory as well as the Cutty Sark whisky warehouse, giving employment to both men and women. The community was lively and confident, with good reason.

✦

Charlie Duffin was very kind to me as I learned the ropes of parish life. In his younger days he had been with the Metropolitan Police in London before studying for the priesthood, which he did in Rome, a city he loved. He and Jimmy Reilly were both excellent teachers, pulling the reins in very wisely on my enthusiasm. I wanted to save the world, not paint a hall. But Charlie soon convinced me of the need to immerse myself in all parish activities, no matter how unimportant they might appear. Jimmy taught me the importance of laughter and not to take myself too seriously.

As the youngest and newest I accepted whatever duties the parish priest asked me to perform. When my first Christmas came along Charlie asked me to preach the sermon at Midnight Mass so that he could be the celebrant without having to prepare yet another Christmas sermon. It was my first and was delivered with much nervousness. The church was full with not a seat available, some people even being squeezed into the little Lady Chapel at the front beside the altar. A number of the congregation were non-Catholic partners of Catholics, or people just wanting to continue celebrations, already begun, by being present at a Christmas service.

As I was in 'full cry' with my sermon I noticed a young couple in the Lady Chapel who were obviously not paying attention. They were kissing and cuddling, and I looked away, distracted, and continued with my sermon. When I next looked they were becoming very passionate and were occupying the attention of a number of the congregation nearby. I stopped talking. People, as they do, began to cough nervously, and heads began to turn.

After a prolonged silence I gave my rebuke: 'Most of us are here for one purpose. Perhaps you should have gone elsewhere.'

The poor girl quickly separated herself from the lad's embrace, and there was more silence before I continued with a sermon that no one was hearing any longer.

In the sacristy afterwards Jimmy laughed himself into convulsions. 'Roddy,' he wheezed, 'that was a good sermon but why did you stop our fun?' I was learning. I should have continued as if nothing was happening; instead I had unnecessarily drawn attention to myself and the embarrassed couple.

After a little dram I went to bed. I was to celebrate the first Mass at 8.00 a.m. and I was 'on call' should anyone need a priest during the night. I had just fallen asleep when I was woken by the night bell. When I opened the door I was confronted by a large and apologetic policeman. It must be a throwback to my childhood, but I am always intimidated when faced by a policeman. There was a hard, white frost and he looked colder than I felt, standing there nervously in my dressing gown.

'Father, I'm Sergeant Divers. We need your help.'

'Oh ... in what way can I be of help?'

'We have two youngsters who have been found locked out of their home. A neighbour is looking after them just now. We must find their father. Their mother is dead and the children say he's with his girlfriend, a Mrs Kelly, in the Temple area of Knightswood. He's a Catholic and we don't want to charge him on this night. If we brought you there, could you persuade him to come home?'

'Oh. Right. Eh, just let me get dressed.'

Once in the car with the sergeant and a constable, I asked about the man we were to visit. I realized that I knew the children, who attended St Laurence's Primary School. Their mother had died a year earlier and they had an older sister who might be with the father. Soon we were in an area of Glasgow I had never seen, pulling up outside a tenement block. I followed the policemen up the dark stairs and found myself on a landing, which the sergeant illuminated with his torch. The nameplate confirmed that it was Mrs Kelly's house. Sergeant Divers gave me his torch, explaining that it was likely there was no electricity in the house. They then moved down the stairs a few steps, wishing to remain in the background. Torch in hand, I knocked loudly on the door. After a while it was opened by a woman who appeared to have only one eye.

'Mrs Kelly?'

'Oh, hello, Father.' She spoke as if it was quite normal for a priest to be at her door at 4 o'clock on Christmas morning.

'Hello. Tell me, is Mr _____ here?'

'Who? Oh, yes. Aye, I think he's in that room,' she said, pointing me to a bedroom door.

The electricity had indeed been cut off and I was only able to see by torchlight. Entering the room, I saw a man sitting up in bed, looking very confused and smelling strongly of drink. I felt angry for a moment. How could he stay here and leave his little children out in the freezing cold? But I remained cool and asked him to get dressed as I was taking him home. He began to cry and complied without demur.

'Tell me, is your daughter here with you?' I asked as he struggled into his clothes.

'Aye. She's next door in that room.'

I asked Mrs Kelly, hovering by the door, if she could waken the girl. 'She'll listen to you before taking any heed of me,' she replied as she showed me into another room. I was again aware of the strong smell of alcohol. As I shone the torch I was amazed to see tousled heads, it seemed, all over the bed. There were six females occupying it, a muddle of feet and heads sharing pillows. Mrs Kelly shook the girl, who sat up looking scared, averting her face in protest at the torchlight. By this time her father, now dressed, had entered the room and told his daughter to get dressed and come home with him. The other occupants of the bed continued to sleep soundly.

When we reached the close-mouth the two policemen silently opened the car doors and ushered father and daughter into the back seat, then squeezed into the front beside me. The poor man kept apologizing, pleading with the policemen not to take the children away. They lectured him on his duty of care and told him that this was a last warning that he *must* heed.

I asked how much food he had in the house and was shocked to be told that the cupboards were bare. The sergeant agreed to take me home first so that I might pick up some provisions. I was able to fill a box with essentials, some tins, a cooked chicken from the fridge, and some crisps, chocolates and lemonade from youth club provisions.

While the constable fetched the children from the neighbour I waited with the sergeant in the cold and sparsely furnished house until the tearful reunion had taken place. The police then took me home, thanking me for my assistance. I thanked them in turn for their compassion and understanding in the circumstances. With Mass to be celebrated at 8 o'clock there was no point returning to bed. I had just received a stark lesson in the realities of life. It is a Christmas I have never forgotten.

✦

Being of a younger generation, my taste in music – especially the Beatles and the Rolling Stones – was not to the liking of Charlie or Jimmy. However, they did push all the youth work my way, an area of ministry I found fulfilling. Working in the schools was surprisingly rewarding and I spent time most days in our Primary schools, St Laurence's and St Sixtus', and at least twice a week I taught Religious Education in St Pius Secondary School which served the whole of that area. At that time Drumchapel had a population similar to the city of Perth (about 60,000), and the Catholic schools were very full.

On Wednesday and Friday nights we had youth club activities in our little hall. The Wednesday evenings, involving the younger children, were very lively and straightforward. Friday nights, however, were always more difficult because amongst the teenagers there were the inevitable troublemakers and, on more than one occasion, we had to call for police assistance. I was getting to know the police well.

Gangs were in fashion around Glasgow at that time and Drumchapel had at least two, the 'Drummy' and 'Blue Angels'. They each had their own patch and were often involved in skirmishes over territory. I used to refer to them as cowboys and Indians. These little wars caused nuisance and occasionally some damage to property. Sometimes, however, a more ugly and frightening incident took place.

One Friday evening I was called from the hall because someone wished to speak with me in the waiting room. In my absence some lads whom I had earlier barred from the youth club managed to sneak into the hall, where everyone was dancing to music provided by a local disc jockey. The intruders took over the stage and began chanting 'Drummy, Drummy', trying to goad members of the local gang, the Blue Angels.

Frantic knocking on the door brought me from the waiting room and the scene that met my eyes was amazing. Young people were streaming from the hall, the girls crying and screaming, and some of the boys wisely trying to get as far away as possible. Inside the hall gang members were throwing chairs and exchanging blows. I dashed into their midst and shouted for them to stop with all the authority I could muster. One of the youth leaders ran to the house and phoned the police as I continued to try and restore some kind of order to the chaos. The hall emptied suddenly, the streetwise lads well aware of the imminent arrival of the police. The result was that the innocents suffered, including myself, as Charlie Duffin suspended the Friday night club. It took four weeks to persuade him to relent and allow the young people to return.

✦

I learned a great deal in my first year, and a little man living in Lillyburn Place taught me a vital lesson. The parish was divided into three areas, each being assigned to a priest for house visitation and the care of the sick. I was given the visiting books for the part known as 'the hill'. To this day I can clearly remember Achamore Road, Inchfad Drive, Lillyburn Place, Monymusk Place and Fettercairn Avenue, because I visited every Catholic household in my first six months. One Saturday afternoon Charlie asked me to see a lady in the waiting room who wished to speak to a priest. She lived in Lillyburn Place so he thought I should deal with the matter. Entering the room, I asked her how I could help.

'Father,' she replied, 'will you talk to my husband? He's drinking too much and not at all nice to me. My life is a misery. I don't want to leave him but I'm afraid I must. Can you speak with him?'

I listened further to her tale of woe concerning the state of their marriage. 'Now,' I said, 'you go home and I'll follow in about a quarter of an hour.'

I walked briskly up the hill to their house formulating my thoughts and when I confronted the husband in their living room my words of admonition immediately poured forth. I gave him no chance to speak. He just sat very patiently and listened.

Then his wife intervened: 'How dare you speak to my man like that! He's not that kind of person.' I was taken aback and, frankly, left speechless in confusion.

'Father,' said the husband eventually, 'what do you know about Clyde navigation?'

'Not much, really,' I replied, startled.

'Aye. And you don't know much about marriage either.'

I left that house, my ego and zeal sadly deflated. But I learned a very important lesson – never to interfere so confrontationally in other people's domestic problems. After that, whenever I was asked to help in such matters, I asked both partners to come to the waiting room and there I would listen. Listening is usually more important than talking. I continue to be grateful to that man for his advice.

✦

The Sacrament of Penance – or, as it has become known in post-Vatican II years, the Sacrament of Reconciliation – has always been important to me. For many non-Catholics Confession (as it is usually called) is a puzzling, if not ridiculous, intrusion into people's lives, but I am sure it has proved significant for many Catholics, like myself, who were reared with the Sacrament as a habitual part of life. The need to say sorry in a meaningful way is essential in any relationship. If I have a conscience and, therefore, an awareness of right and wrong, I need to be able to reach out to God and to those I have offended by my sins. The Seal of Confession, or to put it simply, the strict obligation of silence imposed on the confessor, is also a vital aspect of the process. After more than three decades in the active ministry I understand the importance of Confession as a healing, strengthening and consoling factor in my own and other people's lives.

In my first year as an active priest the confessional played a large and very rewarding part in my pastoral ministry. Our church was on a busy bus route and all the buses stopped outside it, so many people from outside the parish used St Laurence's to attend Mass or go to Confession because it was convenient. On Saturday nights three hours, between 6 and 9 o'clock, were set aside for the Sacrament of Penance. Jimmy and I were kept very busy, often not getting a break.

I remember so clearly, on my first night, bringing a little Moral Theology book with me in case I was faced with some problem for which I had no answer. I never brought it again. It was not necessary. A good confessor is a good listener, a spiritual person not a cold judge. If advice is requested it is given, never imposed. In my own experience of being the penitent I have come across only a few instances of a confessor being imposing or intrusive. My presence on both sides of the confessional screen has brought me healing and, I hope, real humility. I find it sad that fewer and fewer Catholics approach the Sacrament today. It is a great loss to the balance of spiritual life.

✦

Looking back to that time I am still surprised at how I managed to deal with the various problems that came my way in the pastoral ministry. Illness, death and their effect on individuals and families became a regular concern. Since those early days I have never ceased to be uplifted by the courage and fortitude shown by those knowingly approaching death from a terminal illness. Jimmy Reilly set me an excellent example in caring for the sick, and I learned to visit sufferers regularly to administer the Sacraments.

Suicide is one form of death that I find so difficult to understand – the desperation, hopelessness and loneliness must be overwhelming. In 'my' area of the parish I had to deal with three such deaths in the first year. One was by hanging, the others by gassing. All three victims lived in poor conditions and life was a struggle.

One case in particular left me feeling angry because it could have been avoided. We both shared the same name – Roderick. He was a patient in Gartnaval Psychiatric Hospital and had been allowed home for the weekend. On the Saturday afternoon his wife came to our house, deeply concerned because he had told her he was determined to kill himself. She asked me to phone the hospital on her behalf and get them to take her husband back immediately. I spoke to the nurse in charge, relaying the wife's message and her definite concern. I was told in no uncertain terms that it was really not my business to make such a request. In the judgement of his doctor the man was sufficiently recovered to be at home. In vain I tried to explain once more that I was not making a clinical judgement but relaying the real fear felt by his wife. The conversation ended abruptly with the nurse telling me they would see Roderick on Monday when he was due back.

Disconsolate, the woman returned home. About two hours later a neighbour arrived to inform me that Roderick had killed himself. Please could I come to the house? I hurried up the hill and, entering the house, was confronted by the distraught wife and two little children weeping loudly. Having been afraid to leave the children with her husband, she had taken them with her to do some shopping. Returning an hour later, the smell of gas had met her as soon as she opened the door. She found him lying in the kitchen, his head resting on a pillow in the oven. He was already dead.

As we waited for the doctor and the police, I administered the last rites to Roderick where he lay. By the time I left the house a number of neighbours had gathered to give their support. I immediately phoned the hospital and spoke to the same nurse as before.

'Roderick will not be returning on Monday. He killed himself this afternoon.'

'Oh. I'm sorry to hear that.'

'Perhaps his wife did know better than the doctor or any of us.'

My anger did not permit me to wait for her reply. I was too distressed at the terrible waste of life and apparent lack of care. This occurred over 30 years ago, yet today the same needless tragedies are still happening to some of those termed as being 'in the care of the community'.

Members of the working class, as we used to be called, always tried to maintain high standards of cleanliness and tidiness at home. But when real poverty sets in the resulting problems can appear almost impossible to overcome, and hopelessness and despair can so often take over. The community in Drumchapel was full of hope in those days, but there were still cases of severe poverty. Usually the condition had followed people from where they had previously lived – it cannot be made to evaporate with a change of address.

It was in such circumstances that Anne had lived all her young life. I was called to the house in an emergency one day, and found her mother frantically trying to control the asthmatic attack which had left Anne completely exhausted and barely conscious. My knock on the door brought the mother running, thinking I was the ambulanceman. The family's extreme poverty was immediately obvious in the sparsely furnished house, an old television set balanced on a box in the corner, some patchy carpeting, just two hard wooden chairs. In the bedroom I found a little girl, who I thought was about seven years old, convulsing on top of the bed, desperately gasping for air. Utterly distressed, her mother ran from the room and I lifted Anne from the bed. As I did so she gave a violent shudder and then went limp with a little exhalation of breath. She was dead. The ambulance crew arrived but could do nothing.

I tried to console her poor mother, and discovered to my horror that Anne, so tiny, was in fact 14 years old. She was so underdeveloped and so burdened by ill-health that she could never have experienced much joy in her life. Her death certainly had a real effect on one young priest, as did the poverty in which she had lived.

◆

After 10 months in St Laurence's I passed my driving test at the second attempt and bought a little, two-year-old grey mini-van. It was cheap and basic but meant the world to me, and made such a difference to my life. Does everyone remember their first set of wheels with such pride?

Wednesday was my free day and I usually joined other priests of my age in a game of golf at Troon. There were usually four of us and we travelled together in one of their cars, not my modest wee van. I have never been a good golfer and have never even owned a set of clubs, but the company and the sea air were a welcome break from normal duties. In the evening I went home to Hardridge Road to be with my mother and the family, a visit I always enjoyed. Chrissie married in April 1965, having postponed her wedding from the previous August because of our father's death. Effie and Donald John still lived at home with my mother. Donald John had gained his Radio Officer's ticket but, again because of my father's death, he decided to stay at home instead of joining the Merchant Navy and managed to find work as an engineer with the Post Office. We were a close family and it was important to us all that we support each other.

After a year I was happily settled into the parish and felt very much at home with Charlie and Jimmy. The youth activities were developing well and this gave me real satisfaction in my pastoral work. We gradually built up an excellent organization, competing with other clubs in various sports, especially football. The Glasgow team that most of us supported – Celtic – were at the beginning of their magnificent run of success at home and in Europe. Unfortunately, on some Saturdays I would have difficulty putting forward a full team for one of our league games because so many would be at Celtic Park. Other clubs had the same difficulty, however, so eventually we rearranged matters and played our games on Sunday afternoons instead. I was manager, physio and, on occasions, referee.

I played quite regularly myself with other priests, in a Clergy XI, and although it may sound boastful, we were a good side. Our games were so-called 'friendlies' against such teams as The Ministers, The Fire Brigade, The Teachers, and, quite regularly, The Police. 'Friendly' was possibly a misnomer. In one game against the constabulary, a number of fouls were committed and things became quite tousy. An overexcited team-mate, thinking I was too slow to intercept a pass, shouted loudly at me, 'Aw, Roddy, you're running as if the hairs in your arse are tied together!' I was furious and shouted back with some strong language, though not quite as descriptive. Afterwards, as we left the park, one of the policemen said to me, 'Where did you guys learn that kind of language?' I could only reply with another question: 'Where did *you* learn?'

✦

Visitation of every home in the parish was required at least once a year. I found myself welcome in most homes but realized that some people saw me coming and pretended not to be at home. A few were forthright in saying that they did not wish to be visited by the priest. On one such occasion I asked if they wished me to eliminate their names from the list of parishioners and received the immediate reply: 'Oh, no, Father. If we need a priest we'll expect one to come. We just don't need one now.'

About this time John Brown's Shipyard was involved in fitting out the newly built liner, the *Queen Elizabeth II*, and many parishioners were involved in this work. As I visited homes it soon came to my notice that quite a number had the same carpet running from the outside door to the living room. After observing this in several houses, I was curious. 'Tell me,' I asked one lady, 'did you all get your carpets from the same store? I've noticed that your neighbours and a few others in Inchfad Drive have the same.'

'Oh, aye, Father. We got it from the *Q.E.* They've got miles of the stuff. They'll no miss a few yards. Look at my bathroom – isn't it nice?' In the bathroom she proudly showed me gold-plated taps and a towel rail.

'Do you buy it at a special rate?'

'Buy it? No. They have plenty and won't miss it.'

'Don't you think that's stealing?'

'No, Father, when they're finished with the work they'll just dump a lot of it anyway. They know the men take wee cuttings.'

These were not 'wee cuttings', but I could not argue further – they saw it as a perk of the job. I confess I had a good laugh to myself on the way home, thinking of gold-plated taps from the staterooms of a luxury liner adorning bathrooms in Drumchapel. Some time later, however, it was revealed that such pilfering was part of the reason for the huge losses which contributed to the demise of John Brown's Shipyard. It was no laughing matter when it affected employment and livelihood.

✦

Out of the blue on a Monday morning in March 1966 I received a letter from 19 Park Circus, the Archdiocesan Office. It was from Archbishop Scanlan and informed me that on the Friday I was to move to St Jude's, Barlanark, as assistant priest. This was a complete shock to me and left me quite distressed. It was also a shock to Charlie, who received a similar letter, informing him that I was leaving and that my replacement would be Father James Cowan, a Mill Hill Mission Father who had been granted indefinite leave by his congregation after many years' work in Uganda.

I had just four days to pack my bags and make my farewells. This was the normal time of notice given to curates and I had never considered what an upheaval it might prove to be. Although I had only been in Drumchapel for just over a year and a half, I had grown to love the parish and the people. I was surprised to find myself resentful towards the Church authorities for making the decision to move me so soon from a place where I felt I belonged and where I felt I was making a successful contribution.

◆

Barlanark is situated on the east side of Glasgow, the opposite side to Drumchapel. It is really a part of the huge housing scheme of Easterhouse but, because it is separated by the width of the main Glasgow to Edinburgh road, it has maintained its own identity and independence. In 1966 the parish was only half the size of St Laurence's in population and area, and there was only the one Primary school.

When I phoned some of my priest friends to tell them sadly that I was moving, I was further dismayed to discover that Father Martin Doherty, my new parish priest, was regarded as a 'dinosaur'. He was apparently gruff, difficult to live with and had entrenched views on a number of subjects. I was the third curate to be appointed in the space of 12 months. My worry was aggravated by a phone call from the auxiliary bishop, James Ward, on the day after I received my letter. He wished me well, but told me not to complain or ask for a move for at least a year. The good people of Barlanark deserved that, he said, because a change of priest too often was harmful to parish stability.

With my eyes full of tears and my head full of misgivings, I left St Laurence's on the Friday afternoon, my little grey van laden with all my worldly goods. I had never been to Barlanark, but carefully followed the directions given me by Jimmy Reilly. I have felt grateful to Charlie Duffin and Jimmy Reilly ever since for all the kindness they showed me in those first happy months of my priesthood.

Now, it seemed, I was heading off into a far less welcoming and potentially difficult situation.

The first week of my appointment in Barlanark was spent at home in Hardridge Road. When I arrived at St Jude's on the Friday I was greeted by Father Doherty with the news that, as there was a Parish Mission being led by two Vincentian Fathers, there was 'no room at the inn' for me. So I inflicted myself on my mother for that first, strange week, something we both enjoyed.

The Mission over, I moved properly to St Jude's, smaller in every way than St Laurence's. The church and house were situated immediately above the Glasgow to Airdrie railway line. My room upstairs overlooked this and I grew accustomed to the regular disturbance of trains passing, as often as every quarter of an hour at peak times. Very nervously, and feeling not at all at home, I began my time there wondering how I would cope. Scare stories about Father Doherty and the departure of the previous curates loomed large in my mind. How could I do any better? Soon I realized I should not have had such fears.

The first encouragement came when I discovered that the parishioners were of the same ilk as those I had left in Drumchapel: the same backgrounds, the same roots, the same hopes and, of course, some suffered from the effects of the same poverty. Barlanark lacked some of Drumchapel's vitality, however. When I arrived in March 1966 there was only one very basic shop serving the whole community. Families had to travel by bus to Shettleston or Parkhead to do their shopping. There were also no pubs of any kind, and community activities could only take place in one of the two schools. The buses returning to Barlanark on Friday or Saturday nights could be very raucous, full of the menfolk heading home at closing time from the many pubs in Shettleston and Parkhead. 'He's gone out for a pint', a comment so often used to explain a husband's absence, was never intended as an accurate description of the amount consumed!

One notable fact is that in those days there was not one professional person such as a teacher, lawyer, or doctor as head of a household in Barlanark. It was very much a working-class parish. However, there were sons and daughters studying at university who today are prominent in their professions. I often read now of a Sheriff in Glasgow who was one of a large family in Barlanark and was studying Law during my time there. Those parents were a great example in the way they strove to provide opportunities for their children which had not been available in their own youth.

The three and a half years I spent in St Jude's were fulfilling and, after the first year, happy. That first period was made more difficult than it needed to be for no other reason than my attitude. I had gone there full of foolish resentment at being moved and an inflated fear of the reputation of Martin Doherty. He was certainly a gruff man on the surface, and it was not all plain sailing, but he was very kind to me, generous in every way, and agreeable to some innovations which I introduced in liturgy and other spheres of parish life. When two different people live together there are bound to be some personality clashes, and acceptance of this fact enables confrontation to be avoided with a bit of give and take. I learned this lesson during my first year at St Jude's and subsequently settled happily and worked well in the parish.

◆

There were a number of parishes in the east end of the city with active youth clubs, and this gave me the impetus to bring such a group into being in our own parish. As we had no hall, apart from a large room beneath the church, and no community centre we depended on the generosity of the Education Department, who allowed us to use the school for a nominal fee. With some volunteer leaders I began to gather together our little youth club, meeting twice a week. We even produced a play, a comedy, which was very well received by the community.

Surrounding parishes such as St Paul's and St Barnabas' in Shettleston, St Joseph's in Tollcross and St Michael's in Parkhead were long founded and parish activities were all well established. St Jude's was comparatively new and therefore lacked the tradition that comes with age. One thing we all shared, however, was the presence of territorial gangs. The 'Border', the 'Tigers', the 'Wee Men', the 'Toi' and the 'Bar-L' were slogans seen, crudely painted, on so many walls throughout the east end. Gang members carried all kinds of weapons, many home-made. The injuries, occasionally fatal, were mainly inflicted on each other, although innocent bystanders were too often caught up in their skirmishes. On one occasion all traffic on the busy A8 (now the M8 motorway) was brought to a halt as the Toi from Easterhouse and the Bar-L from Barlanark carried out a mini-war on the road. Bottles and stones flew from both sides, followed by wooden stakes, preparing the ground for man-to-man combat. When it was over there was a police chase through the housing schemes as ambulances collected the wounded. The road had then to be cleared of debris before the traffic was allowed to continue. The gangs were a menace.

Around the same time the parishes came together to organize a Youth Mission. It took a great deal of work, with the local clergy, youth clubs and other parish organizations all participating. We hired the Wellshot Halls in Shettleston for the occasion and it was very well attended each night of the week. During that week prominent people in various fields came along to participate in discussions and workshops. Some of the Celtic footballers came along and were a great attraction. However, members of the various gangs were always in the hall and it came to my ears that there was a possibility of trouble after the meetings. The result was that each evening the police were required to be outside as the crowd left. Their method of keeping the various gang members apart was to hold them back until each gang had cleared the area, allowing them to leave in a kind of relay. The local gang were the last to leave. Yes, this was a Church Youth mission.

On the closing night the Archbishop came to celebrate Mass. At the end of his sermon a group of girls in the very centre of the hall stuck their hands up and began chanting, 'Tigers! Tigers! Tigers!' Fearing major trouble, a number of us moved very quickly into their midst and managed to quell the disturbance. At the end the Archbishop asked if some of the congregation were charismatic!

The following summer the gangs provided a nationwide show. Frankie Vaughan, a popular singer for the previous 20 years, gave his name and weight to a move to persuade the young people of the east end, especially Easterhouse, to channel their energies in other directions. With the promise of funding and the provision of facilities for youth activities, a show of armistice was staged between the warring gangs. Television coverage ensured that the day and time for the handing over of weapons were widely announced. Strangely, those of us dealing on a day-to-day basis with the gangs were never consulted.

The show proceeded, the lads duly dumped their 'weapons' in the bins provided, interviews were given, and the event got national coverage. It was a very good day indeed for the media and the icecream sellers, who were prominently in attendance. Many of the 'weapons' had been stolen earlier from yards and building sites: there were noticeable quantities of picks, screwdrivers and hammers in the dumping bins. The real weapons were back in use a few days later. Nothing much seemed to come of the great initiative. The Toi, the Wee Men, the Border, the Tigers and the Bar-L continued to skirmish in my remaining time there. But at least the ice-cream sellers had made a tidy profit.

✦

During these first years of my priesthood I had grown up in many ways. The annual retreats were very spiritual times for me, in the silence of Kinnoull Monastery just outside Perth. This was the venue for all clergy retreats, spaced out between Easter and mid-June every year. After my five days there I returned to the parish renewed and refreshed, and my sermons and ideas benefited from the chance to reflect.

My education in social justice was probably the most important factor in my life in those years. No book or lecturer can surpass learning through experience. My involvement with the people of Drumchapel and Barlanark instilled in me an awareness of the effects of injustice and poverty, which condemn some good people to a hopeless situation in life with little chance of improvement.

As time went on, it came to me that, although the Church did much vital work to console and encourage people in their difficulties, in certain areas its rulings seemed only to cause hardship rather than alleviate it. One of the greatest problems faced by married people was all too apparent in my role of confessor – birth control. Their loyalty to the Church, their desire to practice their faith in all its aspects, and the daily facts of a life spent struggling to support a large family were very often in conflict. Their consciences were genuinely troubled and this added to the burden of an already difficult life.

My own misgivings concerning the Church's teaching on this essential part of life were certainly compounded by my pastoral experience in Drumchapel and Barlanark. Married couples would bring up the subject not only at Confession, but also during house visitation, explaining their difficulties (often health or financial problems) and asking if there was any likelihood of the Church relenting on the strict rules. At this time some priests were speaking out openly against the law forbidding any kind of contraception, while others, although remaining publicly silent, were voicing their views and concerns privately. I made no public statements, but certainly communicated my sympathetic understanding to my struggling parishioners.

A conference was arranged for all priests in the Archdiocese and we each received a letter telling us to attend on one of two days. The main purpose of the event was to be guided by two professors of Moral Theology from Maynooth College in Dublin on the teaching of the Church on 'topical moral questions'. They deliberately prepared us for a major change in the teaching on birth control. In the confessional we were to prepare those asking for advice for such a change. Most of us came away from that conference, which was presided over by Archbishop Scanlan, relieved and very hopeful. In different ways we conveyed this news to our parishioners, especially in the confessional. Those waiting and hoping for such a change were elated because their sacramental life was all-important to them.

We were therefore dismayed when Pope Paul VI's encyclical *Humanae Vitae* appeared shortly afterwards. Its publication was quickly followed by a Pastoral Letter from the Archbishop reiterating the traditional and, now, continuing teaching of the Church. I remember the difficulty with which I read that letter at the Sunday Masses and the disappointment must have been apparent in my voice. It left many people confused.

Not long afterwards Cardinal Heenan of Westminster gave an interview which again raised the hopes of some but, for me, only added further confusion. He inferred that personal conscience was overriding in the matter, suggesting that the use of contraception could be permitted in certain circumstances. My reading of *Humanae Vitae* certainly did not open such a door.

Thirty years later the teaching of the Church has not changed but the attitude of the faithful has altered greatly. Today few confessors are asked to give advice on the matter and couples make up their own minds.

◆

In August 1969 my life as a priest changed dramatically. One Monday morning, on my return from the school, Martin Doherty told me that the Archbishop's secretary had phoned. I was to phone back as soon as possible.

Nervously I called the Archdiocesan Office. 'Ah, hello. This is Father Wright. I've been told to contact...'

'Oh yes. The Archbishop wants to see you today at 19 Park Circus. Can you be here at 3 o'clock?'

'Today?'

'Yes. Please be here at 3 o'clock.'

My mind racing, I prepared myself for some kind of rebuke. What had I done? Had someone reported me for some wrongdoing? Had my views on *Humanae Vitae* and the birth control issue created a problem? Why would he ask me to attend at such short notice?

On my arrival in Park Circus I was shown into a large drawing room. Sitting there, dressed in my best, I concentrated on the works of art on the walls and the quality of the furnishings to distract myself. They were far removed from my rather humble attic in Barlanark. After a wait of about 15 minutes the door opened and the impressive figure of the Archbishop shuffled into view. I sprang to my feet.

'Ah, Father Wright. Please sit down.' Social pleasantries thus dealt with, he said, 'You are needed in Blairs. I have been asked by Cardinal Gray to release you from your duties in the Archdiocese for a number of years so that you can join the staff in Blairs.'

'Your Grace! What am I being asked to do there?' The idea of teaching Latin, Greek, French or Maths appalled me.

'Oh, I presume you are to teach.'

'But I can't teach. What am I to teach?'

'I don't know. You'll be expected to teach as required.'

'But, your Grace. I've had no training.'

'Every priest should be able to teach and communicate.'

'Your Grace, you've got the wrong man.'

'Stand up!' I obeyed the command, wondering what was to happen next. He looked at me closely. 'You fit the description perfectly. It is you they want.'

The realization struck me that my Archbishop did not know me, and would not have recognized me if we had met elsewhere that day.

'When am I expected there?' I asked with some despair.

'It will be helpful if you arrive on Friday. The school term began today.' He stood up and handed me a letter. 'Will you post this on your way home? I wish you well.'

He left the room and his secretary came to usher me to the door. Making my way to my grey mini-van, discreetly parked round the corner, I glanced at the letter in my hand. It was addressed to Cardinal Gray and I guessed it was the Archbishop's confirmation of my appointment to Blairs College.

When I related my news to Martin Doherty he burst out laughing. 'Oh, Professor Wright!' Well, well, who would have thought it?' He stopped laughing when I told him I was leaving within four days.

'Well, they'd better replace you here by Friday,' he said in his gruff way. I knew he was upset by the news of my leaving. My own upset was obvious. Rural Deeside would take a bit of getting used to after the east end of Glasgow. Four days seemed like terribly short notice to me. As we were having a cup of tea and chatting about my interview the phone rang and I answered it.

'This is the Archbishop. Is that you, Father Wright?'

'Yes, your Grace.'

'Tell me, do you know the difference between a bull and a cow?'

'What? Yes!'

'Excellent. You're the perfect man for the job! Can I speak to Canon Doherty?'

Martin then came to the phone and was officially informed of my appointment. I would be replaced in St Jude's by Father Ward. Afterwards, as Martin wondered about Father Ward, whom neither of us knew, I considered the significance of knowing the difference between a bull and a cow. In the evening I phoned Blairs and spoke to the Rector, Father James Brennan, and everything became clear. He was very welcoming and explained that I would be Procurator and Spiritual Director. This meant that I would be in charge of the College Farm and the Blairs Estate, and I would also be the official confessor and adviser to the students. It sounded daunting and I wondered briefly if perhaps teaching Greek was more attractive after all.

The next few days were busy and sad. Once again I had to gather all my belongings and pack them for the journey north. There was sadness because I was moving so far from my mother and family and because I was leaving people whom I had come to love. It had been difficult in the parish at times, with the ongoing problem of the gangs and the struggle some people had to make something of their lives. But amongst them I found good people I have never forgotten. I had come to Barlanark full of trepidation and fear. I drove away that Friday full of sorrow, with a lump in my throat and tears in my eyes. I would miss St Jude's.

4

✦

BACK TO BLAIRS

THE JOURNEY TO BLAIRS TOOK ME ABOUT FOUR HOURS. During that drive my thoughts were a mixture as I mulled over the reality of what I had left and the uncertainty about my future role. What was I getting into? It was a strange journey. I had not been back to Blairs since the day I left in 1958. Now, as I steered my van up the drive, it was as if I had never left: everything seemed as it had always been.

My arrival at Blairs meant a return to institutional life, and I was sure I would find this difficult after five years of virtual independence, living in a house with only one or two others. There were 13 other priests on the college staff, about 170 students, and a community of nuns, all living in one very large building. We were governed by a strict timetable and this, I thought, would be particularly hard after the flexibility of parish life. So I was surprised by the ease with which I settled into college life again. Soon it felt as if I had never been away.

My day began with Morning Prayer in the oratory or main church at 6.50 a.m. each day except Sunday. It ended with collegiate Night Prayer at 9.30 p.m. I soon discovered that there were not sufficient hours in the day. If I did not know what was expected of me at the time of my appointment, I most certainly did by the end of the first week in Blairs.

The role of Spiritual Director is very important in seminary life. Not only did I speak to the student body most days, I was also the official confidant of the students and my door was open to them whenever they wished to talk with me. In a real way I was in the same position as any confessor, unlike the other priests, who as teachers and housemasters were far more familiar. Further, I was outside the disciplinary code of the college and never spoke about individual students or made statements at staff meetings about their worthiness. Indeed, if I judged that acts of discipline were harsh I sided with the students. Much to my surprise I enjoyed being Spiritual Director and was happy with that part of my work throughout my time there. However, especially during my first year, I missed the wider pastoral work of parish life.

My work as Procurator was a completely new experience and, frankly, one for which I had no training. My knowledge of agricultural matters was minimal. My basic experience had been gained on an island croft and could not be compared with being in charge of a large farm. Jim Brennan, the Rector, was a marvellous help, having been in the post I now held for 10 years. He introduced me to the farm workers – the grieve (manager), the tractorman and the dairyman – on my first day. From then on I would talk with these men on most days and often work alongside them. Perhaps Jim's most important introduction was to a lecturer at the College of Agriculture in Aberdeen who was of inestimable assistance to me in my ignorant state. It really was a matter of reading and learning as I went from day to day. I found my brain reacted very well under pressure! Learning by my mistakes became a daily fact of life. After Mass each morning I visited the farm before breakfast, at around 7.40 a.m., removing my soutane and donning more practical working clothes.

✦

In 1969 the Catholic population of Aberdeen was only about 5 per cent of the total. The city had never been affected like other towns and cities in Scotland by the Highland and Irish immigrations. It was, even then, a fishing and agricultural society and it had one of the oldest and best universities in the country. Only a handful of priests served the Catholic community and I discovered that many Aberdonians had seldom seen a priest, let alone spoken to one. It was quite a contrast to the city of Glasgow which I had just left. Of course, a new immigration was just beginning which would affect Aberdeen more than any other city in Britain. The North-Sea oil industry was already attracting Texans, French, Norwegians, Spaniards and South Americans to the area. The Catholic population of the city was about to increase noticeably.

The farm workers were not Catholics even though they were employed by the National Junior Seminary. They came from the Buchan area and had their own distinctive dialect. I think it is the closest to the old Scottish language and was, for me, very difficult to understand. Sometimes when they spoke to each other in my presence I was unable to follow the conversation. Perhaps they had the same problem when listening to the students, who were mainly from Glasgow and the industrial central belt of the country. My main difficulty, however, was that the grieve thought I knew very little about farming – and he was right. With guidance from the College of Agriculture I began drawing up graphs for milk production and crop growing. When I decided that some fields should be rested, on the basis of a three-year cycle, the grieve considered such policy a terrible waste.

We had another run-in about the dairy herd. A regular visitor to the farm was the 'AI man'. The dairy cows were served by artificial insemination. It was costly and at best only 75 per cent successful. Jim Brennan was aware of the market growth in beef production and, with his advice, I travelled to a sale of bulls in Fife. We were involved in both dairy and beef and had decided to replace the present Ayrshire milk herd with Friesian cows, later introducing a cross with Hereford. I returned from that journey with a young Friesian bull and 10 heifers-in-calf of the same breed. I explained to the grieve that the bull was almost full grown and that I had been assured there was no further need of the AI man. He looked very dubious.

The following morning I was at my desk making up the weekly wages, as I did every Friday. (I had to learn quickly about National Insurance and PAYE, which most people of my age had learned to understand much earlier in life.) There was a knock on my door and in walked the grieve, cap in hand.

'Father, it's nae workin'.'

'What's not working?'

'The bull, mon. It's too wee.' My heart almost stopped. We had spent a great deal of money on the creature. It had to be successful!

'What do you mean, "it's too wee"?'

'He cannae get on the coo's back. He's too wee.' I breathed a sigh of relief, having imagined something worse.

'I told you he hasn't fully grown, but we should manage.'

'Naw, he's just too wee. Ah've sent for the AI man. We cannae wait.'

I told him that when I was finished at the desk I would come across to the farm. As soon as he had gone I phoned the College of Agriculture, explaining our predicament to my helpful friend. After some chuckling he suggested that we dig a pit or find a convenient piece of low land where the cow could stand.

I explained this to the workers over at the farm, speaking very firmly, as if I really knew what I was talking about. The grieve and dairyman clearly thought that I was of unsound mind. I was beginning to think so myself. Now committed to my folly, however, I soldiered on, said we should begin immediately and, finding myself a spade, began to dig inside a walled area that was once a piggery. Very reluctantly the others joined me and we dug an area 12 foot long and over one foot deep. It was obvious from the silence, apart from some bad-tempered grunts and sighs, that my companions regarded the exercise as a waste of time. During our exertions the AI man arrived to tend to the cow who was too big. I could see him talking animatedly with the dairyman and giving me some derisive looks. The task completed, I returned to my desk, secretly very unsure as to the outcome of our exercise. I heard no more that day.

The following morning I visited the farm before breakfast as usual. The dairyman was busy cleaning his workplace after the morning milking. He greeted me with a cheerful 'good morning' and continued hosing down the walls without further conversation. I continued with my round of the farm buildings and the grieve came out of the bull pen to greet me.

'Aye. It works,' he said to me.

'What works?'

'Aye, the pit works.'

'Good. But does the bull work?'

'Oh, aye, he works. He's a grand wee beast.'

'I'm glad to hear it.'

I returned to my room chuckling, knowing the story would be related to local farmers and perhaps further afield. Perhaps, only perhaps, I had gone up in their estimation.

Our fields were on a north-facing slope immediately above the lovely River Dee, and were divided by marvellous old 'dry stane dykes'. Fields on a slope are more easily ploughed by driving with the slope, rather than against, and for years this had been the custom. The result was that some of the dykes were beginning to crumble with the weight of the earth lying against them, pushed there by such regular ploughing in the same direction. We had just procured a large Ford tractor and we decided it was time to plough against the slope. The tractorman was not too pleased, voicing his doubts in no uncertain terms. It would be too much for the tractor or the plough; there were too many stones in the field; it would take too long and time was important. I insisted that this was how it should be done.

Mid-morning the following day I walked up through the fields to see how the ploughing was going. The tractorman was standing by his vehicle smoking a cigarette. Beneath the tractor there was a pool of oil slowly seeping into the ground.

'What's gone wrong?' I asked.

'The sump's broken and I've lost all the oil.'

'How did that happen?'

'It hit a stane. Ah tellt ye this widnae work.'

I was furious and told him that any driver should be careful of obstacles, and the stone which caused the problem was certainly very visible. Ordering him to remove the cracked sump, I hurried back to the college, collected the van and drove back up to the field, where he was still tinkering with some spanners. Silently I took the spanners from him and, with the help of a hammer, removed the sump and put it in the back of the van. I told the tractorman to find the grieve and jack up the tractor ready for a new sump to be installed. I drove to Harper's Garage in Aberdeen some six miles away, still seething. Carrying the broken sump, I stood in the agricultural parts department waiting to be served. Nearby, two farmers began to study me intently. I ignored them. After a while one of them approached and began a conversation.

'Aye, mon,' he said.

'Aye,' was my reply (the true north-eastern farmer gives little away in conversation, usually sticking to monosyllables.)

'Trouble?'

'Aye.'

'Ye ploughin'?'

'Aye.'

'Sump?'

'Aye.'

'Hit a stane?'

'Aye.'

There was a pause in this flow of words and then he asked, 'Fit be you?' (What are you?)

'A priest.'

'Aye.' Turning to his companion across the room, he shouted, 'Ah tellt you. Nae *meenister* would dirty his hauns like that!'

Without another word he left me alone. I became conscious that I was standing there in my clerical shirt and collar, denim jeans and very dirty wellington boots, my hands and arms covered in black oil. It must have looked very odd, and his stream of questions had only been a lead up to the single one he wanted answered.

I began to laugh as someone came to serve me, my anger at the tractorman suddenly lifted. I returned to Blairs with the new sump and, the tractor repaired, the ploughing continued. The driver, still disgruntled, followed my directions. There were no further accidents.

Gradually I developed a good relationship with the workers and this was enhanced when I arranged a substantial pay rise for them. Farm labourers were generally poorly paid and the Church was no better in this respect than other employers. They did have good houses, however, which were regarded as part of their wages under the tied system, as they did not pay rent. They also had subsidized milk and free fuel in the form of wood logs. The actual money they received was very low, and I did what I could in that respect. I would have given them much more, but I also had to be constantly aware of the financial needs of the college, which depended on the farm being profitable. Life had been much simpler as a curate.

◆

At the end of my first year in Blairs I had settled well and felt more confident with my allotted work. The staff were very kind and supportive in many different ways and we got on well together. Without the direction given me by Jim Brennan in those early days I would have been like a ship without a rudder. Despite his own onerous duties he gave me all kinds of assistance and when I made mistakes, which was more often than I would have wished, he helped me to rectify matters.

The fact that there were 14 of us on the staff meant that conversation flowed easily when we were together at mealtimes. Indeed, apart from the few evenings in the year when we had occasion to have 'a dram', meals were our only time for communal conversation and we made the most of the chance to relax. Some of my fellow diners were experts in banter and we always enjoyed a good laugh. One evening at supper Father Peter Moran, who was serious and studious by nature – and whose oboe playing kept me awake when I occasionally retired to bed early – saw me staring vacantly into space as the talk flowed round me.

'Roddy,' he called, 'what do you miss most about parish life?'

'Mini skirts!' was my flippant reply.

It stopped the conversation and brought laughter from my neighbours at table but, in a sense, it was the truth. The variety of parish life was missing. My life was now wholly centred on the farm and the college and the only females were the good nuns who looked after us so well. In the parish I had dealt with all ages, male and female, and had relished the richness of 'normal' life. Of course my parish experience, especially the school work, did prove useful when it came to dealing with the students, and I was glad to have the chance to exercise my pastoral skills in some capacity at least.

The students in 1970 seemed quite different from those with whom I had shared Blairs in the 1950s. Television, the telephone and pocket money were facts of daily life by then and, although there were restrictions, the students were allowed access to such 'luxuries' and encouraged to use them wisely. From the beginning I decided to approach the role of Spiritual Director just as if I were a local school chaplain. My previous work in St Pius', Drumchapel, and St Gregory's in the east end had prepared me well, and I had no trouble communicating with the 14- to 18-year-old boys. I found the majority of them to be normal, healthy lads.

Every year a number would decide to leave because they no longer wished to be priests, just as it used to happen when I had been a student. Often this decision was reached after consultation with myself or one of the other priests on the staff. A few were sent home because they were judged by the staff to be unsuitable. Because of my position I took no part in such decisions, but sometimes I had the task of driving them to the station and seeing them off on the train, usually to Glasgow or Edinburgh. The five-mile journey was often difficult in these circumstances and I always felt sorry for the lad who was leaving. As in the rest of life, however, there were instances of real humour on such occasions.

One 15-year-old boy had been expelled for entertaining some of his classmates after 'lights out' with a cache of alcohol hidden in his dormitory cubicle. His father owned a bar and he had returned from the Christmas holiday with a large supply of miniature bottles of whisky, brandy, vodka and rum, among other things. Discovered and consequently expelled, he was surprisingly chirpy on the journey to the station. When I escorted him to the train and helped him aboard with his luggage, he said, 'Will you give these to the priests? I'm sure they'll find them useful.' He thrust a package into my hands.

'Yes, I'll be glad to do that,' I replied. 'You take care. I hope all goes well with you.'

I returned to my car and looked at what he had given me to pass on to the priests: pens advertising his father's bar. When the pens were turned upside down, a lady was seen to divest herself of her garments! There was some hilarity at coffee-break that morning when I handed round the boy's gifts.

✦

My day off was Sunday. (In the parish some people had thought this was my one day of work!) However, on many Sundays I helped serve some of the parishes in Aberdeen Diocese. It is a huge area, reaching from Angus in the south to the Shetland Islands in the north, and west to Ullapool and Dornie. It is also an area steeped in history. Parts of Banffshire were firmly Catholic in the past and that tradition was still evident in places such as Dufftown, Glenlivet, Keith and Huntly, although perhaps these are better known today for their splendid malt whiskies. What has become known as Royal Deeside also had its own rich Catholic history, in the parishes of Banchory, Aboyne, Ballater and Braemar. During my time in Blairs I regularly helped out in all these places, especially in Keith and Banchory.

The parish priest of St Thomas', Keith, had served that parish for many years. Age and terminal illness had taken their toll and, having struggled on for some time to the best of his ability, he eventually called for help. I was very happy to volunteer myself and often drove there on Sunday mornings, leaving Blairs early, to celebrate the two Masses in St Thomas'. The drive through the beautiful countryside could be hazardous in winter. On a few occasions I had to tackle the Glens of Foundland in heavy snow and Jim

Brennan furnished me with wheel chains, which I put to good use. One Sunday, when the road was hard going, I arrived some 15 minutes late. I was met at the door of the church by a disgruntled parishioner.

'Fit kept you? Ah wis just aboot tae leave.'

I apologized as I hurried into the vestry to prepare for Mass. Even a 50-mile drive through a blizzard is no excuse for being late when others are waiting. In fact, I felt privileged to assist in such a parish.

Later I was to help Monsignor Tom McLoughlin, parish preist of Banchory and Aboyne. Banchory is only about 16 miles up-river from Blairs, a pleasant drive on any day and not nearly so dangerous as the road to Keith. Monsignor Tom was 80 years old and frail, but he had a marvellously clear mind and a glorious fund of stories. He was well known and loved by generations of priests.

He once told me the story of how he arrived in Blairs to study for the priesthood, giving me a real insight into a time past – a tale laced with humour, but which demonstrated very clearly how dramatically things had changed now, and were still changing. Tom's father was a soldier, based at the turn of the century in Fort William, which was then a garrison town. Tom was born there and went to school in the town. He served regularly at the morning Mass and afterwards the priest, Monsignor MacIntosh, often sent him to fetch some items from one of the shops. One morning he asked Tom, 'Will you go to Blairs?' The boy said 'yes', thinking it was a shop. He stood patiently outside the house waiting for further instructions but, after a long while when nothing was forthcoming, made his way to school.

Thinking no more about it, he was surprised some days later when the priest visited his parents at home and told them, 'I've arranged for Tom to go to Blairs.'

'Where is Blairs?' asked Mrs McLoughlin. Tom also knew nothing about it, or what it was.

The outcome was that in August of that year the young boy left Fort William for the Junior Seminary, where he spent the next five years without returning home. All holidays were spent in the college. Having completed his course there he travelled to Rome, again without coming home. Seven years later, when his studies were complete, he was ordained priest for the Diocese of Aberdeen.

By this time his family had moved to Edinburgh. Tom travelled there from Rome and, having found the house, rang the doorbell.

A little boy opened the door. Tom asked, 'Is your mother at home?'

'Who are you?'

'I think I'm your big brother.'

'But you're old. I've never seen you!'

Tom was meeting his brother Tony for the first time. In fact, Tony later followed him into the priesthood. I find this story a wonderful insight into the attitudes and circumstances which existed at the beginning of the century now about to end.

These Sunday trips up Deeside or into Banffshire were a welcome break from the normal college routine. On other occasions I assisted in one of the city parishes in Aberdeen itself and on three occasions I relieved the priest who acted as chaplain to the Catholic prisoners in Craiginches Jail, a stark Victorian building in the south-east of Aberdeen. This was quite a contrast to lovely Kincardineshire and Banffshire: keys, locks and clanging doors; the smell, a mixture of polish and urine; and the noise, constant shouts and tuneless whistling – all far removed from the open and fresh countryside, so near and yet so far.

The prison church was interdenominational and the Mass followed the Church of Scotland service. There was a sizeable congregation. It is strange how many Catholics attend Mass when in prison, when they probably would not 'outside'. On my first visit a prisoner, identifying himself as the altar server, came into the little room where I was vesting.

'Hello, I'm Jimmy. Eh, Father Wright? It *is* you. It's great to see you! What are you doing here?'

'What are *you* doing here, Jimmy?'

'Oh, that's a long story. I got life for knifing my wife's fancy man in Clydebank. Did you no hear?'

Jimmy had been a parishioner of St Laurence's and in my short stay in Drumchapel I had got to know him. He was often in trouble, but on this occasion he had gone much further than usual. Without any embarrassment he continued to talk as I got ready.

'Father, there's a lot here should go to Confession.'

'Have they asked for Confession?'

'Naw. But ah'll get them to go, so ah will!'

'No. Only those who, themselves, want to go to Confession, Jimmy.'

'But they'll go if I tell them.'

I shook my head, went into the church and, smiling at the assembled congregation, asked, 'Do any of you wish to go to

Confession?' Silence, apart from some embarrassed shuffling of feet. 'Do we have hymnbooks? Good, we'll sing a few hymns.' I chatted with them as I chose these and then returned to the room to continue vesting.

'Ah told you, father, they'd have come if *ah'd* asked them!'

'Jimmy, do *you* want to go to Confession?' I asked finally.

'Oh no, ah'm okay!' There was no answer to this.

After my few visits I left the prison with a sense of hopelessness, finding the atmosphere of the place and the look in the eyes of so many inmates profoundly depressing. Life is indeed an education.

✦

Apart from my 'Sunday work', I spent most days in the college and on the farm. I also had to manage the Blairs Estate, dealing with the tenant farmers and working in conjunction with the Forestry Department to develop acres of woodland, thinning, felling and planting. My work was time consuming yet surprisingly fulfilling. On many occasions I only had time for a very quick wash after a day on the farm before addressing the students. Often it was only during a rapid bath that I had the time to gather my thoughts on what I wished to say that evening, but sometimes as I worked away on the farm or estate, I would really be concentrating on planning my evening discourse.

My work as Spiritual Director was important to me and benefited me personally. The daily programme of prayer and talks brought regularity into my own spiritual life, and it was natural to return to a habit of reading which I had neglected in the bustle of parish life. This broadened my horizons in many ways. The liturgy of the Church had been transformed since the time of the Second Vatican Council (1962–5) and my knowledge and practice were greatly enhanced by my experience in Blairs. I love plainchant, but in the college church I was introduced to some beautiful music provided for the Sung Mass in the vernacular. With some excellent musicians on the staff, our liturgy was often very uplifting.

Part of my remit was to lead the students in 'Days of Recollection'. At least twice a school term we had such a day, a Sunday set aside for prayer, reading and some talks. This time was spent in silence, which ended at supper, and I had to arrange the timetable and direct the various exercises. Twice a year there was a three-day retreat, again organized by me and during which I had to be present. A priest was brought from elsewhere to lead the retreat, however, and this was refreshing for both students and staff. (The latter had a holiday during these days and some of them used the occasion to improve their golf handicap.)

As a result of my role as Spiritual Director I was invited to lead retreats by a number of different groups. I was free to accept such invitations only on a few occasions and I enjoyed every one of them. The contrast of leading a group of nuns in their five-day retreat and a group of adult laypeople over a weekend was real and fascinating. The sisters were obviously accustomed to regular prayer and meditation, whereas the laypeople, coming from many different walks of life, were in a strange world for two days. Both groups provided me with a special experience because of their wholehearted participation, prayerfulness and thoughtful, reveal-ing discussions. Such days never failed to leave me feeling very humble.

As far as I am aware I had a good relationships with most of the students, especially those in the Senior House. By that age they had developed their individual personalities and, as always, some were more extrovert than others. On one occasion I was passing the sixth-form washplace, where they often gathered after supper, and noticed that one boy was holding court. There was a great deal of laughter, which died suddenly when they saw me standing at the door. I made some light conversation before continuing on my way. It took me a few seconds to realize what had caused such hilarity. Donald, the student entertaining them, was an excellent mimic and had been giving an impression of the Spiritual Director in full flow in the church! I have always used my hands to talk and this had proved easy to imitate. I joined in the laughter as I climbed the stairs to my room.

During tea one evening I overheard the Rector and the Master of Discipline discussing a problem. Earlier that week the students had a holiday and were allowed to go to Aberdeen for the afternoon. On their return some magazines such as *Playboy* and *Men Only* were reported to be in circulation amongst lads in the junior form – the usual inquisitive adolescents. The Master of Discipline was to raid desks that night and any student found to have such material in his possession would be in serious trouble and would, perhaps, be expelled.

I could take no part in disciplinary matters, but knowing these boys to be foolish rather than bad, I decided to intervene in some way. That night, at the end of my talk to the juniors, I explained that I would be in my room after supper. If anyone wished to rid himself of any contraband, such as these magazines, he need only knock on my door and place it in my room. I would sit with my back to the door, as I had work to do at my desk, and would not look round. There were 12 knocks on my door that evening and by the time for Night Prayer 18 magazines were lying on my floor. I had kept to my promise and not looked round.

After Night Prayer a dram was being provided in the staff sitting room because we had a guest, an unmissable occasion. It was late when I retired to bed and the next day I went to the farm after morning Mass and then straight to breakfast. As I made my way to my room after that I passed Sister Perpetua, who looked after the rooms in my corridor. She was normally very talkative and cheery but, on this occasion, barely answered my greeting. I entered my room and immediately understood why she had been so quiet: on my desk, in a neat pile, were the magazines which had been left untidily on the floor the previous evening. I had completely forgotten about them. I rushed off to seek out a rather flustered nun and proclaim my innocence. As for the offending material, I took it in a bag across to the farmyard, where I discovered how difficult it is to burn the paper used in these magazines. I was busy using a long stick to turn them in the fire when the grieve arrived in a talkative mood. As he spoke I vainly tried to cover up some of the photographs which persisted in emerging from the flames. My red face was due as much to my embarrassment as to my exertions – and I am not at all sure what the grieve made of it.

At supper that evening the Rector announced that a student was being sent home the following day. He had purchased some pornography and distributed it amongst his classmates. After this solemn announcement he turned to me and whispered sternly that he knew of my activities the previous evening. I was relieved to see a twinkle in his eye.

◆

By the time I had been in Blairs a year or two, some small farmers were finding life difficult: high beef and dairy production was dependent not only on numbers of cattle but also on acreage. Indeed, the Blairs farm was becoming too small as the herd grew healthily. In addition to the young Friesian bull I later bought a

Hereford bull, a gentle creature now spending his days happily amongst the heifers.

Maidenfold Farm was on the Blairs Estate, bordering on the college grounds. Charlie Shaw farmed it, as his family had done for generations. A gentle and hard-working man, he was well respected in the local community. But, like others, he was beginning to struggle and after amicable and considered discussions, he agreed that Maidenfold should be amalgamated with the college farm. He would become farm manager and have life tenancy of his house for himself and his family. By this time we were building a new dairy, fully equipped and meeting all government requirements for cleanliness and storage. Other modern buildings were now also necessary and it was decided that one of these would be built at Maidenfold.

When all the details of the farm handover were properly and legally agreed, Charlie announced that he was having a 'roup' – the term used for the sale of goods and possessions on such occasions. Amongst other things he had machinery and a tractor that were surplus to requirements now the farms were amalgamated. When the day of the roup came along I went to give support to Charlie. The plan was for me to bid for some of the machinery until a price was reached which would be to his benefit, at which stage I would drop my interest. This did help in the sale of a number of pieces and I was pleased for Charlie. When the auctioneer came to the tractor I bid immediately, pushing the price towards its true value. Two other farmers remained in the bidding and, confident now, I continued upwards. Suddenly, to my horror, the others dropped out, leaving me with an overpriced tractor that I most certainly did not want. They had noticed earlier what I was doing in the bidding and had decided to turn the tables on me. It was a salutary lesson; I was obviously still naive in some respects, and later sold the tractor at a loss.

✦

Early in 1971 I received word that Paddy Sharkey had died in Donegal. He was the cousin of my mother's cousin, Margaret, and it was in their home that I had spent many happy holidays on my regular visits to that lovely part of Ireland. I made arrangements to travel across for the funeral, driving to Glasgow airport through the night and catching the 6.30 a.m. flight to Belfast. The north of

Ireland was in turmoil at the time and security was intense. From Belfast I took the train to Derry, where I boarded a bus for Letterkenny, across the border in Donegal.

From the moment I left Glasgow I felt apprehensive and quite uncomfortable. Apart from some ill-mannered and uncouth behaviour towards me by a fellow passenger, however, I arrived in Derry without incident. Before boarding the Letterkenny bus I did notice that there was a great deal of helicopter activity around, suggesting that a security operation was in progress. As we approached the border, but before reaching the inevitable army check post, the bus was stopped and two armed soldiers came on board. Having asked for identification from some of the male passengers they loudly asked me to leave the bus. I was pushed quite roughly against a hedge at the roadside and carefully searched. On either side a soldier knelt, gun pointed away from me. It was small comfort.

One questioned me in a broad Aberdonian accent.

'Where have you come from?'

'Aberdeen.'

'Fae Aberdeen? You dinna sound it then! Ah'm fae there. Fit are you doin' here?'

'I'm going to Donegal.'

'What's your purpose there?'

'I'm going to a funeral.'

'How long will you stay?'

'Two days.'

I was still spreadeagled against the hedge and feeling more angry by the second. The soldier suddenly released the pressure from my back. 'Get aboard,' he ordered.

'Thank you,' I replied politely. 'By the way, what are you doing here?'

'Get aboard.'

As I made my way to my seat I was embarrassed by some cheering passengers. I could feel their anger in the air. Correctly they assumed that I had been chosen because of my clerical garb. Regular travellers told me that they were accustomed to such searches and rough behaviour. I found it extraordinarily unsettling.

After the Requiem Mass in Annagary, as we moved into the adjacent graveyard a flag I had never seen before was solemnly draped over Paddy's coffin and a salute was given by a group of elderly men. When I asked later about the significance of that little ceremony, one of his sons explained that Paddy was one of the old brigade who had fought in the uprising of 1916 and in the Civil War of 1921. At its conclusion he had fled for his life, spending some time in America, but returning home to Donegal as soon as it was safe. In all the years I had known Paddy I had never heard him speak of those days, or of his real part in Irish history. He was a gentle and hardworking man and I now held him in even greater esteem.

Some weeks later I received a letter from Dublin. It was written in Irish and my understanding of Scots Gaelic only enabled me to pick out a few words and phrases. I brought the letter to Jim Brennan, who was Irish and could easily read his native language.

As he read he glanced at me over his glasses several times, with a mischievous smile playing on his lips. 'Roddy, what have you been up to?' he asked eventually. 'Do you know what this letter means? It's an invitation from the Provisional IRA to further their cause in Scotland. Good God, you'll have the Special Branch knocking on our door at any time!'

Some of the Irish papers had printed an obituary of Paddy Sharkey, mentioning my relationship and the part I had played in his funeral rites. The letter writer had taken note and thought I might be interested in furthering their cause in the 1970s – a rather different scenario from 1916! Jim and I had a good laugh and I am glad to say the Special Branch did not pay me a visit. I did not hear from Dublin again.

◆

In March 1971 my mother had a mastectomy. Cancer had been found. This came as a surprise to me as she had never complained of feeling unwell. When I visited her in hospital two days after her operation, I found her up and serving tea to other patients as if nothing had happened. Indeed, she returned to work after a quick convalescence, carrying on her life as normal. By the end of that year, however, she was obviously in pain and suffering continuous discomfort which she tried to brush aside, telling us, 'It's only arthritis.' Soon it was impossible to hide and her long struggle against the spreading cancer began. She still tried to make sure that life continued as normally as possible, despite the obvious deterioration and the fact that she could no longer work outside the home. I got into the habit of phoning her each evening just after 6.00 p.m., a link that became very important to us both. Whenever

I was at home I would take her to morning Mass in Our Lady of Lourdes church in Cardonald. She had walked or used public transport all her life but now, more and more, she depended on one of us taking her by car.

In May 1972 Effie married and my mother's brother Donald travelled over from New Zealand for the first time since he had jumped ship there in 1949. It was a very special occasion which all of us enjoyed, especially my mother. I have a picture of her taken shortly afterwards when Effie and her husband, Angus, took her for a short holiday to Rothesay. She looks happy and well but, posing for the photographer, she has hidden the walking stick which by then had become essential. For me, that picture sums up the courage and willpower with which she conducted the last year of her life. During that year I travelled regularly to Glasgow from Aberdeen on Friday evening to spend two nights with my mother, travelling back to Blairs on the Sunday. We both valued those visits.

One Friday in the spring of 1973 I was making my now weekly journey to Glasgow when I was involved in a traffic accident. I was at a crossroads in Perth, waiting in the proper lane to turn left for Glasgow, when an articulated lorry cut across me from the outside lane. A woman standing on the pavement gave me a second's warning of disaster by screaming, pointing and covering her face with her hands. Realization dawned as the trailed ploughed over me. I tried to make myself small, reciting a quick Act of Contrition. My little Ford car was crushed, written off, but somehow I emerged without a scratch.

My mother was in hospital that week and after I had made the necessary arrangements to have the wreck taken away and got the insurance details from the Welsh driver of the lorry, I caught a train and taxi and then walked into the hospital ward carrying my overnight bag and trying to look calm. Immediately my mother asked, 'Roddy, what's wrong with your car?'

'Oh, it broke down and I took the train.' I had no wish to distress her with the details.

'I don't think so, Roddy.' She looked at me sharply. 'Tell me what's wrong with the car. Did you have an accident?'

Again I said that there was nothing wrong, but she knew that was not so. I never did tell her the truth about the incident.

Unknown to me, I only had another two such journeys to make and for those I borrowed a car from one of my colleagues. As things would have it, my last time with her was cut short because of a commitment I had made to lead the sisters in Queen's Cross Convent in Aberdeen on a weekend retreat. When I left her that Saturday I was concerned because she had started to have breathing difficulties. While I was mixing cement at Maidenfold on the Monday, 28 May, I was summoned back to the college where I spoke a few words to my mother, who had rung up in obvious distress. Within minutes, as I was throwing clothes into a bag, the phone rang again. It was my sister, breaking her heart, and telling me that our mother had just died. The death of a mother is a loss that none of us can adequately describe. I loved her dearly. I love her still, 25 years later.

After the painful funeral I returned to Blairs and threw myself into the work on the new farm buildings. The sixth year had completed their exams and were killing time until the end of term. There was no shortage of volunteers amongst them to assist in the work as labourers. Some of them excelled in mixing cement! I have always believed in the value of physical work and I know those lads enjoyed their experience.

At the end of term I had the task of sending accounts of the students to their parents. Sitting at my desk on the eve of my 33rd birthday, I suddenly began to feel very strange. The room began to spin and my breathing quickened for no apparent reason. In a state of panic I made my way to the Rector's room where I found him speaking on the telephone. He signalled me to sit down and when he had finished I blurted out that I was feeling far from well; perhaps I was having a heart attack. He immediately took my pulse and gave his diagnosis: 'It's not a heart attack. Your heart is kicking like a mule!' He advised me to go and lie down, which I did immediately, but the palpitations seemed to increase and with them my panic. The Sister Infirmarian came along, read my temperature and took my pulse, telling me she had sent for the doctor. I asked her to fetch one of the priests to hear my confession. She suggested the Rector, an idea I immediately rejected.

'No. Please ask one of the others to come,' I said.

'If that's the case, Father, you're not dying!' she replied tartly. One of the others came and I made my peace with God.

The doctor arrived and, after a thorough examination, informed me that in his opinion I was suffering from mental and physical exhaustion. He administered an injection which made me sleep for the rest of that day and for all of the night. The following day I felt very weak, something which stayed with me for some months.

In all probability this frightening episode was a reaction to the death of my mother and the stressful months leading up to it, when I was torn between my work and being with her. In addition there was the regular drive down to Glasgow in the middle of a very strenuous work programme. Grief always manifests itself in different ways.

✦

It was obvious to me as the new term began in the autumn of 1973 that I had lost not only my energy but my enthusiasm for the work. I began to yearn for a return to parish life. Now in my fifth year in Blairs, I felt that I had little left to give. This change showed itself in my attitude and in my work, but I continued as best I could, the farm extension and a Forestry Commission programme of felling and planting occupying my time. I found myself concentrating my energies on developing the role of Spiritual Director in college life, reading a great deal and, as a result, learning new things. I felt increasingly desperate to get back to pastoral work in a parish, away from the exhausting physical grind of looking after the farm and the estate.

The Conference of the Scottish Bishops met in Blairs for their two main meetings each year, in March and October. These meetings, as I would learn later at first hand, were very intensive and covered a large agenda. Apart from morning Mass we only met the bishops at mealtimes, as college life continued as normal during the conferences. I do not recall ever having a conversation with any of them, apart from general talk at table and one long chat with Bishop MacPherson concerning developments on the farm.

After the March meeting of 1974 Jim Brennan informed me that he was returning to parish life that summer and asked me if that was also my wish. I know he was aware of my present frustration, although we had never really discussed the matter in any depth.

'I know I should return to parish life,' I told him now, 'and I'll be very happy if that's possible.'

'Fine, Roddy, I'll have a word with them,' he said firmly. 'Leave it to me.'

A few months later the Conference of Bishops met for some special purpose. They were in the college for just two days and on the second evening Archbishop Winning of Glasgow came to my room. 'I hear you are quite willing to come back to the Diocese this year,' he said to me.

'Yes, I'll be very happy to return. I'd love to get back to parish life.'

'We're posting some priests as full-time chaplains in our large Secondary schools, starting after the summer. Would you be glad to do that work?'

'I'd be very happy at this stage to do that work,' I assured him. We left it at that and I did not ask which school he had in mind. As he left I said that I would wait for his letter of appointment before telling anyone.

Just 10 minutes later Bishop MacPherson of Argyll and the Isles walked into my room. 'Roddy,' he said, 'the Rector tells me you want to leave here. I know you have wanted to come into the Diocese from recent conversations with you. Are you still of that mind?'

'Yes, I am. But I've just spoken with the Archbishop and he wants me to return to Glasgow!'

'Oh. Leave it to me. I'll have a word with him during supper.'

At supper I said nothing about my conversation with the two bishops. What would the outcome be? Shortly after returning to my room, I had another visit from the Archbishop feigning annoyance at my lack of loyalty to Glasgow. I was embarrassed by the situation, but he really treated me very kindly, knowing that I was happy to return to the Diocese of my island roots.

After breakfast the following morning Bishop MacPherson informed me that he would be in touch – no further details were forthcoming. Full of hope, I waited patiently. Towards the end of June I received a letter appointing me to Our Lady and St Mun's, Dunoon, and asking me to be there on 12 August. I remained in Blairs to complete my work on the farm and finalize the books so that my successor would not have too much difficulty understanding the systems. Jim Brennan moved to Fochabers in Banffshire and I held the fort until the new Rector, Father Donnachie, came at the beginning of August. Then, using the college van, I moved my goods to Dunoon on the Cowal Peninsula, happy with the move and eager to begin work. The parish priest, Roddy Macdonald, made me very welcome at the house we were to share, and from the moment I entered the door I felt comfortably at home.

5

✦

DUNOON AND
FORT WILLIAM

WHEN I WAS A YOUNG LAD IN UIST I had met Roddy Macdonald as he was at that time the assistant priest in Daliburgh, but our paths had seldom crossed since. From the beginning he made me feel at home and very relaxed about finding my feet once again in a strange place. The contrast to the institutional life at Blairs was stark – and pleasing. It was great to be back in parish life and in a very short time I had learnt a huge amount from Roddy about the diocese, its history and especially about the priests who had served so faithfully in the past. A keen historian, his knowledge of these matters was extensive and fascinating.

Although Dunoon is on the beautiful Cowal Peninsula in Argyll, the people tended to look across the Clyde to Glasgow and Greenock for business and shopping. Indeed, many of them came originally from that side of 'the water', which is how we termed the Firth of Clyde. In 1941 some of the survivors of the Clydebank blitz had been rehoused in the seaside town of Dunoon and by the mid-1970s their children and grandchildren were an integral part of the community. The parishioners made me feel as welcome as Roddy had and it was pleasing to find them so supportive of their priests. In this positive atmosphere, I soon settled down and fitted in with the routine.

In addition to normal parish work, including the schools and the hospital, both of us acted as Catholic chaplains to the US Navy, based in the Holy Loch about two miles from the church, and in my time the ship was the USS *Canopus*. Every Sunday either Roddy or I celebrated Mass aboard for the Catholics on duty. However, the majority, because they lived ashore, preferred to attend St Mun's and were an active and important addition to the parish.

Every second Sunday one of us drove to Strachur to celebrate Mass for the Catholic community living in those lovely parts around Loch Fyne. This took place in the home of Sir Fitzroy MacLean whose wife, Lady Veronica, was a member of the Lovat family, a prominent Catholic family in the Highlands. It was always a homely and happy occasion, with crofters, foresters and estate workers all joining the family for the service.

In the parish we also had the convent of the Franciscan Missionaries and the four sisters there were a real asset, working especially amongst the old and housebound. Sister Eileen was a very good catechist and gave religious instruction to children in the distant parts of the parish such as Tighnabruaich and Strachur, vital work in scattered rural areas. Apart from the instruction itself, it also provided an occasion for the children to come together. I am a firm believer in the benefits of mixing the spiritual and social aspects of life.

An important extension to the parish took place while I was there. At Ardyne on the west coast of the Cowal Peninsula MacAlpine's were building huge concrete oil platforms for the North-Sea industry. A 'camp' was built, which in fact was a very large village, and a large proportion of the workers were Irish, many of them from the north. They worked extremely hard, the day being divided into two shifts of 12 hours. We were asked to provide Mass for the workforce and were happy to oblige. A little wooden church was built on the site and with the agreement of the local Church of Scotland minister it was intended to be for interdenominational use. In reality the facility was only used by the Catholics and the Mass, at 6.00 p.m. every Sunday, was so well attended that some of the men, oilskins dripping with wet cement, had to stand outside. These tough, hard-working men were very faithful and attentive to their little church. It was strange to see an interdenominational church furnished with a purpose-built confessional, Stations of the Cross and statues, but they looked after it most carefully and it was always a pleasure to visit those men on site.

Under construction at the time was the 'Cormorant', destined to serve the Cormorant Field in the North Sea. The platform was immense, its base the size of a football pitch. Frantic activity on site always meant there was 'a pour' taking place – when tons of liquid concrete were poured into pre-prepared, reinforced shutters. Once 'a pour' began it could not be halted until that section was completed, normally over a period of at least 24 hours. Those men certainly earned their wages!

The little sub-post office in the nearby village of Toward was the centre of attention on pay day, as large numbers of Irishmen sent their wages home. Some, of course, did tend to spend part of these hard-earned wages in the local hostelries in Dunoon on their night off and, on a few occasions, there was a little trouble. One morning I had a call from a tabloid newspaper. They had heard that the men at Ardyne were attracting prostitutes to the town and this was upsetting the local people. Did I have a comment to make? I scoffed at the idea, saying that the only beneficiaries were the bars and the post office. 'The girls' had arrived in town many years previously with the Navy and, no doubt, would leave when the sailors did. Of course the story did appear and caused anger amongst the workforce and in the town. At that stage I had not learned that silence is the best answer to any tabloid journalist. This was my first inkling that often they seem to write their headlines and then try to put together a story that fits – with or without facts.

◆

Life in Dunoon was busy and within a short time Blairs was a fading memory. The weight of stress lifted, I relished my return to pastoral work and appreciated the variety of situations which came my way. I particularly enjoyed my encounters with the US Navy, and Sunday Mass aboard the *Canopus* provided me with an opportunity to meet some of the submariners. Alongside, most days, would be at least one Polaris submarine, being serviced before returning to the icy waters of the North Atlantic. The submariners were, in my opinion, a special breed and obviously highly intelligent. I learned that many of them were scientists and engineers, and all had been psychologically vetted to judge their suitability for life in a confined space for long periods. They were regularly under the ice cap and North Atlantic for up to 12 weeks. Aboard each submarine an officer was designated the Eucharistic Minister and the evening before they sailed he would make an appointment with us to call for the Blessed Sacrament, always asking for a specific number of consecrated breads. He would then lead the Eucharistic Service at sea and distribute Holy Communion. He would never say where they were going. My understanding is that they did not know themselves until they were many miles away from Dunoon.

When Roddy or I boarded the *Canopus* we were always taken to the little chapel by an escort. As soon as we stepped aboard we were regarded as being on American soil and during the Mass we prayed for Cardinal Cooke of New York as the local bishop, and for the President (Roddy confessed to forgetting his name at times). On one occasion, as I made my way along the deck, I noticed a submarine below on the starboard side. Its conning tower was missing, looking as if it had been cut off by a tin opener. I turned to my escort and asked, 'What happened there?'

'Oh,' came the nervous reply, 'you've seen nothing – right?'

'If you say so.' I was clearly not on the 'need to know' list.

After Mass I was taken back on the port side so that I would not see the submarine again. About three months later the national news carried a story of an alleged collision between an American and a Russian submarine in the Baltic. I am convinced I witnessed the result of the collision on that odd Sunday morning.

The presence of the US Navy made quite a difference on shore as well. In a roll of about 200 pupils in our Primary school a third were American or Philippino. The Navy employed a large number of men from the Philippines, a gentle people who, I found, set the rest of us a fine example in family life. They were very faithful to their Catholic origins and devout in the way they lived. It was also remarkable how well those children integrated – the Scots, the Americans and the Philippinos. Their ethnic differences simply served to enhance the atmosphere and value of our little school.

'First Confession' in a Catholic School is an important part of the children's introduction to participating in the sacramental life of the Church. At that early age, just before they make their First Holy Communion, they are educated in the method of confessing their sins. Being so young, they are not capable of sin and, in my opinion, should not be introduced to the Sacrament until they are some years older. The practice has long been in use, however, and children continue to be educated in this way. My experience of such 'confessions' in Dunoon was revealing and amusing, but did start me thinking about the real merits of the exercise.

The Scottish child came and, just as I did at that age, proclaimed his/her sinfulness in this way: 'Bless me, Father, for I have sinned.

This is my first confession. I told lies and I didn't do as I was told, and I didn't say my prayers. Please, Father, that's all I can remember.'

The American child came and proclaimed, at rather more length: 'Bless me, Father, for I have sinned. This is my first confession. Well, I have this little sister and she bugs me something awful sometimes, so I bug her back. I'm sorry. And mom and pop, well they argue and shout sometimes – she says he drinks too much – and I hate them for it. I get annoyed, know what I mean? I'm sorry. When my folks don't listen to me I get annoyed – so, I shout at them. It's wrong and I'm sorry. Oh, I took some Pepsi from the fridge and my mom says I stole it. I don't think so but I'm sorry. Mmm, I think that's about everything, Father.'

Such a stark difference in communicating was not apparent in the playground, where the Scots and Americans were just children, playing boisterously together.

Once a year the *Canopus* went for a sail. She was really a factory, an engineering workshop and a dry dock, and most of the crew were engineers and technicians rather than sailors. In the spring of 1975 I was invited to join them on a three-day sail and I jumped at the opportunity. I had never sailed in a ship without portholes before – now was my chance! The sky and sea were only visible up on deck. All light and air in the ship was artificially provided and loving the sea as I do, I spent much of my time on deck, enjoying the strong breeze in my face. Also I wanted to know where we were sailing. With the coastline of the north of Ireland clearly visible on the port side and the Mull of Kintyre on the starboard, we sailed west into the Atlantic before turning north. Some hours later I was able to make out the outline of the Western Isles, with the Uists and Barra easily recognizable. It was a beautiful sight to me, but sadly a number of the crewmen were unable to enjoy the view. They were seasick: some of them had never been to sea before, although they were in the US Navy.

Before sailing I had been informed that this was an exercise, important for the ship and crew, and I thoroughly enjoyed the experience. Some weeks later, however, I felt quite despondent when I was told by a serviceman that the purpose of the sail was to dump nuclear waste at sea. My happy memories of the trip were clouded and my despondency turned to anger as I realized the enormity of such constant dumping. British nuclear submarines were based nearby at Faslane, and I began to wonder if our own naval authorities used the Atlantic for the same purpose. There was a great deal we were not being told, I concluded.

✦

In August 1975, declared by the Pope as a Holy Year, I paid my first visit to Rome, travelling as a pilgrim with a group of others. I had not intended to go and had already made arrangements for a holiday in Donegal, but the bishop asked me to assist Father Colin MacInnes, who had organized a pilgrimage for young people between the ages of 18 and 25 from the Diocese. Twenty-three young people from Dunoon were travelling with more than 50 others from Fort William, South Uist and Oban. We would travel by bus and camp en route until reaching Rome, where we were booked into a youth hostel on the banks of the Tiber.

I lived nearest to Glasgow and was therefore deputed to organize the provisions for the journey as a kind of quartermaster. The proof of the pudding is in the eating, as they say, and I would certainly be judged a failure. The tents I efficiently procured from the Catholic Guides Association in Glasgow turned out to be of the pre-war variety and some looked as if they had not been in use since those days. Somehow I also managed to buy sufficient cornflakes to last just two days and enough toilet rolls to take us round the world. Our buses were provided by West Coast Motors, more used to travelling from Lochgilphead to Oban than on the autobahn.

Our journey began on 1 August with a drive south to the port of Hull, and the first night was spent on the ferry to Zeebrugge – it would be my last sleep in a bed until I boarded the same ferry on the return journey. From Zeebrugge we travelled to a campsite somewhere in Luxembourg. With much hilarity and tangled guy ropes we set up camp, to the amusement and probably puzzlement of the other campers. Our tents looked very quaint alongside the more modern models from Germany and Scandinavia. Colin and I were the cooks and busied ourselves preparing food for 78 hungry people. For both of us it was our first attempt at being chef to so many and it was a stressful experience. Eventually, having dished out the fare, we discovered that we were left with one poor, flat sausage to share between us. Later we discovered that we had a number of 'Oliver Twists' in our company who had managed two portions. It did not happen again.

The following day we drove through beautiful countryside, arriving that evening at Lucerne in Switzerland. The campsite was in a stunning spot above Lake Lucerne and we decided to stay for two or three days. The sun and the rest would do us all good before we made the long journey to Rome. That evening we benefited from the generosity of the American community in Dunoon, who had given me a 'fistful of dollars' to use on the journey. We booked a local restaurant for the whole party, much to the delight of the restaurateur. In truth we were very tired and cooking an evening meal for such a horde could have been disastrous, with tempers already frayed. The bus drivers, we felt, had the better deal: wherever we stopped they retired to a hotel or guesthouse.

The following morning we were able to rest in the luxury of the campsite, making full use of the showers and the swimming pool, and admiring the picture-postcard views. While most of the party went sightseeing in Lucerne, Colin and I had the time and leisure to prepare a decent meal and when the others had drifted back, tired and hungry, we enjoyed the food in the warmth and comfort of the late-afternoon sun.

As I was helping to clear up afterwards two of the girls from Dunoon approached. 'Hey, Father, before we left you promised us we would have discos and things like that. I mean, we've come with nice clothes and we've never had the chance to wear them. And there are some nice places in Lucerne – we saw them today. If there's nothing happening here we're going out tonight.'

They were taken aback by my answer: 'Fine, girls, you go. But make sure you're back before 11 o'clock. Have a nice time.' They ran off to tell the others, who were obviously expecting me to prove difficult. I was amused. At home they could go to a disco any night of the week.

Meanwhile, Colin had gone off to phone the Scots College in Rome to clarify the arrangements for our arrival. To his alarm he was told that we were expected in Rome the following day and that the Pope would be publicly welcoming us in his Wednesday address to the pilgrims in St Peter's Square. This caused the first real fall-out between Colin and me. He was adamant that we must pack up there and then and get on the road. I argued strongly that we could never get to Rome by the next day and anyway none of us was prepared for an overnight journey of such length. But after discussion with the other two priests, Billy Fraser and Donald Ewan Campbell, Colin won the argument. We gathered everybody together and explained the change of plan. Those preparing to disco the night away were far from happy! It then struck me that perhaps we should find the bus drivers and inform them of our new schedule. Colin and I made our way to their hotel, where we found their room occupied by one driver and a lady friend, both of them in a state of undress. Colin told him to get dressed and packed and to find the other driver – more unhappy people!

At about 11.00 p.m. we set off for Rome and, like Hannibal, we had to cross the Alps, moving from the heat of Lucerne through the snow of the mountain-tops before descending into Italy. The beauty was lost on most of my fellow passengers, who managed to sleep most of the night. I missed most of the scenery too, as I was focused on keeping the driver as alert as possible. As the sun was rising we arrived in Como and tired bodies were roused to visit the toilets and find somewhere for breakfast. We were forced to stay for a few hours so the drivers could rest. Colin and I were also able to snatch some sleep, much needed after our night-time trek.

By this time it was obvious that we would not be in St Peter's that night. I resisted the temptation to make any 'I told you so' speeches. Duly refreshed and rested, we set off south through Italy. It was completely dark when we arrived in Rome and even later when we finally managed to find the John XXIII Hostel near the Ponte Sixto. Pope Paul VI had indeed given us a public welcome, apparently, but I reckon we would have been nearer Florence than Rome at the time.

As we disembarked, all of us looking forward to food, a shower and a comfortable bed, Colin and I were dismayed to discover that for us it was not to be. Due to the rising crime rate in Rome, all visiting buses had to be manned when parked overnight. Billy Fraser was not feeling well and Donald Ewan did not wish to do it. The drivers definitely needed to rest, so it was left to us to do the 'manning'. As the party settled down for the night Colin and I rescued a bottle of whisky and some paper cups from one of the buses. In the stifling heat of Rome in August we sat on the pavement to have a comforting dram. Have you ever sipped warm whisky from a paper cup? It is best avoided. As we sat there, bemoaning our wretched situation, we were approached suspiciously by two policemen who emerged from a nearby car. Colin, who is fluent in Spanish, could also make himself understood in Italian and the officers fortunately accepted his explanation. After they had departed and we had finished our drink, we decided to retire to our respective buses. To my relief the back seat was comfortable and I was so tired I felt I could have slept on the pavement.

As I pulled off my shirt I became aware of someone watching me. Looking up, my eyes met those of a man sitting on a wall beside the bus, leering at me. Disturbed, I shouted at him in my best Glaswegian to clear off, but he continued to stare. As I emerged from the bus brandishing a large torch, Colin came out of the other bus.

'Roddy, what on earth is wrong?' he asked.

'That creep is watching me – tell him that if he doesn't clear off I'll put him in the Tiber!'

As Colin did some translating I brandished the torch in a threatening manner and the gentleman, outnumbered, quickly departed. It turned out to be another sleepless night, despite my weariness, as I was uneasily aware of the possibility of the man returning with some assistants. So, this was the Eternal City.

The following few days were far more enjoyable, as we went out sightseeing and made use of the swimming pool at the Scots College. It was decided that we should stay in Rome until the Sunday, leaving after the general audience given by the Pope at noon at his summer residence at Castelgondolfo. When Sunday came we celebrated Mass in one of the many side chapels in St Peter's. It was a lovely and meaningful occasion for all of us. After photographs had been taken, we boarded our buses and went to Castelgondolfo, arriving in plenty of time and finding a good vantage point in the small square. The group was in high spirits, cured of the irritableness which had been all too evident on the long journey between Lucerne and Rome. We cheered the Pope, waving our tartan banners for all to see, and then contentedly boarded our buses for the trip to Florence, where we intended to spend the night and the following morning.

The comedy of errors began just as we left Rome. At a roundabout we lost sight of the other bus, went back round and lost our way. Eventually we found the road north and after about an hour we decided to wait in a lay-by until the other bus came along. They had all the food and we had the tents. And so we waited, munching on watermelons from a roadside stall and debating as to whether we should just continue to Florence without the others. We were still deliberating when a policeman on a motorcycle arrived with a message that a busload of people were waiting for us in Florence. By the time we arrived (with the tents) it was dark and a very disgrunted group set about making camp. The day had begun so well. The last blow came when I discovered that someone had taken my sleeping bag. With the buses locked and the drivers retired for the night, I slept on the ground wrapped in some polythene sheeting which I had managed to borrow. Very early in the morning, feeling cold, stiff and miserable, I set off to find a bakery as we had no bread. My spirits lifted as I found a busy bakery in the town where I was able to buy large sticks of newly baked bread. By the time I started my walk back uphill to the campsite the sun had come up. I became very warm, still wearing my overnight jumper and clasping sticks of hot bread. It was worth it, though – breakfast had already been prepared when I got back to camp and my gift of bread was very welcome. Fed and showered, all of us felt much better and we spent some absorbing hours sightseeing in Florence. It is a beautiful city and, personally, I much prefer it to Rome.

While we were in Rome three of the young people had mislaid their passports. Colin read them the riot act, then took them to the British Embassy where they were eventually given the necessary documentation to take them back to Britain. As we left Florence, Colin muttered to me that he also had left his passport in Rome. By this time we were well on the way to the Swiss border.

'What do we do now, Colin?' I asked, torn between despair and hysteria.

'Well, there isn't much I can do about it now,' he said gloomily. 'But after my strictness with those young ones who lost theirs, I don't want anyone else to know. When the customs come on to the bus, you sit at the front and I'll accompany them round carrying the bus log book which they must examine. My hope is they won't ask me for my passport as well!'

And that is how we travelled to Zeebrugge, passing smoothly through Swiss, German, French and Belgian customs. Not once was Colin asked for his passport: the log book was enough. Apart from sitting in a German car park during a frightening electrical storm, we arrived without further incident at the port. Before sailing, however, we decided that Colin would have to become legal again. I accompanied him by taxi to Ostend, where he 'gave himself up' at the British Consulate. We caused considerable merriment and I think they secretly relished the fact that a priest had travelled through so many countries minus a passport. They were very friendly and gave him the necessary document with little fuss. Apart from myself, no one else in our group was aware of the situation.

Arriving home safely somehow diminishes the troubles experienced on a journey, and our trek to Rome now brings happy memories and a chuckle or two.

✦

While we were enjoying ourselves in Rome, there were less amusing events happening in other parts of the world, of course. While I was in Dunoon the Vietnam war was coming to an end. The Vietcong advanced on Saigon and the Americans made a quick withdrawal. Were there any victors in that war? It was hard to tell. This was brought home to me when I witnessed an officer from the *Canopus* openly crying as he watched the events unfold on the television. This man had spent three years in Vietnam and knew of companions posted missing or dead. His sorrow turned to anger as he railed against the American authorities for allowing such a disastrous turn of events. For myself, I was delighted the conflict was over, but I could not convey my thoughts to this man who, like many others in the naval base, felt ashamed that the war had been lost. The conflict which I had only observed from afar had been a real part of their lives. It was a sobering and thought-provoking time for me. In my pastoral role there was always something new to learn from the people I met and cared for.

I strongly believe that we all learn from each other, and I know I learned a great deal from my experience of working with different priests. Roddy Macdonald taught me much through his humility and his understanding of people, no matter their weaknesses, and I learned a lot from him about the pastoral care of people on a one-to-one basis. He was an excellent preacher, his sermons often peppered with humour and a little education in history. He made an excellent house companion and whenever I had been away I was always glad to return. The people in the parish had made me feel welcome right from the time of my arrival there and I can say with all honesty that I had never been so happy in my work. So it was with dismay that I received a letter in August 1976 from Bishop MacPherson, appointing me as assistant priest in St Mary's, Fort William. It was unexpected news and I felt sad because I was really only just settled into my work. But obedience to my bishop meant that I accepted this next move and change in my life without question.

✦

Near the village of Roybridge, in the Braes of Lochaber, lies the graveyard of Cille Choireil. It is very ancient, some claiming it goes back to pre-Christian times. Whatever its age, it tells its own story of the history of that part of Scotland and the Catholic faith of its people. In a beautiful setting on a hill-top above the Roybridge to Laggan road it is clearly visible to those travelling towards the village in the Braes. On the brow of the hill are the graves of the clergy, with a large Celtic cross in the centre marking the last resting place of Bishop Kenneth Grant. A native of Fort William, he was appointed Bishop of Argyll and the Isles while still a prisoner of war. After the war he was a towering figure in the Diocese until he died of throat cancer in the late 1950s.

In the district of Moidart another ancient graveyard, the Green Isle, marks an early Celtic foundation reputed to go back to the time of St Finnan. The ruins of the monastic church lie at the centre of the last resting place of so many buried there over hundreds of years. Moidart is one of the last Gaelic-speaking areas on mainland Scotland, with a Catholic tradition which remained intact despite the Reformation. In times past the Ardnamurchan Peninsula, where Moidart is situated, was well populated, but many of the glens have long since emptied. Indeed, this began as part of the infamous Highland clearances, and later, like so many rural areas, the depopulation trend accelerated with the coming of industry to larger, more central, towns.

Between these two ancient areas, Fort William gets its name from King William and its days as a garrison town. *An Gearasdain* (The Garrison), as the Gaels called it, was a centre of recruitment for the Highland regiments and any military history bears witness to their importance in wars and skirmishes fought throughout the world in the king's name.

When I moved there in 1976, I was well aware of the history of Fort William and the surrounding area. By this time it had become the tourist centre it still is today. When I travelled by train to Mallaig on my way to Uist as a child, we often met some cousins in Fort William. They would be waiting on the platform to greet us briefly before the train moved on and they returned to the hotels where they were employed during the holiday season. A number of them settled in the area and were parishioners of St Mary's, mingling naturally with the people of the Braes and Moidart. It was in every way a West Highland parish.

✦

Arriving at St Mary's that August, I was given a quiet welcome because the parish priest, John MacLean, was a quiet man. He was a native of Barra and had spent most of his priesthood in the islands apart from a short time in Morar. He had been the last resident parish priest on the island of Eigg, from where he also served Canna and Rhum. I have never met a more self-effacing man, a truly humble person. Further, in an affluent society he lived, by his own choice, a life of poverty. Actually, for the first year I found him quite difficult to live with because he was so quiet, often omitting to inform me of what was happening in the parish. Sometimes I would only learn of parish matters from the Sunday Bulletin which he printed each week. It is not easy to live with a saint! But I did learn to live with him and grew to admire him very much. I certainly benefited from our relationship.

It was soon apparent to me how much John missed the parish of Ardkenneth in South Uist where he had spent the previous 12 years. He loved the sea and felt almost claustrophobic under the looming presence of Ben Nevis. Above all, he loved the Gaelic language and gradually we began to speak it on a daily basis, which was to prove very useful to me later on. I soon got back into the way of it. However, the most important lesson I learned from him was the understanding and patience he had for the poor, especially those regarded as 'down and out'.

I soon had much to keep me occupied in the parish. We had a large Primary school of about 200 pupils and the Senior Secondary, Lochaber High School, which served the islands and hinterland as well as Fort William and nearby Caol. This school had a roll of over 1,200 pupils and about a third of these were Catholic. In those days Friday morning was given over to Religious Education, with a class period of 45 minutes allotted to each year. I had the assistance of some teachers and a nun, Sister Margaret, and John MacLean took one class, and thus we were able to offer the opportunity of teaching to all the Catholic pupils. I loved this part of my work, especially the sessions with the senior pupils who kept me on my toes. At the time there was an excellent debating society in the school and one of the stars was Charles Kennedy who, not much later, would be a leading light in the new Liberal Democrat Party. We had some excellent debates in the classroom and I was not surprised when he chose politics as a career.

Next door to the church house was the Belford Hospital and either John or myself visited on a daily basis and had excellent relations with the staff. When I arrived, Father John MacCormick was a patient in the Medical Ward. He had been the previous parish priest of St Mary's but had suffered a very severe stroke which left him paralysed on the right side. But his keen brain and wonderful sense of humour were still very much alive. Twice a week we wheeled him across to the house where he celebrated Mass in the front room, assisted by one of us. Afterwards we shared a fish meal, often salt herring or salt mackerel, which he loved but was not on the hospital menu!

One of us was always on night call for the hospital and were regularly sent for when the staff judged that we should attend, or whenever a patient requested our presence. No matter how tired we were or at what hour the call came, I never heard John complain and I hope he never heard me react in such a way. His example certainly remained with me throughout my priesthood.

Our house always had an open door for priests and seldom did a day pass without a visit from Father Iain Gillies, Arisaig, or Monsignor Ewan MacInnes, Morar, or Canon John Morrison, who was our neighbour in Corpach. The man I succeeded, Father Billy Fraser, who was now in lovely Mingarry, was also a regular visitor. I soon got to know our other regular visitors – the tramps and those regarded as 'down and outs'. John always made time to give them tea and a sandwich, a habit I quickly acquired. We had a rule not to give them money which, more often than not, they would use to buy cheap drink. Most of them you could not help but like – they were real characters, although one or two could be quite unpleasant. One of these had the nickname 'Killer' amongst the fraternity. I never discovered exactly why he was called that, but his demeanour and aggressiveness when he was refused money gave more than a hint.

Just a few weeks after my arrival, the parish priest of Roybridge, Monsignor Ronnie Hendry, took seriously ill and I was appointed to look after the needs of his parish until other arrangements could be made. Every day I drove the 15 miles to that lovely church to celebrate Mass and on two mornings a week stayed to visit the little Primary school there, as well as Kilmonivaig School in Spean Bridge. This was all in addition to my normal duties in Fort William but I never felt it was a burden. After about six weeks Father Gunther, a retired White Father who had spent about 40 years in Africa, came to stay in Roybridge for an indefinite period and my brief term of office came to an end.

My first funeral in the parish was that of a little baby called John MacPhee, who had only survived a breech birth for a few hours. Father John had ministered to the child and the distraught parents, but because he had to be elsewhere on the day of the funeral, I took the service. I had arrived only a few weeks before and did not know the family. Present in Cille Choireil for the burial were the father and his father and brother, and the father and brothers of baby John's mother, Kathleen. No women were present. They were all at home comforting Kathleen. Many years later this sad and private event would make headlines in a Scottish tabloid newspaper, with the claim that one of the women at the funeral was witness to Kathleen looking significantly into my eyes over the grave of her child. Apart from the fact that I knew neither Kathleen nor her family at this time, the simple truth is that no women attended the funeral. I paid no follow-up visits to the grieving family, as they knew John much better, though several times I did meet Kathleen and other family members briefly in the normal course of parish business, as I did all our active parishioners.

✦

As a centre of tourism, Fort William continues to work when most of the country goes on holiday. I used to complain about the constant flow of traffic outside my window, but the guesthouse proprietors and shopkeepers relished the spring and summer 'season'. Now it is busy all year round. The only road to Inverness and Mallaig runs by the church and the house, so all through traffic passes that way. When I was there, people had difficulty crossing the road to reach the church at Mass times during July and August. Indeed, in the summer months the church was often overflowing.

The huge influx of visitors meant that we met people from all over the country and from many different parts of the world. We regularly had Americans and Canadians asking to look at the old registers, in the hope of finding the names of ancestors who had left for their part of the world during the Highland clearances and subsequent emigrations. It also meant that the hospital next door could be very busy, with increased numbers of road accidents, climbers falling on Ben Nevis, and lost hillwalkers being brought in exhausted. Although the very serious cases were sent to Inverness or Glasgow, the majority were treated in the Belford.

In the peak season all accommodation in the town and surrounding area was taken and on a number of occasions the police
approached us, asking if we could open the church hall and allow
people to sleep there overnight. Occasionally we found campers in
our grounds in the early morning who had obviously taken up residence during the night. Once I was awakened by a German couple
who politely asked for use of the kitchen and toilet as if that were
the norm. I graciously gave them the use of the facilities and went
back to bed.

Sometimes our inadvertent hospitality led to more embarrassing
situations. One Christmas a local joiner offered his services to build
the crib. Using bark-covered wood, he constructed what might
have passed as a log cabin in the large back porch of the church.
When completed it was very attractive, decorated with greenery of
all kinds. On Christmas Eve when I was preparing for Midnight
Mass at about 10.30 p.m., the doorbell rang. Opening it, I was faced
by two ladies who were obviously upset.

'What's wrong, ladies?' I asked.

'Father, there's a drunk man lying in the crib!'

'What? What do you mean he's lying in the crib?'

'He's fast asleep and he's spoiled all your work!'

When I went across I found some of the congregation had come
earlier than expected and all of them were looking at Jacob, fast
asleep in our 'log cabin', the crib figures all pushed aside and
almost hidden in the straw and greenery. Jacob was an Irishman
who lived in sheltered housing provided by the Social Services for
single men, situated well outside Fort William on the Spean Bridge
to Invergarry road. During his life he had worked hard in various
parts of Scotland but was now retired. Both John and I knew him
well because he would call for a cup of tea when he came into town.
Occasionally he borrowed a pound which he would repay on his
next visit. He was mischievous in a likeable way.

Sighing, I wakened him from his stupor and managed to extricate him from the chaos he had caused. With an ever-growing audience, I led him out of the church and across to the house.

'Jacob, you're drunk.'

'Aye, Father, I've had a few. It is Christmas.'

'I know. Did you see the mess you made of the crib?'

'I'm sorry. Sure, I was only trying to give the baby a kiss.'

'Well, Jacob, I don't know if you managed that, but you
knocked St Joseph over and nearly suffocated a poor shepherd!'

'Well, I'm sorry,' he said blearily.

Time was short and I had to make arrangements to get him home. If I allowed him to stay for Mass there was no knowing what he would disturb next. The poor taxi driver who called for him was not at all certain about taking this particular fare – I even paid him a substantial tip to ensure that he would deliver his charge all the way to his home. After he left I began a quick redecoration of the crib as the crowd arrived for Mass. I found the baby Jesus hidden deep in the straw and, alongside, an empty bottle of whisky.

✦

It was a busy parish and I enjoyed my work there. Once I had got used to him, living with John MacLean became a bonus in my life. A quiet and prayerful man, he worked so very hard, above and beyond what the parish demanded. One of his tasks, carried out without the knowledge of many, would have been more than enough for most people. In Ardkenneth he had been a member of a committee brought together to begin the work of translating the Mass texts and the Scripture readings of the Roman Lectionary and Missal from English and Latin to Gaelic. They worked assiduously for a number of years, producing their work on typed sheets of paper which were then sent to the priests in whose parishes the liturgy was said in Gaelic. The work had never been completed, or properly edited, corrected or printed in such a way that the laity could have their own copies.

This had become John's work in Fort William. I can still see him, late at night, French and Irish translations of the Bible by his side as reference books, his own and the committee's translations on the desk before him, working with his very old typewriter to produce enough for the following four Sundays. When completed he would send the material to the printing department of the *Stornoway Gazette*. They faithfully produced the leaflets and sent them out to the parishes. (Stornoway has the largest congregation of the Free Church of Scotland, most of whom regard Catholics as idolaters. It would have surprised many that the printing of the text and readings of the Mass was done there, and at a very reasonable price.)

Before I left, John had completed the translation and improved the work of the original committee, thus producing a complete Gaelic version of the Sunday Masses as required by the Roman Missal. The priests and people of the Diocese had no idea how much he gave of himself to this work or how binding a task it had become. If ever anyone deserved an honorary doctorate from the Divinity or Celtic departments of one of the Scottish universities it was John MacLean. Too late, some of us approached Antigonish University in Cape Breton to recognize his work for the Gaelic language, but it was not to be.

One morning, just after 6 o'clock, I could hear the phone ringing in John's room. As I expected him to pick it up because it was his turn to answer night calls, it took me some time to realize that he was not there. I answered the phone myself, only to discover that it was John who was speaking.

'Hello, Roddy,' he said. 'Will you bring me my toilet bag and pyjamas?'

'Why? Where *are* you?'

'I'm in the Surgical Ward of the Belford.'

'What's wrong?'

'Oh, I've been in a lot of pain and they tell me I need surgery.'

'Right,' I said, worried, 'I'll be across as soon as possible.'

When I found him he was in bed in obvious pain. In the middle of the night he had got out of bed, walked across to the hospital and declared himself in need of assistance. Meantime, next door, I slept on in blissful ignorance. That was the type of person he was – undemanding and quiet, always more willing to help others than make a fuss about himself.

Early in 1979 the bishop asked me to go to Eriskay for a short period while the parish priest was absent on sick leave. By this time John was fully recovered and with help from a supply priest on Sundays could manage the parish. For four weeks I enjoyed the idyllic life on that island. In a real way it was a spiritual retreat for me. The sea has always made me aware of the presence of God in daily life. I find it so calming, despite the many moods it displays. The church in Eriskay is on top of a hill overlooking Haun and Baile. The north-facing windows provide a perfect view of the Sound of Eriskay and the hills of Uist, while on the west side are Barra and its neighbouring islands – one of the outstanding views in the world for me, especially at sunset, and on the east side is a close-up view of the island of Eriskay itself. I could spend hours just standing and looking. The memory still touches my very soul.

In the midst of all this beauty, back to earth with a thud, I played my first ever game of bingo, which was a central part of the island's social life on a Sunday. Old and young gathered in the

Community Hall for the fun, all very natural and relaxed. It was a fishing community and the men were at sea most of the week, so any such social gathering was important. Too soon I was back in Fort William and business went on as usual.

◆

During my time in St Mary's I involved myself in youth work again, an aspect of the pastoral life which I have always enjoyed. The YTS scheme was government policy at the time to give young people training for work. To me it never really seemed to be successful. However, I became involved locally by arranging some work for a group of young people on the Green Isle in Moidart. Along with some other adults, I accompanied them and we spent two days cleaning the ancient burial ground.

It was then that I discovered I had a nickname – Starsky, after the character in the popular American police drama. I had to ask, of course, 'And who is Hutch?'

'Oh, Father MacLean,' they replied.

That night, at supper, John had a good chuckle about this. Unfortunately, my nickname stuck in people's minds, to re-emerge amongst the headlines many years later.

In April 1980 I came back as usual after my morning in Lochaber High School one Friday. Awaiting me was a letter from Bishop MacPherson which I did not bother to open immediately, thinking it was just a church circular. Just before lunch I opened it and read it, then read it again. I did not believe what I was reading. I was to take up my appointment as parish priest of St Michael's, Ardkenneth, South Uist, on 21 May 1980. My heart beat faster. 'No. It must be a hoax,' I cautioned myself. I looked at the envelope again. It had no stamp! Yes, it was a hoax then. One of the other priests must have got hold of some diocesan notepaper and written it. I would not mention it to John. I put it in my inside pocket before going down to lunch.

It being Friday, our lunch was my favourite fish. We chatted about parish matters and I made conversation about my morning in the school. As we drank our coffee I could resist no longer and produced my letter. I said I thought it was a hoax and John agreed. Just two days previously he had been with the bishop and this appointment was not John's understanding of how things were to be. I felt quite deflated because I was truly yearning to go to the islands. We agreed not to mention the letter or its contents to anyone.

The following morning John came into my room with a letter in his hand. 'Roddy,' he said excitedly, 'I don't think your letter was a hoax. I know I'm to move and I've received a letter confirming this. I'm going to Daliburgh. We both move to Uist at the same time. Like yours, this letter has no stamp!'

Over the weekend the telephone was busy as a number of priests called, including Father Kennedy who was coming to Fort William. But Colin MacInnes, whom I was meant to be replacing in Ardkenneth, had not received a letter. Confusion reigned. The bishop was on holiday and could not be reached. It took almost a week for all the priests who were moving to receive their letters. En route to his holiday destination the bishop had posted the letters in Carlisle, forgetting to have them stamped.

6

✦

ARDKENNETH

I ARRIVED IN ARDKENNETH, IOCHDAR, the day before Colin left. My journey from Fort William took me via Kyle and Skye to Lochmaddy in North Uist, and from there I drove south through Grimsay and Benbecula to South Uist. I had never been to Ardkenneth before and actually drove past it the first time, not realizing it was a quarter of a mile off the road. Early the following morning Colin left with his belongings to catch the ferry to Barra, where he had been appointed parish priest of Northbay, and I was left alone. I stood in the large kitchen looking out over Loch Bee, admiring the swans and feeling that I had come home. Although I had spent so much of my youth in Uist, the north side of the island was unknown to me. We had seldom ventured further than Lochboisdale, the main port at the south end of the island. I did not know the people of Iochdar and they did not know me – which perhaps was no bad thing! I was looking forward to exploring.

Ardkenneth stands on a knoll just above the western shore of Loch Bee. To the north and west of the church building are the fields of the croft which belongs to the parish. It was built in 1829, the year of Catholic Emancipation – a fact that would have meant very little to the parishioners of that time. Everyday life was a harsh struggle for them and wider Church issues were not a central concern. They probably carried on for some time with their 'underground' priests until the news of greater freedom filtered through. The building was essentially unchanged when I moved in and I felt that its very stones could tell a remarkable story. It replaced an older and smaller structure just to the south of the village of Gerinish at An Gearraidh Fluich, which had been burned to the ground a few years earlier by the Protestant landlord's agents. When the building of Ardkenneth had been completed the priest, Father James MacGregor – who was to remain there until his death some 40 years later – wrote to his counterpart in Barra: 'I have built a temple to the Lord. It can be seen from the north and from the south, and from the east and the west, and they dare not burn it.' They did not dare and Ardkenneth still stands as a landmark on the north-west shoulder of South Uist. A second church, St Bride's, was built in the parish in the 1960s, to provide for the people living on the south side of Loch Bee. I came to love both churches very much.

The story of Ardkenneth reflects the history of the whole of Uist through many years of struggle and persecution. When James Mac-Gregor arrived in Uist in the early part of the nineteenth century he would have found people in abject poverty, slaves to the landlords in all but name. The islanders lived in small thatched houses, known as black houses, with just a small patch of land on which they grew some roots, mainly potatoes. At that time many lived on the east side behind the hills in Corodale, Hellisdale and Usinish. Today there are no people and no roads except sheep tracks there. In the 1820s the land they rented produced little. The best of the land, the machair on the west side, was preserved for growing wheat, oats and barley, which could only be bought from the landowner. The only industry for the local population was kelp harvesting, which again was for the benefit of the landlord and part-payment of the rent for the poor dwellings in which they lived. After 1830 the kelp income died out and the people were thrown off any machair land they occupied. The landowner had these fertile areas converted into farms and shepherds were brought in from the mainland to run them. By 1886, nine-tenths of South Uist's population occupied just two-fifths of the land.

In the middle of the century, to add to the islanders' plight, the Potato Famine struck. The blight destroyed their main source of food, just as it did for the poor in Ireland. In the Ardkenneth register for births in 1848, James MacGregor wrote, 'In this year there were only 88 Baptisms – the year of the potato disease.' Previous years had recorded up to 150 births. The population was being severely diminished by starvation. Further decrease was about to occur in a brutal extension of the Highland clearances.

The owner of Uist and Barra was Colonel Gordon of Cluny in Aberdeenshire. He had 500 people banished from the area between Loch Eynort, in the middle of the island, to the Point of Usinish in the north. These abandoned habitations on the east side of the island can be identified today by remnant stones from the little houses and the still visible outlines of the 'lazy beds' where they grew their potatoes. The people were moved to make room for sheep. Some of them ended up in the little island of Eriskay, some were sent to till the barren soil of Lochboisdale, but the majority were sent to Canada, many dying en route or soon after arrival. The deportations were violent, and Donald MacLeod describes the scene in *Gloomy Memories in the Highlands of Scotland* (Toronto, 1857): 'They were catching them and securing them with ropes. There was no pier or wharf at Loch Boisdale, so they were taking them out to the ships in small boats.' The priests did their utmost to defend their people against this persecution. The natives were mostly Catholic and Father Chisolm, who had come to Bornish in 1836, and Father MacGregor could only protest and do their utmost to minister to their people in such plight. They had no power in the face of the Establishment. These expulsions continued under the acceptable name of 'emigrations' until as late as 1923.

After the First World War, during which so many young men lost their lives, those few returning began to claim the land for themselves. As in Skye and Lewis, in Uist there were 'land raids' by the men returning from the trenches, as they staked their claims for crofts. In many cases they were successful and crofting became the norm. It is a fact that the earlier cruel deportations were the price of the present way of life.

When I arrived in Ardkenneth in 1980 there were 350 parishioners, a far cry from the population which had existed before the decimation of the famine, the clearances and the wars. In 1979 just three children were born in the community. Nonetheless, the people amongst whom I now lived had a marvellous sense of their own history. They were steeped in tradition and were determined to preserve their language and culture. On most days I would only speak in Gaelic.

That proved to be my first hurdle on arriving. I speak the language fluently – it was the language of my childhood and John

MacLean and I had spoken it together in Fort William. But I had never had the opportunity to learn to read or write it, as it was not on my school curriculum. In Uist the liturgy was mostly in Gaelic! On my second day in the parish I sat down with the Mass text and the Readings for the coming Sunday in the company of a local teacher who kindly led me through the texts, correcting me word after word. For six months I depended on the teacher's assistance as I prepared painstakingly for each Sunday's liturgy. Then, all of a sudden, I no longer seemed to need that constant assistance and could read almost as fluently as I spoke. Soon I not only spoke and read in Gaelic, I thought in it and it was also the language of my dreams. This was important in my pastoral work, especially amongst the older generation. The oldest parishioners had difficulty in speaking English fluently, although the younger generation was at ease in both languages. I was deeply moved by these old islanders' devotion to prayer, in particular the rosary. Some of them knew wonderful old Gaelic prayers, passed on through the generations and so full of poetry and meaning.

Close acquaintance with my parishioners came later, though. Of more immediate concern on my arrival (apart from my Gaelic illiteracy) was the fact that as well as a parish, I now had a croft and a flock of over 100 sheep. My morning call was the bleating of lambs and the call of the ewes. Overnight, I felt at home on the croft and one of my first visits was to Angus John, the local crofter who supervised the church's croft and stock. I quickly learned from him the importance of shepherding, of looking out for the trapped or lost lamb. Angus John's first request was that I have the fields properly fenced. He produced the necessary forms for claiming a subsidy from the Department of Agriculture and Fisheries, and so began my regular dealings with that vital organ of the Government. My first constructive work in the parish was the erection of those fences and gates, and I revelled in it.

✦

Just two weeks after my arrival in Uist Father John MacCormick died in Fort William. Arrangements were made to bury him in Cille Choireil after the Requiem Mass in St Mary's. On the Sunday I told the parishioners I would be going to the funeral and that I would therefore be absent from the parish for two days. That night, however, my throat became very sore and closed up. I knew in the early hours of the morning that I would not be able to travel. Indeed, I felt really ill and was unable to rise from my bed. I wanted to phone the doctor but found that I could not utter a word. At around 10 o'clock the lady who had looked after the house for Father Colin came to collect my washing and do some tidying, which she had agreed to continue doing for me on two mornings a week. Presuming I had left for Fort William, she walked into my bedroom and was shocked to find me lying there looking dreadful. Her concern grew when she discovered I could not talk – I think she thought I had had a stroke.

After failing to understand my sign language she brought me paper and pen and I scribbled 'Please phone the doctor'. Half an hour later I was in an ambulance, making the 20-mile journey to Daliburgh Hospital. I had never been so ill before as to need hospital treatment. As we drove down the Ardkenneth road I could see neighbours stopping to stare, standing in the fields and outside their doors. They all thought I was on my way to Fort William, and an ambulance always creates curiosity in a scattered rural area. I was certainly making myself conspicuous, so soon after arriving! A dose of antibiotics had me back on my feet in two days and I returned to work, sad that I had missed Father John's funeral, but relieved to be back in good health.

✦

There were not too many young people in the parish so I quickly got to know all of them. Despite the shortage of children, we had two schools in the parish – a four-year Secondary combined with a Primary school, and another on the south-west side of Loch Bee in West Gerinish. I do not think I have ever met such well-behaved children and it was a pleasure to work with them. The Secondary school provided for the young people of Benbecula and those from the north end of South Uist, although they had to travel to Stornoway for their fifth and sixth years. Amongst the pupils from Benbecula were the children of military personnel. There was quite a large military establishment then, a very important employer for the men and women of the islands. It was attached to the Rocket Range situated on Gerinish Machair, just adjacent to Ardkenneth with just a strip of loch and a few fields separating us. The whole building would vibrate when some of those rockets were fired out into the Atlantic.

As is the case in most parishes, visiting the parishioners in their homes was one of my first and most important tasks. Although there were only 350 parishioners, they were scattered over a large area, from Aird a Mhachair on the Atlantic coast to Caolas and Loch Skipport on the hilly east side, and from Carnan in the north to Stilligarry in the south. Only my nearest neighbours could be visited on foot.

In some of the houses I felt I was visiting the past. Very little in the way of furnishings or decoration had changed since the 1940s and I would sit on the bench (*an beingidh*) just as I had done so often in my childhood in my grandfather's house. The conversation being good, I could sit there for a long time listening to stories of the Somme, Passchendaele or Flanders, as if the events had occurred yesterday. Other homes were so modern and beautifully furnished that I wondered if I was still in Uist. Some of the children brought a similar confusion to my mind. Amongst them were the singers, dancers and pipers who, on request, would perform these traditional arts quite beautifully. Others, just a few years older, found it difficult to extricate themselves from the earplugs through which they listened to the 1980s music enjoyed by teenagers round the world. The few times they spoke, they did so in English, thinking it more 'macho' (much as I probably had at a similar age).

Ceilidhs were still important social events for the whole community, though, and powerful singers amongst the men and women would entertain the gathering with songs from the distant past. The Gaelic language is very descriptive and, when sung well, highly evocative. I was surprised by the older people's agility and ability on the dance floor. They were always first on their feet, completing the most intricate set dances and reels with apparent ease. If they enjoyed themselves, so did those of us who could only watch. Today, I wonder if the young people will continue to keep their culture alive with such enthusiasm.

Some traditions are possibly held onto for too long, however, and during my first year I upset some of the older people by changing a long-held custom. Unlike the rest of Britain — and indeed the rest of Uist — clocks in Iochdar were not changed on the appointed day until after Mass. When we were due to turn the clocks back by one hour in October 1980 I was told by a number of parishioners that this *never* happened in Iochdar until after the last Mass on Sunday. I complied and was most confused when BBC Radio 4 gave the time that morning. The following spring, when the change to summer time came around, I gave a few weeks' notice of my intention to comply with what was the norm for the rest of the nation. There were murmurings of disapproval. Change is never popular!

Old habits die hard, and many of the older people much preferred to use cash rather than cheques. They were generous by nature, as I came to know too well, but also very careful with their money because in their young days everything had been such a struggle. If they used the bank it was normally the deposit account that they favoured which, of course, was wise. I think few, if any, would have used a credit card. Some preferred the Post Office, which they had always used in the past for transactions when necessary. I was once asked by a sister and her two brothers to help them with their brother's estate shortly after his funeral. They trusted me, and wanted to keep the business private. Sitting in the kitchen with all surviving members of the family present and watching, I set about counting. The money was all contained in plastic bags taken from a bedroom. I began my task at 2.00 p.m. and around 4.00 p.m., as darkness closed in, I asked for some light. Some time after that I finally completed the job. All the man's debts had been paid and the family wanted a straight three-way split of what was left. It was dark when I departed, leaving each of them sitting with a bundle of notes amounting to over £16,000. Their brother had left almost £50,000, many of the notes so old that I had never seen their like. I strongly advised them to bank the money, but I am not too sure they ever did.

In Ardnamonie lived one family I grew very fond of, and of whom I have such lovely memories. Angus, Donald, Morag and Kate Effie MacCormick lived in one of the few remaining thatched houses on what is termed a half-croft. Outside the house were the peat stack and the old thatched byre, ducks disapproving of visitors with a shake of their tail feathers, hens clucking and pecking, a dog with a permanent black eye, and a few cats occasionally scattering their feathered neighbours. In June, when I paid the first of many visits, two tiny lambs lay at the door waiting to be bottle fed. I had to stoop to enter the house and, once inside, found myself in another world. All four of them stood, Donald and Angus doffing their caps in reverence to the priest. Morag sat down immediately, telling me she was far from well and showing me the various bottles of tablets and lotions which the doctor had prescribed. Whatever the illness was, it had lasted for more than 20 years and I would regularly be called to the house to minister to Morag.

Conversation with these brothers and sisters, who were very simple but wise, was always enjoyable and revealing for me. They loved company and rarely did an evening pass without some neighbour calling in to pass the time with them. Sitting on the Mac-Cormicks' *beingidh*, I was able to view a perfectly preserved croft house of the 1930s or '40s: the painted V-lined walls, adorned with some religious pictures and a few photos from the distant past; opposite me, the dresser with the dishes guarded at each end by the china 'wally dogs'; the floor covered in linoleum with a mat in front of the old black stove which was permanently lit, constantly fed from the peat stack outside. Our conversation was always in Gaelic – they had real difficulty conversing in English. Time passed so pleasantly in the warmth of that room and I often felt quite lonely when I left.

Within the first two months I visited every home and soon got to know every household. Of the 350 parishioners only six did not practise their faith by attending Mass on a regular basis. There were a number of elderly people who were unable to attend and I ministered to them regularly. Pastorally it was an excellent situation, but I had to be one of them and willing to attend to their needs. I soon learned what was required. In illness many of them would call the priest before the doctor. Indeed, I quickly got to know the doctors as we often arrived at a house together. The faith of these people always impressed me, making me feel very humble in the living out of my own faith. The prayerfulness of the household when I called on such occasions was profoundly moving. The hospital was 20 miles away in Daliburgh, as I had reason to know. We Catholics knew it as The Sacred Heart Hospital, although it was first called Bute Hospital and is now known simply as Daliburgh Hospital. It had been founded at the end of the nineteenth century by Lord Bute in the midst of terrible poverty worsened by the upheaval of the recent clearances. The Sisters of the Sacred Hearts of Jesus and Mary came from France to run it and to this day they have a presence in the island and are still held in great esteem. The most respected was one of the early Sisters, Casimir, after whom a road adjacent to the hospital has been named. I visited the hospital at least once a week, but would make the journey more often if a parishioner was seriously ill. All too clearly I remember the sad case of two hard-working brothers who suffered from what is known as 'farmer's lung'. Working amongst old hay, they had contracted this fatal illness, which caused fungus to grow in their lungs. The two men, Seumas and Seonnaidh MacDonald, shared a room in the hospital and witnessed each other's suffering and approach to death. Most days I spent time with them. I was with Seonnaidh when he died, his brother Seumas lying helplessly behind a curtain just a few feet away, aware of all that was happening. Seumas died within two weeks of his brother. They were only about 40 years old.

✦

Under the energetic direction of my predecessor, Colin MacInnes, and with help from the Van Leer Foundation and the Highlands and Islands Development Board, the people of Iochdar had set up a Community Association and the Co-Chomunn (co-op). At this time, communities throughout the islands were being encouraged to set up local co-operatives based on individual shares which were then matched with equal contributions from the HIDB. Once this was done, and a proper constitution drawn up by the members, a committee was elected to run the business for a year. When I arrived Iochdar Community Hall had just been opened, built under the auspices of the Community Association and the Co-Chomunn. They had been set up as separate bodies, but in truth they appeared to me to be the same thing – an excellent way of ensuring the necessary funding for different projects!

The hall was a much needed resource for the community and it was here that Co-Chomunn set up its office and began business with a tea room which soon became popular with both locals and tourists. Having bought my shares worth £50 I was asked to join the committee as Secretary. This I did willingly because my predecessor had been so important in setting it up and most of the members were parishioners. It was a decision I was to rue as my workload increased alarmingly. Not only did I have to attend the weekly meeting and take the minutes, I was also co-opted on to a subcommittee which met separately, and I had to attend to the correspondence. Soon my desk was overflowing.

The Co-Chomunn meetings were a revelation. Why do committees, elected to work as a body, turn out to be so divided? I quickly learned a great deal that I would not have discovered from the pulpit. Little power struggles became apparent, and enmity which had lingered on between parties over something that had happened in the distant past. I became very good at sitting on the fence. The meetings began at 8.00 p.m. and often lasted until after 11.00, regularly ending without matters resolved. Yet it was remarkable how well we progressed and the voluntary efforts of the community can only be praised.

Soon after I joined, HIDB officials came to the islands to hold public meetings concerning their assistance to the communities. I was asked to address the gathering in Creagorry Hotel as a representative of our community. To be honest, I had only heard criticism of the Board during my short time at Ardkenneth, and portrayed this in my address. The local Development Officer, the Chairman and the Secretary all sought meetings with me immediately afterwards. I see now how unfair I was in my address, and of course it was reported in the local press and I was interviewed by local radio. But never mind – the outcome was beneficial to Co-Chomunn and relations between us and the Board improved.

At about this time the Department of Agriculture and Fisheries advertised the sale of their crofting stores throughout the islands. One of these was in Carnan and, having been assured of grant aid by HIDB, we put in a formal bid for this local store. The other stores in the islands were quickly disposed of, but we could not understand why there was no movement on the property at Carnan. At this time we were struggling to set up the viable business essential to our survival. We already ran a subsidized bus service which was of vital importance to the older people in far-flung places like Aird a Mhachair, Loch Carnan, Loch Skipport and Stilligarry. With our plans for the store at Carnan, we hoped to give employment and improve services to the community in general. The store would provide for building and crofting needs, and our business plans had been professionally drawn up with the assistance of the HIDB and local business people. Why was our bid not progressing?

We asked the Board to chase the Department of Agriculture and Fisheries on our behalf, but were informed that no two government departments could deal with each other on such matters. I spoke to the Secretary of Lord Mansfield, the Minister for Agriculture and Fisheries, but he obviously knew nothing about the sale – or even where Uist was. Some days later Mrs Winnie Ewing, our SNP member for the European Parliament, was holding a constituency surgery. I explained our situation to her and she promised to look into the matter. Within a week we had recognition of our bid and within the month it was accepted. Whatever Mrs Ewing said it was successful!

The Western Isles Crofters Ltd already owned two stores, one in Lochboisdale and the other in North Uist. Our plans for Carnan

Stores did not please them: they wanted no competition. I am sure that the reluctance to sell to us was due to their objections, but we came through in the end. In Iochdar today Co-Chumunn continues to thrive, while the Western Isles Crofters have long since gone into liquidation.

✦

In addition to my heavy involvement with the Co-Chomunn I was appointed to the Education Committee of the Western Isles Council, Comhairle nan Eilean. This meant I had to fly to Stornoway in Lewis on the first Tuesday of each month for the full meeting of the Committee. I was quite nervous of my role as the representative of the Catholic Church on this important body. The Comhairle has elected representatives from all the communities in the islands – local councillors. By reason of population size the majority of councillors are from the island of Lewis, which is one of the last areas in Britain where there is deep suspicion of most things Catholic, with the Free Church of Scotland a very powerful voice in all matters.

My first journey there was eventful. The flight from Benbecula was on the little Loganair plane nicknamed 'The Paraffin Budgie', which carried nine passengers. I was sitting beside Hugh Morrison, a councillor from Castlebay on Barra, my large frame squeezed into the bucket seat. It was a very windy day and I could feel the little plane being moved by the gale even while we were stationary on the ground. Hugh reassured me that we were perfectly safe; he had often made the journey in terrible weather. After my head hit the roof in a violent bumping episode over the hills of Harris and I heard gasps and shouts from some of my fellow passengers, I have to confess I was frightened. The taxi which took us to the Crown Hotel in Stornoway was a welcome change of transport. On subsequent flights I came to trust 'The Paraffin Budgie' which, on beautiful days, afforded me a marvellous aerial view of sea and islands (although I never did find a comfortable sitting position).

On that first visit to Stornoway as I made my way along Cromwell Street to the Comhairle's headquarters, I was accosted by a very respectable-looking elderly lady who said to me in Gaelic: 'Excuse me, are you a papist priest?'

'I am.'

'Where are you from?'

'South Uist.'

'Well, there's no need for the likes of you here!'

'Madam,' I replied politely, 'I have no wish to be here. I'll be back in Uist tomorrow. Good day to you.'

I was not upset by the encounter; she was expressing her heartfelt views. I continued my walk along Cromwell Street a little more nervously, however. Arriving at the building, I was given a warm welcome by some of the other councillors. The representatives of the Church of Scotland and the Episcopalian Church also greeted me kindly, but the representatives of the Free Church and the more extreme Free Presbyterian Church avoided me as the Israelites of old did the lepers. Ecumenism was truly alive and well in the Western Isles! This entrenched difference did cause some problems in the council chamber, but I always refused to be rattled by it, preferring to concentrate on the reason I was there in the first place – representing the educational interests of my parishioners.

I had always wondered how effectively local councillors could make critical decisions on such matters as education and health. My eyes were about to be opened. Some spoke fluently and with knowledge, but too many showed their ignorance and refused to listen to the logic of others. In one particular debate on the closure of schools in our southern isles I heard one of the older councillors, just returned from the bar, who had probably last entered a classroom in the 1920s, vaguely ask his neighbour: 'What way should I vote here?' On such is built our wonderful democratic way of making decisions on vital issues affecting the lives of others, I thought to myself. I am not a professional 'educationalist', but by then I had spent many hours in different schools in various parts of Scotland and had listened to parents and teachers voicing their concerns. I never spoke on the Committee on important and relevant matters without seeking the opinions of those directly involved in our island schools.

In 1983 or 1984, we in the southern isles objected strongly to that year's school schedule, which meant that the pupils of the Nicholson Institute in Stornoway had to return to school after their Easter break on Maundy Thursday, three days *before* Easter. Fifth- and sixth-year students from our islands had to go to Stornoway because the southern schools only provided education until the fourth year. There were over 100 pupils from the southern isles at the Institute and most of these were Catholic. Holy Week, especially the Sacred Triduum from Maundy Thursday leading up to Easter Sunday, is the most solemn and important celebration in our

Church's calendar. It is also an important family occasion and both pupils and parents were upset that their Easter holiday did not include Easter Sunday. The Free Church does not celebrate Easter as other Christian denominations do, stating as it does that every Sunday is a celebration of the Resurrection. If school began on Maundy Thursday or Good Friday it was of no consequence to them. We argued our case strongly, but the Education Department would not relent: the school plane would collect the pupils as planned on the Wednesday of Holy Week.

John MacLean in Daliburgh eventually suggested that we raise some money and cover the pupils' fares back to Stornoway on Easter Monday ourselves. The parents enthusiastically set about various fund-raising efforts. The chartered plane paid for by the Comhairle left Benbecula on the Wednesday of Holy Week almost empty. The southern pupils stayed at home, celebrated Easter, and on Easter Monday a boat hired by us made two sailings across the Sound of Harris from North Uist. From Harris the pupils continued their journey by bus to Stornoway. The total cost was less than that paid by the Education Department for their charter plane. To the best of my knowledge, the school term has not begun again before Easter since that time. On my next visit to Stornoway I received a rather frosty welcome from some of the councillors. It was a pointed victory, but there were perhaps more pressing concerns on the table.

Nothing upsets a small community like the closure of their school. In many cases it is at the heart of a village, not only because of its importance to the children but also because the building is often the focus of local activity. Further, none of us likes change and the school has often served generations. The Education Department announced such closures in the early 1980s and there was strong reaction to the news throughout the islands. A few closures were to take effect in Lewis, but the majority were in the southern isles, the Uists and Barra being particularly targeted. West Gerinish School in my parish was one of those listed and the immediate response of local people was to set up a committee to fight the closure. Other communities reacted in the same way and in the Uists a remarkable co-operation between the different communities was soon apparent. It was agreed that a large number of their representatives should gather in Stornoway on the day of the next full Council meeting.

Part of the context for the anger over these closures was that for many years the people of the Uists had been arguing their case for a six-year Secondary school. There were three four-year schools serving the islands, but many of the young people then had to leave home, sometimes for good. The communities suffered, losing the vitality and enthusiasm of those young people. About the same time as the closures were announced, the Secretary of State for Scotland gave approval for a six-year Secondary school to be situated in the Uists. It was eventually decided that the new school would be built in Liniclate, Benbecula. At least the children from North and South Uist, Eriskay and Barra would be able to return home each weekend instead of once a term. When it came to our resistance to the closure of the small schools, officials and councillors from Stornoway were not slow to argue that we should realize the expense to which they were going in providing this new school. It was a patronizing and false position. The six-year school was long overdue and a separate issue, a fact I argued strongly in the Council chambers.

On the day of the Council meeting a large group of people from the Uists arrived in Stornoway, having travelled by sea and by air in order to make their views on the closures known. I met them outside the building and had a few words with them before making my way to the chamber. Inside, a Lewis councillor approached me and said, 'I see you've brought the hooligans with you.'

'It's my opinion,' I told him crisply, 'that if there are any hooligans they're in here. Those outside are parents and concerned people who have a right to be heard.' His only response was a grunt.

It was the most heated debate in which I have ever participated. Our voice was heard, but – inevitably, I suppose – we were outvoted and the islands lost their small schools. Amongst some of our opponents there was an air of triumphalism which left me feeling very unhappy.

These were important issues for those amongst whom I lived and worked, and I got fully involved. On the whole, however, my visits to Stornoway were without incident and I certainly found the majority of the councillors and officials helpful and friendly. Whenever I was there I always called on Father Capaldi sj, who had been parish priest in Stornoway for more than 20 years. The little Catholic church was hidden from view behind buildings in Kenneth Street. On his arrival so many years before he had suffered some indignities and much antagonism, as had his predecessor, Father Whittaker. These men were really missionaries working in a foreign atmosphere. The hard-working Father Capaldi had long since silenced his critics, even if he had not overcome their suspicions, and by the 1980s was regarded with respect in the town. Since 1974, when the Western Isles had gained its own unitary authority, the number of parishioners had increased, bringing much-needed stability to the isolated parish. It was important that Father Capaldi meet with other priests, however, and whenever any of us visited the town we made sure to give him a call. The little church of Our Holy Redeemer was falling into a state of disrepair and it was his hope that a new church would be built. It was a pleasure to me some years later when I was able to help fulfil that hope.

✦

From time to time, in the midst of the whirl of activity as I travelled round the parish and did my duties with the Co-Chomunn and the Comhairle, I would take a moment to stop and drink in the beauty of the place. Sometimes it was hard to convince myself that I was really here, living in a place which meant so much to me and doing work which I dearly loved. I have certainly never lived in a church house with such a warm feeling. The house in Ardkenneth was not discernible from a distance because it was such an integrated part of the building: it actually forms the gable end of the church. Because of its age it has not only character but a living sense of history and, apart from the addition of a kitchen and a little porch, it is in essence just as it was almost two centuries ago. It has three storeys although the top one, the 'loft', was in my time just a storeroom, with old statues and books scattered around in an untidy gathering. On the ground floor was a public room, an office and the large kitchen. From my stance at the sink as I washed dishes I had a wonderful view of the flat lands between myself and the Minch. On a clear day I could even see the clear outline of the Cuillins in Skye, and beyond them the Five Sisters of Kintail on the mainland. From the other windows I had a view south to the hills of Uist beyond Loch Bee and the bluish outline of Barra, seeming to float on the sea. I had an even more panoramic view of the same from the sitting room window upstairs. In spring and summer I could never tire of that view, especially the ever-changing colours of the machair, brushed by the breeze. From my bedroom window, which faced north, I could see the hills of North Uist and sometimes caught a glimpse of the higher hills of Harris. More remarkably, I had a good view of the north-west Atlantic and could see the

Monach Isles, and occasionally the unmistakable shape of St Kilda, more than 70 miles away. I doubt if there are many houses with such marvellous views from all sides. I never left that house without longing to return.

✦

I have been writing as if I were the only priest in Uist and this most certainly was not the case. To the north in the parish of St Mary's, Benbecula, was Father Calum MacNeil, a gentle and scholarly man. He arrived in the parish on the same day that I arrived in Ardkenneth and I could not have asked for a better neighbour. He was much loved. A devotee of our Celtic heritage, he produced writings and sketches which were later published. During that first year I knew he had not been keeping well and I did my best to encourage him as he struggled to cope with the large parish of Benbecula, greater than mine in population and area. He also had to serve the Catholics in North Uist and care for the patients in the Geriatric Hospital in Lochmaddy, which entailed a round trip of 50 miles, often in the middle of the night. In time the bishop agreed to his request for a smaller parish and he was replaced by Father Iain Mac-Master, a contemporary of my own whom I was glad to welcome.

My near neighbour to the south was Canon Malcolm Morrison, an elderly priest who had been there for almost 20 years. I had known him since I was a young boy, his brother being married to my mother's sister. His dry wit and undoubtable wisdom, and the warm welcome he always gave me, brought me to visit him often – though it was foolish to visit him if you wanted an early night.

Further south was St Peter's, Daliburgh, where John MacLean was parish priest. His was one of the largest parishes in the diocese, with over 1,200 Catholics. This was an area I knew intimately, the Uist of my childhood. Although I had lived with John for four years in Fort William, I now grew closer to him in many ways, despite living 20 miles away. When I was visiting the hospital or my relatives, I would frequently call to see him for a chat. His advice was always worth considering. On one occasion, a sunny afternoon, I found him scraping and cleaning his little sailing boat at Ludag on the southerly tip of the island. He just seemed so much at home as he prepared his vessel for sailing. The very thought obviously gave him pleasure – it was his way of relaxing, and I felt envious of him as I discussed one of the thorny problems in my life at that time: those school closures. At other times I would find him working in his potato patch. Wherever he was he always managed to grow his crop of potatoes each year. He was a man close to nature and to God.

These were my neighbours and our togetherness was a real plus in my life. The most positive aspect for me was their prayerfulness, their example clarifying the necessity for such dedication in my own life. The daily Mass and the praying of the Daily Prayer of the Church were not only priestly duties, but an essential part of life.

◆

The tradition of the rosary as a prayer has played an important part in the living faith of the people of the West Highlands and the islands. It is reported that when Propaganda Fide (a missionary society in Rome) sent priests to these fringes of Europe in the eighteenth century they found a simple and living faith amongst the people despite the absence of local priests for many years. They suffered real persecution, especially from the landlords, but this only seems to have strengthened their resolve. In Lochaber and Moidart, Uist and Barra, the Mass rocks where the underground priests celebrated the Eucharist are still revered. And the names of Fathers Duggan and White live on, not only in stories but in place names. They were Irish Vincentians who worked amongst the people of Moidart and the islands during those years when the Catholic Faith was proscribed. Throughout those dangerous times a simple (some would say ignorant and poor) people enriched their lives through their devotion to the rosary. It is sad that in these 'enlightened' times that devotion has diminished. I carry my beads with me everywhere, not just from habit but because I need them.

On one occasion I was called out to Loch Carnan where a man had died very suddenly. When I reached the house I could see there were already a number of callers and as I opened the door I could hear them praying. Quietly I entered the room to find a group of neighbours on their knees. Donald John, the deceased, had been laid out on the bed. On his chest was a dish of salt, five large nails and a crucifix. His now cold hands clasped his rosary beads. As soon as I entered the room they stopped praying, but I told the man leading the rosary to continue and knelt down beside those nearest the door. He did continue, with beautiful prayers for the dead that I had never heard, soft Gaelic words so full of meaning. The symbolism of the salt and the nails are old Celtic signs representing the elements and the five wounds on Christ's crucified body.

I was to come across these symbols on other similar occasions. In the island communities death is treated with natural acceptance. To this day they continue with the 'wake' as they do in rural Ireland. Everyone remains in the graveyard until the turf is replaced and during the filling of the grave mourners go and pray at their own relatives' graves before returning for the last beautiful prayer, which is said when the turf has been laid. In Iochdar each mourner is offered cheese as they leave the graveyard to help them on their journey, a throwback to the days when there were no fast means of transport. I found all this sensible simplicity very natural and comforting. These people and their faith made me feel close to God and I understood that even in these complex times there is a place in life for simple devotions.

On Rueval, a hill overlooking West Gerinish, there is a huge granite statue of Our Lady of the Isles. It was erected there in the 1950s as a result of the enthusiasm and drive of the late Canon John Morrison who was then parish priest of Ardkenneth. The statue shows the Virgin holding the Child high, facing west towards the Atlantic just a short distance away. I remember going with my grandfather to the opening ceremony. I have always found it a powerful symbol, and it is ironic that in later years the Ministry of Defence erected alongside it a tracking station with the usual satellite dishes and aerials, guarded by a very secure fence. Twice a year, on a Sunday in May and on the Sunday nearest to the feast of the Assumption in the middle of August, people gathered to pray the rosary on Rueval, no matter the weather. Some came from Benbecula and Eriskay to join the people of Uist, and old and young knelt on the hillside together, their heads bent at times against the wind and the rain, reciting the prayer which has been so important to many generations.

I called regularly with the Sacraments to an old man in Ardnamonie, a neighbour of the friendly MacCormick family. One morning his wife Peggy offered me a cup of coffee in the kitchen. It was cold and windy outside and I was glad to accept.

'Father,' she said as I sipped at the hot liquid, 'I have rosary beads that I want you to have.'

'But I have plenty of rosaries.'

'I know that, but these are special.'

'Why are they so special? Surely if they are you should keep them.'

'Someone close to you gave them to me – your good father, Andrew.'

Amazed, I took the beads, well worn because they were so often used. The figure was missing from the cross, but the old beads and strong chain were still intact. Peggy told me their story. Sometime in the early 1930s a group of young men and women in Glasgow met up to go to the Gaelic service which was held every month in St Margaret's, Kinning Park, followed by a ceilidh. My father was in town waiting to join a ship and he had accompanied Peggy to the church. Peggy had no rosary beads and my father gave her his own, saying, 'They were given me when I first left Eriskay and I've had them since.' Afterwards Peggy forgot to return them, my father went to sea and they never met again. She took good care of them and now they are one of my few prized possessions.

✦

Two or three times a year I would visit the priests in Eriskay and Barra. My journey to Barra was on the little ferry from Ludag on the south end of South Uist, to Eoligarry on the north coast of Barra. In good weather the journey would take about 40 minutes, but when the weather was rough it could take longer. It was always a special trip. Wildlife enthusiasts could happily spend days in this meeting place of the Minch and the Atlantic. There were seals curiously looking on from their rocky perches or popping up from the waves to have a close look at us passers-by. Sometimes we would have the privilege of being entertained by a school of porpoises, or seeing gannets diving fiercely into a trough of waves, already swallowing their catch as they surfaced to rest a while on the sea. Oystercatchers, known as 'St Bride's birds', would call to us from above, and always around were the sleek, oily cormorants disappearing on their long dives. Occasionally we caught a glimpse of a fin and the surging back of a basking shark. And all the time there was the beautiful view of Uist with its hills behind, of Eriskay with the Weaver's Castle to the east, and islets blocking our way to the sand and greenery of Eoligarry. Every time I made that journey it was different, beautiful even in bad weather. On one such journey Donald, the boatman, took us very close to some rocks to view the white seal pups not long arrived in their habitat, which he had noticed on one of his trips the previous day. The mother barked at us to go away. On every journey I learned something new. The shorter voyage to Eriskay was always like a homecoming. Every house was familiar and most faces still known to me.

✦

In the weeks leading up to the Falklands War we were aware of much military movement in Uist. During the night the roar of Hercules aircraft wakened us as they swooped down on practice runs. Firing on the Rocket Range increased. As we watched the news develop on our television screens our neighbours in the Royal Artillery were preparing for a star role.

One morning I was woken by the noise of disturbed baa-ing and running hooves. Looking out of the bedroom window I saw my sheep all gathered in one corner of the field, usually the sign that a stray dog was around. Quickly I threw some clothes on and rushed downstairs to investigate. In the little light of dawn I made my way round the back of the house to the wooden garage. Suddenly I had the fright of my life as a wetsuited figure loomed in front of me, rifle in hand. He was dripping water and in a hoarse whisper said in a southern accent, 'You haven't seen me! I'm on an exercise and there are guys out there trying to find me. If they come to the door you've seen and heard nothing!'

'But who are they ... who are you?'

'It's military. Don't worry, we're legit.'

I returned to my kitchen and rather shakily made myself a cup of coffee. Shortly afterwards, I saw the sheep were moving about normally in the field again. Whoever had caused the disturbance, they were gone. I guessed it was some kind of commando exercise or even the SAS. Never mind the enemy, they certainly frightened me! Not long after that we heard that men from the local army base were already in Ascension Island ready to transport south to the Falklands. Those islands, so far south in the Atlantic, were similar to our own in terrain – hence the night flights and daily activity of the previous weeks. We had been part of the dummy run.

During my six years in Ardkenneth I had a number of invitations to functions in the Officers' Mess at the Royal Artillery base in Benbecula. I never have been one to enjoy such occasions and accepted only twice, rapidly regretting both. The second time I was there I was placed at a table with a group of officers, some of whom were visitors to Benbecula. I was a listener rather than a contributor to the conversation, until I became very riled by the direction in which we were being taken by one of the military gentlemen. He was pontificating on how the islands could be put to much better economic use. His theory was that with fishing, game and the wildlife, they should become a kind of National Park for entertainment and sport. I could not believe my ears, and broke my silence.

'Excuse me, sir, but what on earth gives you the right to talk about people's lives like that?' I said when he paused for breath.

'Just that I don't think you realize what you have here. I mean, look what we've done in Kenya.'

'I confess I don't know what you've done in Kenya. It's far from here.'

'Well,' he said confidently, 'we've given their economy a great boost. Safaris, game-spotting – and film-making has brought them prosperity. The same could happen here.'

'Who have become prosperous? The tribespeople, or whoever "we" are?'

'Sacrifices are always necessary.'

'These sacrifices – eh, would they mean movement of the people here? Obviously, townships would have to be cleared and crofts taken over if the land was to be used for these games. Oh, and I presume sheep and cattle would also be sent to pastures new?' I was really quite angry by this time.

'Yes,' came the breezy answer. 'There's no economic future here once the army goes, and we won't be here for ever.'

'But what of the people here now? Their forebears struggled to keep this "poor land". It's less than a century since many were cleared from their homes at the whim of a landowner. Do you honestly think some kind of repeat would be a way forward? And we existed fairly well before the Rocket Range was set up here!'

He seemed taken aback by my vehemence.

'Well, mmm, I was just saying what a number of us think would be a way forward for these islands.'

'Thank you. I was asking because I'm astounded that anyone could think as you and your friends do.' There was an embarrassed silence after this until others began talking of something else. As soon as I could I made my excuses and left.

I was angry with myself for accepting the second invitation because on the first occasion I had not even reached the table. I had been invited to their Christmas Party and was accompanied there by the local doctor. Having hung up my coat, I made my way to the lounge. The Christmas decorations left me cold – everything was black, skulls and crossbones and black drapes. 'Whose idea of Christmas is this?' I asked the doctor.

'Oh, it was the RAF boys who decorated this year. Their idea of fun!'

'Well, to me it rings of black magic or something even worse. I don't like it! Sorry, please give them my apologies.' I returned to the cloakroom, collected my coat and left. There seemed to be a real clash of cultures, and this was too much to cope with in the context of the ancient peace and beauty of the islands, with their long tradition of faith.

✦

It will be clear to anyone that I was passionate about island life and loved my time in Uist. Spiritually it was a very important time in my life – I would call it a reawakening and a renewal. Living in Ardkenneth I became so aware of the power of nature, both dark and beautiful. On calm days the smallest bird could be heard calling, the song of the lark carried clearly and from somewhere hidden the unmistakable sound of the corncrake accompanied the setting sun. On other days there was the frightening, awesome power of the wind and sea, bringing home the fact of man's feebleness in the face of God's creation. In the calm or the storm it is easy to be aware of God in such surroundings.

In the first days of January one year we had a spate of gales which reached hurricane force. This is not unusual in the far north-west of the country, but at times such wind creates great danger and causes serious structural damage. On 3 January I was woken during the night by the violence of the storm. The rattling windows did not usually keep me awake but a loud bang and a cold rush of air into my bedroom had me on my feet and running downstairs – into the teeth of the gale.

The noise from the church made me look there first. So strong was the wind inside the church that I had great difficulty pushing the door open. The electricity was out, but I could see the window that had been blown in, with its frame still intact. It had landed with such force that it had split the bench below. The wind had played havoc with the crib, which was scattered all round the front of the church. In vain I tried to board up the gap left by the window, but the strength of the gale kept forcing me back. I knew it was far too dangerous to venture outside so I just bolted the doors and returned to bed.

At daybreak I went down and inspected the damage from the outside. Part of the roof had been stripped, with north-facing slates scattered and broken on the south side of the building. I called a local joiner who came and boarded up the window. Many houses on the island were damaged that night when winds of over 120 miles per hour were recorded. We had the added inconvenience of being without electricity for a number of days, a common occurrence in such weather. The hurricane lessened to a gale which lasted for days, and our roads were strewn with debris thrown up by the raging sea. Temporary repairs and repeated clearing up were the order of the day.

Eleven days later we were struck by another hurricane, on this occasion from the south-east. With no electricity and therefore no heating, I retired to bed with my book and a candle. At about 1.00 a.m. I had a call from Gerinish. A woman there appeared to have had a heart attack. Could I please come? I set out on perhaps the most frightening drive of my life. The car rocked with the ferocity of the gusts and, going south, I was heading into the teeth of the gale. As I approached the causeway which crosses Loch Bee I could see the tail-lights of another car ahead going slowly and carefully. Slivers of ice were blowing off the loch, making the road very dangerous and whipping against the car with an alarming noise. Turning into Gerinish, I noticed the car ahead stop at the same house for which I was heading: it was the doctor. By the time I had manoeuvred the car close to the wall of the house for shelter the doctor was already in the house. One of the family met me at the door with a torch and showed me into the kitchen, where I waited with them until the doctor had finished. Eventually he emerged and I asked how the patient was faring.

'She's had a fright.'

'A fright? What do you mean?'

'This storm has given her a bad fright. Not half as bad as the fright I suffered coming here!' I heartily agreed.

After administering the Sacraments to a now calm patient I returned to my car. As I turned back to the road I was appalled to see two mobile homes lift off the ground and then smash into each other, collapsing like a pack of cards. I sat where I was as debris flew everywhere. After a while I ventured out and joined others making their way as best they could towards the scene. It was almost impossible to stand in the wind, never mind walk. Thankfully, because of the weather, the occupants had evacuated earlier and no one was hurt.

Struggling back to my car was even more hazardous and I fell more than once. The doctor was waiting when I reached the causeway and we crossed slowly together to be sure of each other's safety. The following morning a quick inspection revealed more damage to the church and house, with the south side of the roof now also partially stripped. It seemed to my despairing eyes that there were as many slates on the ground as there were left on the roof.

Just a week later the scene had changed dramatically. In the dusk of a clear winter's afternoon a neighbour pointed out to me the strange behaviour of the swans on Loch Bee. Normally they were scattered all around this large loch but that day they were gathering together, more than a hundred of them, near an island. The weather was dead calm. Next morning I woke to discover South Uist covered by a hard frost. The loch seemed to be completely frozen, a surprise to me since it opens out to the sea (it is well known for its flounders!). Not many of the older population could remember ever seeing it like this. Near that little island on the loch the swan population was still clustered together – their body heat had prevented the water freezing in that area and they were at home in the water. The loch remained frozen for six days and there they remained. Isn't nature wonderful? Throughout those days the view from wherever I was in the house was stunningly beautiful. Skye and Kintail, Barra, North Uist and even St Kilda were all visible in the freezing atmosphere.

◆

One afternoon in 1986 the phone rang. It was the bishop. He passed the time of day with a few generalities but, with a sinking heart, I knew that was not his reason for calling. He asked if I was alone.

'Yes, my lord.'

'I know you're happy there, so I'm sorry to ask if you'll be willing to move?'

'If I must. But I'll be very sad to leave here, where I've spent the happiest time of my life.'

'I understand that, but I do need you elsewhere. It's important that you go to St Anne's, Corpach.' My heart sank even further.

'Oh no! It's the last place in the diocese that I'd choose at this time.'

'Och, you'll be fine. I'll come back to you. Say nothing about this meantime.'

Shocked and deeply saddened, I put the phone down. It was not just that I was leaving the island and the way of life that I loved. I was being asked to go to an unhappy parish suffering from recent and serious divisions. There had been some kind of conflict between the old parish priest and his assistant which had resulted in the young priest moving elsewhere. Then a group of parishioners had drawn up a petition and presented it to the bishop, asking that the parish priest be moved – something that is very difficult to effect under Canon Law unless the priest co-operates. The numbers attending Mass had dropped as many made their way to St Mary's in Fort William rather than attending their own church in Corpach. It was a situation that no priest would wish to inherit. There was silence for a few weeks after the bishop's initial phone call and I pushed the matter to the back of my mind. Perhaps it would not happen. I did ensure that my book work was brought up to date, just in case.

About a month later the bishop arrived unannounced and made me a proposition. Would I be willing to move to Corpach, live in a separate house, but allow the older man, who was in ill-health, to continue as Parish Priest Emeritus (a title given to important priests who retire, but not quite)? For the first time in my life I said 'no' to a bishop. It would never work and would only make things in the parish much worse. He would have to retire before I would move. After the bishop left I drove to Daliburgh to ask John MacLean for his advice. He agreed with the stance I had taken.

Two weeks later I was due to be in Fort William for the marriage of a cousin. It was arranged that I should meet with Canon John Morrison (the same man who had erected the statue at Rueval, and now the parish priest in question at Corpach) and Bishop Colin in St Mary's. During the meeting I again refused to accept the position until Canon Morrison had retired. It was finally agreed that he would retire on St Andrew's Day, 30 November 1986 and I would assume my responsibilities on 1 December. With a very heavy heart I returned to Uist to prepare for departure.

That parting was far from sweet. I felt so very sad. Packing up was done with a struggle and the good-byes were painful. I spent my last evening in Uist in the company of John MacLean, who sympathized and vainly tried to encourage me. I cannot remember much of my journey to Fort William, sunk as I was in profound gloom. I was given a warm welcome by John MacNeil, the parish priest of St Mary's, and he would play a very important part in my life from then onwards. But as I sat at his table that day I was not cheered by his friendliness, and I envied the man who would now be in the kitchen at Ardkenneth.

7

✦

CORPACH AND THE
LION'S DEN

ON I DECEMBER I MOVED MY FEW BELONGINGS into a council
house in Corpach for which the parish had been paying rent since
the departure of the assistant priest. It was damp from lack of use
but I tried to make it homely for the short time I knew I would be
there. December is not a good month to move house and Canon
Morrison still occupied the church house for the time being.

A week after my arrival there was an ordination in St Mary's,
Fort William. Sandy Culley, a popular local man, had completed his
studies for the priesthood. Bishop Colin MacPherson chose to
ordain him in his home parish and most of the priests of the Diocese
gathered to support him. John MacLean came over from Uist for the
occasion: Sandy was going to join him as assistant in Daliburgh. It
was a joyous occasion and I spent a good deal of the time afterwards
in John's company. He was travelling back to Uist with another
priest the following day.

The weather was bad and they were stranded overnight in Uig
because the ferry was unable to sail. By the time they arrived in
Lochmaddy John was in pain. He claimed it was indigestion and
was treating himself with some tablets. After the long journey he
immediately set out to administer the Sacraments to housebound
parishioners, who had been expecting him that morning. Having
completed his round he called into the hospital, by now in very

severe pain. He had suffered a severe heart attack. Nobody could understand how he had managed to go on working. The doctor had him put to bed immediately, but he died during the night. His parishioners and all his many friends were devastated. His death certainly left an aching gap in my life. A close friend for some years by then, I had valued his advice, respected his insights, and admired his deep faith.

Just over a week after leaving Uist I returned in the company of John MacNeil and Monsignor Ewan MacInnes, a sad journey. Immediately after John's funeral, which seemed to be attended by everyone in Uist and Barra, we left again to catch the last ferry from Lochmaddy. Passing Iochdar, I had a lump in my throat at seeing the dearly familiar territory. It just added to the distress over John's sudden death. It was too painful and I simply wanted to leave. But once more the weather intervened. The conditions meant that there could be no sailing until 6.30 the following morning at the earliest. It was suggested we return to Daliburgh, but I could not bring myself to do this and persuaded the others to spend the night in the local hotel. It was a relief when the ferry did sail the following morning.

✦

Shortly before Christmas I moved properly into St Anne's (Canon Morrison and his sister had moved to a pleasant house on the hill above me). Both house and church were very basic. The bungalow was linked by a short passageway to the church, which had a beautiful altar and statues, peeling walls in bad need of repair and a rather porous copper roof. It had been erected as a utility building in the early 1950s to serve the communities of Corpach and Caol and the nearby area of Annat which, at that time, was due to be extended to house the workforce of a large pulp mill about to be constructed. In the event it was Caol which was expanded to house those coming to work in this new industry. The intended development of Annat never materialized and this meant that St Anne's was now on the edge of the parish rather than at the centre. The bulk of the population lived around the other church, St John's, situated in Caol.

In light of the previous divisions I made certain I took no sides, trying to settle in and work as normal. Healing is never easy, but it was time for the parish to move on. If one or other 'side' tried to put their view I would answer, 'I don't want to know. It's of no value to what we're now about, nothing at all.' It took time and patience, and sometimes I seemed to be making no progress at all in terms of drawing the parish together again. Sometimes it was painful, both for me and the parishioners who had been so upset. I knew what had to be done, however, and stuck to the approach I knew to be right: if I just carried on, things would get better in time. Neighbouring priests were strongly supportive, and I was encouraged by that.

Gradually the parish did come together and bonded as a community once more. As this happened and good results finally came out of the struggle, my continuing ache for Ardkenneth and Uist diminished and I started to feel genuinely enthusiastic about my work in Corpach. Once we knew each other, people became friendly and co-operative. To this day I am indebted to them for their friendship and support. Looking back, I believe this determination to keep going in the face of a mountain of difficulty – drawn on by the faith that a better time was waiting round the corner – helped me later to cope with even darker days.

Most days in Corpach were spent visiting parishioners and attending to the schools. Shortly after my arrival I made arrangements with the headmaster of Lochaber High School to resume teaching Religious Education to the Catholic pupils as part of the curriculum. The earlier agreement which existed when I was at St Mary's had lapsed, but I insisted that Catholic pupils had a right to be taught by a Catholic priest and agreed to fit in with the school's timetable. This entailed my presence in the school for periods of 55 minutes 9 times a week. Most of my days had to be arranged around these class times, a difficult exercise when I also had to officiate at funerals. It also meant that I could not take a break during the school year, but it was certainly worthwhile.

John MacNeil in St Mary's became my friend and companion. He was generous and affable and almost every day he provided lunch for us both in his kitchen in St Mary's – sometimes rushed because I had to return to Lochaber High School for the first afternoon class. His companionship and encouragement were very important to me during those early days when everything was new and hectic, and especially when difficulties arose. There was much to plan, and one particularly acute problem was the practical matter of church upkeep, something which proved to be an ongoing headache, despite our best efforts.

All round the Diocese one enduringly popular and successful way of raising money was to hold a 'sale of work'. During my time in the islands I was astounded by people's generosity. In every parish they made huge efforts when funds were needed, raising impressive sums of money for such small populations. In Ardkenneth they raised over £6,000 on three such occasions during my time, essential funding for the upkeep of church buildings in small parishes. Efforts were rewarded when the beautiful old church in Ardkenneth was painted and renewed. Now in Corpach I was faced with the need to repair two churches, and paralysed by the shocking discovery that the parish was in debt to the tune of £140,000. Both churches were in a desperate state of repair, however, and I decided that despite the debt something must be done urgently about the impressive building of St John's in Caol.

The hitherto 'divided' parish came together in a way that surprised me, with no shortage of volunteers, and the result of their efforts was that more than £6,000 was raised. St John's, with its vast roof, could finally be re-painted. The work took two weeks, and on the middle Sunday Mass had to be celebrated in the school. All of us were delighted by the outcome. Two years later we repeated the exercise and raised a similar sum of money, which we used to re-roof St John's, by this time regarded as the principal church of the parish.

But what of St Anne's? Any priest who closes a church knows the unpopularity of such a move. After two years in the parish I decided that the debt was such that we could not afford two churches. After receiving some estimates of the costs of repair and renewal it was obvious that soon a decision would have to be made on the church's future. With the estimates at hand I wrote a report which I forwarded to Bishop MacPherson. His first reaction was to refuse my suggestion of closure, despite the debt of £140,000 which was like a millstone round our necks. The report was filed. We continued to use both churches, one now in excellent condition, the other in a depressing state of delapidation. Those caring for St Anne's toiled so hard to make the place presentable: they could only be admired for their patience and devotion.

◆

During my second or third year in Corpach, John MacNeil asked me to take his place on a pilgrimage to Lourdes. I love the shrine, but did not relish the journey (shades of that Rome trip!) by bus from Ben Nevis to the Pyrenees, staying near Calais on the first night, halfway down the country on the second night, then spending four nights in Lourdes before returning via Lisieux to Cherbourg for the ferry. I agreed to John's request nonetheless, and on a Saturday morning we set off from outside St Mary's.

My fellow pilgrims were mostly from St Mary's and surrounding parishes, some from my own of Corpach and Caol. They were of all ages and one, George, was dying, but all were determined to make the most of this journey. It turned out to be one of my most spiritual experiences, not only because Lourdes is such a place, but also because of the faith, humour and patience of my fellow pilgrims. Each Mass we celebrated, be it in the Rue du Bac or in Lourdes, was special. Despite obvious weariness it was very touching to see how gently and carefully some of the men in the group tended to George. Though so very ill, he remained cheerful throughout. I felt humble and unworthy in comparison.

When we reached Cherbourg on the return journey, we discovered our sailing was delayed because of appalling weather conditions. I went with Calum, an ex-sailor, to inquire about the length of the delay and we were informed that there were signs of abatement; the wait should not be too long. (We were also told that a German freighter had gone down in the Channel, but decided to keep this news to ourselves!) It was a dreadful crossing and quite a number were sick and miserable. The morning stop on the motorway was a very welcome break. It was late that night when we disembarked outside St Mary's, very tired but feeling happy and fulfilled. It had been a wonderful trip. Most of us would later be reunited at George's funeral. It had been a privilege to make that last journey with him.

◆

Very early one morning in March 1990 I was woken by the phone ringing. It was John MacNeil.

'Roddy,' he said, 'the bishop died a short time ago.'

'Oh, God rest him. I didn't realize he was so ill.'

'He must have been.'

Colin MacPherson died on the 50th anniversary of his ordination as a priest. We had known he was in hospital in Oban suffering from pneumonia, but the previous day had heard that he was making a recovery. The news of his death came as a shock. Little did I realize that day how severely it would affect my life. A few days later we gathered in St Columba's Cathedral in Oban for the concelebrated Requiem Mass. The other Scottish bishops were present for the occasion, along with the diocesan priests and many others from all over the country. Indeed, so many were there that I found myself standing with my back pressed against the cold granite wall behind the main altar, only able to see the backs of people's heads. Afterwards, in a cold and biting wind, I stood near the open grave and paid my last respects to a man who had been kind to me at all times.

The Chapter of Canons gathered immediately afterwards to elect an Administrator to run the Diocese until the ordination of the next bishop. Later that evening John MacNeil phoned to say he had been chosen as Administrator. His life would not be the same again.

For the rest of us life continued as normal, daily duties once again requiring our attention. John took on his role as Administrator with gusto. His assistant in the parish was a young priest, Donald Campbell, ordained just the previous year, and he assumed many of the parish duties while John was occupied elsewhere. Naturally there was much speculation as to who would be the next bishop. A short while later I received a form from Archbishop Barbarito, the Apostolic Delegate (the Pope's representative in Britain), naming a priest and asking for my opinion of his suitability to be bishop. Knowing the man well I gave a full and positive report, hoping he would be selected. To this day I am truly sorry he was not chosen. Time passed, and we became used to having no bishop. The initial curiosity about the next candidate diminished.

Meantime, John MacNeil agreed in his role as Administrator that I should again consider the closure and sale of St Anne's church and house. I prepared a new report, emphasizing the financial situation and the fact that, of those attending services in St Anne's, the majority were travelling from Caol simply because the time of Mass was more suitable for them. That Sunday, at the end of each Mass, I argued the case for closure and sale. The majority accepted the situation although, naturally, a minority remained opposed. These soon made themselves known, trying to organize a petition which came to nothing in the end. They did meet with myself and John MacNeil and argued their case vociferously, some of them claiming that I had spent too much on St John's – a church which a few of them then vowed never to attend. I could understand such views:

people have strong nostalgic feelings about the church where they were baptized, received their First Holy Communion, were married, and from whence they had buried their loved ones.

We remained firm and put the premises on the market. A great deal of interest was shown considering the condition of the buildings, but it was on an excellent site on the tourist route and this made it attractive. Eventually we had a firm buyer with an offer of £140,000. They wanted to turn the building into a museum of rocks and stones, which pleased the local hotelier who had feared it being converted into a rival hotel. The offer was good and would pay off the parish debt. We started to look forward to having that weight removed and the relief of only having to pay for the upkeep of one church.

Then another obstacle appeared to dash our hopes. The Administrator had to consult with the senior clergy on such an issue because the Diocese had no bishop. The most senior priest refused his consent, arguing quite properly that such a matter should only be decided by the new bishop. The potential buyers were not pleased by the prospect of delay and said they would look elsewhere for property. Once again I accepted the situation, having no other choice, and continued to use both places.

Sometime in early November John MacNeil mentioned enthusiastically that it looked as if I might be the next bishop. The idea appalled me and I said so in no uncertain terms. 'Anyway, how can you know, John?' I asked.

'Well,' he said, 'I do speak with Archbishop Barbarito.'

'Aye. Well if he knows he'll make the approach.'

'Well, Roddy, if you are asked would you accept?'

'No, John, it's not for me.'

'But if the priest and people want you, surely you would accept?'

'I don't think I could. Anyway, it won't happen because there are far better candidates.'

'Roddy, would you accept?'

'No.'

The matter rested there. John was prone to wind me up at times and I presumed – I hoped – that was what was happening.

Shortly afterwards John came back more strongly on the subject and I became seriously concerned. I avoided the subject when talking with the other priests, but obviously John was in contact with a number of them on a regular basis.

'Roddy,' he pressed me harder this time, 'if you're asked to follow Colin it *is* your duty to accept. We would want that.'

'John. What about you?'

'I'm too old. We need some freshness.'

'Look, John, I'm serious. There are others far more suitable. I think you might get a surprise.' How could I get my strong feelings across to him without offending, without saying what I knew must not be said?

'No, Roddy. You will be asked.'

'Och, John, I would *not* be a good choice. I mean that. And I don't want to leave parish life. It's all I know and what I'm best at.' He pushed the point no further that day, but I had a frightening feeling that I had not heard the last of this.

◆

I was moving house at the time because the one by St Anne's in Corpach was in such a disastrous state of disrepair. With no money available, I was unable to do much about the situation. I found a one-bedroomed flat just beside St John's which I was able to rent. It was comfortable, neat and furnished, and the move was simple. I felt no sadness leaving the little house in Corpach: it had been a roof over my head but never a home like the house in Ardkenneth. I would be backwards and forwards anyway, because the church there was still in use. Only three nights after I left the house was broken into, the intruder smashing a window at the back. He found nothing of interest to take.

After moving all my belongings I was in the new flat – to be honest I was sleeping in my chair, waiting to open the church for evening Mass – when John came in, his heavy steps rousing me. He looked so serious and, only half awake, I asked him if there was anything wrong.

'No. No. I'm just tired.'

'Sit down. I'll make a coffee. I've got Mass in an hour.'

'Aye, Roddy, that would be good.' He sank into a chair.

I made the coffee and turned off the television, which I had not been watching anyway. Sitting down again, I offered him a cigarette and lit one for myself.

'Roddy,' he began, 'I'm here on official business.'

'Oh, is the sale of St Anne's progressing?' I asked hopefully, this being uppermost in my mind at the time.

'No, it's not that,' he replied soberly. 'The Apostolic Delegate has sent me and wants an answer tonight. Will you be bishop?'

My heart sank. 'No, John. Not that again.'

'This is genuine. I have to tell you the priests and the people have had a strong say in this. I hope you can agree.'

'John,' I said in growing alarm, 'I'd rather not – honestly!'

'We'll all help you, Roddy. It's a new start for all of us.'

'No, I'm so reluctant.'

John, oddly enough, did not press me to explain why. He knew nothing of my real difficulties with the proposal – no one did. If he had asked me straight out for the truth, I am not sure what I would have said. As it was, I kept that truth to myself and let John go on thinking I was simply doubtful about my ability to fill the position. How wrong that was. At the time I could think of no good way out. John trusted me to be the person I appeared to be and so, obviously, did countless other people who had been consulted about my potential as bishop. If I was not brave enough to reveal the real reason, there was no objection I could raise which John would not be able to argue aside.

'We all have to do what we find difficult,' John told me gently.

'Yeah ... would *you* accept?'

'If I had to, yes. You'll disappoint many if you refuse. Now, will you accept?'

I knew for certain that I should not. I needed space to think, but John had come for an immediate answer. He had pushed his argument so eagerly and had no reason to suspect that there was any real impediment to me accepting the position. He never did know the truth. He repeated his confident assurance that I would be given all the support I needed, and continued to look at me earnestly.

Suddenly I found myself saying, 'Yes, John, I will, and may God help me!'

John rose, shook my hand and went to the phone. Through the fog in my head I could hear him talking with Archbishop Barbarito. Returning, he told me the appointment was strictly secret and the announcement would be made publicly in three weeks' time. He then left me to my thoughts, asking me to visit him that evening after Mass.

My mind in chaos, I went straight across to the church and prayed. I knew I had made a dreadful mistake. I had no right whatsoever to accept the position of bishop, yet I had done so. What if my secret came out? I have a vivid recollection even now of the turmoil which seemed to assail my whole being. I prayed for forgiveness; I prayed desperately for help.

Somehow I got through the evening Mass, then went across to St Mary's. Still I said nothing. John and I spoke at length about the Diocese – practical matters only. There were many things that had to be done, even before the announcement was made, and we were soon swept up in a hectic schedule of planning and preparation.

◆

I continued to work as normal, coping with my distraction as best I could. The school work and the visitation of the sick had to take priority as long as I was parish priest. But strangely, the heart had gone out of me in many ways. My appointment did solve one problem, a small point of light in the midst of the darkness in which I seemed to be living. As bishop I would certainly give my consent to the sale of St Anne's! John, still Administrator, suggested that we open negotiations again with those who had shown such keenness to buy. I left the business to him. Very soon the matter was in the hands of the lawyers and the sale was underway. Being tied to my appointment, however, nothing could be said publicly until that was announced.

As the three weeks progressed, I grew more nervous by the day. I could not eat, could not concentrate. I slept tensely, if at all, and woke exhausted. Twice I lifted the telephone to call the Apostolic Delegate and have my appointment cancelled. On both occasions my nerve failed me and I never completed the dialling, a fact that I have rued ever since. At the time I rationalized my cowardice, telling myself that perhaps after all it was easier to go on rather than call a halt, be forced to explain myself and face – whatever I would face.

In private conversations John and I talked about a date for the ordination and we decided on 15 January 1991, a little over a month after the announcement was to be made. The actual time of the announcement was determined by the official publication of the fact in Rome, 12 noon in Italy being 11.00 a.m. in Scotland.

On the evening before the announcement I received a call from Father Tom Connolly, the Catholic Media Officer for Scotland. He congratulated me and said that the press were now informed, although they had accepted an embargo which meant they could not release the news until 11.00 a.m. the following day. They would be present in St Mary's at the time of the announcement, however, and he encouraged me to co-operate with them in every way. After his call I heard from a surprised Archbishop Winning in Glasgow. He had only heard the news a little earlier, a fact that surprised me as I thought the senior churchman in Scotland would have been informed by then.

The following morning, 11 December 1990, I arrived in St Mary's at about 10.45 and John told me to go upstairs and relax until the press arrived. I decided to phone my family, but Chrissie was not at home. I did manage to reach Effie, who disbelievingly and tearfully received the news. Nervously I lit a cigarette as I heard people arrive downstairs, voices I did not recognize. There was really no way out now.

At 11 o'clock I met the press in a group for the first time in my life. About five or six journalists were gathered in the front room. One of them was a woman I recognized as the local reporter on the *Oban Times*. There was a hush in the conversation as I entered. Taking a deep breath, I smiled and said, 'Good morning. What can I do for you?'

'Eh, we were told to meet some bishop here,' said the woman from the *Oban Times*.

'Aye. That's me.'

'You, Father Wright! Really?' She seemed very surprised.

'Yes,' was my short reply. I gave them some quotes for their editors and a very general CV. The photographers did their duty and they all departed.

I was having a very welcome cup of coffee with John and Donald in the kitchen afterwards when there was another caller at the front door. A photographer from *The Herald* had arrived late. Mindful of my instructions from Tom Connolly, I was co-operative with what he wanted. This entailed posing somewhere in Glen Nevis and on the edge of the local pier with some creels at my feet, all in pouring rain accompanied by a biting wind. I felt miserable and awkward in front of the camera. By the time we returned to St Mary's I was quite exhausted.

That night, as I walked out to lead the rosary before Mass, the little congregation began to clap. I frowned and signed sharply for silence, saying only, 'We will pray the rosary.' This was ungracious and unkind, and I knew it. Amongst other things, we prayed for the new bishop and the Diocese. Afterwards I went over to the house at St Anne's, because most people did not have the phone number of my flat in Caol. The phone was ringing as I entered and continued to do so until about 11.00 p.m. – priests, family and friends all ringing to congratulate me and offer their best wishes. Throughout it all, as I struggled to make conversation and sound normal, my mind was in turmoil and my cigarette packet emptying. People I had not heard from for years called, obviously delighted. They had heard about the appointment on the television or radio. As well as my friends, I realized that all sorts of strangers round the country would also now have heard my name and seen my picture. The thought unsettled me profoundly. That night I slept very fitfully, uneasily aware that the morning papers would also carry my name and photograph – shades of things to come, of course.

After morning Mass, John and I set off for Glasgow where I was to be fitted out with the garments required for office. On the way home we called to leave my hat size with the nuns at Carmel Monastery, Dumbarton, who were going to make my mitre. John told me on the journey that Archbishop Barbarito wished to be the ordaining prelate and I agreed. Now I know I should have consulted Archbishop O'Brien on the matter since he was my Metropolitan, but frankly I was so bewildered at that point that I was not too bothered who would be ordaining me.

On my return there was a message from BBC2. They wished to make a programme about me. This was the last thing I wanted: as a private person just doing my work, publicity was something I had shied clear of most of my life and I did not want it now. It was impossible to avoid, however. A full day was given to the BBC2 programme, and I was interviewed in the wild beauty of Glen Nevis and then in a classroom with a group of children from Primary 7. I actually enjoyed that part. One little girl made a statement which still amuses me. 'My mum thinks you'll look ridiculous in a pokey hat!' she told me. How true – 'out of the mouths of babes ...' as the saying goes. The programme went out on the Wednesday before Christmas. I was saying Mass in St John's at the time. The producer sent me a video, but I have never watched it.

I made arrangements to leave the parish immediately after New Year and go to Dublin for five days of retreat. I chose Father Tom Dougan, a Vincentian Father I had got to know on his annual visits to Barra and Fort William. He was a holy man, learned and humble, and I liked him very much. The retreat would be a chance to stop and breathe, to take stock. Would it calm my soul?

Meanwhile Christmas, as ever, was busy and I gave all of myself to the parish preparations. Perhaps I could find respite from my thoughts in frantic activity. There was sadness amongst some parishioners when I announced that the official closure of St Anne's would be on the last Sunday of the year, 28 December, the Feast of the Holy Innocents. After that the two Masses, at 9.00 a.m. and 5.00 p.m., would be transferred to St John's in Caol. I was sad too because a church was being closed. At least most parishioners were in favour of the change now, and only a few persisted with their vehement criticism.

I said my farewells to the parish that same Sunday, having arranged to travel to Dublin on 2 January. Immediately Christmas was over I completed my packing. A retired priest was to take my place in Caol temporarily until a new parish priest could be appointed. On my return from Ireland I would go straight to Oban for the final preparations before my ordination as Bishop of Argyll and the Isles.

✦

Why was I so very reluctant to be bishop? I love my Faith, I love the Church. Throughout my years as priest I gave myself fully to my work. The daily celebration of Mass was the important factor in any day, and I always made sure I was available for the sick and housebound, giving as much attention as they needed to those who were terminally ill. School work was something I actively enjoyed, as was the rest of the work with young people. For the most part I always found my life as a priest very fulfilling, and it had been satisfying to see each different parish flourishing in its own way. In this respect I was just like any other dedicated priest. Few who love their parish work truly harbour ambitions to 'rise in the ranks', away from daily contact with the ordinary people who make up the Church.

I *was* different, though. Attentive and devoted priest as I was, I carried a dark secret. I had a son. He was born in the south of England in 1981 and my behaviour regarding this fact remains a matter of shame. I had known his mother for a short while when I was at St Mary's, Fort William, but was not aware of any inkling of attraction at that time. She had moved south, unknown to me, before my appointment to the parish in South Uist. Months after I was settled in Ardkenneth I received a letter from her, telling me how she was and inviting me, if ever I was down south, to give her a call. Some time after that I had occasion to travel south and we did meet. This led to a brief relationship and the birth of our son.

My shame is that I did not face up to my responsibilities at that time. I did not acknowledge my son, nor did I seek appropriate advice and direction by confiding in someone straight away. I did not even contemplate doing this. A long silence developed between me and his mother and I foolishly numbed myself to the fact of my obligations. Later on I started to help support my son financially, and saw him twice. But I never confessed my secret to anyone and buried myself in my work – a crazy escape route, and one I should never have taken without clarifying my moral dilemma. My apologies to my son and his mother for this are heartfelt – although some will see them as lame, and apologies cannot eradicate the hurt I have caused.

That I accepted my appointment as bishop says something about my muddled state of mind. How could I have been so foolish, so stupid? The fact is that I could have continued as a priest despite the situation: the relationship between myself and my son's mother was not ongoing and would never have led to marriage. But I should not have kept the truth secret. I should have owned up to the existence of my son immediately and gone on from there. At the very least I should have explained the truth to John when he was offering me the bishopric. Now, having accepted the post, I was embroiled in a far more serious situation. The harm that would be caused if the secret was exposed now would be far greater than it would have been when I was a parish priest. No matter people's wishes, no matter John's persuasiveness, I knew in my heart that I should not be bishop, that it was entirely wrong of me to accept. For this I am guilty of doing great damage to a people and Church that I love. From the moment of my acceptance a darkness loomed over me and from that day, as I judge it now, my meaningful ministry was deeply affected.

The guilt I already carried became weightier by the day. I was facing the task and responsibility of being a leader in the Church: how could I do that with honesty, knowing my ministry was flawed? During that January retreat in Ireland with Father Tom Dougan, this trouble was foremost in my mind. I prayed and prayed, but no prayer would lighten my load. Yet still I could not bring myself to confess.

Father Tom was a great listener with a wonderful sense of humour. We spent time together each afternoon and in the evenings.

My mornings were spent in prayer and reading. Much of the time I was surprised to find my thoughts positive, although the shadow of guilt and fear was never far away. There was a public park nearby and I walked there every morning, praying the rosary. On one morning my thoughts drifted back to the conversation on the previous evening when Tom had spoken with obvious fondness of the Celtic monks who had left his shores for mine so long ago. He spoke as if it had all happened yesterday, enthusing at their strength and courage in the face of nature's elements – the power of wind and sea, the isolation of those small islands, the hostile reception from the inhabitants. Despite all these difficulties, Christianity grew and grew, its presence still strong in those places today.

'Roddy,' said Tom, 'this is *your* Diocese I'm speaking about. You have that background to work on. What are you afraid of?' I answered lamely that I had nothing to fear except myself. The good Father Tom did not know how true that was. I left the retreat uncomforted, no further forward with my dilemma.

◆

On my return from Ireland I drove to Oban and moved into the Bishop's House adjoining the Cathedral House and the cathedral itself, a large and imposing building, a landmark on the Oban seafront. It must be the finest of the Catholic cathedrals in Scotland. The house felt cold and dark to me – and so very large. I felt desperately isolated.

I had little over a week to prepare myself for ordination and there was a great deal to get through. Little time was left over for brooding, which came as something of a relief. I had received more than 1,000 cards and letters from all over Scotland, but I knew that I could not possibly reply to them all. There was no such person as a secretary – or any staff, for that matter. Father Ted Murphy, the parish priest in Lochgilphead, was the Diocesan Master of Ceremonies and called to see me the day after I arrived, to assist me with my preparations for the actual ceremony. He was very thorough and over the next week gave me excellent lessons on what I had to do and say. Each of his visits, however, also served to increase my apprehension. There was a beautiful little chapel in the house and here I spent a number of hours alone during those final days. It was peaceful and I could pray – but it was also a constant reminder of my situation. In a state of screaming tension, entirely lacking in inner peace, I prayed continuously for forgiveness and help.

John MacNeil was, as always, unfailingly helpful, reminding me of matters still to be resolved. We drove again to Glasgow and I was kitted out with the now completed robes. They never did seem to fit. On the return journey we again called into Carmel, where I collected the mitre to be placed on my head during the ordination.

My family all came to Oban for the occasion. They had to book into local guesthouses because I could not accommodate them, despite the many rooms in the house. John had arranged for the Apostolic Delegate and a number of bishops to stay there overnight before the ordination. On 14 January I was in the cathedral with Ted Murphy when a choir arrived to rehearse. They had come from Uist and Eriskay to sing some of the liturgy in Gaelic. It was a real surprise and a delight to see them. I was given to understand that a large number of people were making the journey from the islands, despite the time of year.

That evening John and my sisters produced a lovely meal for the assembled bishops. I joined them at table with hardly any appetite, but all of them treated me with kindness. Did they think it was normal for bishops to be this nervous on the day before their ordination? After dinner the Apostolic Delegate invited me to join him in his sitting room at the top of the building. He spoke with me for almost an hour, telling me how the Diocese should be administered. His words spilled out, full of advice and vehement instructions. I always had difficulty in understanding him because of his strong Italian accent, but I actually heard very little that night, my mind being elsewhere. When my sisters had left and the bishops retired for the night, John and I had a last blether and a dram before going to our beds. I slept very fitfully and was up making coffee for myself by 6 o'clock the next morning.

15 January 1991 turned out to be a beautiful, clear and sunny winter's day. The previous days had been dark, cold and wet, suiting my mood. I excused myself from joining the others at breakfast, preferring to stay in my room. Somehow I had to compose myself for this very public day. From my study window I had a marvellous view of Oban Bay, with the island of Kerrera opposite, and a glimpse of the mountains of Mull beyond. It is a beautiful sight at any time and restored my sense of balance in a small way. From my vantage point I could also view those arriving for the ceremony. Well over an hour before it was to begin there were already clusters

of people along the promenade. I recognized people from Uist and Eriskay, others from Glasgow, relatives from Donegal, and a group of my nephews walking along to take their place in the cathedral. Seeing them only left me feeling even more nervous, however, and I drew away from the window. Instead, I descended the stairs to the chapel for a last period of silence and prayer. 'Walk with me, oh my Lord.'

All too soon it was time, and Ted Murphy had everyone in place in the cathedral. The principal procession set off and Ted led me in with my two escorts: Sean Fitzgerald, a friend since my first years in the priesthood, and Calum MacLellan, the only priest alive to have been born in Eriskay. They felt privileged that I had asked them to be with me and did their best to put me at my ease. We were at the head of the procession, followed by the mitred bishops, a piper welcoming us at the steps of the cathedral. The piper, my cousin's son Angus, had travelled from Uist especially to play for us. Entering those doors, I was suffocatingly aware of the large crowd. Every seat in the great building was taken.

It was a slow march up the aisle to the sanctuary, full of the priests and clergymen from different denominations who had accepted invitations to attend. I just felt incredibly tense and weak. Afterwards I was told that this had been very obvious to the onlookers. As the Mass began, however, I was lifted up by the enthusiasm of the congregation, the place so alive with their singing and responses. During the ceremony I had to lie on the floor while the clergy sang the Litany of the Saints. Lying there, I just prayed and prayed, not hearing the names of the Saints, but asking our Lady, the Virgin Mother, to pray for me. When at last I stood and stepped forward for the laying on of hands I felt quite dizzy. For a moment, an intense panic seized me, but suddenly I seemed to gain strength. The rest of the ceremony was completed with dignity and I was able to pay attention to the lovely liturgy.

As I emerged at the end into the bright sunshine I was met by television cameras and had to give interviews in Gaelic and English, then pose for the photographers — alone, with my family, with the diocesan clergy — and all the time the piper played on in the winter sunshine. The haunting music seemed most appropriate in that magnificent setting.

There was a buffet reception in the nearby Corran Halls and by the time I arrived the bishops had already been fed and departed. I managed a little something to eat myself by joining the end of the queue! I still had very little appetite, however, much preferring to spend the time with my family. That night a ceilidh was organized in one of the local hotels. The islanders, whose boat sailed at midnight, attended and I joined them for a short time with Father Angus MacQueen. He and Calum MacLellan were staying the night with me and at midnight we stood in my study to watch the ferry pass on the beginning of its seven-hour journey. I felt very humble, and so grateful that the islanders had made the long journey to be present for me. I was beginning another kind of journey.

In the days that followed I read no newspapers. I did not wish to see any photographs or read anything about myself. A video recording was made of the ceremony. I have never watched it and it embarrasses me that such even exists. Just a few days afterwards Tom Connolly phoned to say that a television company was interested in making a documentary about my apostolate in the Diocese. Using helicopters to transport us, they could film me in parishes as far flung as Stornoway in the north, other island parishes, and then as far south as Campbeltown. I know he was disappointed when I refused to co-operate. He thought the programme would help others understand how the Church worked in such scattered areas. I wanted nothing to do with it, however, and in any case I was already preoccupied with all that had to be done in reality, never mind on the small screen.

8

✦

THE RELUCTANT BISHOP

I DO NOT KNOW OF ANYONE WHO WOULD CLAIM that administration is a forte of mine. Yet now I found myself in charge of all the affairs of the Diocese. In financial matters the Diocesan Central Fund was both basis and provider. All monies gathered in the Sunday collections and through fund-raising were lodged in the Central Fund, which was a Trust governed by official regulations. From this source all the priests received the same amount each month for the normal running of house and church, including car and telephone. In such a large and scattered area with little population it is a fair method of seeing to the needs of priests and property. About four or five of the larger parishes were the main contributors to this fund because of their size and people's generosity. Some of the smaller parishes had little over 100 people, who would not normally be capable of supporting a priest and church. Before my ordination John MacNeil had already revealed to me his discovery that the Central Fund was badly in debt. Something had to be done immediately. My first letter to the clergy informed them of the situation and asked them to forgo any extra expenditure for the next year. They responded with excellent co-operation which made our task of recovery much simpler.

Money had been well spent, however, on two special churches in urgent need of assistance. My first trip as bishop was to the island of Barra to rededicate the refurbished church in Craigston. This is the oldest church still in use in the Diocese, built in 1810. The event was organized by Calum MacLellan, the parish priest, and was a wonderful occasion, celebrated without pomp and with much devotion. Barra is predominantly Catholic and everyone seemed to have turned out with enthusiasm for the rededication.

Also at this time the first Catholic church to be built in Lewis since the Reformation was near completion. During his time as Administrator, John had been very much the driving force behind this project. The architect had to give the building a last inspection before we decided on an opening date and John and I accompanied him on an early-morning flight from Glasgow to Stornoway. Here we saw a delightful building, a tasteful and beautiful church. Most of the internal furnishings – the altar, the heavy wooden pews, the Stations of the Cross – had been taken from the Corpach church which I had closed. It was especially pleasing for me to see these now in such a lovely setting. The architect assured us that all was complete apart from a few alterations, and we decided that the opening should take place shortly after Easter.

We returned to Glasgow on the afternoon flight. It was a fantastically clear day and the British Airways captain gave us a wonderful return journey, flying low over Skye, then south over Mallaig, Morar, Arisaig, Locheilside and Corpach, all of them so familiar to me. To entertain us, he then took us close to the north face of Ben Nevis, returning over the summit of the highest mountain in Britain and affording us a panoramic view of mountain ranges for miles around. Finally he headed for Glasgow – via Oban. We stared at a stunning aerial view of the cathedral and the town before passing over Bute and Dunoon on our way back into Glasgow. Unknowingly, that captain had given the Bishop of Argyll and the Isles a spectacular tour of his wide and scattered Diocese.

These first months as bishop were unrelentingly busy. Having committed myself, there was an important job to be done and I wanted to do it well, not wishing to let down all those who trusted and supported me. As things began to happen because of hard work and the co-operation of others, I was surprised to feel a certain satisfaction. But the secret weight was still there and as I had expected I missed the normal pastoral contact with people. I had never enjoyed desk work, but now I had to regard it as a daily chore and it was difficult to discipline myself in this matter as I should have done.

✦

In March, in the fifth week of Lent, I attended my first three-day meeting of the Conference of Scottish Bishops. Apart from the months of July and August, there was a monthly meeting lasting a day, but twice a year the Conference met for three full days. This took place in Chesters College, the Seminary at Bearsden near Glasgow (Blairs had closed several years earlier). For three days I witnessed the care and hard work, listened to the thoughts and views, and recognized the hopes and aspirations of a group of men for whom I have had the highest regard ever since. Each of them has his own gifts, all of them have obvious ability, and during those three intensive days I never understood where some of them got their energy.

Personally I found such meetings quite tiring and at that early stage I had little to contribute. I also had to contend with the added difficulty of being in charge of a Diocese which was difficult to organize because of its geographical make-up. Most of the other Scottish Dioceses, apart from Aberdeen which covers the largest area, had an obvious centre and it was fairly easy to gather parish representatives in one place. Almost half the Catholic population of Argyll and the Isles live in the Western Isles and there is a great deal of water between them and the mainland – a sail of seven hours to Oban, or a shorter sail of two hours to Skye with hours of driving to follow. Often the bishops discussed and arranged events which I knew would hardly be possible in our Diocese. Nevertheless, I learned a great deal and there was no lack of offers of assistance from the others. They made me feel at home and I shall always be grateful to them for that.

When the Conference finished, at lunchtime on the Wednesday, I returned immediately to Oban for the Mass of Chrism which was being celebrated in the cathedral that evening. Given the long distances some people had to travel, I was amazed and delighted when I realized that a number of people had made the journey from Fort William and Dunoon to be present for the occasion. During this Mass the sacred oils to be used in Baptism, Confirmation and the Anointing of the Sick throughout the Diocese for the next year were consecrated and blessed. Once again the congregation brought the cathedral alive with their singing and responses, and once again I felt humble in my position. A strong feeling of unworthiness never left me that night, or throughout the following Holy Week, when I presided at the solemn Easter ceremonies.

✦

After Easter I was absent from Oban every weekend until the Feast of Pentecost in May, when the children of the cathedral parish were confirmed, and after that until the end of July. My first engagement was the opening of Our Holy Redeemer's Church in Stornoway, now completely finished. Father Capaldi was still the parish priest, having worked on through several decades in very difficult circumstances, with Catholics in a minority and regarded with suspicion. To have a church rather than a converted printing shed was a great joy to him and his parishioners. Monsignor MacInnes, John Mac-Neil and I travelled together, flying from Inverness. On our arrival I discovered that the local council officials – apart from Catholics from the southern isles – and the local clergy of the Church of Scotland would not be present. The Episcopalian clergyman, closely related to the Anglican Church, did attend. I was not surprised that the others had not accepted the invitation. I was well aware of the strength of opposition to Catholicism in Lewis, and I know that a number of them were torn because of their situation, wishing they could be there. Some, I know, had a real fear of being seen in a Catholic church. It turned out to be a very happy occasion for those who did attend, the priests from Uist and Barra mingling happily with the Stornoway parishioners.

The following week I was once more on my way to Lourdes with a group of pilgrims from the Diocese, this time mainly from Lochaber. The journey was much easier as we went by bus only as far as Manchester, where we caught a plane to Lourdes. I was rather preoccupied during the pilgrimage and failed to appreciate it as much as the last. Just before leaving, I had made some changes which involved moving many of the priests to other parishes. Some priests had been too long in their present posts and there were vacancies which had to be filled. Having carefully consulted all the priests beforehand, I made the final decisions and sent out the letters of appointment which were to take effect in May. On the very day that I posted these letters a young priest, able and excellent in so many ways, called to see me on an urgent matter. He wished to leave the priesthood. Naturally I was concerned for him – but also for my careful organization of the moves: I had just appointed him to an island parish and his letter was in the post. I spent some time listening to his difficulties and trying to dissuade him. He agreed to go and talk with the priest who had been his Spiritual Director when he was a student in Rome before making any firm decisions, but he was adamant that he should not accept any new appointment at that stage. I knew this would upset the chain of my planned moves, and this was much on my mind during the pilgrimage as I tried to think of a way round the problem.

My meeting with the young priest had disturbed me in a deeper way too. I was still struggling to live with the dilemma of my secret, and here was this young man being courageously open and taking the proper course. His attitude highlighted my own secrecy and, yes, deviousness. This was an added thorn, alongside the guilt already wounding my conscience. Set apart by this but able to talk to no one, the loneliness of my position was beginning to affect me in a real way only months after my ordination as bishop. As a priest I had never been happier than during my years in Ardkenneth, when I had lived in a physically very isolated spot. I never once felt alone there. Now I was continuously surrounded by people, always busy, always on the move, and I had never felt so lonely. Even when things were going well – and I did have many positive experiences – I never felt truly comfortable in my role. Always at the back of my mind was the knowledge that I was wrong. I was living untruthfully. But trapped by my own acceptance of the post, and perhaps by other people's expectations, I could see no way out.

Perhaps the others on the Lourdes pilgrimage noticed that their bishop was out of sorts – I am not sure. Perhaps they thought I was always so reticent! One of the pilgrims was Kathleen MacPhee, mother of the baby whose funeral I had conducted shortly after arriving at St Mary's, Fort William, back in the mid-1970s. I knew her family quite well by then as they had been parishioners in Corpach (Kathleen's mother had travelled on the first pilgrimage I had accompanied to Lourdes), but as with everyone else during that busy pilgrimage week, I had few conversations with her.

On my return I began a round of administering the Sacrament of Confirmation – more travelling and regular absences from the cold house in Oban. These visits to parishes were very enjoyable for me and I was touched by the enthusiasm of the children and parishioners. Where possible I made the effort to meet the confirmation candidates in their schools beforehand, and this helped put us all at our ease when we met at the altar the following Sunday. In Uist and Lochaber I found I was confirming children I had baptized myself.

Halfway through this programme in May, the priests changed parishes which, as I well knew, is quite an upheaval in life and sometimes unwelcome. By the time I had completed my visits to the parishes at the end of June all the priests were settled in place, all vacancies filled. It had been an extraordinary six months and I was exhausted. As June came to an end I flew to Stornoway for the weekend. At the opening of the church I had promised Father Capaldi that I would come and relieve him so that he could take a short break. On my first night there I took part in a Gaelic chat show on the local radio. It was a new experience for me, difficult because a number of questions concerned my own life – an area I was reluctant to discuss. The rest of the weekend proved to be an enjoyable respite, however: I was just another priest for those parishioners.

◆

One part of the Diocese seldom visited by a bishop was the Inner Hebrides. Most of these islands closest to the mainland had few Catholics and they were only able to go to Mass when a priest could call – about twice a month in most cases. The island of Iona, that centre of Celtic Christianity, had only one Catholic resident in the early 1990s. Many Catholics visit, but they only stay for a week or two at the most. During my first summer as bishop I decided to take the opportunity of visiting Catholics living in such isolation.

My first visit was to Tobermory in Mull. Tobar Mhoire, 'The Well of Mary the Virgin', is the Gaelic name for this little town, a reminder of its Catholic past. The priests of the cathedral in Oban serve this island on a fortnightly basis and I replaced the man due to say Mass that weekend.

The following weekend I spent three days in Islay. It is an island I had never visited before and I loved my time there. The greenness of the island was striking, and there was a welcome lack of over-commercialization with regard to its tourist industry. Of course, Islay is famous for its main industry – malt whisky. Historically it has evocative links to the ancient Celtic Church, having been home to the early Irish saints Colmcille, Brendan, Maolrubha and Ronan. There are a number of Columban sites on the island linking it to the monks of Iona in early times. On the east coast is the renowned Kildalton Cross, which has stood there for over a thousand years, linking the present to the repentance and reflection practised by those early Christians. Today I do not know of one native-born 'Ialach' who is Catholic. Our congregation there was completely made up of incomers and I admired the spirit and faithfulness of that little group. Mass was celebrated in the little Episcopalian church near Bowmore, the priest from Campbeltown making the two-hour crossing twice a month. My lasting memory of Islay is the sight of the hundreds of geese who visit the island on transit every year. The crofters and farmers are naturally not so keen on their presence.

The small islands of Eigg and Canna are served by the priests of Arisaig and Morar respectively. A few children on Eigg had been prepared to receive their First Holy Communion and two of them were ready to receive the Sacrament of Confirmation. With the parish priest of Arisaig I made the crossing on a small ferry to the island, so recognizable because of its famous peaked cliff of An Sgurr at the north end of the island. It is a small community, a mixture of natives and incomers much in the news in recent years because of their protests at the neglect of absentee landlords. The lack of basic amenities has only served to emphasize the resilience of the residents. On that Sunday all of them turned out – Catholics, non-Catholics and those without religion. It is that kind of community and we had a wonderful day of celebration. After Mass everyone gathered for food and a ceilidh which continued all day until we boarded the ferry on its way back to Arisaig.

I travelled to Canna the weekend after that, accompanied by John MacNeil who was now the parish priest in Morar, having moved from Fort William in the recent clergy changes. He would make this three-hour journey twice a month. We sailed on a fishing boat from Mallaig, a wonderful way to travel in that part of the world. On a calm, clear day we sailed north of Eigg and the mountainous Rhum, past the south end of Skye and out into the Minch. This was the same journey I had made on the *Lochmor* as a boy, and as a teenager when I fished out of Eriskay. Canna appears from a distance to be a little green table of land floating on the sea, with the hills of Uist in the far distance as a backdrop. In 1991 it had a population of about 25 people, all but one of them Catholic, most of them natives, with the landowner John Lorne Campbell being a permanent resident. A noted Gaelic scholar and writer, he and his wife have spent most of their lives there as important and respected members of the small community. The island is now in the care of the National Trust of Scotland, with an agreement between John Campbell and that body to conserve the crofting way of life and, therefore, the livelihood of the inhabitants after his death.

In times past there was a much larger population, revealed by the size of the now derelict church of St Edmund built in the nineteenth century by Lord Bute. That is also now in the ownership of the National Trust. John Lorne Campbell had another little building refurbished as a church which is lovingly cared for by the people. It was here that we celebrated Mass, followed by refreshments in a parishioner's house. Regretfully we set off on our three-hour journey back to the mainland, but a surprise was in store and we were a little delayed en route. A whale was spotted just off Rhum and the skipper went out of his way to give us a closer look. It was a remarkable sight, the huge back and tail clearly visible as this giant of the sea played to the enthralled audience. Eventually the whale turned west and we sailed for home with dusk closing in on us, arriving back at about 11.00 p.m. It had been a long but beautiful day.

In all the travelling I undertook as bishop these remote islands, floating on the fringe of Europe, stood out for me because they all have Celtic connections with the Christian communities of the early Church. These were the islands where the monks of Columba had places of worship and study, and that history was still tangible. They were expert seamen, those monks of the past, and their love of nature and the sea in particular continues amongst the communities living there today.

◆

As I journeyed on round the Diocese throughout the summer, I had the opportunity of meeting all the priests in the relaxed atmosphere of their own homes. We all knew each other and therefore there was no strangeness to overcome, but I was no longer 'one of them' and I felt the loss keenly. A feeling of envy grew up in me: these men were still working, as I now could not, in the pastoral field, caring for their parishioners and fully caught up in everyday church life.

The weight of the Diocese felt heavy on my shoulders and I was always aware of my secret, pulling me down. I was being contacted more often by my son's mother. Understandably life was difficult for them and the financial demands increased. This could only come from my own pocket and the reality was that I was poorer now than I had been as a parish priest. Stipends were often given at baptisms, marriages and funerals, which had been a great help.

I was seldom involved now on such occasions, however, and had to manage my house, food, telephone and car on the flat £500 provision which like all priests I received every month. Nonetheless, I began to send more per month for my son and struggled to keep things together as best I could in Oban.

✦

Colin MacInnes, a native of South Uist and my predecessor in Ardkenneth, was by this time working in Quito, Ecuador. When he was parish priest of Northbay in Barra, he had received permission from Bishop Colin MacPherson to volunteer for missionary work with the Society of St James in Latin America. On his visit home during the summer of 1991 he invited me to visit him in Quito, and we arranged that I would travel there the following February.

Colin has always shown remarkable initiative and energy. It was he who had begun the whole concept of co-operatives and local community projects in Iochdar during his time as parish priest. During his short time in Barra he had concentrated his energies on the Gaelic language and liturgy, producing an excellent hymnal which was now used regularly. In Ecuador I was to experience his work in a different and much wider field.

I was met off the plane by Colin, who drove me to his home in the Comite del Pueblo, a huge area of shacks and half-built houses on the edge of Quito. As part of my preparations I had taken the various antidotes for tropical diseases, only to discover that the city was over 10,000 feet above sea level: not a mosquito in sight. All I suffered from in the first day or two was some breathlessness and dizziness related to the thinness of the air.

Colin is priest for about 65,000 people spread across the hillside. Padre Colin was very important to those people because his initiatives were changing their lives. When he arrived there in 1985 he found himself a shack and some land, living without running water and only a little electricity like most of his parishioners. He built a one-storey house – kitchen, waiting room, meeting room and bedroom. All around him were similar structures. The inhabitants were mostly of Indian origin, the mountain people of the Andes. They had come to the city to find work and make a living but, like their counterparts throughout the world, they were disappointed. Poor and displaced, there was nowhere else to go, so they stayed.

To help give them an identity Colin worked to instil in them a sense of community and belonging. In his first years there he had much opposition from the Communists, who were trying to form the people for their own purposes. Some of this opposition was life threatening and he was assaulted and, of course, there was the usual weapon of slander. Despite this, a church was built on a hill within the Comite, and here Colin set up an organization which included teachers, a doctor, nurses, a legal adviser and an engineer. A school was started in rooms below the church, the younger children making use of it in the earlier part of the day, followed by their older brothers and sisters. Each morning before starting work the group at the church would meet after Mass to pray, read the Scriptures and discuss what they had read. Then they would discuss the business of the day. Their work was tied to their faith, with Christ at the centre of everything. In my fragile and lonely state I admired and envied their strength of purpose, their commitment, and their uninhibited support for every person in the team.

By the time I arrived Colin had built another storey on the house, which was to be used as a clinic providing much-needed health care. Throughout the day there were always people around, working or looking for Padre Colin. His day began at sunrise around 6.00 a.m. There being very little electricity the people lived their lives by the light of the day. The bells on the church, St Joseph the Worker, rang out at that early hour and the day started with the celebration of Mass. I watched as people emerged from the shacks all around to make their way to the church. Everyone had a smile, a wave or a shouted greeting, displaying a real cheerfulness despite their obvious poverty. What a contrast, I thought, to the glum faces of so many of us in the comfortable world that is Britain.

The people's attitude and behaviour inside the church was also a revelation to me. Colin is a very active person with great foresight and initiative, but I had never regarded him as a great preacher. Now I had my eyes opened. Preaching to this congregation was actually a two-way exercise and Colin obviously loved it. Some of the listeners would question him on what he was saying, asking for clarification of a particular point. One elderly lady leapt to her feet and, pointing vigorously to her Bible, spoke in a very excited manner. Colin's reply sounded just as excited. Not being a Spanish speaker, I was unable to understand what they were saying, but at least the congregation were clearly paying attention!

I am still amazed at what Colin and his parishioners have managed to achieve. Under his direction there are now three credit banks in operation, staffed by the people themselves and enabling them to develop their shacks into houses without suffering crippling interest rates. Further, by persuasion, cajoling and begging, Colin has brought about a better electricity supply, though it is still inefficient at times. When I was there a huge project was under way to provide running water and a sewerage system for everyone in the Comite. On top of all these practical matters he has ensured that these people, too often discarded, are aware of their own dignity and have real purpose in their lives.

Once a year the priests of the Society of St James working in Latin America came together for a retreat and rest period in Lima, Peru. This was to take place during my visit and I was invited to join them. In four happy and fascinating days I was able to meet priests from Scotland, England, Ireland, America, Australia and New Zealand, who had all volunteered to work for a period of years in this part of the world. Hearing of their work in Peru, Bolivia and Ecuador, in the cities, on the coast, or high in the mountains, I was impressed by their commitment and their faith. They all had stories to tell and I thoroughly enjoyed being in their company. Unfortunately we were unable to see much of Lima because the Maoist revolutionaries, known as Shining Path, were active there and priests were amongst their targets. We were confined to the retreat house and grounds (luxurious in comparison to the conditions in which Colin lived).

Talking with these missionary priests, and having already seen Colin's dedication in the Comite del Pueblo, I found myself deeply touched by the way they had decided to express their Faith and live out the gospel. My few short weeks in Ecuador and Peru left a profound and lasting impression on me. Everyone was so enthusiastic and it was easy to become absorbed in the work that was going on. For myself, I was enthralled – and grateful for the distraction from my difficulties back home. It was a welcome respite from the pressures of my role as bishop.

Colin's easy company helped me to relax after a year of being permanently on edge. He was a good friend and we talked and laughed a great deal, sharing news and funny stories. I had also brought messages from people in various parts of the Diocese who, interested in his work, regularly collected money to help with projects in the Comite.

As well as swapping amusing stories, we spoke about more serious matters. I was interested in how well the Church was developing in Ecuador. Quito is a very large city, the seat of government and learning, its buildings reminiscent of its Spanish colonial past. It was obvious to me that there were differences amongst members of the Church in their attitude to the poor. The poor people, the 'displaced', were mostly served by foreign priests like Colin and those I met in Lima. The traditional parishes, usually with churches dating back to colonial times, were served by native clergy. The obvious presence in government and academic circles, however, was the Order of Opus Dei, fast growing in influence in South America and encouraged by the Vatican as an antidote to the influence of Liberation Theology. (Founded after the Second World War by a Spaniard, this right-wing Order is now a considerable wielder of power in the Vatican and the wider Church.) In the past 10 years newly appointed bishops in Latin America have tended to come from their ranks. I saw nothing of them amongst the thousands of poor in the Comite del Pueblo. Opus Dei invariably seems to focus on the elite in any society, which has always left me feeling uncomfortable. I was only there for a short while, but my personal impression was that there were in fact three Churches at work in the Quito area: the missionary church, working at the coal face amongst the poor; the colonial church, caught in a time warp and rather stagnant; and the politically motivated church of Opus Dei. Time will tell, but if I have a judgement to make now, it is that division weakens.

◆

I left Ecuador with a lump in my throat, grateful to Colin for giving me the opportunity to sample life in such surroundings and amongst such lovely people. I journeyed sadly home to the shock of Scotland in late winter – but there is something about Argyll and the Isles that I found curiously comforting. Perhaps it was simply the welcome of familiar sights, pleasing to see despite my apprehension at returning to the seat of my difficulties.

On my arrival in Glasgow I discovered that Bishop Charles Renfrew, the auxiliary to Archbishop Winning in Glasgow, had died. He had suffered from a very serious kidney disease for a number of years, but had continued to work with great cheerfulness despite the weakening effect of such illness and the onset of blindness.

Every second day he had to spend hours in hospital having dialysis treatment, something he made light of and accepted with patience. Many people were very saddened by his death, which in the end had been sudden. I drove back to Oban, and returned to Glasgow early the next morning for his Requiem Mass and funeral. The turnout was astonishing for a weekday, the church crowded to overflowing and the streets outside lined with mourners – ordinarily people come to say farewell to someone they obviously loved.

After the warmth of Ecuador, I was back to old winter clothes and porridge! It was quite a culture shock, and as I moved around the house in Oban I felt guilty about the amount of space allotted to me in comparison to the little shacks I had left behind in Quito. I began to give serious consideration to selling or leasing Bishop's House. Some of the older priests were unhappy with this in view of the history of the property, which had been in the ownership of the Church since the restoration of the Hierarchy in 1878. The economics of 1992 made sense of a sale or lease, however. The necessary repairs and refurbishment were, in my estimation, far too expensive considering the financial situation of our small Diocese. It was also the coldest and darkest house I had ever lived in and I would have been more than happy to move.

I thought I had the opportunity to do so when I agreed to Father Gerard McKay, a very talented Canon lawyer, leaving his parish of Taynuilt to work for Cardinal Ratzinger in Rome. Whenever possible, from that day until I left, I said the Sunday Mass there and attended to a few Baptisms and funerals as required. It was something I was very happy to do, and in any case I was unable to appoint anyone else because of the shortage of priests. I also gave serious thought to moving there, only seven miles from Oban, which would have enabled me to put Bishop's House up for sale without then having to spend the money on another house for me. However, I discovered that the Taynuilt property needed considerable repairs and renewal, and decided to let matters rest for the present.

◆

Every five years a country's National Conference of Bishops has to travel to Rome and report in person to the departments of the Church's administration in the Vatican known as Congregations (the Congregation of the Sacraments, the Congregation of the Clergy, of the Laity, etc.). We were due to report in 1992 and towards the end of October I joined the other bishops in Rome. We were to be there for eight days, staying in the Scots College which is some distance from the Vatican. I had not, like most of the bishops, studied in Rome, and had only visited the Eternal City once before, with the youth pilgrimage in 1975. Most people would be excited about such a visit, eagerly anticipating the chance to see a little of the internal workings of the Vatican, but I felt apprehensive. Travelling to the heart of the Church, I felt out of place and conscious of the heavy weight of my guilt. Once there, I was stifled by the atmosphere of history and power, intimidated at meeting such famous Cardinals. There were moments of relaxation, but I always felt somehow on guard.

The Rector, staff and students of the Scots College were very welcoming and treated us throughout the week in a most hospitable way. On our first day I had no appointments and travelled into Rome, where I made my way to St Peter's and took a leisurely, solitary stroll around the famous basilica, visiting the burial crypts of the Popes of my lifetime – Pius XII, John XIII, Paul VI and the short-lived John Paul I. There was a great sense of history about the place, but I preferred St Mary Major's and St Paul's outside the Walls, which I also managed to visit that day. They too have a wonderful history, but I found them to have a more prayerful atmosphere. I have a poor sense of direction and, making my way back to the college, I took the wrong bus, ended up in another part of Rome and had to take a taxi back (even then, I was not too clear about telling the driver my destination, but accepted the blame when I was overcharged for the fare)!

The following day business began. We had to travel into Rome dressed in our robes of office as this was required by protocol. The Swiss Guards saluted us as we entered the Vatican portals. Not being sure if I should return the salute, I just nodded and said 'Hello.'

Each morning there were two meetings, or interviews, with the various departments of administration. The head of each Congregation is normally a Cardinal of the Curia, one of the Pope's close advisers. I was very glad that I did not have to present my personal *Ad Limina* report on this occasion, as I had been in office for less than two years, but I accompanied the others for the experience. On that first morning I found myself sitting at a table with Cardinal Ratzinger, regarded by many as the 'power behind the throne'. Few of those present were required to say much, because he did most of the talking. I had the impression that he was speaking at us rather than to us, yet I sensed the essential goodness of the man. Those Cardinals in the Curia certainly carry power, but they actually have a very frugal lifestyle.

I have to say that I felt a coldness, almost clinical, for most of the time I was there in the business centre of the Vatican. At another of these meetings, however, I did enjoy meeting Cardinal Gantin, a tall man from Africa who impressed me a great deal because of his humanity, humility and noticeable warmth. In the past he had been regarded as *Papabile*, a possible Pope. I thought that he would have been marvellous for the Church, but the Holy Spirit works in His own way.

I was struck by the number of different nationalities I saw in those corridors – it truly is a catholic Church. It was particularly noticeable how many nuns from the Far East were working within the administration departments. Remarking on this, I said I found it strange that they were not back at home where they were surely most needed. One of my fellow bishops replied with a wry smile that perhaps they felt more comfortable in the Vatican. Perhaps that was the case, but I certainly did not.

On the Friday of that week, the meetings completed, we met Pope John Paul II, spending a good part of the day with him. At about 5.30 a.m. we were shown into the part of the Vatican containing the Pope's private apartments. His secretary, a Polish priest, greeted us and led us into a little chapel where the Pope celebrates Mass at about 6.00 a.m. on most days. Close to the Pontiff, we sat or knelt at prayer in the silence of the dawn. It was a holy moment, on a very deep and personal level which I could not begin to put into words. I know I prayed fervently and these were the most important minutes of my visit to Rome. The Pope rose and walked out in silence. His secretary led us to the adjoining sacristy where, still in silence, we vested for Mass. We concelebrated the Mass with the successor of St Peter, a momentous occasion which was at the same time simple and profoundly prayerful. Afterwards Archbishop Winning introduced us to him individually.

We left then, returning to the college for breakfast. At 11 o'clock we were back in the Vatican, again greeted by saluting Swiss Guards, and shown into a large room on the second floor where we waited for our private audience. We each met the Pope alone, called in turn for a brief, individual meeting. I was the last to be shown into the room, where I found the Holy Father standing by a table looking at a map of Scotland. He greeted me warmly and asked me some questions about the Diocese which I answered nervously. Did the Pontiff know that someone had dubbed me 'The Reluctant Bishop'?

He put me at my ease by pointing to the map, saying, 'There is much water and little land where you live.'

'Yes, your Holiness,' I replied.

'And not too many people.'

'No, your Holiness. Only about 11,000!'

'Ha. More sheep than people.'

'Yes, your Holiness.'

To my relief our private conversation ended then and the others entered the room. After the obligatory photographs we left, with an invitation to join the Pope shortly at table for lunch.

Bishop Devine and myself were the only smokers in our group. It had been a long morning and we were desperate to have a puff, so the two of us made our way down to the Papal garden, where we found a secluded corner and smoked a welcome cigarette. I wonder how many others have managed that? I suppose it is quite ridiculous that two bishops should act like schoolboys behind the bike shed, but we could see no alternative!

Lunch was a simple meal of pasta and chicken. The nine of us sat around the table with Pope John Paul and his secretary. I was still very nervous and picked at what was placed before me. During that meal I think the only words I spoke were 'thank you' and 'no thanks' – rather unusual for me. The Pope is an excellent conversationalist, however, and his command of English is very good. He led us over a range of topics and did not hesitate to debate with some of the bishops when there was disagreement. Some of them were not afraid to raise controversial subjects and I think this pleased the Pope, although he was firm in his replies, as ever. I think he enjoyed our company. We sat down at table at one o'clock and it was after three before we rose and said our farewells.

Those hours with the Pope, especially the Mass, were the highlight of my visit to Rome, despite my state of nerves. I did not enjoy the cold atmosphere of the Vatican in general. This is a very personal feeling and no doubt had something to do with my sense of guilt, amongst other things. My perception of coldness (bureaucracy always leaves me with that feeling) does not mean that those working there are without human warmth, however. Indeed, there are saints working there, serving the Church with their expertise in theology and law, talents I do not have and perhaps, therefore, did not appreciate fully during my limited experience of Vatican life.

✦

In addition to my trips to the islands and the longer journeys to Ecuador and Rome, constant travelling also became a way of life for me closer to home. The Conference of Bishops had appointed Bishop Conti of Aberdeen and myself to represent them in the sale of lands and buildings at Blairs Seminary. It had been closed since the mid-1980s and, although interest had been shown, a firm buyer had not been found. The Trust demanded that all proceeds from such a sale be used for the education of those studying for the priesthood. The bishops were the trustees and therefore had to be directly involved in the sale. At this time we were also in the process of setting up a National Seminary at Chesters College, Bearsden, near Glasgow. This was proving to be difficult because at the time the college was an interdiocesan establishment for the west of Scotland. The eastern Dioceses had their seminary at Gillis College in Edinburgh and were pressing strongly for the National Seminary to be sited there. It became a heated argument, although all concerned admitted the illogicality of having two such establishments in such a small country and at such a cost. When Blairs was sold the proceeds would go to the new National Seminary – wherever it was eventually situated.

My involvement in the sale entailed attending business meetings in Edinburgh as well as several visits to Blairs to meet with Bishop Conti, advisers and potential buyers. On the first occasion it was a very strange sensation going up that neglected drive to be faced with the familiar, grand granite edifice, still looking as solid as ever. It was now only a shell, however, cold and vacant. After that first visit I wanted it sold as soon as possible. Having known Blairs when it was full and alive, I could not bear to hear my footsteps echo through the emptiness. The church remained open, still beautiful and in use every Sunday but, I thought, somehow lacking. My nostalgia for my alma mater was no longer so strong that I wanted to keep Blairs in church hands regardless. It was time to sell up and move on.

There were also regular journeys to Glasgow for monthly meetings of the Conference of Bishops. For the one-day meetings I would leave Oban at about 6.30 a.m., often stopping at Tyndrum for some breakfast. I soon lost count of how often I passed through Tyndrum, Crianlarich, Inverarnan, Tarbet, Luss, and on to Bearsden.

Then I had to drive very regularly to Fort William where the Diocesan Office was situated. Efficiency, of course, demanded that it be in Oban, but Margaret Macdonald had worked with Bishop MacPherson's Chancellor, Monsignor Hendry, in Roybridge for years and her expertise in all things financial was something I relied on. I quickly came to depend on her knowledge and, above all, her discretion, which is so important in such work. In that area of administration she was more efficient and valuable than any priest. It was for this reason that I appointed her as the official Diocesan Treasurer, the only layperson to hold that position in the Catholic Church in Scotland. John MacNeil suggested at the beginning that the office be situated in Fort William, as Margaret lived in Roybridge just 15 miles away. After a few years I felt that I knew every tree and house on the hour-long journey from Oban. Indeed, I sometimes arrived at St Mary's without realizing that I had already passed alongside Loch Creran, through Appin and Kentallen, over the Ballachulish Bridge, through Onich and Corran Ferry and into Fort William.

Sometimes, having finished business in the office, I would travel on to Morar, passing through Corpach, Locheilside, Lochailort and Arisaig, taking the road to Bracora and branching off at St Cumin's, where I would spend the night with John MacNeil. He knew how a number of the clergy were reacting to my administration and was an excellent sounding board. I relied very much on his support and advice – at times his house in Morar was a haven.

On 4 March 1993 the phone rang at about 6.30 p.m., shortly after I had finished washing up from my evening meal. It was Monsignor Wynne, the parish priest of Arisaig.

'I'm sorry to be the bearer of bad news,' he said. 'John is dead.'

My mind on something else, I did not immediately grasp what he was telling me.

'Sorry, eh … who is John? Who is dead?'

'John MacNeil – we've just found him in the sacristy. He must have had a heart attack.'

'Oh, no. I was speaking with him on the phone last night. He seemed to be fine. May God rest him. I'll be up as soon as possible.'

I put the phone down, feeling devastated and then guilty. Our conversation the previous evening had been brief. He had phoned to give advice on some diocesan matter. Perhaps he had wanted to talk, to say more, and I had not given him that opportunity; perhaps he had already been feeling unwell. I was overwhelmed by a feeling of great loss.

I packed a bag because I knew I would have to stay in Morar that night. All the lights were on when I eventually arrived at John's house and I could hear voices in the kitchen. As I entered I was surprised to see so many parishioners there with Monsignor Wynne. They told me how John had been found, and it was obvious that they were deeply affected by his death. Apparently John had celebrated a Funeral Mass for an old lady in Mallaig that morning. There was no burial afterwards because her remains were being taken to South Uist for interment. On his way back to Morar John had called to see a couple and had eaten some soup with them before returning home. It was clear that he had lain on top of his bed and, they surmised, felt ill. Then, perhaps knowing it was serious, he had tried to make his way into the church – more important to him than making a phone call to ask for help. He never reached the door of the church, collapsing and dying in the sacristy. It was there that he was found, having been dead for several hours. By the time I arrived his body had been taken to Inverness for a post-mortem examination.

I went upstairs to his sitting room and sat at a surprisingly tidy desk. In front of me was a notebook recording Masses to be said and the stipend. It was so up to date that the last Mass he had said the previous day was marked as being fulfilled. All his Mass obligations had been met. I had never known John to be so meticulous. In the top right-hand drawer I found a diary I had never known that he kept, and his last entry was for the day before his death. The only other thing in that drawer was a large envelope containing his will and instructions for his executor. John had everything prepared for his death, of that I am certain.

The following morning I spoke with his doctor in Fort William. Although he lived in Morar, John had remained with the practice he had attended (not very often) over the previous 10 years. The doctor was very upset as he and John had been friends. He told me that the day before his death John had travelled to Fort William to see him. On arriving at the surgery to discover that his doctor was not there, John had left without seeing one of the other doctors. To make such a journey he must have been feeling unwell. According to one of the parishioners John had taken some kind of weak turn in his car on Mallaig pier the week before. He had just sat in his car for over an hour before driving home. Yet he did not complain to me or to anyone else. I am sure that John knew his death was near, and that is why everything necessary was easily accessible in that tidy desk.

After Requiem Masses in St Mary's, Fort William, and in Morar, we took his remains home to Barra where he was laid to rest beside his parents in his native soil. All of us who knew him miss him very much. May he rest in peace.

✦

Occasionally, when I was in Fort William, I would take the chance to visit my former parishioners who were seriously ill in hospital. From the spring of 1991 I saw Kathleen MacPhee there on several different occasions, knowing her and her family as I did from my time in Corpach. Kathleen and her husband ran a very busy guesthouse and she was an outgoing, giving person, always willing to volunteer when help was needed for parish events. Her children were bright, and happy in our school. Kathleen herself attended daily Mass, having learned the importance of faith from her parents, John and Theresa MacDonald. Her father had died two years before I arrived in Corpach, but Theresa was an active member of St Mary's in Fort William, also attending Mass daily. Mother and daughter both joined other parishioners on our pilgrimages to Lourdes.

In my last year in Corpach I was called on to help with a family problem in a pastoral way. Kathleen and her husband had been married for 19 years, but early in that year after a serious incident in the home, Kathleen and the children left and went to live with her mother. Her husband visited me on a few occasions asking for my help and eventually I encouraged and persuaded Kathleen to return. To the rest of us they seemed to be fine, but some months later there was a similar and more serious incident and again she left home with the children. Her husband did not ask for my help this time. He was persuaded to leave the house and Kathleen moved back with the children. In the previous four years I had called only on a few occasions and I think I only visited twice after their separation. Shortly afterwards I moved to the flat in Caol and within a short time I was involved in the whole business of becoming bishop. Later some press reports tried to claim that we were already involved with each other at this time: we most certainly were not, and on the occasion of the second separation I counselled neither party.

When I visited Kathleen in the Belford Hospital in the spring of 1991 she was very ill. Afterwards I went to see the priest in St Mary's and advised him to administer the Last Rites. I called to see her a few times during the 10 days she was there, and eventually the symptoms subsided, although the doctors were still mystified as to the cause. That summer she continued to run the guesthouse on her own, as ever having a busy season. I called occasionally for a cup of coffee and a chat on my way to Morar. Her separation from her husband was permanent by then and under Scottish law the property had to be sold and the proceeds equally divided. This was done towards the end of the year and Kathleen and the children moved into a smaller house in Inverlochy, Fort William.

A few months later, towards Easter 1992, Kathleen was back in hospital with the same mysterious illness and the same symptoms of massive stomach distension, severe pain and very high temperature. The Mass of Chrism was being celebrated that year in St Mary's, next door to the hospital, and beforehand I called to see her. She did not seem to recognize me and the staff were more than concerned. After the Mass the parish priest administered the Sacraments to her – she was indeed very ill. I returned to Oban with feelings of real worry. Little did she or her children know that she would have to return to hospital on another 15 occasions before any kind of solution to her illness was found.

It was far from unusual for me to take such care to visit former parishioners in hospital. Although I was no longer their parish priest, I still knew them all and my pastoral concern for them continued. I was particularly fond of Kathleen because – along with others in the parish – she had been a great help and support during my time with the troubled church in Corpach. I was naturally concerned for her and her children as they struggled to cope with these bouts of serious illness. We got on well and as I visited her in hospital I felt no need to hide a genuine liking for her.

Meanwhile, my work as bishop was continuing: I travelled all round the Diocese; I went to Ecuador; I went to Rome; I struggled to cope with the volume of desk work; I tried to come to terms with the sadness of John MacNeil's death in the spring of 1993. A month after he died I asked Roddy Macdonald, the parish priest of Glencoe, to replace John as Vicar General. Roddy has wisdom and integrity, and we knew each other well after working together in

Dunoon. I came to rely on him very much, but later I would leave him burdened with problems he had never sought.

◆

In July 1993 Cardinal Gordon Joseph Gray died. He had been Archbishop of St Andrew's and Edinburgh from 1951 until his retirement in 1985. In 1969 he had been created Cardinal, the first in Scotland since the Reformation. With the other bishops I travelled to the Requiem Mass and burial in St Mary's Cathedral. It was a very moving occasion. In many ways Gordon Joseph Gray had been a giant in the Scottish Catholic Church. He had led the Church through the traumatic changes initiated by the Second Vatican Council in the early 1960s and was very well respected by all shades of opinion in Scottish public life. I had only met him once since my ordination as bishop, although our paths had crossed a few times when I was Procurator in Blairs. On such an occasion as this, celebrating the life of such a great man, I felt my unworthiness and guilt even more. As I returned to Oban I know I shared with many others the thought that it was the end of a wonderful era in the Catholic Church in Scotland.

Amongst some of the clergy the question was then raised: who will be the next Cardinal? Would Archbishop O'Brien follow in the footsteps of his predecessor? Would Rome appoint another Cardinal? I never heard the subject discussed amongst the bishops, but by then our attention was firmly focused on the very serious and painful matter of child sexual abuse. Although I knew that this problem was raising its ugly head elsewhere I had not come across it in Scotland. Suddenly, it seemed, there were two or three cases, one of which received very widespread publicity. With the advice of a working party headed by a top social worker and other experts in the field, we were in the process of drawing up definitive and strict guidelines. These would be followed by all the Scottish Dioceses where any such accusations were made against a priest or church worker. In the press we bishops were criticized for not having such guidelines already in place, and were charged with covering up for those accused of being involved. It is true that such instructions were not previously in place, but it is also a fact that Strathclyde Social Department, the largest in Scotland, had only recently drawn up guidelines itself. The two cases before the courts concerned events that had taken place more than 20 years before.

Of course such rules should have been in place long before, but at least a working party was now dealing urgently with the matter.

During the long process of drawing up the document I received word, out of the blue, that an accusation of sexual abuse was being made against a priest in my Diocese. Roddy Macdonald phoned me with the upsetting news. Could I come to his house the following day and meet the woman making these allegations? We agreed that Roddy would remain with me throughout the interview.

Roddy and I met the woman the following morning in the sitting room of Roddy's house in Ballachulish and we listened to her story of sexual abuse which, she said, had occurred some 30 years previously when she was about 9 years of age, continuing until she was about 12. When she had completed her account, which I believed, I asked her if she wished to press charges. She was adamant that she did not; she wanted no publicity. She also refused the offer of professional counselling, simply saying, 'I just want him out of the pulpit.' I spoke with her for a while, apologizing wholeheartedly and with real sorrow for her terrible ordeal at the hands of a priest. I promised that I would remove this man from the active priesthood, and she seemed much happier when she left.

The next day I drove the long distance to the accused priest's parish and arrived unannounced at his door. In the privacy of his house I confronted him with the allegations. He was shocked, but neither denied nor admitted culpability. I told him he must leave and retire from the active ministry. He agreed, saying that because of poor health he had been contemplating retirement anyway (he was about 70 years old). He had his own house in Bute and would move there as soon as arrangements could be made. I told him to begin packing and that I would find a replacement for his parish.

He was the only priest I had to deal with regarding the sexual abuse of children and I acted in accordance with the guidelines being drawn up and soon to be published. As far as I was aware, only the woman, Roddy Macdonald and myself knew of the true reasons for this man's departure. No charges were brought at that stage, because the woman had clearly said she did not want this to happen. I thought this was the end of the case, but I was wrong and a few years later the event would make headlines, causing further pain.

✦

In early November 1994 it was announced that Thomas J. Winning, Archbishop of Glasgow, had been created a Cardinal by Pope John Paul II. Personally, I was very happy with the news. I liked the man and felt that his leadership in certain areas was excellent. His elevation was also a recognition by the universal Church of the Catholic Church in Scotland.

Along with the other bishops and more than 1,500 Scottish pilgrims I was present during the Consistory in the Paul VI Audience Hall in Rome when Glasgow's Archbishop was given the red hat by Pope John Paul. A total of 30 Cardinals were created that day, with Cardinal Winning eighth in line. It was a very long service, but fascinating in terms of its historic importance. Amongst the red of the Cardinals were a few faces that I recognized, but most were unknown to me: Glemp of Warsaw, familiar from the days of Solidarity in Poland, Law of Boston, Hume of Westminster, Ratzinger and Gantin from the Curia. But I was shocked by the appearance of Pope John Paul, who appeared to have diminished in size and vitality since I had last seen him in 1992. Despite that, I was aware of the power of the Church residing in these men before me. I felt that somehow it was a more temporal than spiritual occasion.

In contrast I was touched by the presence of so many of the ordinary folk of Scotland who had sacrificed much to be there, just weeks before Christmas. I am sure that many of them could ill afford to make such a journey, but it was important for them to witness the creation of 'their' Cardinal. Officials acknowledged that these determined Scots made Vatican City history by being the largest contingent from any country outside Italy to participate in such an event. They made it one big party, as only they can!

The following morning we came together again at 9.30 a.m. in St Peter's Basilica for the solemn Mass concelebrated by the Pope and the new Cardinals. Afterwards the Scots seemed to take over St Peter's Square, tartan everywhere and the music of the pipes all around. That afternoon there was an official reception, after which I packed my bags for home. Bishop Logan and myself were travelling back the following morning while the others were being given a special audience by Pope John Paul. It was to be my last visit to Rome.

On 11 December I travelled to the Scottish Exhibition and Conference Centre in Glasgow where over 9,000 people attended a Mass of Thanksgiving with the new Cardinal. Politicians and civic leaders gathered with the ordinary people for a remarkable celebration.

Halfway up some stairs in the midst of this vast crowd I managed to meet my two sisters, Chrissie and Effie, and we had the chance of a cup of coffee and a chat together. Earlier, before the ceremony began, I had met a few people from our Diocese, amongst them Theresa MacDonald (Kathleen's mother) and her sister Bridie. Theresa told me of her concern for Kathleen, who was still not keeping well.

It was a very wet and windy day in Glasgow, yet the crowds in the SECC were in high spirits. I sensed a real spirit of solidarity amongst them which was encouraging because, after great publicity and much praise for the new Cardinal, he had returned to Scotland to find a difficult press due to a much-publicized paedophile case. Criticism of the bishops was still ongoing, with accusations of a cover up and a lack of proper guidelines. I was very conscious of this bad press as I travelled to Glasgow that day. We needed the wisdom and supportive leadership of Cardinal Winning.

◆

During that year, 1994, Kathleen had to be taken to hospital on a number of occasions, repeatedly falling ill with the same mystifying symptoms. More treatment was given, but still no answer was found. By this time she and I had become quite close. We had not yet spoken about it in so many words, but we knew we were attracted to each other and were growing to rely on the relationship. I visited her at home and in hospital as regularly as my round of duties allowed, and our phone conversations became more frequent, especially when I was away for lengthy periods. It had suddenly become important to be able to talk to each other about everyday concerns. I was very worried about this continuing illness, as were her mother and family. Life was difficult for Kathleen and the children. She was now working, often when quite ill, as an auxiliary nurse with geriatric patients – work which, even for the healthiest, can be exhausting.

At the end of June Kathleen was once more in the Belford Hospital, suffering with the same symptoms. Already she had spent time in hospitals in Edinburgh and Inverness, all to no avail. Now, back in the Belford, a visiting surgeon decided on a Sunday morning that her condition demanded immediate surgery. He was convinced that adhesions, resulting from several operations earlier in her life, were the cause of her present condition. In great pain and distress, Kathleen agreed to the operation in the hope that an answer would be found, but it was not to be and the unnecessary surgery only added to the problems. Later in the year she was diagnosed as suffering from endometriosis. The diagnosis was not a cure, but at least it was an answer and treatment could be given, albeit with little success. I had never heard of such a disease before and was distressed for her obvious and almost constant pain. I could only admire her strength of will in the face of such difficulties.

By the time 1994 came to an end, Kathleen and I were well aware of the bond between us. I could talk freely to her, and it was important for me to know how she was and to support her with my encouragement as her illness went on, seemingly without hope of a cure. We spoke a great deal on the phone, wrote letters, and I visited her at home as often as I could – a fact which must have been noticed and wondered about by her neighbours in Inverlochy. Both of us were coming to realize the consequences of allowing our love to grow: if we could not stay apart, the effects on ourselves and, in a wider sense, on many others could prove to be devastating.

I am sure that friends and family noticed a change in me at this time. Looking back, I realize I was becoming distant and losing contact with those who had supported me in different ways over the years. I see very clearly now how I must have caused hurt, especially to my own family. Somehow, I saw less and less of them and it was my own fault. I can honestly say that it was not a deliberate act on my part, but it happened. The other bishops also must have taken note of how little I contributed to deliberations at our meetings and how seldom I offered my services when a volunteer was called for. I was no longer giving of myself as I had always done in the past. I knew this to be the case, but seemed able to do very little to lift myself out of my apparent lethargy. It was more confusion than lethargy: even if I had not yet fully acknowledged it to myself, I was being pulled in two directions and eventually would have to make a decision between them. My attention was divided. I had always felt uncomfortable with my role as bishop, but had worked as best I could. Now I was preoccupied with Kathleen's frightening illness and the increasing depth of my feelings for her.

The year 1995 was busy with the normal round of engagements in the Diocese, mostly to administer the Sacrament of Confirmation, which I did that year in the Uists, Stornoway, Fort William, Oban, Mingarry, Dunoon, Lochgilphead and Campbeltown, spending time with the priests and parishioners in each place. Wherever I was, whatever I was doing, always churning away inside me was a deep-felt conflict over my role and the needs of the people and priests. What was I doing? Who was I to be acting this part? What were they thinking? Was I letting people down? My distraction must have been obvious to those I visited that year, and I certainly felt that the easy familiarity of previous times had diminished. I felt awkward; sometimes I could not respond to an innocently warm welcome with any genuine warmth of my own. The problem was entirely within me: I knew I was withdrawing myself and as far as the people of my Diocese were concerned this was making me something of a lame duck. Throughout my priesthood I had been an able preacher, but even that was becoming a struggle in many ways.

I was confused about my role in the Church, and burdened by the responsibility I had towards the people under my care, but as the pressure built up inside me my personal Faith never wavered. Often, in that large, unfriendly house in Oban, I would take refuge in the little chapel. It was a profoundly peaceful place, and I found it restful to sit in there and read or pray in private. I never once spoke to my priest friends and advisers about my inner turmoil. I spoke only to God.

◆

In June 1995 Kathleen was sent to Stobhill Hospital in Glasgow to be examined by a respected gynaecologist. Some days later, while she was at work in the geriatric ward, she received a telephone call from her doctor's surgery informing her that she had been found to have abnormal cells growing in the area of her womb. She was shocked to receive such news in this way and immediately went to see her doctor, who advised her of the need for surgery as soon as possible. She was understandably worried. She was a single parent looking after two children at home, and she knew how her older son, working in the North Sea, would be affected. He had his own flat, but at least she knew she could rely on him to care for the other two while she was in hospital.

Her biggest concern was the extent of those 'abnormal cells', so often a euphemism for cancer. How far had it spread? Would surgery be sufficient? Did this mean other treatments, such as radiotherapy or chemotherapy? Sometime in the second half of July I collected Kathleen from her home and drove her to the hospital in

Glasgow. She has a strong faith, and prayer and the Sacraments were always an important part of her life. In this way she prepared herself for surgery. The consultant was excellent, explaining what he would do and giving her reassurance. He performed a full hysterectomy and probed further to satisfy himself that there were no more abnormal cells. It was also his hope that the endometriosis which had plagued her life in recent years might be completely removed by the operation.

A few days after the surgery I called to see her in the hospital. She was already up and about, looking remarkably well. However, the following day she became quite ill, suffering from a haematoma which, thankfully, burst through just above her wound. This can be very dangerous, however, and she was confined to bed to receive further treatment. With the wound reopened she would be kept in hospital longer than expected.

On Sunday 30 July, six days after the operation, her brother-in-law took Kathleen's mother and her children to visit. After their arrival she made up her mind to return to Fort William with them, very much against the wishes and advice of the nursing staff. Kathleen can be thrawn, however. She stuck to her plans, reassuring the nurses that she would obey their instructions and co-operate with the local nurse who would visit her every day. Armed with the necessary dressings and painkillers, she set off for home. Much later that evening I received a call from her – she was at home, but confined to bed. I can only say I was surprised!

Early the following morning the phone rang again. It was Kathleen, sobbing uncontrollably. Her brother-in-law, who had taken her home from hospital just the previous day, had died very suddenly in his sleep. Aged only 43, he was apparently fit and had no history of illness. His wife and two sons were devastated with grief, as indeed were both families. A neighbour took Kathleen across to her sister's house and there she would remain, stubbornly on her feet, until after that very sad funeral and for many weeks afterwards. Feeling very much for the bereaved family, whom I knew well, I was also most concerned for Kathleen. Her wound had to be cleaned and dressed daily; she had just undergone major surgery and was supposed to be convalescing. She had other priorities, though, and I was amazed at her resilience, despite thinking it foolish and even dangerous. It was important to her that she be with her sister, and during the months that followed I did not see Kathleen very often, although we were regularly in contact by phone.

✦

Misfortune seemed to be close to us at that time. In December my sister Chrissie, to whom I had always been close, complained of feeling unwell. A year before, after 30 years of marriage and 9 children, she had left home with the two remaining boys and her two daughters. The older boys had left home in previous years and it was to them she now turned. Between them they gave her shelter and love until she managed to find a house for herself. She had just completed decorating and furnishing her council home when she fell ill. During a telephone conversation I realized she was hiding something from me and, as I was going to Glasgow for a bishops' meeting, I made a point of visiting her. I was shocked by her appearance. She had lost weight and said she constantly felt tired, although she continued with her work as a home help. The doctor thought she was suffering from a nervous bowel disorder. A few days after Christmas I called to see her again and was even more alarmed. I encouraged her son to phone the doctor there and then and have him come and visit her at home.

At the beginning of January 1996 I spent three days with the bishops in Seamill. On my way there I called to see Chrissie, but was told by one of the boys that the ambulance had just left and was taking her to the Southern General Hospital. The following afternoon I drove up from Seamill to visit her. I was appalled by the deterioration in her condition, feeling full of foreboding and an unspoken realization that she was terminally ill. Chrissie was hopeful and cheerful, as ever. Her only concern was for the family at home. That morning they had performed a biopsy and she was waiting for the results. I returned the following afternoon and on the stairs to her ward I met her son Roddy, brokenhearted but trying to be brave. He had just been told that his mother had inoperable cancer of the liver. They had not yet managed to discover the primary cause. When he left I went in to see Chrissie and found her quietly weeping. I sat by her bed and held her hands as we prayed together. All she was asking for was a little more time with her children, especially the girls, twins born after her seven sons.

Three weeks later, on 7 February, Chrissie died with those lovely children around her bed. During the last two weeks, when they had her at home, they nursed her, helped her in and out of bed, turned her when it was necessary, handling her fast-wasting body with a tenderness beyond their years. I visited and stayed with her several times, shocked at the rapidity with which the disease had spread. Two days before her death we were told that the primary cause was ovarian cancer, that silent type which does not show itself until the end. She died in the early hours of the morning with her seven sons and two daughters around her bed. They prayed the rosary and she spoke to all of them. A few minutes later she was dead. May she rest in peace.

I have never found it so difficult to celebrate the Requiem Mass. By the time we laid Chrissie to rest in the same grave as our parents my throat had closed and I found myself unable to speak. The pain and emotion of the last few weeks could no longer be kept in control. I returned bleakly to Oban that evening. The following morning I offered the usual Sunday Mass in Taynuilt. Life has to go on and I found some comfort in the familiar words and movements.

9

✦

THE END AND
THE BEGINNING

KATHLEEN AND I KNEW BEYOND DOUBT by then that our feelings
for each other had gone beyond mere friendship. We had fallen in
love. Early in 1995, aware that this was happening, we had agreed
to see less of each other and she had gone away for a while. It was a
strange, tense year and we both found the separation very painful.
Then other events, as I have described, took over – Kathleen's operation, the death of her brother-in-law, Chrissie's illness and death.
We were not able to see each other very often even then, but the
telephone was a lifeline. We needed each other's support; we
needed to encourage each other. In the midst of these dreadful
troubles, our love was growing stronger.

What were we to do? The separation had been hard to cope
with, but perhaps more difficult was the lie we were now living:
we were becoming furtive in our behaviour as we tried to be
together but continue leading our lives 'as normal' so that others
would not notice and be upset. Kathleen had gained her divorce in
1992 and in society's eyes was free to live her life as she wished.
The same society would not accept her love for a priest, let alone
a bishop. She was concerned for her children (Stephen was 23 then,
Donald 18, and Julie Anne 15), her family and her Faith. In addition
to the ongoing guilt over my son, I now faced the conflicting

realities of my priesthood, my vows and my love for Kathleen. The time for choice was coming close.

✦

In March 1996 I went for the last time to the three-day meeting of the Conference of Bishops. We would meet on other occasions, but I was almost certain that I would not be at the major meeting later in the year. I was on edge and withdrawn throughout the conference, and must have seemed inexcusably brusque. I could talk to no one. Feeling even more burdened by guilt, I thought how much pain and disappointment my leaving would cause these men who had always shown me friendship and ready support.

In April I faced Kathleen with my secret. Until that moment she had no inkling that I had a son, and my revelation shocked her as I knew it would. I had spent a long time agonizing about how and when to tell her. I had never spoken about the matter to anyone at all before then, but not only was it essential for me to bare my soul to Kathleen, it was also by now her right to know such an important fact about me. I should have told her much earlier. Too often in life many of us allow the coward in us to prevail. Procrastination is so very futile, however, and does not in any way lessen the shock or hurt. My greatest fear was that she would cease to love me, and her love was vital to me now. At last I was facing truth and realizing its importance.

My agonizing and fear had been foolish and needlessly exhausting. Kathleen's shock and tears evaporated quickly in her generous forgiveness, a beautiful quality of her love for which I will always be grateful. Her acceptance of my weakness and her positive attitude made me feel suddenly much more purposeful. A great weight, it seemed, had been lifted from my shoulders.

In late May I paid what was to be my final visit to the islands, to administer the Sacrament of Confirmation in the two parishes of Barra. As always, I was given a very warm welcome by the two priests, Angus MacQueen and Donald MacKay, who treated me with their normal generous hospitality. I was glad to be back on that beautiful island, but struggled with a feeling of sorrow that I could not shake off.

On a free day during my visit I had the opportunity to travel over to Uist. The sail from Eoligarry in Barra to Ludag in Uist was as enjoyable as it always was. It was a fine day and I stood at the front of the little ferry, revelling in the invigorating feel of the wind and sea on my face and gazing at the hills of Uist, a view that has always pulled at my very soul. Twice that day I would pass the island of Eriskay, and also Ghearraidh na Monaidh just below South Boisdale. Both places had been a special part of my life since early childhood. Too clearly I remembered carefree, barefoot days of happiness and thought how far away from those I was now. My roots were here, on this island of hills and machair and miles of white sand. Would I ever be able to return?

Time and circumstances were pushing me to make a decision. I no longer wanted to live with secrets. Lies wear at the spirit and damage all parts of life. The reality of my love for Kathleen clarified for me the injustice I was committing against her by continuing to keep our relationship hidden: she had the right to a committed future. And so many others were long overdue the truth. In this frame of mind I was searingly aware of the beauty of the islands, the honest warmth of the people I met and the contentment I had experienced there as a child and as an adult. It hurt so much to think that I might be saying goodbye for ever. When it was time to leave for the mainland, I did not look back.

◆

As the year progressed, Kathleen and I talked and prayed together about our situation. We could not deny what was between us. We had formed a deep relationship. Things could not go on as they were. The strain of having to hide the truth was now too much to bear and we either had to part or make our togetherness public.

We sat in my kitchen one day and reached our decision. It was a dark, comfortless room at the back of the house, not much of a place for making life-changing plans. As we sat at the old table with our cups of coffee, Kathleen spoke. 'Roddy, what are we to do?'

I put down my cup. 'Kathleen, we can't continue like this. We mustn't. Neither of us is living in the real sense!'

'We have each other,' she said, 'we're certain of that. And we have no illusions about what might happen.'

'I know too well what all of this will cost your family. We've spoken of it over and over. Whatever, we must be sure of these things. And I know what pain I'll cause my own family, and so many others. God knows we've prayed and thought about it. We want to be together, and that means we must leave. I want us to spend the rest of our days together. But what about you, Kathleen? Will it cost too much in your life?'

'Roddy, you know the answer to that very well.'

We had finally decided. It was a release. It was past time to be honest, despite the upheaval a public announcement would make. We knew we faced a mountain of problems and pain and did not make our decision lightly. My position in the Church meant that there would inevitably be a scandal and people would be deeply hurt – not only ourselves, but also our families, our friends, and the people and priests of Argyll and the Isles.

We discussed what we should do, now that we had come to a decision. I suggested that I should resign and leave the country, to be joined by Kathleen shortly afterwards. Kathleen disagreed, however, and in the end we decided that we should leave together, set up home, then inform our families first before making a public announcement. After long deliberation we decided to leave at the beginning of September when Kathleen had some holiday booked. The first practical step was to find somewhere to live, outside our home area in Scotland. Our finances were limited and Kathleen knew that it would be essential for her to find work. It was unlikely that I would find employment. The Lake District had similarities to our own part of the country and we found a suitable house to rent in Kendal. It was out of the way, but still within feasible reach of family in Scotland. Kathleen's main hope was that her family would accept her decision and that her daughter, Julie Anne, would join us.

Kathleen continued to work at the hospital, trying to act as normally as possible as we laid our plans. I carried on with my duties as bishop, relieved that the secrecy was soon to come to an end, but plagued by thoughts of how those around us would react: how much would I be hurting the priests and people of my Diocese, those I had worked with and become close to over the years? However alienated I had felt over the last few years, it was not from lack of love for the Church and people I served. As August came to an end and we made our final preparations, I was still torn, but knew we had chosen the only possible path.

◆

Secretly Kathleen began to ferry clothes and belongings down to Oban, where they were stored in one of the many empty rooms of

Bishop's House. I gradually gathered my own belongings and packed them in boxes and cases. On 1 September Kathleen drove me to Glasgow to hire a van, which I then drove to Oban as she made her way back to Fort William. The following morning I took the van to Inverlochy and we loaded it with some heavy furniture which Kathleen wished to take with her. I returned to Oban in the van and she followed in her own fully loaded car later in the day. We filled the van with as much as we could from what had already been stored in the house, but the van was too small to take it all and we knew we would have to make a second journey.

Early the next morning we set off for Kendal, leaving Kathleen's car in the garage beside the house. We arrived at 7 Mountain View shortly after lunchtime and immediately began unloading. The only suitable access was at the rear, by way of a very narrow lane, because the front entrance was on a busy main road. We unloaded and carried most things in ourselves, down the steep, overgrown back garden. However, we knew we would not manage the heavy furniture alone down the awkward slope. There were some construction workers on a nearby site and I went and asked if two of them could give us some assistance – a decision which would later rebound on us. They came willingly and were very happy with what we paid them. At last the van was unloaded. After a bite to eat, we collapsed on a mattress on the floor and slept for a few hours, knowing it all had to be done again the next day.

Once again we set off very early in the morning, arriving in Oban in the middle of a lovely sunny day. We set about loading the van with the rest of our possessions, then Kathleen began the task of tidying up that large house. The doorbell rang and when I opened it I was startled to see two ladies from Justice and Peace, Scotland, who sometime before had arranged to meet me that day. They required my signature on certain documents and had been waiting around for hours. I had completely forgotten about this and felt very embarrassed. They must have thought I looked very strange – dressed in old clothes, dusty from the baggage, dishevelled and red-eyed from lack of sleep. Hastily I explained that I was just doing some 'sorting out' and got the business over with as soon as I could.

Once the general tidying was completed I left all my keys, cheque books and cash cards on the kitchen table and my car in the garage. Having made sure that the house was secure and locked, I bade a final farewell to Oban. On this journey Kathleen drove ahead of me in her own car, fully loaded. It was very late when we arrived in Kendal and we unpacked the van in darkness, using the front door this time as the road was quiet.

The move was made. We had taken the first step and there was no going back. The next day we would have to return the van to Glasgow, then drive back to Kendal and start unpacking our new life. We were too tired that night even to finish a relaxing bottle of wine. I felt sad, relieved and apprehensive all at once, but too bone weary to sort out any of these conflicting emotions. Speechless, we fell into an exhausted sleep.

Over the next week we worked to make the house at 7 Mountain View as comfortable as possible. Everything was pretty basic, but when the table and chairs were in place and cutlery and dishes unpacked we started to feel at home. After the gruelling round trips of the previous days it was luxury to be able to stay in one place – and to be alone without the pressure of time or other duties. The next thing to do was to write to our families informing them privately of our decision. Once this had been done I would publicly resign, making my reasons known to the world.

Meanwhile, Kathleen had already applied to the local hospital for work and was waiting for the necessary forms. We set out to discover where the hospital was, where the supermarkets were, and generally explored the area. At that stage no one gave us a second glance. We already knew where the church was and went to Mass on the first Sunday. We sat at the back of the church and did not speak with the priest. I knew I would not miss my position as bishop, but immediately felt the loss of not being able to act as a priest. It would be a lasting ache, but I was particularly aware of it that first day in church – although I had already accepted my passive role as inevitable.

✦

On the morning of Saturday 14 September, I was shocked to hear my name mentioned on the radio. According to the report, I had been posted as 'missing'. Not being able to find me anywhere, members of the Diocese had become concerned and one priest had forced his way into Bishop's House, only to see the pile of cards and keys carefully left on the table. Kathleen was upstairs and I ran up to tell her what I had just heard. We stared nervously at each other. Now what would happen? For some reason it had not occurred to us that the news of our disappearance might leak out before we had announced it properly ourselves.

I would have to contact someone straight away and try to put things right before the speculation got out of hand. I dialled the number of the Catholic Press Officer, but only reached a terse answer-phone message: 'I have no idea as to the whereabouts of Bishop Wright.'

I tried Archbishop O'Brien, my Metropolitan, next and got straight through to him. As soon as he realized who was calling, he said, 'Are you resigning?'

'Yes,' I replied, and made an appointment to meet him and Cardinal Winning in Glasgow the following evening.

The next day Kathleen and I drove north once again, arriving at the Cardinal's house at about 7.00 p.m. We parked down the road out of sight and Kathleen stayed in the car while I went up to the house. Despite the circumstances, I was warmly greeted by the Cardinal. We were both quite emotional. He told me that the Sunday papers had all headlined my disappearance, were now looking for me and had all assumed that Kathleen was with me. I said immediately that this was so and I wished to write my resignation letter to the Pope. In it I set down the full reasons for my decision – my love for Kathleen and the fact that I had a son. I asked for an assurance that the full statement of my reasons would be given to the various press agencies by the Press Office. It was important to us both that there should be no more hiding, and no ambiguity to fuel useless speculation.

None of us wanted to prolong that difficult meeting. I had always liked and respected Cardinal Winning and I knew I was causing him pain. We both knew the harm my actions would bring to the Church in Scotland. He tried to persuade me to change my mind and stay, as a priest not as bishop. But I had made my decision and Kathleen was waiting outside. He understood and accepted that I wanted to make a clean break.

There was little else to discuss, so we said our goodbyes and the Cardinal kindly walked me to the gate. He is a warm-hearted man, with a genuine care for his priests. His parting comment was, 'Keep in touch. And don't do anything drastic.' I walked back to the car, relieved that the next step was over, but now worried in case there were photographers about.

We made the long journey south, arriving back in Kendal at around midnight. What would happen next? We were unsure what to expect now that we were no longer holding the strings. Our own

plans were in disarray since the news of our departure had already
been splashed across the newspapers in a riot of lurid speculation.
All we could do was to hope that the official announcement about
my leaving would put a stop to this with the plain truth. We had
no wish to be the latest tabloid scandal. All we wanted was a dignified announcement of the change in our lives and then to be left in
privacy. How naive we were! We were devastated on the Monday
when the news of my resignation from the Church was broadcast:
it was just a bald statement, no word of my love for Kathleen, no
word of the existence of my son. Why had they not done what
I asked? Now the press would be on our tail, hunting out the
'truth'. Little did we realize just how hunted we were going to feel.

The following day, Tuesday, Kathleen and I went shopping. I
remained in the car while she – very bravely in my opinion – went
into the supermarket. She returned to the car very upset. On the
newspaper rack she had seen the headline of one of the Scottish
tabloids: 'MOTHER LEAVES CHILDREN FOR BISHOP' it shouted in bold
black print. It seemed we were now public property and our feelings, and those of our families, were irrelevant.

On the Thursday evening an exclusive television interview was
given by my son's mother on the BBC news. It was sensational,
of course, an explosive 'new revelation', and opinion apparently
turned against us even more. I felt quite desperate: it was only a
'revelation' because my full statement had not been made public.
I had wanted my own explanation to be given to avoid just this
kind of excitement. Kathleen was really suffering because she was
now at the heart of a scandal in which she had played no part. We
both felt more isolated than ever that evening, but at least we were
together and supporting each other.

That Friday, 20 September, I was standing at the upstairs window looking blankly across the road. We were in a row of terraced
houses high above a very busy junction. Opposite us was a telephone kiosk and suddenly I noticed that one of the men who had
helped us carry furniture into the house was making a call. As he
spoke he was referring to the newspaper in his hand and looking
up at our house. It dawned on me – I felt it so strongly – that he
was giving information to the press, no doubt for a price.

We were just about to go out and I said, 'Kathleen, I think that
fellow is making a call about us.'

'Who?' She came over to look. 'Isn't that one of those men who
helped us move the furniture? Yes, I think you're right.'

We went out anyway and drove to Lancaster to do our shopping. Again, I remained in the car while Kathleen hurriedly bought some essentials. Once more she had to pass the newspaper rack, all editions carrying headlines about us and the fact that I had earlier fathered a son. Guessing that our movements would have to be restricted from now on, we made a plan to try and dodge any waiting media. On our return I left the car before we got to the house, carrying the shopping, and Kathleen continued up the hill to park the car some distance away. It would not be moved during the next two weeks. Unknown to us there was already a photographer in place and later we discovered that he had photographed Kathleen on her way into the house, but had missed my earlier entry.

✦

We had been right about that workman in the kiosk, and within a few hours of our return we were under siege. Both of us were afraid of what was happening. It was no longer in our control, indeed we soon realized that it was not in anyone's control. With hindsight, we can see that we went about everything in the wrong way, but at the time, with the press on our doorstep, we felt trapped and increasingly panicked. The decisions we eventually took seemed to us to offer the only way out of this trap, although in the days that followed we soon knew we had made a bad mistake. But that was to come later. Now, as the watching media began to gather outside, we decided we should just sit it out. Surely if we did not appear, did not communicate, they would eventually get bored and go away?

Kathleen was very calm, remarkably strong and positive. She collected the kettle, a jar of coffee, some biscuits and my ash tray and took them upstairs where we could sit without being glimpsed by the besiegers. But as time passed, there was within us both a fast-growing fear for our immediate future. Our own plans for how we would reveal our decision to leave Scotland and live together had been ripped out of our hands. Most people feel afraid when they know they have no control over events in their own lives and we were no different. As the numbers grew outside we prayed the rosary together, asking for God's help. Looking back today, we believe our prayers were answered. Through the whole ordeal that was to come, through the confusion, the panic, the good decisions and the bad, we were conscious of an inner strength that kept us going.

The events of the next nine days were bizarre and stressful in the extreme. At times it all felt unreal. I kept a diary of what took place, starting that Friday, partly because I could not quite believe it was actually happening. Reading it now, I can recall vividly the tension of waiting, the rush of events and our dawning realization that our 'escape' was not what had been promised.

FRIDAY 20 SEPTEMBER

At around 4.00 p.m. photographers and reporters arrived. We went into hiding within the house. At 8.00 p.m. there was a loud knock on the door. We remained hidden and alert throughout the night. Peering through a gap in the curtains upstairs we could see two cars parked across the way, men chatting on the pavement outside. They continued to knock on the back and front doors and on the windows.

SATURDAY 21 SEPTEMBER

The first knock on the door was at 8.00 a.m. Thereafter they knocked on the door every 30 minutes approximately. We noticed a letter had been pushed through the letterbox early in the morning but left it where it was. Outside, more and more press arrived, some at the front of the house and others at the rear. Outside we could hear cameras clicking, and the downstairs windows and doors continued to be knocked. Any movements downstairs required us moving on all fours. The front door was half glass and we did not wish anyone to see our movements. By midday we felt exhausted and very afraid. In the early afternoon I crept downstairs and retrieved the letter pushed through the door in the morning. It was from a Sunday tabloid paper which neither of us were accustomed to read. We discussed its contents at length, both of us quite unwilling to speak with them. The letter contained a promise to take us out of there, and even out of the country, if that was our wish, provided we agreed to give them one interview. For this one interview we would be paid £10,000. After more discussion we agreed to meet the writer. From there on our lives and decisions were no longer our own!

Mr B., the tabloid paper's reporter, got himself in along with two other colleagues. He immediately began negotiating with Kathleen using the promises clearly written in his letter. I remained upstairs at this time.

By now others were shouting and banging on the doors. After about 30 minutes of conversation, Kathleen and Mr B. came to an agreement – viz. £15,000 and help to get away from the situation. Of the money I wanted nothing and Mr B. understood this. I then came downstairs where I met him and his colleagues. They were introduced to me and from now on I call the reporter Mr H. and the photographer Billy the Camera.

We gave our interviews sitting at the top of the stairs. Immediately before this Kathleen and I had to pose, very reluctantly, for pictures. It was a terrible experience, and the first time we had ever been photographed together. During the interviews three mobile phones were constantly ringing, and also the house phone, the reporter Mr B. having already given our number to his office. The banging on the doors and the shouting continued so much that eventually I called the police. They kindly sent someone around who cleared our front door. Our three guests informed us that by now Sky TV and ITV were outside. Even amongst the crowd of locals now swelling the numbers outside were a few who shouted their obscene advice. During my interview Kathleen was busy preventing the other two snooping around the house.

Billy the Camera brought in a Chinese carry-out for himself, Mr H. and the two of us, a meal I paid for. Afterwards, Kathleen and I were told to rest in preparation for leaving. However, we found this very difficult with the noise outside, flash bulbs going off, and TV arc lights concentrating on the front of the house. Kathleen was also concerned about the antics of those left downstairs. We decided that we couldn't rest and in the dark made our way down to join them.

SUNDAY 22 SEPTEMBER

We were given 10 minutes to pack our bags, which we did in the dark. At 2 o'clock in the morning our by now 'good friends' smuggled us out in the dark and through an allotment at the back of the house. I was taken first, and 10 minutes later, Kathleen was taken out by a different route. At 4.00 a.m. we arrived in separate cars at a Manchester airport hotel. I was booked in as David Jansen ('The Fugitive'), and Kathleen was booked in as Mrs B.

Later that morning we were informed that my wish to be taken to Santander in north-west Spain, which we had discussed the previous evening, could not be granted. It seems that Bilbao Airport closes down every Sunday at 2.00 p.m.! Instead, we were going to France in a private plane and our three 'minders' were accompanying us. Again we were taken in separate cars, this time to Blackpool. They ensured we were kept apart in the separate cars during a long wait before being taken aboard a small 'twin prop.' plane which had six seats. Including the pilot, we and our three 'friends' filled it. Later, in the air, we discovered that our craft was built in 1970! Its usual runs were taking parcel post around England, and foolhardy tourists around Blackpool Tower. Our journey to Bordeaux took

over four hours, in very cramped conditions, and we arrived there about
9.00 p.m. local time. Eventually we were given a room in the local Mer-
cury Hotel. Two days had passed since the arrival of the press. We didn't
know where we were, or what was happening.

MONDAY 23 SEPTEMBER

*The following morning after breakfast the charming Mr B., of whom both
Kathleen and myself were now very suspicious, appeared with a hired
vehicle – a seven-seater Renault Espace. When we made our agreement in
Kendal on the Saturday we had no idea that we would have these three as
travelling companions. On the Sunday, when this was revealed, we were
told that we would be given complete privacy. Very rarely was that the
case. They informed us that they were there to protect us from other press
and assured us there were to be no other interviews. Oh, we were politely
asked where we wanted to go – both of us, strangers in that part of
the world, didn't know where we were! However, by this time, we knew
that everything was pre-organized and that we would be told where we
were going.*

*In our spacy Renault Espace we were taken for a long drive, eventu-
ally arriving near a little town called Castillon. It was obvious that Mr
B. had planned and chosen this location and the chateau, as he called it,
where we were to stay. Actually it was a cold, old house. Kathleen and
I rejected the invite to go for a swim or a walk. We didn't feel inclined to
relax in this way and, already, we knew that Billy the Camera would be,
as ever, vigilant. He was a Liverpudlian, charming and witty. Earlier, he
had identified with my Clydeside background but I soon knew otherwise.
The two weary 'lovers' were fast growing apart from their keepers – but
not from each other! Kathleen and myself tended now to talk about
mundane things – Celtic, Scotland (especially the Highlands) and other
generalities.*

*That evening we ate duck, Mr B. choosing the wine. He thought him-
self quite an expert on French cuisine and wines, mais oui! Actually,
Kathleen had far better knowledge of these and quietly let him know.
I enjoyed that with a little smile to myself. It soon became apparent that
our three companions were going to enjoy themselves on their expense
account! Apart from our keep we did not accept any money from them
during our stay.*

TUESDAY 24 SEPTEMBER

*After breakfast we went for a drive. It would have pleased Mr B. better if
we had gone for a swim. We drove some 20 kilometres to a little town.*

There we were left alone! 'Just take some time together. I need to go to a bank and the others have things to do,' said Mr B. Then pointing to a café opposite he suggested we meet there in half an hour.

We went for a walk, glad to be away from them, and finding a church we went in and knelt to pray. We lit candles, praying for ourselves and our families, and heard the door close. Lo and behold Mr B. appeared. He has a great interest in French churches! We immediately left and he followed us, inviting us to join Mr H. and himself at the café for a coffee. We did. Shortly afterwards we were joined by the elusive Billy the Camera.

As we sat there, not speaking, Kathleen noticed a French Telecommunications van pass where we were sitting three times before parking opposite us on the other side of the square. The driver then stood, leaning against the vehicle. He kept looking towards us. I remarked that he seemed to be watching us, to which Kathleen agreed. After a while he walked up the steps of the church. He was an obvious stranger, not knowing where the door marked 'Entrée' was situated. At this point Mr H. stopped writing the postcards he would never send and said he would investigate. He walked to the deserted van and soon returned to inform us that the man was indeed a Telecommunications employee! By this time the man had emerged to sit on a wall near the church.

Mr B. then changed the subject, telling us that there was a lovely walk by the river which he had discovered in our absence. He managed that as well as finding a bank! Once again, under his instructions, we moved. Kathleen and I were determined to walk apart because we noticed that Billy the Camera had begun disappearing. We found there was very little area to walk beside a dirty river. I sat on steps beside Kathleen. After about a minute she told me to move as she felt that Billy the Camera who, we knew, had his camera in the vehicle, might be at work. I immediately got up and walked away, sitting on my own by the water and hidden from view. Shortly afterwards I heard approaching footsteps and there was Mr H., solicitous as ever. He asked some questions to which I replied by asking if he knew what kind of ducks were in the water in front of us! Soon he realized I was not in a co-operative mood. Meanwhile, Mr B. was sitting with Kathleen praising me for being 'a man's man'. He was trying his best to get her to talk but discovered she was unco-operative.

The elusive Billy the Camera arrived with the vehicle — time to move on. When we took our seats he informed us that the 'telecom' man had gone, which was no longer of any concern to us. We drove back to the 'chateau' in silence. When we arrived there Kathleen took 'The Camera' aside and accused him of being part of a set-up regarding the Telecommunications man in the square earlier. He agreed it was staged to make us concerned that others might be looking for us! And he actually apologized to her.

The menu for the evening meal was duck or fish. This time I chose fish, which was served with the same sauce as I had with the duck the previous night. Mr H. enjoyed a full bottle of white wine, while Mr B. and Billy the Camera enjoyed two bottles of red wine. Kathleen and Roddy were not in the mood for wine. It was a rather silent meal. The atmosphere was heavy. Even Billy the Camera had little to say at the end.

WEDNESDAY 25 SEPTEMBER

We did not join the others for breakfast. Instead, I brought coffee to our room. Afterwards, although we were booked to stay there until the following day, we were informed that we were moving on. Obviously the lack of photograph opportunities and the unused swimming pool did not satisfy the journalists. Our destination now was 'a nice hotel' in a town called Albi. Mr B. knew it well. Surprise, surprise. And so we were driven there, to the Hotel La Reserve. It was nice. It had a lovely swimming pool. As always now, we were booked into one double and three single rooms. During our stay Kathleen and I would not eat in the dining room there.

After a short time Mr B. appeared and informed us we would be eating in a restaurant in Albi which he knew well. We were taken by taxi accompanied by him, the others following later. While we waited for the others to arrive he showed us the outside of the magnificent cathedral, asking us if we wanted a tour. We declined the invitation firmly. Both of us knew it would be the perfect photo-opportunity for our friend with the camera. Indeed, shortly afterwards we were joined by the other two who obviously knew where to find us.

Before going to the restaurant we went for drinks. Unsuccessfully they tried to ply us with drinks. I had two whiskies and Kathleen had a brandy. They had a couple of beers each. Then we were led to a fish restaurant, the kind that has fish nets and creels as decor, but many miles away from the sea. Billy the Camera made an embarrassing fuss over the lack of raw garlic for his meal. Kathleen and I said very little during that meal. While we were at the table Kathleen noticed that a red light was flashing in Mr B.'s pocket. She turned to him and said, 'You can switch that thing off!' Without any embarrassment he pretended to do so. Our conversation was over. Kathleen later informed me that he had not switched his tape recorder off. We then left them there and returned to our hotel by taxi. The three of them headed off for a night on the town, no doubt courtesy of their employers.

THURSDAY 26 SEPTEMBER

We had coffee in our room in the morning which I fetched from the dining room. There was no sign of the others, who were obviously having a long lie! We got a taxi to town where we found a bank, our first opportunity since arriving in France. With some money of our own we bought a phonecard. Kathleen wanted to speak with her lawyer in Fort William because she had left certain matters in her care, like payment of bills and such things. The call was useful in another way because she informed Kathleen of what was being said in the papers and of the activities of the press in Fort William. The lawyer was very valuable because she was our only contact back home. From her we discovered what the tabloid paper now 'caring' for us had written the previous weekend. Our companions had never mentioned their reporting of things and would have been very annoyed to discover that we knew anything. During that conversation Kathleen informed the lawyer that we were intent on escaping from our 'keepers'.

We then ate lunch in a café, returning to the hotel in the afternoon. On our return we discovered that Mr H. was packed and ready to leave for Manchester. His excuse was that he had a holiday planned in Torremolinos with some pub friends. The atmosphere between us all was now decidedly cooler. We declined the invitation to eat that night.

FRIDAY 27 SEPTEMBER

Again, for breakfast, we remained in our room. I brought some coffee up from the dining room. Shortly afterwards there was a knock at the door and Mr B. entered. He was going to Toulouse to arrange travel home. There he would find out what flights were possible for us the following week to Manchester, on Tuesday or Wednesday. However, he needed our passports to obtain the tickets. Kathleen was firmly against this but I relented. Of course this meant that we had no way of making our escape that day.

Left to keep an eye on us was Billy the Camera. Without his knowing we got a taxi into town where I made enquiries about bus travel to Santander. I was informed that a bus left Toulouse at 10.00 p.m. on Saturday, arriving in Santander at 5.30 a.m. on Sunday. We decided to travel in this way. There were trains regularly to Toulouse from the station just down the road.

On our return to the Hotel La Reserve we discovered Mr B. had returned from Toulouse. We were just in our room when he appeared at the door with the information that, as yet, he hadn't any tickets. He wanted to know if we wished to travel back via London or Manchester.

Kathleen asked why he had not made the reservations as he had intended earlier in the day. Wasn't that why he needed the passports? Mr B. replied that the travel arrangements could be made in a local agency in Albi, which we had known from the beginning. He then said that he would make the arrangements for us to fly to Manchester on the Sunday. No doubt his employers had told him during his last conversation that this was what he should organize. But we were adamant that we would only travel back later in the week. We were not willing to fly into hordes of waiting press on the Sunday. Mr B. relented, saying he would make the arrangements the following morning, which was Saturday. He left the room.

We decided to eat on our own that night, again at our own expense. As we left the hotel for the waiting taxi Mr B. met us in the foyer, casually dressed and obviously eating in the hotel. He was waiting for Billy the Camera and could not hide his surprise at our intentions to dine elsewhere.

The taxi driver took us to a quiet little Thai restaurant. We had just completed our second course when Kathleen saw Mr B. come out of a taxi just opposite. He was talking with a swarthy fellow in a green vest. Then Billy the Camera appeared from the taxi, giving this fellow what looked like sheets of paper. Kathleen was convinced that these were photographs of us. Once more the presence of these gentlemen spoiled our meal. The three of them looked around and then disappeared.

Just as we were finishing our coffee Kathleen, who was able from her seat to see what was happening in the street outside, saw Mr B. pass the window. Immediately afterwards the man in the green vest entered the restaurant. Kathleen realized what was happening – he had been sent in to have a good look at us. After making enquiries about the availability of a table he turned to leave, giving me a long hard stare. I returned his stare fully. As he left I turned and pulled back the lace curtain on the window and there was The Camera making his approach to rendezvous with the man and Mr B. I stood up and gave him a 'thumbs-up' sign and waved, letting him know of my awareness of the situation. Obviously, with Mr H. gone, and Billy the Camera about to leave, Mr B. would need some assistance in keeping tabs on the two of us! We returned to the hotel by taxi.

SATURDAY 28 SEPTEMBER
Early on Saturday morning I went downstairs and brought some coffee to our room. Our two remaining companions had not appeared for breakfast. Later I returned downstairs to find Billy the Camera staring at a cup of coffee, looking very hungover. In reply to my question he replied

that Mr B. was out on business. I patted him on the head saying, 'Feeling rough? Don't worry, you'll feel better soon!' About 11 o'clock Kathleen met Mr B. in the foyer, his suit in a dishevelled state, obviously hungover and smelling of stale drink. She approached him and demanded our passports. He said he would return them later with our air tickets.

We then called a taxi, went into Albi, found out where the bus and railway stations were situated, had a cup of coffee and returned by taxi to the hotel.

A fresher-looking Mr B. met us at the desk downstairs. Obviously he had been looking for us and making enquiries of the receptionist. A short time before he had taken Billy the Camera to the station to catch a train for Toulouse airport. He produced tickets for a flight to Manchester on the Sunday. We refused them, saying that we would not return until Tuesday or Wednesday. However, he did, reluctantly, return our passports. About an hour later he came to our room with tickets for a flight to Manchester on the Tuesday. We took these, knowing that we would never use them, and promised to meet him later.

Kathleen then packed our bags. From our balcony I could see Mr B. sitting by the swimming pool reading a book. I went downstairs and joined him, speaking of generalities. He made no mention of their strange behaviour the previous night. During this conversation Kathleen took her bag downstairs, slipped unnoticed past the desk, and hid it in bushes close to the road. She then returned to the room and spoke from the balcony to me below. This was a signal that she had managed to remove her bag. She then phoned a taxi. As she did this I took my bag downstairs, hiding it in the bushes. When I returned to our room Kathleen left, taking her jacket and handbag. She recovered her bag from the bushes and took up a position outside the main gate. I followed five minutes later and, having collected my bag, joined her outside where we were hidden from view. There we stood, for what seemed an eternity, until the taxi came.

The time was now 4.45 p.m. We were deposited at Albi railway station where we bought two single tickets on the 5.17 train to Toulouse. We arrived there almost two hours later, only to discover that we could not travel to Santander that weekend after all. On further enquiry we found out that a bus left for Andorra at 8.00 a.m. on Sunday. We found terrible accommodation close to the bus station and after eating a snack in a nearby café we tried to get some sleep.

SUNDAY 29 SEPTEMBER
After a sleepless night we rose early and were in the bus station half an hour before we were due to leave. Shortly after 8 o'clock we were on the

road to Andorra. Until that time we had been nervous because we thought Mr B., left behind in Albi, might have tried to find our whereabouts.

I enjoyed the journey through the Pyrenees with such beautiful scenery all around. We arrived in Andorra shortly before midday and made our way to the Tourist Information Centre, where we were given addresses for self-catering holiday flats. I hailed a taxi and gave the driver the address of a block of flats where there were vacancies. Later we discovered that he managed to deliver us to an address about 200 yards from the tourist office by driving around the town! When we eventually reached there a notice on the door informed us that the caretaker would be absent until 4.00 p.m.

Dragging our weary bodies and suitcases, we made our way to a family-run restaurant where we enjoyed our first real meal for a long time – paella. On the table was a jug of wine which the waiter filled as we drank. The wine went straight to our heads and by the time we had eaten our meal we were both quite tipsy! We walked back to the flats and, thankfully, found the caretaker had returned. The accommodation had all the necessary amenities, including a television set, and looked comfortable. We paid a week's rent. In a very real way we felt free again and in control of our own movements.

◆

Andorra is picturesque and very compact. It attracts visitors not only because of the scenery but also because of its duty-free facilities. On the Monday morning after our arrival we went shopping in a nearby supermarket. Kathleen was delighted to find such variety and at such reasonable prices. She really enjoys cooking and we returned home with all that she needed to produce some lovely meals. It was a relief to be doing something so simple and normal. We then went for a walk to discover this little town, our temporary home. It was great to walk freely once more, and we did plenty of window shopping, marvelling at the number of jewellery shops, fashion stores and perfumeries. After the tension of the previous week we managed to relax a little in this lovely place.

Close to our flat was a little tobacco and newspaper kiosk. Here we purchased a phonecard and Kathleen called her lawyer in Fort William. She was able to inform us that the 'friend' we had left in Albi had written another front-page 'exclusive' in his tabloid. Of course, the agreement had been that they would only run one such article, which they had done on the previous Sunday. However, we had been aware of their intentions from the moment we left Britain and had told them nothing, taking steps to ensure they had few opportunities to take photographs. From what the lawyer told Kathleen it was obvious that we had been quite successful. Billy the Camera must have been very frustrated! They did publish a poor picture of us walking down some street, but it could have been anywhere. The highlight of their revelations was a claim by them that I preferred Celtic football club and whisky to being a bishop. It is remarkable what money these people can spend on nothing. The next day we wondered if Mr B. was with other journalists vainly awaiting our arrival at Manchester airport.

On the Wednesday, while we were out walking, Kathleen decided to phone her lawyer again for an update on the situation and I went to the little kiosk to buy a phonecard. As the man was serving another customer I looked around at the newspapers and magazines. Right in front of the counter was a pile of magazines showing a full-colour picture of myself and Kathleen on the front cover. My heart sank. Why was anybody interested here? Was nowhere safe?

Quickly making my purchase, I went out to where Kathleen was standing. 'I've just seen our picture. Some magazine called *El Pronto*, I think.'

'What? Oh no. We just can't get away from them, Roddy.'

We felt vulnerable all over again and slowly made our way over to the telephone and called Kathleen's lawyer. As they spoke I remained close by and very soon could see a look of disbelief on Kathleen's face. I joined her in the small space of the kiosk, but of course could only follow Kathleen's side of the conversation. The lawyer had been approached by a television company and a Scottish Sunday tabloid wanting to arrange a deal with us; for exclusive interviews they would fly us home secretly and safely and pay us a sum of £10,000.

This was the last thing we wanted. Having given the lawyer our firm refusal of such a proposal, Kathleen replaced the receiver and we walked tiredly back to the flat. We were now, we felt, completely alone and that thought weighed heavy on us.

During the evening we decided to watch television, flicking around the channels in the hope of finding something we might understand. Suddenly, there on the screen was our own picture. The commentator was speaking Spanish so he could have been saying anything. There and then we decided we must return home as soon as possible. There was obviously no escape and it seemed somehow better to be facing whatever difficulties were at home rather than staying out on a limb like this. We went to the Tourist Office the following morning and made enquiries about bus services to France and the timetable of trains to Paris. It was time to move again.

✦

On the Friday evening, as dusk settled on the Pyrenees, we boarded a bus which took us back along the scenic route we had admired on the previous Sunday. Just over the border we disembarked at a very quiet little station where we could join the night train to Paris. After a wait of almost an hour, by which time we were feeling quite chilled in the cold air, the train arrived. We were happy to find the compartment quiet and warm. Making ourselves comfortable, we looked forward to getting some sleep. Unfortunately, our first stop was Toulouse, where our comfort and quietness were quick to disappear. The train was boarded by a crowd of young soldiers obviously going on leave. In their neat uniforms and with their closely cropped hair, they looked smart and disciplined: they were anything but. As the beer went down they became louder and the smoke became thicker. They crowded into our carriage and one of them jumped on a seat and began dismantling some of the lights. By this stage my nerves were taut and my temper short! When this young man began vandalizing the compartment Kathleen had to restrain me as I began to remonstrate. I have never accepted needless vandalism. On this occasion, however, I took Kathleen's advice and stayed silent. As the night progressed they became quieter and we got some peace, but our journey to Paris felt long and very tiring. Once there we had some coffee and croissants in a little restaurant before making our way to the Eurotunnel terminus to board the train for London Waterloo.

We were both surprised by the speed at which we travelled in very comfortable conditions. On arrival at Waterloo, not wishing to hang around, we quickly took a taxi to Euston where we could board a northbound train. Here, in a station frequented by fellow Scots, we felt suddenly very exposed and vulnerable. Such fear was groundless, of course. Most people in the railway station are intent on catching a train, not spotting 'wanted' faces! But that is how we felt – like fugitives.

The first train north was to Carlisle, which pleased us as there were unlikely to be many Scots aboard. We settled ourselves in a quiet carriage, a surprise on a Saturday afternoon, and the journey passed without incident until we arrived at Preston. Here we were joined by some Scots, an old couple and a younger woman. They were obviously under the influence of alcohol and continued to drink from cans and a half bottle of spirits. They were facing me and I laid my head on my arms on the table in front of me in the hope that they would not recognize me. I think they were actually quite oblivious. Listening to their loud conversation, so completely divorced from our own problems, I began to giggle for no reason. I could not help myself: nerves and tiredness were taking over. Kathleen at this point was much calmer.

'It's a bloody disgrace,' the older woman was saying. 'Ah mean, who wants tae take a bus fae Carlisle tae Glesga. Know whit ah mean? Ah'm goin' tae write tae them. Ah mean, we bought tickets tae Glesga. It's no oor fault if there's somethin' wrang wae the rails!'

'Aye. You're dead right, so ye are,' said the younger woman. 'It's a bloody inconvenience. It'll be midnight afore we're hame. Eh, paw, naw, naw, ye put it in your ear!' This last sentence was addressed to the old man, who was obviously very pleased with the Walkman he had bought during his holiday but could not work out how to use it.

'Whit?'

'Ye put it in your EAR! Aye, yer EAR!'

'He cannae hear you,' said the older woman. 'Jist let him play wae it. Here, gie's the bottle. Anyway, ah'm gonnae write an official complaint. Naebody does this tae me – naebody...' I chuckled on, quietly. It was a pleasant relief to hear Glaswegian voices again, and they did not care who we were at all.

As the train approached Oxenholme Station in Kendal, Kathleen and I collected our luggage, glad to be near home. We were exhausted, having been travelling for 30 hours. We were the only passengers leaving the train. Ahead of us I noticed a man watching each coach of the train as it pulled out of the station. It did not strike me as odd until he turned and looked at us, and then hurried out of the station. What now? When we got outside there were two taxis awaiting fares. I moved to the leading one, but Kathleen said, 'No, Roddy. We'll take this one,' and walked to the second. The driver was the man who had been watching the train so closely a few moments ago. He seemed surprised as we opened the rear door of his car, clearly expecting us to take the other taxi. I said briefly,

'Mountain View please,' and we spoke very little on the journey. I asked him to stop beyond the house, not wishing to give the exact address.

As we climbed the steps to the front door we were both wondering what would be waiting for us inside. It was just as we had left it two weeks earlier, cold and dark, with a makeshift curtain still covering the window. In the kitchen were some unwashed dishes and a carton of sour milk. Behind the front door was a pile of mail which we brought through to our sitting room. My heart sank at the sight of so many letters, and I expected all of them to be hostile. Surprisingly, most were supportive and some were kind and understanding. Of course, others were condemnatory and a few were downright vicious. Somebody wrote anonymously from Glasgow threatening to bomb us into eternity, and somebody from Liverpool, also anonymous, promised to shoot us both. Nonetheless, our hearts were lifted by the number of supportive and forgiving letters.

As we were reading the letters and drinking black coffee, there was a sharp knock on the door. We had been home for about 20 minutes. The press! It was as if we had never gone away. We looked at each other and, as I switched off the light, Kathleen said, 'I was right. The taxi driver.' She had known instinctively that he was looking for us, and had insisted on using his taxi so that he could not call the press immediately. Instead, he had to delay his call at least until he had delivered us home. The driver confirmed this the following evening on the television news and no doubt enjoyed his 30 pieces. We had travelled unnoticed from Andorra, through France, through England, but in the darkness of Oxenholme Station someone had been waiting and watching. Weary to the very soul, we made our way to bed in the darkness. The only food in the house was a packet of stale Ryvita and a jar of coffee.

◆

In the morning the first knock on the door was at 7.30. We had decided not to give ourselves away if we could possibly help it. The curtains had remained closed since our previous departure, and on my knees I peered out from the side. Across the road, parked on yellow lines, were two cars. On the pavement a little group, some with the inevitable cameras slung over their shoulders, were talking with each other as they looked across at our house. I just said to Kathleen, 'They're gathering again.' Quietly we washed and changed into fresh clothes.

Having taken the kettle, the coffee and the stale Ryvita upstairs, we prepared once again to camp there. The front door was rapped with regularity. Soon we heard the letters being pushed through the letterbox. We left them lying on the floor. Occasionally some-one would shout through the letterbox, giving his name and the tabloid he represented. Outside the numbers were increasing, some of them locals just glad to have something to do on a quiet Sunday in October. The passing traffic moved slowly as people gaped up at 7 Mountain View. We heard a few of them shout at the gathering press, 'Leave them alone!' Below our window I could hear quite clearly our next-door neighbour being interviewed by a woman reporter, but there was little information to give. For part of the morning Kathleen and I passed the time by doing crosswords. The black coffee began to taste sour in our mouths.

By the middle of the day we knew we could not continue, despite our resolution not to give ourselves away. The incessant knocking, the constant noise, and the sight of so many people gath-ered on all sides of us, had once again brought on an acute sense of isolation and fear. Eventually Kathleen spoke. 'Roddy, we'll have to do something. We can't go on like this!'

'I know, Kathleen. They won't go away. I'm so sorry that you have to go through this.'

'We're together and that's all I want,' she told me. 'Whatever lies ahead we go through it together. I love you.'

'I love you, Kathleen. They can't destroy that.'

I kissed her and held her close, drawing strength from her. Then I crept downstairs and collected our mail. Very few people have so many letters delivered on a Sunday. Amongst them I found an invitation from *The Herald*, a Scottish broadsheet. Another was addressed to Kathleen, asking if she would be willing to be inter-viewed 'woman to woman' for the *Daily Mail*. After some thought, and because we had to decide one way or another, we agreed we would speak to both *The Herald* and the Scottish edition of the *Mail*.

Both letters contained mobile phone numbers. I called *The Her-ald* and asked to speak with Ron McKenna, whose name was in the letter. 'Oh, he isn't here at the moment,' said a rather bored voice. 'Can I take a message?'

'This is Roddy Wright. I'd like to speak with him.'

'Oh, really. *Really*! Eh...'

'Look, take this number down. Tell him I want to speak with him soon.' Whoever had answered my call was obviously very surprised and rang off with some excitement.

Kathleen reached the woman from the *Mail* immediately. They agreed to meet, but Kathleen stipulated she would call back with a time later. Ron McKenna rang shortly after that. I told him I would give him the interview he had requested, but he was clearly disappointed when I told him that the *Mail* would be there also, interviewing Kathleen: we were denying him his exclusive, and perhaps he already suspected that the *Mail* reporter would not play fair. Nonetheless, he agreed to contact the woman reporter and then call us back. A few minutes later he was back on the phone, asking me to be ready to open the door for him and the woman in five minutes' time. I must open immediately, he warned me, because others might try and enter at the same time. How right he was!

As soon as Ron McKenna knocked on the door and shouted his name, I opened it. He came in quickly, but then there was a rush of bodies trying to follow. With his help I tried to close the door, but the weight of bodies on the other side was too much and it remained ajar as, with all our strength, the two of us tried to keep the pack at bay. The woman reporter was caught up in the melee but we managed to squeeze her in eventually. She was petrified and ran straight up the stairs. It was frightening for all of us inside the house, and the shouting and cursing had to be heard to be believed. I called to Kathleen to ring the police, which she did immediately. Meanwhile we just tried to keep the door from opening further. A pane of glass on the door cracked, fragments of glass falling on the carpet. Fortunately the police arrived very soon and the mob – for that is how they behaved – relented and we were able to close and lock the door. We were very shaken. Even the two journalists were shocked by the behaviour of their colleagues. I just found myself toweringly angry.

Once calm had returned, introductions were made and we asked if one of them could bring some food. The door was now clear as the police had ordered the others right back to the street. The *Herald* photographer was on his way, so Ron McKenna talked to him on the mobile and asked him to bring us some bread and milk. When he arrived we had some proper coffee and fresh bread, our first real bite to eat in 24 hours.

The journalists had their work to do and a deadline to meet, so we got on with the job. The photographer did his work first. This was something we both found difficult and we were happy when he declared himself satisfied. He then set off for Glasgow and we were told that Ian Wilson, the Chief Reporter on *The Herald*, was on his way south and would be with us soon.

Kathleen took the woman reporter upstairs to give her interview. I remained downstairs with Ron McKenna, and found the interview much easier to give than on the previous occasion. To my relief, Kathleen told me afterwards that she had also found it easier than before. The interviews were over and we were just chatting when Ian Wilson rang Ron to say he had just parked his car and would be with us in a short time. Ron went to the door and waited there, ready to open it as soon as Ian arrived. There was no stampede this time. Once Ian was with us, the two other reporters left to return to their hotels and send their interview material to their respective editors. No money at all was involved in either of these interviews.

Both of us were quite relaxed with Ian Wilson. He seemed like a man we could trust, gave us good advice, and stayed on to help even after *The Herald* had what it wanted. From then on he proved to be an important support to us as we faced the media. The pack outside had quietened down considerably although they had not gone away. They knew we had spoken to the two newspapers, so they had lost that part of the game. They would not leave, however, until we had spoken to all of them. A note came through the door to this effect. It was not over yet, then. There was more for us to do before we could hope to be left alone.

When the two journalists came back, having sent off their copy, they brought a Chinese meal which we were happy to share with them. By now it was dark. Kathleen and I knew that by then our interviews were already being printed in the next day's first editions. Soon after he returned, Ron McKenna asked to speak privately with me. I joined him in the next room, and he told me we should be careful what we said because the woman journalist was recording the conversation. Not again, I thought. For the remainder of the time she was in the house I watched my words.

We discussed how we should deal with the still-waiting press. We knew we would not be able to speak with them until the following day after *The Herald* and the *Mail* were on the streets. I suggested that we do it late morning because I wanted time to write out my statement. With that agreed, the two journalists left for their hotels, but Ian Wilson kindly stayed with us that night. He was particularly helpful to me as we prepared a draft statement for me to read to the media the following day. I made a bed on the floor for him and we all retired for the night. The crowd outside had thinned considerably, preferring the lure of the local hostelries to a cold wait in the dark. A fair number stayed around, though, vigilant as ever. Perhaps they thought we might escape again.

✦

We rose early that Monday morning and, looking out, I could see that a number of the journalists and photographers had done the same. One of them had already procured a copy of that day's *Daily Mail*, which he put through the door. A picture of Kathleen was at the top of the front page, advertising the 'exclusive interview' on the Features page inside. After reading it Kathleen was upset and angry. What had been given out as a 'woman-to-woman' interview read very differently. Indeed, much of what was written was, with a caustic slant, about me. My reasonable smoking habit had turned into chain smoking. Apparently I was always touching Kathleen whenever I passed her. On the mantelpiece in a room upstairs were a bottle of whisky and a bottle of brandy, both partially consumed, which had been there since we left for France two weeks previously. This reporter wrote as if we had been guzzling down the booze while she was there. She had clearly been snooping around – without our permission – in a house which had not been inhabited for two weeks. Little of the interview giving Kathleen's view was in print.

Shortly after we had finished reading, the writer of this ridiculous article arrived. She had brought some bacon and sausages, for which we paid. That was thoughtful of her, but Kathleen tackled her immediately about the article. She had not expected this and looked very surprised that we already knew what the article said. She had not brought a copy with her. Flustered, she laid the blame on her editor, saying he had rewritten some of the article. Kathleen made her own view very clear and the woman was certainly embarrassed.

By this time the crowd outside was growing again and we agreed to face them all at midday. Ian thought we would need that time to prepare my final statement. He and I went into the front room with the draft from the night before and set to work. Using my typewriter he wrote out everything that I wanted mentioned in the statement. We worked over it together until I was happy with what had been produced. He is a professional and I am still grateful for his assistance that day. I wanted the statement to be absolutely clear, and began by apologizing to the Catholic Church, especially the priests and people of Argyll and the Isles, to our families and to all our friends for the hurt our decision had caused. I proclaimed my love for Kathleen and stated that we hoped to marry when that was possible.

Ron then informed the waiting media that we would meet them at midday. Ian phoned the police to explain our intentions. We had decided to meet the press at the back of the house, which pleased the police because it would leave the roads in front less congested. They promised to be on hand to control matters, and we were relieved. They had been very supportive throughout the siege.

We drank some more coffee and waited for high noon. Kathleen and I learned from the others what had been written during our absence from the country. Ian said that he could not recall a story running for so long with such intensity. I learned of the supposed statement of one of the priests in Oban who had branded me 'a Judas'. The MP Ann Widdecombe had also entered the fray, demanding my excommunication. This was in response to a report that Kathleen and I had received £500,000 – or was it £300,000? – from the Sunday tabloid which had taken us to France. This was so ridiculous that I found it difficult to believe anyone would think it was true. In fact we had received nothing and were out of pocket by £2,000 because of our refusal to co-operate with the tabloid journalists in France.

At midday Kathleen and I emerged into daylight for the first time in several days. We came through the back door and walked to the top end of the sloping garden. Both of us were shocked by the number of media people present, even though we had watched them all crowding the street on previous days. Shortly before leaving the house I had noticed a large BBC van parked on the pavement opposite the house – everyone was here! They had taken up positions in the lane at the back and in the two neighbouring gardens. The flashing and clicking of cameras greeted us as we walked, in what was an otherwise eerie silence, to a point near the top of the garden. They could all see and hear us from there. The ground was a bit rough and we chose our steps gingerly. Throughout I held Kathleen's hand, a simple reassurance to us both.

I read my statement, aware of the faces all around us, in what was the most nerve-wracking moment of our lives. Afterwards

I answered a number of questions, and Kathleen replied when appropriate. I was so proud of her because I had been accustomed to public speaking for most of my life (although nothing of this intensity), which of course she was not.

Towards the end of the questioning one gentleman asked, 'Why did you choose Kendal?'

'Because we thought it was a quiet place!' I gave this reply with a wry smile for the 300-plus representatives of the British media crammed into the small gardens. At an agreed signal from Ron, I thanked them all, asking them to give us and our neighbours some peace now.

We made it back to the house and I flopped into a chair. I kissed Kathleen, full of admiration for the way she had carried herself. We both felt completely drained. Ron switched on the television and there in front of us was the scene of just minutes ago. They had already edited my statement, obviously omitting what they regarded as unimportant – but I should have expected that. Ever since then Kathleen and I cannot watch the BBC news, or *News at Ten*, without remembering our own faces staring back at us from above the presenter's head. The *Mail* journalist left soon afterwards, but Ian Wilson and Ron McKenna stayed until they judged that peace had returned to Mountain View and only a few stragglers remained, cameras slung over their shoulders. We said our good-byes to them, expressing our gratitude for the way they had treated us, and for their support and direction throughout the last couple of days. It seemed much longer than that.

Finally we were alone. Perhaps the worst was over. Looking out of the upstairs window, however, I was dismayed to see that people in passing cars were craning their necks as they stared at our house. For both of us, so private in our own lives, it was very diffi-cult to accept. I would never have got through this stressful time without Kathleen's strength of mind and support. She was still remarkably calm, and that steadied me. We prayed the rosary together every day, and that habit has stayed with us into more peaceful times, a vital part of our lives.

10

✦

AFTERMATH

IN THE SILENCE after all the journalists had gone we just sat looking at each other, exhausted. We jumped when someone started knocking on the door. Not again! We let them knock until eventually they walked away. Later I discovered that it was my sister Effie and a cousin who had travelled from Glasgow to speak with me. Unfortunately, we had presumed that it was yet another media hound and they did not try to tell us otherwise.

We went round opening curtains and windows, and it was a relief to allow air and light back into our lives. The previous three weeks had been so unreal. All we wanted was a return to some kind of normality.

Amongst the mail we had opened on our arrival that Saturday night was a letter from one of Kathleen's family. It was friendly in tone and asked her to get in contact as soon as possible. But it also gave us a distressing glimpse of the pressure they had been put under in our absence. A daily tabloid had approached them with an offer to give us and them a holiday in Dublin with an open cheque at our disposal. Dismayed by this news, we were uplifted by the letter nevertheless, because it was the first contact with Kathleen's family. Throughout those weeks when it had not been possible to explain ourselves, we had worried about our loved ones – afraid of all the publicity and harassment they might be receiving, and also afraid that the hurt would be too much, especially for Kathleen's children.

The following day Kathleen decided she must pluck up the courage to make contact with Stephen, the oldest of her children. She was naturally very apprehensive but need not have been so worried. Stephen answered the phone and greeted her warmly and happily. He told her how worried he had been, only concerned for her welfare. Before my eyes Kathleen visibly relaxed during the conversation. It meant so much to her to be back in contact with her children. Her younger son Donald and her daughter, Julie Anne, were living with their father at this stage. All three children had managed to avoid the prying press through the clamour of recent weeks, a remarkable achievement for these young people. Stephen told Kathleen that her brother had taken her mother Theresa to the south of Scotland, where she was living with her sister, in the hope that the media would not be able to bother her there. During that phone call Stephen assured us that he only wanted us to be left alone to live our lives and be happy. Kathleen and I just felt humble and very grateful for that.

The next evening, again apprehensively, Kathleen phoned her mother. Theresa was marvellous, and chatted away as if they had only spoken the day before. She was just so happy to hear her daughter was safe. 'But Kathleen,' she said, 'why didn't you tell me? I wouldn't have told anyone!' That conversation helped us both, encouraging and strengthening us in a way that words cannot describe. A mother's love is indeed a blessing.

After that call to her mother, Kathleen phoned her sisters, apologizing for all the trouble our departure had brought them. They told us that after the initial shock of our leaving they were worried in case we were in danger, not knowing where we were or what was happening. Certain that we were together, they had contacted the Church authorities, Bishop's House had been searched and we were posted as 'missing', kicking off the media frenzy. Both of us are still very embarrassed by the upheaval caused to our families. Speaking to Kathleen's sister that week I accepted the blame, because it had been my intention to make the announcement myself once we were safely away. Caught off balance when the media broke the news instead, I then handled everything wrongly – 'back to front' was how I described it at the time. I cannot emphasize enough how the supportive reaction and understanding of Kathleen's family lifted our hearts when she first spoke with them.

✦

During that week after our television appearance more letters arrived. Most of them were supportive and included one from a priest of the Diocese which touched me deeply. Learning of my whereabouts through press reports he had driven south to see me, but had not been able to get near the house because of the crush of media people. Almost daily there were invitations to appear on television shows and documentaries, or on radio programmes to which I had often listened. There were even invitations from German and Irish television, as well as the usual magazines and newspapers. In most cases money was dangled before me as a carrot. Then, as ever since, I have politely declined such invitations, no matter the sums of money mentioned. The last interview of any kind that I gave before writing this book was the appearance in the back garden on Monday 7 October 1996 (despite two newspapers claiming otherwise).

It was still difficult to leave the house, because as soon as we opened the door passing motorists would stare at us. During the day there was a regular queue of cars outside, moving slowly because of the busy junction between Queen's Road and Windermere Road. Outside our house we had to descend some steps to the road below, in full view of everyone. There was no parking space nearby and we had to park further up Queen's Road or across the main road in Kendal Green. We felt we were running a gauntlet whenever we left the house. I soon learned not to look at the people or cars and to ignore the curious stares and pointing fingers.

We were very fortunate indeed to have such good and patient neighbours, despite the upheaval we had brought to their lives. Throughout our time there they were friendly and understanding. Indeed, when journalists arrived at their doors they were generally supportive by refusing to speak with them.

For months afterwards I never saw the inside of a store. I would remain in the car while Kathleen went round the shop and joined the queue at the cash desk. If we had gone in together we would have been recognized instantly. The only shop I visited regularly was the little corner shop where I had ordered *The Herald* to be collected daily. It had been a favourite of mine for its sports page and the crossword, and now we had respect for its journalists. I often managed to finish the crossword in a car park while poor Kathleen was shopping.

Within that first week of normality Kathleen received from the Health Trust the application forms for work as a Nursing Assistant in the local hospital. She immediately wrote to Sister Pat McAuslan, who was in charge of the Geriatric Ward in Fort William where Kathleen had last worked. Although her letter was mainly a request for a reference, she also apologized for any hurt or problems caused by her sudden departure. The reply came by return of post, assuring her of a reference and wishing her well in every way. Pat also told her that none of the staff had spoken to the press despite constant requests. It was from such people as these that Kathleen received much encouragement during those early days.

◆

One day I received a telephone call from my sister Effie. It was a difficult conversation which lasted more than an hour. For most of that time I just listened. From the beginning I had known I would cause much distress and hurt, a fact that continues to make me sad. My sister ended the call by saying she was coming to see me. I told her she would be most welcome and we agreed she would come two days later. I was very nervous during those days in anticipation of the meeting.

On the day we managed to make our humble abode look quite attractive. Kathleen prepared food, as only she can, and we anxiously awaited Effie's arrival. I stood in the front room, where we had temporarily stored some furniture, and watched until I saw her coming. She was accompanied by a cousin. Opening the door, I embraced them both. That was the last sign of warmth to be experienced during their stay. Effie refused to shake Kathleen's hand, saying she had only come to speak with me. This was very hurtful to us both. Diplomatically, and because she wanted me to be able to spend time with my sister, Kathleen withdrew upstairs.

When we were alone Effie poured out her heart: I had betrayed the Church; I was bringing shame on the family and on our dead parents. She needed to give vent to her anger, and I found it very painful as I listened to the hurt, the disappointment and the accusations. I love Effie, I understand her hurt and I am deeply sorry for the distress I have caused. Nothing I said was of help that day. Once she understood that I had chosen to live with Kathleen because I love her, she left with my cousin. It is painful even to think about that meeting, let alone write about it.

◆

Kathleen was determined to find work and, having made one application, also applied to the Mental Health Trust who have a Psychiatric Unit in the local hospital. Within a matter of days she received invitations to interviews with both Trusts, both taking place in early November. This was positive news and gave us both a welcome boost. Meanwhile, Kathleen's family were asking us to return to Scotland for a visit. Very naturally they wanted to see her and spend time together, but we foresaw difficulties. The job interviews were to take place in two weeks' time, and how could we travel to Fort William with so much press interest in just such a visit? The train was too public, and no doubt Kathleen's car would be recognized.

Kathleen's family came to the rescue. Her sister Anne's daughter lived in Grimsby where she was a teacher. The half-term holiday was beginning the following Friday and Michelle and her boyfriend arranged to come across to Kendal and take us up to Scotland that Friday night.

Michelle and her boyfriend arrived at about 7.00 p.m. We left shortly afterwards and drove north in darkness and rain. Just south of Carlisle our young driver skilfully avoided a crash when very suddenly we found ourselves just behind a recent pile-up. I certainly woke up from my snooze, and all of us received a jolt and a fright. All was well, however, and once past Glasgow Kathleen and I were in familiar territory, well-loved landmarks obvious even in the darkness. This was especially true going through Glencoe and Ballachulish and over the bridge to Onich. For much of the journey I held Kathleen's hand, knowing that she was excited but nervous about meeting her family. I too was apprehensive. Although I knew all of them, our meetings had taken place when I was a priest in their parish or during my time as bishop. How would they react to me now?

It was after midnight when we arrived at Kathleen's sister's house. I remained in the car at first, allowing Kathleen and Michelle time to meet everyone – we could see by the cars parked at the house that most of the family were there. When I did go in I found them all in the kitchen, hugging Kathleen in turns, the atmosphere very emotional. Kathleen's longest embrace was for her two sons, Stephen and Donald. I stood quietly by the door, shaking the hands of those closest to me. Stephen came across to me and shook my hand warmly, which meant a great deal. Donald, at this stage, did not look in my direction, but I understood. In his mind I had taken his mother from him.

When we all settled down around the table Kathleen and I were plied with questions, all natural and proper. Kathleen's sister-in-law did grill me much more than the others! Michelle and her boyfriend soon left with Anne, then suddenly Donald came across and shook my hand, a gesture I appreciated very much. He said he intended staying with a friend nearby, but I sensed he might be going to town beforehand. We then relaxed with a drink and it was past 2.00 a.m. before we retired to bed.

Despite going to bed so late, Kathleen and I woke and rose early. As we relaxed in the kitchen there was a loud knock on the door which Kathleen's sister answered. It was the press – at 8 a.m. on a Saturday. The reporter, from a Scottish tabloid, said he had information that we were home. Would it be possible to speak to us? Kathleen's sister denied the story and closed the door. Once more we had to go into hiding. We were there for a week and only ventured out under cover of darkness on two occasions. For the whole of Saturday a car full of journalists remained nearby keeping an eye on the house. They even followed Stephen's car when, after a short visit, he returned to his flat on the other side of Fort William. They came to the door three times that day and trespassed on neighbours' property at the back of the house, trying to look through the kitchen window. We closed the blinds.

That evening Kathleen's mother Theresa joined the family for a meal. It was a lovely occasion. She was completely natural with us, relaxed as ever, her laugh brightening the whole room. She spoke to me as if I were still the local parish priest, telling me all the news. It was lovely to hear her cheerful banter with her daughters at the table. For both Kathleen and myself, her presence that evening was very important.

When her sister and nephew went to Mass on the Sunday morning, Kathleen and I had to remain in the house. It was as painful as it had been on previous Sundays when we were unable to attend Mass, but we prayed the rosary together. A knock on the door disturbed us and we retreated into our room. The press were back again. After a while, and some muttering, we heard their footsteps on the gravel outside our window. We held our breath, but they continued past and apparently left. Stephen returned with the others after Mass. As breakfast was being prepared there was another loud knock on the door. Stephen opened it, only to be faced by a reporter and photographer from yet another tabloid. He closed the door immediately, leaving them open mouthed, words lost in thin air. We were virtual prisoners for the rest of that day. Despite their efforts they never got a glimpse of us and had no proof of our being there. Neither Kathleen nor I have ever bothered to find out who gave them the information. That was not what was important.

Kathleen enjoyed seeing her family and that pleased me – I spent quite a bit of time watching videos and reading so that she could have some time alone with them. Under cover of darkness we were taken out twice for meals. On the first occasion we spent an enjoyable evening with Kathleen's brother and his family in Spean Bridge, and on the night before we left we had dinner at Anne's house in Fort William with the whole family. Theresa was the life and soul of the party that evening. It was a fitting way to say our goodbyes. Michelle and her boyfriend were kindly taking us south early the next morning. I shall always be grateful to them all for the love they showed Kathleen and the welcome they gave me.

Kathleen's only sadness was that her daughter Julie Anne, just coming up to her sixteenth birthday, still could not bring herself to meet her. Kathleen understood and accepted this. She had written to Julie Anne and, although there had been no reply, continued to send letters regularly with love, making no demands.

During our visit to Fort William we had the chance to read exactly what the papers had been saying over the weeks since we had left. Kathleen's sister had kept most of them for us. I could not bring myself to read them in detail: the awful headlines were enough. Kathleen did read them, however, and was particularly upset by one carrying an old picture of her on a beach dressed in a skimpy top and shorts, and portraying her as a 'good-time girl'. The story and picture were both untruthful. Kathleen is certainly no 'good-time girl' and never has been: the photo was taken during her marriage and she was faithful to her husband throughout the 19 years they were together. The original snapshot (of which Kathleen has a copy) shows a whole group of people on the beach – and the photographer, a married man, was having an affair with one of them. With Kathleen suddenly 'famous', this man sold the picture to the tabloid for a large sum of money, the photo was doctored to show her alone and used to support a completely inaccurate story. Kathleen felt angry at the injustice of being put at the centre of such hypocrisy and lies.

This is only one example of the nonsense which had been written about us. The sheer volume of it all made me numb. It was unbelievable that so much suffocating interest should be shown in us. It was a dreadful time for our families and friends. We were pleased that Kathleen's children has successfully managed to dodge the press. They had only got a snap of Stephen as he left the train at Fort William one day, returning from a business course. The headline with the picture was 'HOME ALONE!' Stephen was 24 years old by then and had been living in his own flat for at least two years.

✦

At the beginning of the week after we returned from Fort William, I drove Kathleen to the hospital for the first of her two interviews. Ultimately she wanted full-time work, but at this stage was happy to start on the 'bank' system, working in any hospital department whenever there was a shortage of Nursing Assistants. Faced by a panel of three, she introduced herself and told them of the recent publicity, thinking that was only fair. Much to her surprise she was offered the position immediately at the end of the interview. Could she begin work the following Friday? Gladly, she said. As she left, the principal interviewer took her aside and told her there was no need to reveal anything about herself to her new colleagues. A jubilant Kathleen returned to the car where, as usual, I was reading *The Herald*. It was great to see her so elated. I can only reiterate my admiration for her, so determined to go through with what must have been an ordeal. It was vital to us that she did have work, because we had no money coming in then and our outlay had already eaten into much of our savings.

At the beginning of the following week she attended the interview with the Mental Health Trust. On this occasion she made no reference to her immediate history. The interview went well and she was offered a contract there and then for 30 hours a week. She felt very fortunate that she had received two offers of work within a week. She had already worked two 'bank' shifts in the Geriatric Unit in the hospital, an experience she enjoyed, but now she had been offered a contract. Mental health was an area of nursing which was new to her, but she was interested and the reality of a steady contract was important. She decided to accept and wrote to the other Trust, thanking them for their kindness and removing her name from the 'bank'.

She and her colleague Angie still enjoy a laugh when they remember that interview for the Mental Health Trust. Unknown to Kathleen this was Angie's first experience of being on an interviewing panel and she was nervous – even more so when she discovered beforehand who was being interviewed. From the first day, however, Kathleen received marvellous support from the Trust and her colleagues which she appreciates very much. Very shortly after she began her work in the Psychiatric Unit another colleague, Nikki, took her aside. 'Kathleen, can I speak to you?' she said. 'We all know who you are and we're behind you. No one is saying anything, but we accept you for who you are. Anyway, I can't understand all the media coverage.' This conversation put Kathleen at her ease and she quickly made many friends, working with them as a team until she left recently to study Psychiatric Nursing.

✦

I was delighted for Kathleen that she had found work so soon after the media ordeal. This success encouraged us both and Kathleen loved the work. I regretted very much that my own prospects for employment were so slim. It was odd to be suddenly at a loose end during the day and took some getting used to. All my adult life I had been active, immersed in my work for the Church, sometimes working 16-hour days. I missed the pastoral work which had always meant so much to me – I still do – and it was frustrating to think that I would not be able to put to use in a fulfilling way the experience and ability I had gained over the years. I made a number of applications for different positions but seldom received a reply. My age and notoriety were major stumbling blocks.

In the meantime, I made an appointment with the local Job Centre to clarify my position and set about satisfying all the conditions which must be fulfilled by any unemployed person seeking work. Immediately I learned that I had no right to any benefit because Kathleen was working 30 hours a week, even though I had paid a self-employed contribution to the National Insurance for 33 years. I could have my National Insurance paid provided I attended the Job Centre every two weeks to 'sign on' and proved that I was seriously seeking work. I accepted this and filled in the necessary form, stating my previous employment, my previous salary (£500 a month) and present costs (£300 monthly rent plus Council Tax). Two weeks later, on a Friday afternoon, I went to 'sign on', taking my place in the queue with others in a similar situation.

On the Monday morning after that visit I noticed a red car parked suspiciously across the road. It remained there on the yellow lines throughout the morning, the inevitable two gentlemen sitting inside. They were back! That morning I had driven Kathleen to work at 6.30 a.m. and on my return had parked across the road in Kendal Green. I was due to collect her at the hospital at 2.30 p.m. but I could not reach the car by my normal route without passing the reporters. Leaving early, I went out of the back door, sneaked up through the allotment and cut across a field, managing to cross Windermere Road out of sight of the watchers. I walked down a side road to reach the car and to avoid passing them. I collected Kathleen and on the way back we took a different route, parking the car somewhere else to give us easy access to the allotment and so to the back door of the house. The two in the car, oblivious to our movements, carried on sitting and waiting. They left at 4.30 p.m., returning at 9.00 a.m. the following day.

Over the next few days as they continued to keep vigilant watch, we took the back route to and from the house, not wishing to disturb them. On the Wednesday afternoon a supervisor at the Job Centre phoned to inform me that the press were snooping around making enquiries. I told her I was aware of their presence. 'It isn't often that our clients park a Mercedes outside!' she said wryly. I was told not to come for my next appointment: they would send the appropriate form to my address.

Now I understood why those journalists were there – they hoped to catch me going to the Job Centre. They left promptly every day at 4.30 p.m. No one can 'sign on' after that time. I quite enjoyed the next two days. I saw them whenever I chose, but they never managed to catch a glimpse of me or Kathleen. On the Friday afternoon they actually came to the door at 4.30. It had been a long vigil! Perhaps they wished to say goodbye. We paid no attention to their persistent knocking and they left. The following morning when I looked out the red car was not in place. Job Centres do not open on Saturdays.

To our amazement yet another article on Roddy and Kathleen appeared the following week in a national tabloid newspaper, which of course was also printed in the sister paper in Scotland. Kathleen's sister sent us a copy. With the article was a picture of the back view of a man, about my height, entering the Kendal Job Centre. He was accompanied by two little boys. The article claimed it was me, although it was perfectly obvious that this was not true. Both Kathleen and I were very angry that this report claimed I was receiving £78.00 of dole money a week – another lie as I was not receiving any state benefit, apart from the payment of National Insurance for three months. The most worrying fact was that amongst this fabrication they revealed confidential information concerning my previous salary and the amount of rent we paid each month in Mountain View. These figures had been given by me in a confidential document at the Job Centre. How is it possible for a newspaper to print such information? That was the question I asked of both the Area Supervisor and the Manager of the Job Centre. Their replies were far from satisfactory. I remain convinced that this newspaper had gained access to such information in an illegal way.

◆

Soon after that I hired a van in Kendal and once more we drove north, arriving at Kathleen's sister's house in the early evening. Then we drove on in the dark to Kathleen's house in Inverlochy, where we loaded up some furniture and possessions she had left behind. With the help of Stephen, Donald and Kathleen's brother and brother-in-law, it did not take us too long. A neighbour came out to see what was happening and was relieved to discover that it was just Kathleen removing things from her own house. The following morning we drove back to Kendal and unloaded the van, carrying everything into the house ourselves this time (no more workmen for us!).

Someone who had seen us at the house in Inverlochy must have alerted the press, but the birds had flown by the time they visited the nest. On this occasion they wrote that I was seen being driven around Fort William by Kathleen's ex-husband – but I do not think anyone believed *that* story. The same paper greeted Christmas that year with yet another fanciful article, superimposing my face on to a picture of a lollipop man and caricaturing me as a Santa Claus, suggesting that perhaps I should seek work in these areas instead of being on the dole. There were plenty of serious things going on in the world at the time, I thought: why could they not concentrate on the real news?

◆

Kathleen had continued to write to Julie Anne through November and December. A week before Christmas she received a letter back. It was a beautiful and forgiving letter from a daughter to her mother, and meant so much to both of us. Kathleen will always keep that precious letter. Stephen had already said that he and his fiancée, Kerrie, would come down on Boxing Day with Donald and stay with us for a few days. Now here was Julie Anne saying she would be joining them. Our Christmas promised to be much brighter than we had expected.

We did some last-minute shopping on Christmas Eve, happily absorbed in preparations. About five minutes after we had come home there was a knock on the door. Reluctantly I answered it, very wary of the press. I was astonished to see two police detectives standing there. They had travelled all the way from Inverness to interview me. What was this all about? Policemen always seemed to make me feel immediately nervous. I asked them in and introduced them to Kathleen. They would not discuss the matter in her presence and asked me to accompany them to the local police station. This sounded ominous and I know Kathleen was very apprehensive. Before their arrival she had been planning to go back into town on her own to buy a few more presents. She drove me to the police station and continued into town, intending to pick me up again on her way back.

I was taken into an interview room and finally discovered what was going on. The priest I had 'retired' some years before, after allegations from a woman that she had been sexually abused by him as a child, was now charged on several counts of abuse. The woman Roddy Macdonald and I had met had changed her mind about not going public and she now brought charges. The police wanted to interview me about her evidence and the priest's reaction when I dismissed him. Others had apparently come forward with similar allegations and they asked if I had any knowledge of these. I had not. I answered all their questions and then made a formal statement which one of the detectives wrote down. By the time it was ready for me to sign we had been in that interview room for almost three hours. Unknown to me Kathleen had called at the police station and demanded to know why they were holding me for such a length of time! The two detectives dropped me off at Mountain View on their way back to Inverness. It was 5.45 p.m. on Christmas Eve. What would they have done if they had driven all that distance only to discover that we had gone on holiday to France or, better still, Inverness?

◆

It was the first Christmas in 33 years that I would not celebrate Midnight Mass. This made me very sad, but I accepted it as part of the choice I had made. We had a lovely day of celebration, just ourselves, and Kathleen phoned all her family. I called my sister and brother. The situation between us had eased a bit, but it was still tense.

On Boxing Day we excitedly awaited the arrival of Kathleen's children. When they did arrive I joined Stephen to show him where to park, leaving Julie Anne to have an emotional reunion with her mother. She greeted me very warmly when I returned with Stephen. We celebrated our real Christmas dinner that evening, with all of them sharing our table. It was a healing time for us and will always be a special memory.

Before they came we had made up beds in the constricted space as best we could. I had suggested that Julie Anne should sleep with Kathleen because their few days together were very important and they needed the opportunity to be alone. This was agreed and I made a bed for myself on the floor downstairs. During the next few days, as 1996 drew to a close, those young people brought an air of normality to a house which in recent months had been anything but normal. Gradually some of the nervous tension eased out of us.

After Stephen and the girls left we still had Donald, who wanted some more time with his mother. We had accepted an invitation from Kathleen's sister to spend the New Year holiday with her and Donald decided to stay and travel up with us. We set off north on Hogmanay and arrived in Fort William at about 10 o'clock. It was a difficult time for Kathleen's sister, who had been widowed so suddenly just a year and a half before. Such celebratory occasions are always so painful for the bereaved and it was good that Kathleen was able to be there. Another sister and her husband, along with some friends, 'first-footed' us and we had a pleasant time. Kathleen and I were more relaxed this time because we knew that the press were also having a holiday. On New Year's Day, Theresa and the rest of the family all called round and I was made to feel very much at home. We headed back to Kendal the next day, praying that 1997 would bring us a more settled life after the emotional upheavals of the previous year.

◆

About a month after we had come to Kendal we had accepted an invitation from Alex and Jan Walker to visit them at their home in

Carnforth. Alex is a former priest who is very involved in Advent, a group of former priests seeking a more active role in the Church. He and his wife were very welcoming at a time when we felt terribly alone. After our return from Scotland in the New Year they visited us in Mountain View.

With the approach of Lent we were very anxious to find somewhere to attend Mass together. Since the start of the media frenzy we had not been able to go to the church in Kendal because I did not wish to have others in the congregation distracted or disturbed by some prying journalist. During one of our conversations Alex mentioned another former priest, Ed Harrison, who lives with his wife and children in Preston. Ed and Maureen had written to us, but we had not had a chance to reply with all that was happening at the time. We phoned them and they invited us to stay with them on a Saturday evening and attend Mass there on the Sunday. Our weekend was made complete when their parish priest, Father Peter, gave us a warm and genuine welcome.

It meant so much to us both to attend Mass and we knew that despite the distance we would return as often as possible. Alex, Jan, Ed and Maureen were a very great support to us as we struggled to find our feet again. Not only did they make it possible for us to attend Mass, but they helped us in many practical ways too – not least by taking us for our first meal out, a welcome taste of freedom and normality which gave us hope at a dark time.

◆

In early March a Scottish tabloid produced another little masterpiece of journalism. This time the headline read, 'KATH'S PAD WON'T SELL'. Apparently people were not interested in buying the house in Inverlochy because of our notoriety. In truth Kathleen had only recently put the house on the market. The estate agents had fully agreed with the delay as they were aware of the possibility of journalists posing as interested buyers to gain an opportunity to photograph the interior of the house.

We were glad we had far more important things to think about. The dates of Mother's Day and Kathleen's birthday are close to each other in March and she was given a lovely surprise when her mother Theresa and Julie Anne decided to come to Kendal to celebrate the occasion. We drove up to Glasgow to meet them off the Fort William bus.

Theresa sat with me in the front of the car while Kathleen and Julie Anne enjoyed their own conversation in the back. Meanwhile, Theresa entertained me with her reminiscences, speaking as if I was still active in the Church and presuming I knew every priest she mentioned. And she spoke of Lanarkshire where she was born, of the poverty and struggle there in pre-war days. I really enjoyed the journey and before I knew it we had crossed the border and were close to Kendal. Those few days they spent with us in Mountain View were so enjoyable and homely, a treat for both Kathleen and myself.

That Saturday night we decided to go to the Vigil Mass in the local church. Would it be all right? I was not sure, but the others wanted to go, so I went with them in the car. I parked opposite the church and could see the two priests standing at the door of the brightly lit building, shaking everyone's hands as they went in. I was still feeling very raw then, and suddenly knew I could not go through with it. It was too local, too public. Kathleen instinctively knew what I was thinking. Turning to me, she said quietly, 'If you don't want to go in, Roddy, you don't have to.'

I stayed in the car and watched Kathleen, Theresa and Julie Anne go into the church. Once they were inside, I turned on the little interior light and went through the readings of the Mass for the Third Sunday in Lent for myself. I felt so isolated, even more so when they returned afterwards obviously having enjoyed the occasion, especially the sermon. It had been nothing but cowardice on my part and I was ashamed and angry with myself. I should have gone into the church.

My spirits were lifted the following day, however, which dawned bright and cheerful. We decided to go for a run to Morecambe and Kathleen and Theresa went to fetch the car while I waited for Julie Anne, who was still getting ready. When we left the house, we were faced with the usual queue of cars waiting at the junction. I could see faces turned in our direction, watching us walk down the steps. Julie Anne also noticed.

'Would you look at them!' she exclaimed.

'Just think, Julie Anne,' I said, 'they'll be saying to each other, "My, hasn't she got young!" ' They must certainly have been wondering what we were laughing about as we crossed the road.

The visit of her mother and daughter together worked wonders for Kathleen. The bond between them was obvious to see and Theresa's infectious laugh raised our spirits. I think we had discovered that laughter is a vital part of life. We were only sorry that our small house did not offer them more comfort at the time. We both felt rather sad when we returned with them to Scotland, leaving Theresa in Hamilton with her sister Bridie and taking Julie Anne on into Glasgow to catch the bus back to Fort William.

11

◆

NEW LIFE IN CARNFORTH

EASTER WAS APPROACHING and we were becoming concerned about having a place to live. The lease on 7 Mountain View would run out at the end of March and so it was a relief when we managed to have that extended until the end of April. Fortunately Kathleen's house in Inverlochy was close to being sold, and this encouraged us to look for a house in the same price range. Almost daily we looked at houses for sale in the area, but found most to be too expensive or unsuitable.

We began looking outside Kendal and especially in Carnforth where Alex and Jan Walker lived. The sale on Kathleen's house went through and we were just making up our minds between two houses in Carnforth when the estate agent informed us that another house, not yet on the market, was being sold to the builders as part of a deal on a new house. We made arrangements to view it as soon as possible and discovered to our delight that it was only two houses away from Alex and Jan Walker. The price was right and the house was in good condition, so we went ahead with the purchase as quickly as we could push it along.

We were already pressurized by the fact that we had to leave 7 Mountain View on 30 April. Nigel and Simone, the couple whose house we were buying, were understanding and co-operative, and agreed to have the house available for entry on that date. This was a great relief to us and we were grateful for their help. It would have been difficult to find rented accommodation for an interim period, as well as being now beyond our means.

Alex Walker arranged help for us on the day we were to move. His friend Andy Williams, whom we had met earlier, along with some of his sons, would provide transport and labour to move us from Mountain View. Alex, Andy and the boys arrived on 30 April at about 7.00 p.m. We hoped we would be less conspicuous in the dark. I had hired a van and Andy brought his own spacious transport. We began to load up and Kathleen drove to Carnforth to prepare for our arrival. With the expert help I had to hand we soon moved everything out of the house, and by 10 o'clock we were carrying everything into our new house in Carnforth. Neighbours and passers-by must have seen by our activities that we were leaving, but we had only told our immediate next-door neighbours where we were going. They had always been very kind to us during the seven months we lived in Kendal.

The following morning we returned to Mountain View for the last time to clean the now empty house. While I returned the hired van, Kathleen handed in the keys to the estate agents. Neither of us will ever forget that address in Kendal.

Over the next few days we set about putting our new house in order. Kathleen was to return to work at the beginning of the coming week. Very soon we felt at home in this house, at long last able to put in place all the furniture which had been stored in the front room in Mountain View.

◆

We had hoped the move to Carnforth would mean that our life was settling down into something like normality and that the media harassment was petering out. Over the next months, however, we were to find our existence repeatedly disturbed by the intrusion of inquisitive journalists, which not only bothered our neighbours but also involved some potentially dangerous incidents on the road. It did not take them long to track us down after we had left Kendal.

Kathleen returned to work on Monday afternoon. About an hour later a man came to the door and told me that the press were at the top of the road. He was involved in the Neighbourhood Watch and a local mother had complained that there were two men sitting in a car looking suspicious. He had approached them and asked their business, discovering who they were, what newspaper they worked for and what their purpose was. They were from a Scottish tabloid and were looking for us, of course. I thanked the man for the warning and the information. Shortly afterwards, an elderly gentleman came to the door. He lived in a mobile home on a little hill at the end of our road. Discovering someone lurking in the bushes close to his home, he had asked the lurker what he was doing. The man in the bushes had given him a card to prove he was an employee of the newspaper. He was obviously trying to get a photograph of Kathleen and myself. I phoned Kathleen at work to warn her, but the journalists had retired to their hotel, and no doubt the bar, by the time she returned that night.

Kathleen was working the early shift the next day and left the house at 6.30 a.m. Mid-morning I heard knocking on the door which, of course, I ignored. Later they returned, and then again, and again ... Meanwhile, they justified their wages by disturbing the neighbours, going from door to door. They were still around when Kathleen phoned to check and she wondered how she could get into the house without them seeing her. Unfortunately, there was no way of doing that with them parked where they were, but for some happy reason they were not there when she got back. They must have been surprised to see the car parked outside when they turned up again later. Once more we ignored the inevitable knock on the door, nerves grating. When would they let up? Things were to get worse over the next two days, however, when the 'campaign' took a worrying new turn.

Kathleen was working a late shift on the Wednesday and I decided to drive her to the hospital in Kendal. We passed the journalists' car at the road end and decided to take the country road via Milnthorpe. In my mirror I could see that we were being followed, a few cars between us and the pursuers. I took the first opportunity to turn off where there were some buildings which might hide us from view. The pursuing car passed at speed and I drove back on to the road, returning the way I had come in order to take another route. In the rear mirror I could see them trying, frantically I am sure, to turn their car on the narrow road. Having managed to put some distance between them and us, I took a slip road on to the M6 and headed for Kendal. All this time Kathleen was keeping an eye on the road behind. I was angry to find myself forced to participate in such ridiculous and dangerous behaviour. Who did they think they were? Who did they think *we* were? It was like something out of a film.

They must have given up on the chase because we reached the hospital without further trouble. Just in case, I dropped Kathleen off at the main door where she could make a quicker entrance. I took the country road back but saw nothing of the reporters. As I turned into the road close to our house, however, their car passed me, with the driver looking frantically around. 'Surely I'm not all that important!' I thought to myself disbelievingly.

On the Thursday Kathleen drove herself to work, early in the morning. Sometime later she looked out of the window of Ward 4 to see the press car sitting at the far end of the employees' car park. She told the Ward Manager, Ted Jones, who offered to move her car elsewhere. Unfortunately he could not understand the immobilizer mechanism, so the car stayed where it was! The two watching men snapped alert, clearly aware that something was afoot. Shortly before the end of the shift, Kathleen's colleague Helen offered to help. She went out and opened Kathleen's car door as if she were going home. This caused great excitement in the other car, as they hurriedly took their pictures. Then they drove rapidly out of the car park. Helen returned to the Ward, having enjoyed her experience of being a celebrity. 'Perhaps I'll have my picture plastered all over tomorrow's papers!' was her comment as she and Kathleen finished off their work.

It was not the end of the matter, however, and as Kathleen drove out of the car park she was dismayed to see the press car waiting along the road. They chased her all the way along the M6 and then through Carnforth until she arrived at our house. She was shaken and frightened by their harassing behaviour. Angry that Kathleen had been put at risk by the distraction of these men on her tail, I immediately phoned the local police station to make a complaint. Shortly afterwards a constable arrived and Kathleen described what had happened at the hospital and on the road home. The policeman agreed that their behaviour was ridiculous and dangerous. After he left I drove to the local shop and passed him speaking to the two reporters. They were still standing there when I came back and I gave them a wave. They did not bother us further that day.

On the Friday they were still parked at the top of the road, but busied themselves by annoying the neighbours with their questions instead. Kathleen and I felt so embarrassed that we were the reason for the disturbance in their lives. The press did not return to our door that day, but we both noticed excited activity outside at teatime. The photographer ran past our house, camera at the ready.

Their attention had clearly turned from us to Alex and Jan Walker. Here was a former priest living just two doors away from a former bishop! Oh joy! They had something to write about – they might even get a photograph! We were comforted by the thought that Alex and Jan were probably old pros at all this.

That night the journalists left for Scotland without getting an interview and we had denied them any photo opportunities, despite their hard work. But we knew they would write their story regardless. Early the following week there was the story, along with a headline about the 'Randy Revs'. There was a picture of Alex and his wife and children that they must have procured from another newspaper which had printed an article about the organization Advent. The photographer had been gainfully employed after all, however, because he had managed to photograph the house with our car parked outside. They called our house 'a villa', and the car was described as a 'shiny new Megane'. Perhaps our neighbours would be pleased to hear that their houses are regarded as villas by some of the press! Kathleen had owned her car for well over a year by then and the mileage certainly did not suggest that it was new. We were not living in the kind of luxury they were trying to lead people to believe.

◆

The following week we decided to decorate the living room. We had invited Kathleen's brother and his wife to spend a long week-end with us at the end of May and we wanted to have this decorating completed before their arrival. Somehow we managed to paint and paper without falling out too often!

When Kathleen was at work one day I was determined to finish the painting in the porch. At the time I had an ear infection and had some cotton wool in one ear, having put some drops in. As I was painting, a man arrived at the partially open door. He identified himself as Bill Frost from *The Times*. I tried to move the ladder to close the door, but he insisted that he was not a journalist and represented the paper's literary supplement. They had information that I was writing a book. Would I be interested in having it serialized in *The Times*? I denied that I was writing a book, which was the truth at that point. As I tried to close the door he asked me if I was aware of having paint on my ear, presumably trying to prolong the conversation. I corrected him, saying it was not paint but cotton wool, explaining about my ear infection. He then returned to the subject of the book and gave me his phone number – should I ever write one and want it serialized. I finally managed to get rid of him and continued with the painting. At the time I thought little of the matter: surely no one from *The Times* would be mad enough to write an article about my ear infection.

On the weekend of their visit Kathleen's brother and his wife arrived on the Saturday about noon. That evening, the weather being so good, we enjoyed a delicious barbeque meal and stayed out afterwards to enjoy the evening air and a good old-fashioned blether. The following morning we went to Mass in Lancaster, where Kathleen and I often attend. Later we went to a lovely spot at the side of Lake Windermere for a picnic meal, then we took a run to Ambleside and Grasmere where we enjoyed a stroll around that pretty place. Not a journalist in sight. It was bliss. That evening Kathleen prepared a sumptuous Indian meal, one of her specialities, and again we talked into the early hours of the morning. We bade them a sad farewell on the Monday. It had been a beautiful weekend.

Our guests were not long on the road north when someone came to the door. Opening it, I was faced by two men, one of whom informed me that they were from the *Daily Mail*. I closed the door. Through the glass I could hear him telling me that they wanted to speak with me about the interview I had given to *The Times*. What interview? I thought. When they received no answer from me they pushed a copy of the article through the letterbox. I took it with me to the garden where Kathleen was sitting and we read it together in gathering gloom.

The heading was 'A BRIEF ENCOUNTER IN CARNFORTH'. As always, it was the only picture of Kathleen and myself they had, taken in the back garden of Mountain View when we faced the press back on 7 October 1996. The reference to *Brief Encounter* was clever, of course, since that romantic film had actually been made in Carnforth railway station. The rest of the article was far from clever. It claimed to be an exclusive interview. It claimed that I was a broken man, filled with remorse and guilt (quite a leap from a simple ear infection). And it was written by Bill Frost, who had supposedly been a representative of the *Times Literary Supplement*. I have seldom been so infuriated. I wanted to speak immediately to the editor of *The Times*, and then I thought of contacting the Press Complaints Commission. Not sure what to do, I eventually spoke with Ian Wilson of *The Herald* – who calmly advised me to do nothing! He understood my distress, but went on to say that I should not say a single word when spoken to by journalists, because some of them use a reply such as 'I've nothing to say' as licence to write about an 'interview'. His last piece of advice was not to sue unless I was a millionaire. There was nothing I could do except seethe privately.

In the wake of this 'article' I received an extraordinary flood of mail. Most of it was sympathetic and encouraging, telling me not to be overtaken by such sentiments of guilt. However kindly it was meant, Kathleen and I found such mail distressing because it was in response to nothing I had said but to the written word of someone who did not know anything about me.

◆

It turned out to be a beautiful summer and when Kathleen had the occasional day off work we enjoyed a barbeque in our garden or went exploring. We love walking and have discovered excellent locations here in Lancashire, as well as the fells around Kendal. The nearby Lancaster Canal and Jenny Brown's Point near Silverdale are our favourites for short outings. Now that we have settled in we feel it is a privilege to live in such a lovely part of England. That summer was also made memorable by various special family visits.

At the beginning of July Anne, Kathleen's sister, and her son Andrew came to stay with us for a few days. It was a pleasure for us to share our home with them. Kathleen had a few days off work while they were with us and we drove them to Grimsby where we spent the night at the house of Anne's daughter Michelle. The following morning we went to Leicester, where Michael, Anne's oldest son, was graduating at the university later that day. Michelle joined us there at the house of Teresa, Anne's other daughter. While they and Kathleen attended the ceremony I strolled around a part of Leicester, a city I had never visited before. That evening we shared in the celebratory meal for Michael.

Kathleen and I returned to Carnforth the following day, as she had to report for work. There was more family to come, however. It was not a quiet month! A few days later we drove to Glasgow to collect another sister, Margaret Rose, and her two children, the twins Daniel and Kathleen. They would be with us for a week, and Anne was to join us again in a few days' time. We certainly had a full house, but we were just so glad to see them all.

To give Margaret Rose a rest I took the twins, who were only seven years old, for walks to the nearby swing park and to the canal where we fed the ducks. We were throwing bread to them one day when Daniel asked me why one particular duck, a drake, looked different from the others. I told him this was because the drake was 'a man duck' and he seemed satisfied.

As we walked home later Daniel asked me, 'Do you know all of the ducks by name?'

'Daniel, I don't know any of them by name,' I replied.

'Aye, you do. You called that one Amanda!'

It took me a minute to understand and I have a good chuckle every time I think about it. It was a grand week, and a whole lot more refreshing than having non-conversations with journalists. Our door, which until then had seldom been approached by anyone but the press, suddenly became a centre of attraction for children. The majority of them were neighbouring boys looking for little Kathleen!

Anne joined us halfway through the week and I enjoyed listening to the three sisters laugh as they reminisced and played tricks on each other. One night, quite late, they were arguing about who was their mother's favourite. When they phoned her to find out, Theresa knew their game and answered very diplomatically, as most mothers would! Kathleen and I were very sorry to leave them all in Glasgow at the bus station when the week ended. However, Julie Anne was waiting there to return with us to Carnforth, so we were not entirely bereft. She stayed for three weeks before beginning her college course in Glasgow, and quickly made the spare room her own, as it has been ever since. In the pleasure of having her at home with us, the shadow of the intrusive media receded.

◆

Some weeks later, just after Julie Anne had returned to Scotland, Kathleen and I returned from a walk and saw a strange-looking woman standing in someone's garden a few doors away from us. We went straight out to the back garden and had just sat down when we heard someone at the door. As I went to open it Kathleen called after me to be careful. It was the woman we had noticed earlier, and to me she certainly looked troubled in some way. In her strong Scottish accent she told me she had travelled by train from Glasgow that day. 'Can I speak with you?' she asked.

'Who are you?'

'I would like to speak with you.'

'I want to know who you are.'

'I've something to say to you. Can I come in?'

'No. Who are you?'

She gave a name and said she worked for a Scottish Sunday tabloid. The moment I heard this I closed the door. She continued to speak to me through the closed door, but I went back out to the garden. After five minutes I went to check she had gone, but she was still standing outside. Through the closed door I told her to go away or I would send for the police. She was still standing there five minutes later, so I repeated my threat to call the police. When I next looked out she had gone.

Kathleen and I were quite unnerved by the woman. She looked odd, and indeed Kathleen said she had felt afraid of her. Was she really a journalist? We were both amazed the following Sunday when we were told that this woman had written an 'exclusive interview' in the Sunday paper she had named. Until that time we had thought kindly of that particular paper: it had always appeared to be a cosy little family read. Our opinion changed as we read this 'exclusive'. The woman wrote that I looked well and gave a description of our sitting room as if she had been inside. She must have peered through the window quite carefully and then written the nonsense on her train journey back to Glasgow. Well, we thought, August is known as the 'silly season'...

◆

Stephen and Kerrie visited us for the weekend at the end of August. It was lovely to see them and, from the time they said they were coming, we had looked forward to their visit. On the first day we just relaxed at home and in the evening we enjoyed one of Kathleen's special meals. The following morning, 31 August, I rose early and switched on the radio as I made some coffee. I heard Diana, Princess of Wales mentioned on the news bulletin but took little notice: it was not unusual to hear her name. Then I heard the words 'crash' and 'proclaimed dead' and suddenly paid attention to what was being said. Like many in the country, indeed the world, I was hearing the first news of her death.

When I had grasped the main facts I took some coffee upstairs to Kathleen and broke the news to her. She was very upset and went to tell Stephen, then joined me downstairs where I had turned on the television. By this time suspicions about the behaviour of the paparazzi beforehand were being voiced. The situation was unclear, but we could see what the speculators were driving at, having – to a far lesser degree – suffered from their attentions ourselves. Along with many others our day was spent under a cloud of sadness. In the afternoon we did go out to a funfair and enjoyed a game or two of indoor bowling. On our return the television reminded us of what had become a national bereavement. On the day of the funeral we watched proceedings unfold on the television and found it a deeply moving occasion.

The Monday after the Princess's funeral was sunny and warm and we decided to go for a walk in one of our favourite areas near Silverdale, then take a picnic lunch to Jenny Brown's Point. It was early September now, and one year after our leaving. We should have been prepared. Returning from our walk, we approached our car through a copse and discovered two men standing close to it. They had obviously been examining it but, on our arrival, pretended to be studying the trees instead. We were immediately suspicious. They looked out of place – one, a short, red-haired fellow, was wearing a loud pair of shorts and an equally bright shirt; the other was in a city suit, the jacket draped over one shoulder. They moved away as we approached and made a dash for their own car as we got into ours.

We drove off to Jenny Brown's Point as we had intended and made our way down to some rocks close to the sea where we could eat our lunch. We were certain the two men were from the press. Had they followed us? Were they going to spoil yet another private day? Just as we finished lunch we saw a familiar-looking sunseeker stretch himself out on a nearby rock.

Quietly, Kathleen spoke as she put everything back in our little picnic box. 'You go back to the car and I'll walk the other way. We won't give them the chance of a picture. The other fellow is lurking somewhere near.'

'Fine, Kathleen,' I whispered, 'just you walk now, and I'll slowly make my way to the car. I'll pick you up further along the road.'

As we unexpectedly parted, the red-haired man sat up and began to move. By the time I reached the car he was just a short distance behind me. I did a U-turn on the narrow road, forcing him to stand against the fence until I had completed the manoeuvre and moved off. His companion appeared on the other side, having obviously failed to get his hoped-for picture.

About a quarter of a mile along the road I stopped to allow Kathleen into the car. There was no sign of pursuit. When I turned on to the main road, however, there they were, speeding up behind. On the outskirts of Carnforth I turned quickly into a garage forecourt. Their car sped past. I followed them as they drove very obviously towards our house. Letting them go on ahead, I stopped at the police station: Kathleen had noted down their car registration number and we reported that and the way they had chased us.

When I drove out they were parked across the road and followed us round the one-way system until we were stopped at traffic lights. The little red-haired fellow jumped out of their car and approached my window, which I closed. Knocking on the glass, he said, 'Mr Wright, I promise we won't chase you if—' but I shouted straight back at him, 'Go away! I've reported you to the police!' The lights changed and we left him standing there. Earlier we had cleared the garage, so we squeezed the car in there, out of sight. We saw no more of their white car that day. Perhaps, we hoped, they had heeded the warning about the police.

The next morning Kathleen had an appointment with her doctor. When she was ready to go I opened the garage door from the inside. I should have looked outside first. About 20 yards away I saw the red-haired one emerge from a black car. They had obviously changed cars to fool us. Immediately, I closed the door and told Kathleen. We cancelled the doctor's appointment, feeling angry all over again that our lives were being restricted in this way. Kathleen had been denied the freedom to visit her doctor without being harassed. Not only that, but they had chased us in our car in a dangerous way just two days after the funeral of Diana, Princess of Wales, when such behaviour had been roundly condemned.

The men were from a Scottish tabloid newspaper and we both knew that it was the anniversary of our leaving which had prompted a renewal of the pursuit. We also knew they would print their story although they had not managed to get a single quote from either of us, apart from what I had said through the closed window of the car. And so they did — a repeat of old news and a reproduction of the picture taken in the garden in Kendal a whole year before. Other newspapers printed their 'anniversary story' without bothering to pay us a call.

✦

Despite this rude interruption, we had enjoyed our summer and did feel that life was starting to show signs of normality once again. The family visits had helped a great deal and of course we loved having them all to stay. We were very much at home in Carnforth. The parish priest had been kind and we were now attending Mass regularly in our local church – although we still liked to go sometimes to Father Peter's church in Preston, where we had first been made welcome. We also attended a church in Lancaster on occasions, depending on Kathleen's shift work.

Our Faith, I think, will always be important to us both because it has always been an essential part of our lives. Of course, I feel cut off from the Church in one sense as I can no longer participate actively as I have done for most of my life. I have not contacted many who worked with me and supported me in the past: not from preference, but because I know that my decision caused much pain and great disappointment to them.

This 'separation' does not mean that my Faith has diminished or my beliefs altered. They remain the same. The way we profess our Faith is now private, however, except when we attend Mass. From before the time of our leaving Kathleen and I had prayed together, and since the beginning of the press siege in Kendal have always said the rosary together every day. We know we have both gained comfort from that, and all the way through that first difficult year were aware of a vital inner strength which kept us going, certain that better times would come. We were still aware of it as the summer of 1997 brought a return to relative calm. As we headed off for a late break in October, however, we did not know that there was further sadness ahead for us at the end of the year.

◆

Father Peter in Preston had offered us the use of a house close to Mâcon in central France, a beautiful wine-producing area where the Chardonnay grape is prevalent. We had invited Kathleen's widowed sister and her son to join us for a holiday there in October, and duly set off down the country to catch Le Shuttle. The weather was very poor when we arrived in France and Kathleen took the wheel for the drive south. Pouring rain and an unfamiliar road did not deter us: we were looking forward to this long-overdue break! Despite my poor directions we arrived safely in the early evening.

The house was beautiful and we were so content to have some

real privacy and the opportunity of a rest. Our first task was to light a log fire in the huge fireplace. Warm, comfortable and relaxed, we were all soon lulled into sleep.

The following day, although it was still cloudy, we explored the surrounding countryside. By the time we returned to the house the sun was shining and we were able to sit outside beside our own swimming pool. Kathleen cooked the first of many delicious meals and we sat in the large lounge afterwards playing cards and Scrabble. It was most relaxing, a far cry from our last, unhappy visit to France. In the days that followed we visited Mâcon and other local villages and towns. The house itself was on the outskirts of Pont-de-Vaux and we found the people very friendly. Later, we thought, we might go to Switzerland, which was only a little over an hour's drive away.

We decided to cut the holiday short, however, because Kathleen's sister developed a very severe back pain. The drive back was long and tedious, despite the lovely countryside. We left Pont-de-Vaux at about 8.00 a.m. and reached Carnforth that night at midnight. Early the following morning we set off again, knowing that Kathleen's sister preferred to see her own doctor. We were all very tired when we arrived in Fort William that afternoon, but Kathleen and I decided we should return south immediately, not having come prepared for a stay. As we drove along the side of Loch Linnhe, Kathleen remarked that we should have paid her mother a visit. Both of us were so weary, however, that we were just concentrating on the road. Anyway, we were hoping that she would visit us in Carnforth very soon, so we decided to go straight on home. To this day we rue the fact that we did not visit Theresa then.

We thought no more about it at the time, as we were looking forward to another important visitor. Occasionally through the year my nephew Roddy, one of Chrissie's sons, had written and phoned. This contact meant a great deal to me personally and I was able to find out how those children were progressing after the loss of their mother. Roddy had arranged that he and his fiancée would come to spend a weekend with us. We had not met since I had left. Awaiting their arrival, Kathleen and I were quite nervous and I discovered later that they were both similarly affected. Happily, within an hour of their arrival it was as if we had been seeing them regularly and we all enjoyed those two days, a good mix of laughter and serious conversation, fuelled by Kathleen's excellent food. They have visited us since and we value their company and friendship. It is an important and precious link for me with my family.

◆

As the winter of 1997 arrived we knew that Kathleen's mother would not be able to visit as we had all hoped. In one of our regular telephone calls we asked Theresa if she would come down with Julie Anne and Donald, who were spending a long weekend with us. She said she was not feeling very well and thought the journey would be too much for her. We accepted this, thinking that we would travel up to see her during the Christmas period instead. Donald and Julie Anne did come and we enjoyed their visit as always. It is so important to us both that Kathleen's children feel at home here with us.

On 12 December Kathleen's sister phoned. Her mother had been taken ill in a shop that afternoon. After a thorough examination by her doctor she had been allowed home, but was going to spend a few days with Kathleen's sister until she felt better. Kathleen was at work, and I immediately phoned the hospital to tell her the news. When she returned from work at about 10 o'clock that night Kathleen phoned her sister to ask about her mother. She was happy to hear that she seemed better and asked to speak to her. However, hearing that Theresa had not long returned to bed after speaking with her sister, Bridie, Kathleen decided not to disturb her. She would speak to her in the morning, she said.

When the phone rang in the morning I answered it without a second thought. Immediately I knew that something was seriously wrong. I could hear crying in the background and Kathleen's nephew blurted out the news that Theresa was dead. I took the phone through to Kathleen and told her. There was no way to soften the blow. I gave her the phone and as she spoke with her sister she crumpled before my eyes. A light had gone out in Kathleen's life. I could only hold her close. There was little I could say to relieve the terrible pain of such a sudden death. We packed our bags in silence, secured the house and set out on the long, sad journey north. Kathleen had already phoned Julie Anne, who was still at her college in Glasgow, and we had arranged to collect her on our way to Fort William.

As in any home after the death of a special family member, the atmosphere was sombre yet loving. Theresa's faith was so very central to her life and the family wanted that fact remembered now by having everything done with dignity. After she had embraced everyone, Kathleen went to pay her respects to her mother, whose remains had been placed in her coffin. The candles were already lit and we knelt down to pray, as Theresa would have wanted and expected. Later that evening her parish priest led us in the rosary and the prayers for the dead.

As other relatives and their families arrived – and there were many of them because Theresa had been one of 13 children – the same touching and dignified procedure was followed. The custom in the west of Scotland and in the Highlands is still that of saying the rosary and prayers for the dead every night that the remains of the deceased are still in the house. This we did, as Theresa had done for others in her lifetime. The house we were in had been built just a few years previously. It was here that Kathleen's brother-in-law had died, so unexpectedly, two years before, and now, again so suddenly, her mother had died in the same house. It added an extra poignancy to the occasion.

The dignity of the grieving process was spoiled by an unwelcome visitor. A reporter from *The Herald* actually came to the house to speak with me. I was disappointed, because I expected better of that paper, and I was glad when he was told to go away. But his presence disturbed us all, and there were reports that others from the press were also around. Kathleen's brothers took me aside and quietly suggested that perhaps I should not attend the funeral. They did not wish any such interference to tarnish the solemn occasion. With great sadness I agreed. The last thing I wanted was for my presence to be the excuse for a media circus. I spoke with Kathleen about it and she also agreed that it would be best if I remained in the house during the funeral rites. I paid my last respects to Theresa before they took her to her beloved St Mary's in Fort William.

I felt very strange, alone in the house, when everyone had gone to the Requiem Mass and the burial. It was distressing not to be able to stand beside the woman I love at a time when she needed me. And it hurt that I was unable to attend the funeral of someone who meant so much to me. Shortly after their departure, the phone rang. I did not answer. When the ringing stopped I checked the number to discover that it had been someone using a mobile phone – normal procedure for the press. They were clearly checking on my whereabouts.

During their absence from the house I concentrated my thoughts on Kathleen and all the family, and I prayed the rosary. After Mass Theresa's remains were being taken to the graveyard of Cille

Choireil, just outside Roybridge. There she would be laid to rest with her late husband, John. May she rest in peace.

. The house was soon crowded again after the funeral. All those who had travelled a long distance came back to the house with the family and close friends. Indeed, I sat on the stairs with a few of the other men to allow as many into the sitting area as possible. I was unable to get close to Kathleen at her stance by the cooker and we did not manage any kind of conversation until the numbers eventually dwindled. She had stood up to the ordeal very well so far and once again I was full of admiration for her strength. She had to cope with the added difficulty of being in the public gaze, in a place where everybody knew her, as well as the pain of losing her mother whom she deeply loved.

At 5.00 a.m. the following morning I was trying to persuade a doctor to come to the house. Kathleen was now far from well, showing the same symptoms as she had before the major surgery of two years before. I took some advice over the phone, but to no avail and a few hours later the doctor who had cared for her mother came and spent time examining Kathleen. He did what he could and left some tablets to deaden the pain and, hopefully, the distension. By 5 p.m., however, we had to ask him to return and now he strongly advised her to go to hospital. He knew of us and was very understanding. It would have been most difficult for her to go to the local Belford Hospital or to Raigmore Hospital in Inverness because of our notoriety. Despite this, I wanted her to take the doctor's advice and go to hospital. She was in terrible pain and I was afraid that she might need immediate surgery. Kathleen was adamant that she would not go to a hospital in that area.

Eventually the doctor relented, but asked me if I was willing to travel south that evening and take her to a hospital nearer home. I agreed to try and take her to Lancaster Infirmary and the doctor gave her an injection which he said would last for most of the journey. Then he wrote a report of her condition which I was to give to the Accident and Emergency department on arrival. If there was any deterioration during the journey I must take her to the nearest hospital en route. Within half an hour we were on the road south.

It was a difficult, even frightening, journey that night. Kathleen's pain was diminished by the injection, but not removed. I drove in the dark, trying to concentrate on the road and worrying about her condition. As ever she was brave, telling me she was fine. We passed Balloch, and therefore the Vale of Leven Hospital, and

Glasgow with its infirmaries, then through Lanarkshire and the hospitals there. At each stage I asked Kathleen if she wanted to continue. She said 'yes' firmly every time. After passing Carlisle I realized that we could reach Lancaster after all and said that was were we would go. However, Kathleen thought differently and asked me to take her home to Carnforth. She won the ensuing argument, a sure sign that she was getting better! She was still very tired and weak and promised that, if she must, she would go to hospital the following day. Thankfully, her condition eased and for the next few days she rested at home before seeing her own doctor. This time the danger had passed, but it was a scare neither of us wanted to experience again.

Christmas and New Year passed and we spent those days very quietly, going to Mass in the morning and speaking to the family on the phone. Theresa's death had been a very great loss and the Christmas period was painful for all her scattered family. It was a very difficult time for Kathleen, still feeling weak after her illness.

✦

As I write, the sharp pain of Theresa's death is receding as time passes, although she will surely always be badly missed. There are positive things afoot in our life together, and Kathleen and I are full of hope for the future.

While we were in Kendal I began to do a little writing, but never offered any of it for publication. Towards the end of 1997 I decided to write this book. So much had been written about me and about us as a couple over the previous year, too often based on supposition, defamation and inaccuracy. I felt that I should tell the story from my own perspective, and so I began, in the tenements of Kinning Park where my journey started all those years ago. Life is a journey and very rarely straightforward. Through these pages I have relived the important stages of mine up to the present time. As I reach the close I feel very aware of the past, but am also conscious that there is more of life to be lived, more to learn, more experiences to look forward to.

Kathleen has begun a three-year course of study for her Diploma in Psychiatric Nursing, planning to work part-time as well. This will be demanding, but she is determined to see it through. There will be difficult times ahead for her and I hope I can provide the help and support she needs. Our experience over the past two years, facing seemingly insurmountable difficulties, is that hard times have drawn us closer together and strengthened our love for each other. Whatever the difficulties still to come our way, with God's help these too will be overcome.

At the beginning of 1997, while we were still living in Kendal, we made enquiries through a lawyer – John, who has been most helpful to us – about the possibility of getting married. Could he approach the local Registrar? Was there any possibility of a Special Licence? After investigating, John suggested that perhaps we should try somewhere else in the country. At that time the Registrar was being bothered regularly by members of the press asking if we were intending to be married. One actually followed her to her home some distance from Kendal. Again we felt angry that such people should interfere to this degree, not only in our own lives, but also in other people's. We had already proclaimed our love to the world, in a most public way and in a manner we did not want or choose. We felt very strongly that this important event in our lives should not become another 'act' for the media circus. It seemed, then, that it would be almost impossible for us to marry quietly in Britain.

With the support and knowledge of Kathleen's children, we travelled privately to Antigua, where we were married on 18 June 1998. We made all the arrangements ourselves at the appropriate office there in St John's and, with Julie Anne and Donald as our witnesses, we were married by the local Marriage Officer.

We had expected a rather cold ceremony, mainly to do with the signing of forms. We were wrong. The Officer was a Methodist lay preacher and used verses from the letters of St Paul as the basis for his prepared talk. Both Kathleen and I were touched by this use of Scripture and found it profoundly meaningful. He knew nothing about our background – these were simply his chosen words when he officiated at a civil marriage. Afterwards our guests were the three maids who cleaned our rooms during our stay. It was a beautiful day in an idyllic setting and we were so happy that Kathleen's son and daughter were there to share our joy. On our return we kept the news to ourselves and away from the press. We are thankful that our special day was enjoyed without disturbance and regard this as an added blessing. Now we simply wish to look forward to a peaceful and meaningful life together.

FEET OF CLAY

WHEN I LOOK BACK ON MY LIFE, the most potent factor has been the priesthood, the life that was mine for more than 30 years. The essential nature of that priesthood has never changed. It cannot. The priest conducts the Eucharist, which is central to the life of Faith and has been unchanged since the Last Supper, when Christ 'took a loaf of bread, and when he had given thanks, he broke it and gave it to them, saying, "This is my body, which is given for you. Do this in remembrance of me" ' (Luke 22:19). This command was followed from the very beginning by the early Christians: 'They devoted themselves to the apostles' teaching and fellowship, to the breaking of bread and the prayers' (Acts 2:42). The Eucharist is central to our Faith and so, therefore, is the priesthood.

From an early age I wanted to be a priest. I was attracted by the role of the priest as I saw it at that time, admiring our local priests and excited by stories of missions and foreign adventures. When I came to understand fully the real meaning of being a priest, it only enhanced the attraction, and I particularly came to love my pastoral role among the people of my parish. My years of study and preparation were important because I learned then to live in community and, at the same time, matured in independence. This may appear to be a contradiction, but it is the reality. Living in such a community taught me to be aware of the needs of others and to accept the most menial and difficult tasks as part of life. This kind of formation undoubtedly made me stronger and more independent. But above all this came the formation in spirituality. This is an essential part of each individual's life – or should be – and the education and nurturing I received helped me to realize just how valuable it can be. That has never left me.

In the far-off days of my childhood the priest was a very valued person in the community. His presence at the altar and in the pulpit was the basis of this value and he was given respect because of it. He also had other important roles. He was the youth leader, and guide to the various adult confraternities which were then a big part of parish life. In rural communities such as those I served in the Highlands and islands, his leadership and representation were important in secular matters as well.

Despite these other activities, which change with time, the priest has an essential and unchanging role in the life of the Church, the people of God. He presides at the celebration of the Eucharist and this is the essence of his place in the Church. I cannot stress enough the importance of this role because I cannot emphasize sufficiently the importance of the Mass, the Sacraments and the preaching of God's Word in the living of the Catholic Faith. To fulfil this role we need, more than ever, men who are not only schooled in spirituality but who lead truly spiritual lives.

The priest also has an important pastoral function, through leadership, counselling, encouragement and example. These are significant tasks, although they can also be fulfilled by others who are not priests. In more and more cases this is now happening, priests and laypeople working side by side. After my ordination my education in spirituality continued as I worked in the various parishes, with many dedicated people and more experienced priests. Throughout my active priesthood I saw in other priests what I know I lacked – a prayerfulness, a self-effacing attitude and an unstinting generosity in the giving of themselves. If I lacked these I certainly yearned for them. I was fortunate to live with priests, and to have others as personal friends, whose examples challenged me to become a better person. They were good men whose lives and ministry were of great importance to those amongst whom they lived. No matter how people think of me now, I hope my priesthood was beneficial to the people I was privileged to serve. I leave that judgement to God.

Society has changed in so many ways since I was ordained a priest. Attitudes have altered almost as quickly as fashions. The respect for and status of the priest, once taken for granted, have greatly diminished, if not disappeared. Priests are no longer on a pedestal, automatic objects of reverence. With that change comes an obvious difference in role which in some ways is not a bad thing. More and more, those who value the gospel or seek knowledge of it expect the priest to be a truly and deeply spiritual person. He is under intense scrutiny. How does he live the Faith he preaches? Does he do what he says? This is where example is so very important and I will be judged by many to have failed them in this.

✦

There are two aspects of the priesthood which I must consider more fully: the vows of celibacy and obedience. When I reached the sub-diaconate, a year before entering the priesthood, I willingly accepted the obligation to celibacy (now this is accepted a little later, on ordination to the diaconate). Many people understand celibacy as a vow not to marry, but it is actually a promise to live in chastity, i.e. inclusive of much more than 'not marrying'. It has been part of the Church's law concerning priests for centuries, having grown up as a tradition and been adopted as an obligation since the fourth century AD (the Western Catholic Church still upholds it as a ruling for priests, whereas the Eastern Orthodox Church now allows its priests to marry). It was an obligation I accepted, valued and tried to fulfil for most of my priesthood. The fact that I have broken that promise does not mean that I disagree with the law and teaching of the Church. I accept the law and certainly do not ask that it be changed for my convenience.

The arguments about celibacy will continue. At some time in the future the law may be changed or relaxed; no one knows. I can only live my faith as best I can at this time, under the law as it stands. For this reason I have left the active ministry. I broke that promise to be celibate. I fell in love and both my priesthood and that love demanded truth. Lies destroy so much, especially the spirit.

Whatever happens to the law of celibacy in the future will, I firmly believe, be the work of the Holy Spirit: change will not and should not come about because of the demands of those who, like me, have failed to live up to this aspect of their priesthood. We are just a very small part of the ongoing Church. When Kathleen and I faced the press in that garden behind the house in Kendal I was asked by one reporter, 'Will you leave the Catholic Church and join another like the Anglicans?' My response was brief but heartfelt: 'Never.'

In the Rite of Ordination the candidate promises obedience to his bishop. I have met a number of priests who found this more difficult than celibacy. Personally I did not, except on a few occasions. The reality is that the priest gives his life to the people he serves and the decisions of the bishop are usually for the benefit of those people. The availability of the Sacraments and the preaching of the gospel are the essential tasks of the priest and there is seldom any great difficulty in 'obeying' when the purpose behind the command is the provision of these essentials. Obedience is not a matter of blindly following instructions.

The Church is 'the people of God'. It is Catholic and Apostolic because it exists throughout the world where people are trying to live the gospel of our Lord as passed on through the Apostles and those who have followed them down the centuries. All of us in the Church have one thing in common: the living of our Faith. In the simplest of terms we all believe what we proclaim in the Nicene Creed. We have different roles within the structure of the Church, but we are equal in our belief, just as we are equal in sharing the same God-given nature. This is the beauty of the gospel – it reveals God's love for us, with all our strengths and weaknesses, and it shows us how to love God and our neighbour despite our failings.

The need for authority and order is a reality in all our lives and we depend on the structures which make that authority not only identifiable but also a part of life. In the Church I love, I see the authority of the Pope and the bishops as necessary because the teaching of Christ must continue always as a living truth. The structures of hierarchy and the official teaching – the magisterium – ensure that continuity. The people I served as priest in Glasgow and in the Highlands and islands, the people I met in Quito and in the corridors of the Vatican, all of us depend on the security of knowing that we follow the same gospel, share the same Faith. In this view of the Church the importance of that promise of obedience is easier to understand. There are rules, and an order, and something is lost from the structure when we do not live by them.

✦

As much as Faith is a vibrant and important part of life, so also are the realities of weakness and failure. Indeed, they very often co-exist.

Since my son was born, guilt has remained a part of my life. Guilt is defined in my old Chambers dictionary as 'the state of having done something wrong'. It is something experienced by any one of us who has a conscience. It can be resolved, however, by admitting the wrong and, if possible, trying to make matters right. I did not admit the wrong I had done. When I accepted the bishopric I only added more guilt because that decision was also wrong. Given my priesthood and promise of celibacy, my falling in love with Kathleen was a further guilt to add to the existing catalogue. Kathleen was also affected by guilt because she practised her faith in an open and real way. When we eventually admitted our love for each other, but kept the relationship secret, this parcel of guilt became part of the lie which we were finding so difficult to live. Both of us have living consciences which affect our daily lives.

Our actions affect others and, indeed, can blight their lives. All my life I have tried to avoid hurting people. At this time I am very aware of the enormity of the pain I have caused to so many. Because I was a bishop I have caused great harm to the Church I love. It is a hurt that would not exist to its present extent if I had refused the appointment. Because of the trust put in me by so many of them I have hurt my brother priests in Argyll and the Isles and the people of the Diocese, especially those in whose parishes I served as priest. Then, of course, I have affected my own family – my brother and sister and their families, and the children of my late sister Chrissie. Most families are extended and I know my aunts and uncles and their families have also been distressed by my decision. The turmoil and resultant pain I have created in their lives weighs very heavily. But, of course, I am not alone. There is also the pain caused to Kathleen's family, especially her own children, as well as her mother, her brothers and sisters and their families. Their generous forgiveness has been of immense importance to us in our isolated situation. We carry guilt not only for our own actions but also for the problems caused in the lives of others. Good people, close to us both in our different areas of life, were left feeling abandoned in one way or another. Neither of us could ever have imagined, or wished, that we should be the cause of so much hurt.

There is, therefore, and we admit this openly, a sadness which we pray will heal in time. In asking God's forgiveness we also seek the forgiveness of those we hurt, if not yet their understanding.

Throughout this book I have stressed the importance of Faith in my life. Outwardly I am now restricted in its practice but within myself it is still most important – a daily need. Throughout her life Kathleen has always been active in the practice of her own Faith and she also feels the pain of restrictions. We accept these because we both submit to the teaching of the Church. In the eyes of the Church we are not sacramentally (i.e. truly) married: priests may not marry and my priesthood has not been annulled. According to Church teaching, therefore, we are living wrongly. For this reason neither of us has received Holy Communion since the day we left, although we attend Mass on Sundays and also sometimes on week-days. Each time we are at Mass this is a painful moment when we cannot participate fully by receiving the Sacrament. However, we accept the law of the Church and, therefore, the consequences of our choices. Prayer, the Scriptures and attendance at Mass continue to be essential parts of our lives: we could not do without them.

✦

If I wake in the morning with no hope, how will the day turn out? What meaning or purpose can I then attach to my thoughts and actions? Hope is the spur in life, and the hope of eternal life the powerful encouragement for the true Christian to act in faith and love. Kathleen and I hope for the healing, where possible, of the hurt we have caused, especially that caused because of my position in the Church. In chapter 21 of Luke's Gospel is our Lord's parable of the widow's mite. She put into the treasury very little in comparison to those around her, yet in truth she put in much more because she gave all she had. No one can give more. I hope so much that will be possible for Kathleen and myself now. Kathleen finds fulfilment in her nursing and has chosen to extend her knowledge in that important area of service. Quietly, and out of the awful glare of publicity, I wish to live out the remainder of my life, serving others in whatever way is possible. It will be enough if we can realize that shared hope to give all we can.

C.S. Lewis wrote, 'I find that when I think I am asking God to forgive me I am often in reality … asking Him not to forgive me but to excuse me. But there is all the difference in the world between forgiving and excusing. Forgiveness says "Yes you have done this thing but I accept your apology. I will never hold it against you and everything between us two will be exactly as it was before." But excusing says "I see that you couldn't help it or didn't mean it, you weren't really to blame." If one was not really to blame then there is nothing to forgive. In that sense forgiveness and excusing are almost opposites ... To be a Christian means to forgive the inexcusable, because God has forgiven the inexcusable in you.'

I have not sought to make excuses. I do seek daily God's forgiveness, and I do so because I know he loves me, as he loves all of us, even if we have feet of clay.